MURDO

The Life and Works

Iain Crichton Smith

MURDO

The Life and Works

Edited and introduced by Stewart Conn

Birlinn

First published in 2001 by
Birlinn Limited
8 Canongate Venture
5 New Street
Edinburgh
EH8 8BH

www.birlinn.co.uk

ISBN 1 84158 058 9

British Library Cataloguing-in-Publication Data
A catalogue record for this book is available
from the British Library

The publisher acknowledges subsidy from the Scottish
Arts Council towards the publication of this book

Typeset by Palimpsest Book Production Limited,
Polmont, Stirlingshire
Printed and bound by Omnia Books Ltd, Bishopbriggs

ACKNOWLEDGEMENTS

'Murdo at the BBC' first appeared in Chapman no. 73 in 1993.

Three excerpts from the *Life of Murdo*, selected by Lesley Duncan, were featured with photographs in *The Herald* on 18th–20th April 2000, under the heading 'The Admirable Crichton Smith'.

At a party held by *Cencrastus* to celebrate his 70th birthday Iain Crichton Smith read an instalment in the life of Murdo: this subsequently appeared in issue no. 59 as 'Murdo comes of age'.

CONTENTS

INTRODUCTION

At the time of his death in 1998 Iain Crichton Smith was one of Scotland's most diverse and best-loved literary figures. Two contrasting volumes of his poetry, *The Leaf and the Marble* and *A Country for Old Men*, have been published since. One of his poems was read at the opening of the Scottish Parliament. Tributes have been held in his honour. And he retains a warm place in the hearts of all who knew him – not least in the guise of the anarchic alter-ego cum anti-hero of this volume.

Born in Glasgow on New Year's Day, 1928, Crichton Smith was the second of three sons whose parents had left Lewis to seek work. Shortly afterwards they returned to Upper Bayble in the Point peninsula. On the death of his father, a merchant seaman, from tuberculosis, his mother had to face alone the struggle to bring up her family. The poverty of his early upbringing in this God-fearing Gaelic-speaking island community would leave a lifelong impression on him, and on his writing.

In his essay *Between Sea and Moor* he wrote: 'I would think of my mother working as a fishgirl among those barrels, wearing her flesh-coloured gloves, an inconceivable girl in a world so different from mine, and I would feel guilty as if I had condemned her to that life.' The sea stayed with him as both monster and creator, and a source of fertile symbolism: 'I think of the dead – some I have known – drifting about in it, being refined there forever. One of the best footballers in the island was drowned there one terrible night. Another boy was blinded by an oar. The *Iolaire* sank there on New Year's morning, in 1919, bringing home from the war two hundred men to be drowned on their own doorsteps, a tragedy that breaks the mind.'

Crichton Smith felt too the jolt of arriving monoglot, and having an alien tongue imposed on him. It is no accident that the first of the *Thoughts of Murdo* should be 'Murdo and the Language', and starts:

> When Murdo went to school at the age of four, he being then about three feet high, a starved-looking very tall thin woman loomed up in front of him.
>
> 'You will have to speak English from now on,' she said.
>
> Murdo did not know what to say as he did not know English.
>
> 'The cat sat on the mat,' she later told him in confidence.

He depicts this linguistic phenomenon in terms of colours, not just externally perceived but embodied in him and splitting him in two:

> One half of Murdo, vertically visualised, had the colour red: the other half had the colour black. Also it seemed to him that half his tongue spoke Gaelic, the other half English. There was a smell of salt herring from the black half, and a smell of bacon from the other half . . .
>
> People would say to him, 'Och, you are just suffering from the linguistic disease. It will settle down the older you grow. Eventually the black spots will disappear altogether and you will not feel anything at all.' Still he learned and used long words such as 'dichotomy', 'schizophrenic' and 'traumatic'.

This extract sets a childlike subjectivity alongside a lucid assessment of the pressures on him. The words in the closing sentence indicate an awareness of the terminology on which any exegesis of his work, or the mind behind it, is likely to draw. They are also liable to be brought into play, with regard to his Murdo persona.

In his personal palette the colour *black* stood for the crow-like ministerial garb, and rigidity, of the Free Church. It related also to the metaphoric scythe-bearer not only of childhood experience but of the death-oriented moral climate and atmosphere of the island he grew up on. The 'dichotomy' within him, its 'traumatic' tug between discipline and freedom, rigour and inspiration, was mirrored in the titles of his early volumes of poems, *Thistles and Roses* and *The Law and the Grace*.

At school, he tells us, he was slow at arithmetic but good at writing essays. Later he won a scholarship to the Nicolson Institute in Stornoway, where he found he could do mathematics, loved geometry and became a crossword fanatic. For many years a poem would be to him primarily 'an elegant construction . . . a musical artefact composed of exact language'.

When he was eleven the Second World War broke out. One of his brothers served on a corvette, the other joined the Home Guard. But the war remained remote and unreal in a village of women and girls. Nor in those days did he feel any interest in the past, or in his island's history.

At seventeen Crichton Smith left Lewis for the first time, to go to university in Aberdeen. He has described how his mother, waving him goodbye, looked small and distant. A piper played on the deck of the boat. Soon he would fall in love with Aberdeen, and with learning. Lewis would seem a world away – yet closer also: 'The moor and the granite came together in a new synthesis. And here I really began to write poetry, a great deal of it about Lewis.'

Having received his honours degree he went on to Jordanhill Training College in Glasgow, with a view to becoming an English teacher. Following National Service he joined his mother and younger brother in Dumbarton, and started teaching in Clydebank. After a couple of years his link with Gaelic was restored by a move to Oban, where he joined the staff of the High School. He taught by day, wrote by night. His reputation grew, mainly as a poet, in both languages.

Crichton Smith's first novel, *Consider the Lilies*, came out in

1968. With its limpid style and empathy for old Mrs Scott, it remains his most highly regarded and successful prose work. When his mother died the following year he was devastated – a huge sense of release being countered by an intense loss and feeling of being rudderless. He drove himself harder and harder in his writing.

When he was forty-nine he took early retirement from teaching. Shortly afterwards, in 1977, he married a former school pupil, Donalda Logan. In due course they moved to Taynuilt. Friends noticed how much more relaxed in demeanour he now became; how well groomed and socially at ease. The books kept appearing: fiction, a steady flow of criticism, and in 1981 his first *Selected Poems*. In that same year Murdo was loosed on an unsuspecting public.

Murdo & Other Stories was similar in style to Crichton Smith's previous prose works, but for the title piece, which was hailed as opening up an invigorating new world of surrealistic transpositions and comic invention. The verve of the writing, its at times dream-like imagery and metaphysical musings, gave it a unique stamp. So did the unpredictable gyrations of its central figure.

Murdo Macrae, a demon with numbers, has left the bank. He tries to write, but cannot get beyond the first sentence: 'There was a clerk once and he was working in a bank.' A social and emotional misfit, his eyes meander from the vacant page to the stainless white mountain visible through the window his wife is always polishing. He has a wild and fertile imagination: he puts on a red rubber nose to go to the local shop for a paper; at the library he asks for *The Brothers Karamazov* by Hugh Macleod; late one night he gazes tipsily at the stars and wonders if there is a parallel world on Betelgeuse; he believes Calvin is alive and living in the village.

Interspersed with these fantastical set pieces are symbolic tales he tells his young nephew and touching glimpses of his marriage. One day Murdo proposes he and Janet climb the white mountain. She refuses: it would be too cold. Sensing how happy the world is without him, he suggests they dance. They do so. Another night he wakens, sweating and trembling. He sees masks everywhere. Eventually he says Janet can put the light off, and falls asleep, soothed by her tranquil breathing. But beforehand he has a vision of beaked animals which could be a premonition.

Janet's father, the opposite of Murdo and utterly 'normal', urges her to leave her husband. She refuses, not because she is frightened to, but because she hopes Murdo will one day return to the bank. Either that, or find himself able to write something. It is clear she also pities him. As the novella draws to a close Murdo's own father is dying, with Murdo and Janet by his bedside. Eventually Murdo turns away, weeping. Outside is the white mountain, like a ghost staring at him.

Much of the comedy derives from Murdo's inadequacy in the face of social convention. This in turn reflects and is reflected in his spiritual turmoil. Having no job offends the work ethic, so strong in the Lewis of Crichton Smith's upbringing. Murdo is resented as not merely a wastrel, but one who mocks accepted values. Under the stars, his words parody traditional song: 'The isle of Mull / has no grief or sorrow, / It is so green, / and will be here tomorrow.' Even on a visit to Glasgow, the policeman he notices is the stereotypical Highlander: 'He's got a red neck. And red fists. Big red fists.'

Nor is Murdo simply a misfit within Gaeldom: he senses, and shares, the community's negative perception of him. In the mirror he holds up to society he sees his own despair. From this derive the tragi-comedy and pathos of his situation. And it is in the intimate area of feeling – most significantly through Murdo's grief for his father and the unflinching loyalty of Janet – that the novella achieves not just poignancy but real *gravitas*.

The story is about Murdo, and about writing . . . and togetherness. He wants to cover the white page and – eventually with Janet – climb the white mountain with its mysterious aura, and leave his footprints in the snow. It is also, I think, about the shared pain of ageing and loss. For whatever else is resolved, there remains the white mountain we must all face – 'that grey question', overhanging us at the end.

I remember the typescript of *Thoughts of Murdo* arriving in the post with a scribbled note from the author asking if I thought it 'worth publishing', and whether he should try a Scottish publisher. When we next met I enthused on both counts; and he gleefully revealed the source of his title as the *Little Red Book of the Thoughts of Chairman Mao*.

In the twelve years between *Murdo* and *Thoughts*, the eponymous hero had become something of a cult figure – so much so, in fact, that the new book was written pretty well in response to public demand. Yet despite sharing the main protagonist, there are big differences between the two works.

Thoughts is not a linear development of the earlier work but a kaleidoscopic collection of notes, letters, manifestos, observations and random jottings. A number of set pieces from the novella are included, among them Murdo's letter to Dante and his visit to the library, his dissertation on the potato and the herring, and his *Last Will and Testament*. With the parent work sitting alongside, the duplicated pieces are omitted from this edition, thus reducing its original tally from 67 pieces to 58. The remainder, in common with Crichton Smith's output over all, are uneven. Some of their targets seem very slight. There are no evolving relationships or anything of the 'howling' quality of the novella. But this was never the author's intention. He sets before us a mix of verbal firecrackers, credos and aperçus for the sheer fun of things. These offer at times side-splitting insight into the tight-knit community which bears the brunt of Murdo's often jaundiced and at times self-lacerating satirical observations. The origin of the pieces varies widely. *A Bilingual Poem* pursues the black and red theme (representing too, come to think of it, the 'credit' and 'debit' of his previous existence). In the first wholly 'fictional' piece, Murdo leaves the bank, his exchange with the manager revealing that he did not go voluntarily.

Murdo and the Mod was sparked off when Crichton Smith's stepson Alasdair received a lower mark for Gaelic than for music from a Lewis adjudicator. It comments on those parents who would complain if their offspring's adjudicators were not from their own island. Murdo's notion of the Mod heading for Paris stems from the similarity between the words *église* and *eaglais*. In Brahan Seer mode, his prophecies poke fun at ingrained inefficiency ('The End of the World is near when the MacBrayne's ship will be on time') and enigmatic aphorism ('A fire in the thatch will cause the downfall of two dynasties').

In the novella, Murdo was unable to write. In *Thoughts of Murdo* his output spans poems and a play fragment set in a Chinese restaurant. We also meet a new and inspired creation: the blue-slippered Sam Spaid of Portree, Free Church private eye. There remains Murdo's own predicament. Though he seems gregarious, he is conscious of being excluded or regarded with suspicion by his fellows; of being as much a stereotype as they are. In deriding the corrosion of their cultural values, he realises he is every bit as trapped by their shared inheritance.

Elements of Murdo often found their way into real-life situations. In one story a Major Cartwright from Hampshire lives in a small Highland village. At ceilidhs he introduces the singers and insists on speaking Gaelic. The natives soon tire of him. Sam Spaid speaks to him only in English. At the end of a writers' weekend at Crieff Hydro, in the course of which Crichton Smith read the piece, he was confronted by an actual Major Cartwright from Hampshire who, much to his relief, took the coincidence with good grace.

The ceilidh is the tip of an iceberg. To Crichton Smith the changed nature of the ceilidh was symbolic of the infiltration of Gaelic culture by outsiders – abetted by betrayal from within. He wrote elsewhere that 'the songs at modern ceilidhs have nothing at all to do with those sung at the old ceilidhs . . .

The ceilidh as it is now practised is a treacherous weakening of the present, a memorial, a tombstone on what has once been, pipes playing in a graveyard.' This is not nostalgia or parochialism, but concern at the way he saw Gaelic culture going, and something he tried to counter in his 'Eight Songs for a New Ceilidh' with their wider international themes and vocabulary.

Professor Donald Meek has perceptively observed: 'On the one hand, Iain was writing for the Gaelic community, and he belonged to that community; but on the other, he was coining new literary styles, and subverting some of the most important stylistic hallmarks of the traditional Gaelic community . . . His connections with the Gaelic world remained strong, but he was not wholly part of that world; he was "of that world, but not in it" . . . His work includes satire as well as merciless attacks on the Gael's "sacred cows", including the Church. He was, by any standards, a complex individual.'

In conjunction with this, Crichton Smith shows a breathtaking range of cultural reference. Camus and Proust attracted him for their exploration of the mind as against the external world of their creations. The great Russian novels, and whodunnits, were alike grist to his mill. He ranges effortlessly from Celtic history, Greek tragedy, Galileo, Copernicus and Maupassant to Freud, Catherine Cookson and the verbal constructs of MacDiarmid.

Murdo has many soul-mates, at an oblique angle to the world. It is fun to picture them cavorting in the colourful cabaret of Crichton Smith's mind. He was the first to point me towards Kurt Vonnegut's outrageous satires on America and a universe in disorder. I still have *The Groucho Letters* he passed on to me. The *Thoughts of Murdo* have a certain kinship with Flann O'Brien – though one certainly wouldn't say of them, as Dylan Thomas did of *At Swim-Two-Birds*, 'Just the book to give your sister, if she's a loud, dirty, boozy girl.'

Schweik, malingerer and dog-fancier (his creator Jaroslav Hašek a bank clerk before he took up writing), hovers in the background, but unlike Crichton Smith, Hašek's satire has a savage political edge to it. There may be parallels in Pinter's obliquity of language and its potential for the absurd. But mercifully for Murdo he is never in danger of being taken away by such characters as Goldberg and McCann.

Closer to home, Douglas Gifford noted how 'in the same way that many other writers from Jenkins to Gray have reconciled themselves with their tragi-comic predicament in an unfriendly cultural climate, Smith objectified and distanced immediate and impossible pressures so that incongruity and perspective allowed the unbearable to be handled'. Tom Leonard has lampooned the denigration of working-class Scots speech, the more lunatic elements of the Lallans movement and cultural icons. None of these writers, though, shared the predicament of Crichton Smith, for whom retreat into one tongue could cause alienation, or exile, from the other.

In the early 1980s Crichton Smith suffered the illness which would be the basis for *In the Middle of the Wood*, whose central character Ralph Simmons – a writer living in a Scottish village – heads in a state of extreme paranoia for Glasgow, tries to take his own life, and spends time in a mental hospital. It is as though in the wake of the novel Murdo became the conduit, or the catalyst, for a further exploration of breakdown and recovery.

In 1997 the Traverse premiered *Lazybed*, based on an earlier piece *Tog orm mo Speal* ('Lift on my Scythe'). Derived from *Oblomov*, with Kafka and Monty Python lurking among the peats, it is about a young crofter who won't get out of bed: a condition not unknown in Gaelic culture. Round the initially inert figure of Murdo Macrae – something of a Dostoevskian 'holy fool' – buzz his brother, a neighbour, the minister, a pretty nurse called Judith and a host of familiar themes.

A black-clad figure with a scythe engages him in debate, then takes his mother away. Murdo feels he is to blame. Judith notices a beautiful blue vase is missing. The neighbour has taken it, claiming it had been left to her. Judith demands its return. Murdo goes up on the roof to sweep the chimney. A scream, off. He has fallen. An ambulance is called. Telling the men not to be rough, Judith goes with him to the hospital. The play ends with the neighbour hoping Murdo will be all right, though he took back the blue vase. Death reassures her Judith and Murdo will get married: he hopes to attend their wedding, but as a benevolent, not malign, presence.

The author's preface states: 'I hope the audience enjoys it. That's all I want from it.' But he concedes that, as with the bulk of his work, darker questions are posed: 'And of course, though Death is presented comically, there are times when we can't forget who he is.'

Crichton Smith was a Spike Milligan fan. At the end of *Puckoon* the hero, stuck up a tree, shouts 'You can't leave me like this!', to which the authorial reply is, 'Oh, can't I?'. The device is counter to Murdo's oneness with his creator, for whom the question 'Who wrote me?' *(Co sgrìobh mi?)* had very different and far-reaching implications. The one West End play I saw Milligan in was *Son of Oblomov*. A few minutes in, he not only heckled latecomers but had the curtain brought down so that the show could start again uninterrupted.

The detachment of *In the Middle of the Wood* is achieved through its third-person narration. Part of the joy of *Murdo* and *Thoughts* is guessing to what extent fact is embellished. And though elements of *Lazybed* are drawn from real life, it is not a documentary but a drama. The philosopher Kant has a cameo role. And climbing up to mend the roof is the last thing I'd imagine Crichton Smith doing (although had he attempted it, the venture might well have ended similarly).

Prefacing his autobiography, Crichton Smith states that the choice of 'Murdo' rather than 'I' – their identification now clearly total – was so that he could be objective about himself, and 'to make comedy of painful experience'. The at times erratic directness of the narrative, the many carelessnesses and at one point an inadvertent switch from third to first person, persuaded me it had been typed in haste. It appears, though, that it was compiled slowly, with gaps between sections, and with the author's heart not necessarily in it.

Did it occupy a spell when there was nothing else to write? At one point, late 1997 is indicated. In that year *Columcille* had also been premiered. There would still be poems. But was there a sense of tasks completed, of marking time, or tying up loose ends? A premonition even (hinted at in a poem found later, 'I see my library among the gravestones') of what was to come?

At the age of seventy 'Murdo' scans his life. The early pages show a skinny boy 'with a rather scared expression' in slummy Dumbarton then in Lewis, with books his solace. His closeness to his mother is conveyed, as are a residual guilt and an ambivalence towards his later 'imprisonment' by her.

His account of National Service comically sets his own gaucheness alongside the boredom, and mad logic, of military life. Against this we sense the strengthening of his views on the dignity of the individual in the face of whatever form regimentation takes. And evident throughout is his resilience in the face of adversity and the destructive forces he had to combat.

Of his teaching years he concedes Murdo was not the world's best disciplinarian. There are '60s sessions in Edinburgh pubs, with telling pen-portraits of Hugh MacDiarmid, Norman MacCaig and Sydney Goodsir Smith. He and Donalda share with Robert Garioch revelries so farcical as to be rhapsodic. George Mackay Brown is vividly glimpsed in Stromness.

There is also full corroboration of something all Crichton Smith's and Donalda's friends realised: 'There is no question but that meeting Donalda was a turning point in Murdo's life ... In his flat in Combie St, he would listen for [her] footsteps on the stone stairs. In her yellow dress she was like an actual physical ray of sunshine entering his house.' The image of the 'yellow dress' would appear in a lovely poem to her. Later, in drives round Argyll, they shared an appreciation of nature's lushness and 'the extravagance of wild flowers and varied bird-life: a world of decorative colour and scent new to him'. He even learned that not all flowers were rhododendrons.

Then comes a dramatic change of setting and flavour. Before their marriage Crichton Smith and Donalda visited his Uncle Torquil, now a big, craggy 87-year-old, in White Rock in Canada; his generation a microcosm of the diaspora:

> On his mother's side there were Torquil, who had gone
> to Canada, Angus who had gone to South Africa, Alisdair
> who had been drowned young, John who lived in Lewis,
> Katie Ann, a sister who had also gone to Canada, and
> one or two others.

Torquil tells of his childhood days in Lewis when, for pouring milk on the clay floor of the black house, 'his mother had hung him in a creel over the fire as a punishment for being so improvident with the food God had given him'. Leaving to join up, he took nothing but his accordion. He could be from an Annie Proulx novel.

Torquil's zest for life is patent, as is his nephew's affection for him. When he takes them to hear a woman preacher, the old colours recur: 'If you sinned you were in the *red*, if you were virtuous you were in the *black*.' The night before they leave there is a ceilidh, and Gaelic singing. And a pale moon that might be 'the moon of Lewis, "the moon of the ripening of the barley"'.

Back home, things come full circle. Crichton Smith describes himself switching between English and Gaelic, 'as if riding a linguistic and psychic bicycle'. Noting that neither Sorley MacLean nor Hugh MacDiarmid, 'Scotland's two great poets of the 20th Century', wrote in English, he reiterates that 'we grow up in a web of language to which feelings are attached, and that the most powerful feelings are those of childhood'. Language and feeling, and memory, as ever inextricably intertwined.

Nowhere has Crichton Smith's writing a hint of malice, subterfuge or self-aggrandisement. Among other attractions I like to think it manifests two aspects of his personality. Firstly, he was himself every bit as much a 'holy innocent' as Murdo. Secondly, and as Catherine Lockerbie, previewing *Lazybed*, observed: 'Many Scots are well and diligently aware that Iain Crichton Smith is one of our most eminent authors; that he is a rare polymath, writing poetry, short stories, novels and plays; that he has umpteen awards, including the Queen's Medal and an OBE; and that due respect should therefore be accorded. But that he is one of the funniest men alive is a secret too well cradled to the bosom of literary society.'

I trust this volume will reach and delight a much wider than purely 'literary' audience of aficionados and new converts alike. It is, after all, a hilarious and moving celebration of a wonderful and compassionate writer – and man.

Stewart Conn
April 2001

MURDO

With his pen in his hand Murdo looked out at the tall white snow-covered mountain that he could see ahead of him through the window.

He was trying to write a story.

He looked down at the green pen in his hand. The day was cold and white, and now and again he could see a black bird flying across the intensely blue sky.

His wife was working in the kitchen. After she had finishèd cooking she would polish the table and chairs and the rest of the furniture. Now and again she would come to the door and say,

'Are you finished yet?'

And Murdo would say, 'I haven't even started,' and he would look out at the mountain again, he would resume his enchanted scrutiny of it. The white stainless mountain that was so cold and high.

Murdo had left his work as a bank clerk and was trying to write. When he had arrived home and told his wife that he would not be going back to the bank any more, she had begun to weep and scream but Murdo had simply walked past her to his room and had taken out a pen and a sheet of paper. He had left his work in the bank on an autumn day when the brown leaves were lying on the ground, and now it was winter.

He would sit at his desk at a little past nine o'clock every morning.

The white paper lay on the wood in front of him, as white as the mountain that he could see through the window which itself was entirely clean since his wife was always polishing it. He had not written a single page so far.

'Your tea's ready,' said his wife at eleven o'clock.

'Right,' said Murdo.

He went into the kitchen where she was. The room was as

neat as a pin, as it always was. He couldn't understand how she could spend her time so remorselessly cleaning rooms, as if it had never occurred to her that a particular table or a particular set of chairs could be elsewhere rather than where they were: that they could be in another house, in another country, on another planet even.

From the time of the dinosaurs, Murdo said to himself, was it predestined that this table should be standing by this window, that these chairs should be settled in the centre of this room? This was the sort of question that perplexed him and made his head sore.

He didn't say any of this to his wife for he knew that she wouldn't understand it.

They sat at the table opposite each other, and between them the pot of tea. His wife, Janet, was as neat and tidy as the room.

'When are you going back to your work?' she asked him as she did so often.

'I don't know,' said Murdo, putting a spoonful of sugar in his tea. His wife didn't take sugar, but kept saccharins for occasions like these. The saccharins were kept in a tiny blue box.

'Oh?' said his wife. 'You know of course that people are talking about you.'

'I don't care,' said Murdo drinking his tea.

'But I care,' said his wife. 'They're always asking me if you're ill. You aren't ill, are you?'

'Apart from a touch of the Black Death there's nothing wrong with me,' said Murdo.

'And my mother and father are always asking me when you intend to go back to the office.'

'Are they?' said Murdo, thinking of the red cross on the door. There was green paint on the wall. Why had he in those early days of happiness put green paint on the wall? Why not blue paint or yellow? Ah, the soul of man cannot be plumbed, Murdo sighed to himself. A clock, colour of gold, was ticking between two clay horses that he had once won in a fair.

Her father was a large red angry man who would sometimes become bloated with rage. He had been on the fishing boats in his youth.

Janet had left school at fifteen. When she married Murdo she expected that her life would be as limpid as a stream, that there would be money coming into the house regularly, that Murdo would at weekends be working stolidly in the garden reclaiming it from the wilderness, that they would have a daughter and a son, and that she would sit knitting by the fire when she wasn't talking to the neighbours.

She was a very capable housewife, small and alert. A good woman.

Murdo was trying to write a story about a bank clerk who had one day left his work and had begun to try and write. But one morning he had been enchanted by the white tall mountain with the snow on it and he had written nothing.

'This tea is very good,' he told Janet.

'Huh,' said Janet.

She would now begin to cook the dinner, and that was her life, and that life perplexed and astonished Murdo.

Why were the two horses set exactly like that, one on each side of the silently ticking clock?

'I'm going out tonight,' said Janet.

'Where?' said Murdo.

'Out,' she said. 'You can carry on with your writing.' She spoke simply, without irony.

'Where are you going?'

'I'm going to call on Mother,' said Janet.

'Oh,' said Murdo. 'I thought you had called on her on Monday.'

'I did,' said Janet. 'But I'm going to call on her again tonight.'

Your eyes are blue and cunning; said Murdo to himself.

She was still pretty with her blue eyes, her dark hair, her red healthy cheeks.

'That's all right,' he said.

He rose and went back to his room.

He sat at his desk and gazed at the white mountain.

I should really, he thought, leave the house this minute and climb the mountain. I should leave my prints in the snow.

It occurred to him that his wife might have been lying, that she wasn't going to see her mother at all. But he said nothing about his suspicion to her at lunch or at tea. She left the house at five o'clock and he went back to his room again.

The red sun was lying across the snow like blood.

What am I going to do? Murdo asked himself. Am I going to stay here staring at this mountain without writing anything?

The house felt empty after his wife had left it. He wandered about in it, looking at the made bed, the still ornaments, the mirrors, the dishes, the books.

The whole machinery of her world was impeccably in its place, his wife had built a clean orderly world around them.

But this world wasn't as clean as the mountain.

At half-past five he left the house and went to his mother-in-law's house and rang the bell at the side of the door. There were actually two bells but only one of them worked. His father-in-law came to the door and his face was as red as the sun that shone on the white mountain.

'Is Janet there?' Murdo asked timidly.

'No, she isn't,' said his father-in-law and didn't ask Murdo to come in. Murdo could see through the window that the TV was on.

'Oh,' he said. 'I only thought . . .'

'You thought wrong,' said his father-in-law. The houses around them were quiet and grey. Murdo saw a man going past with a large brown dog. 'Oh,' he said again, shivering in the cold since he wasn't wearing a coat. He turned away and walked down the street. Where was Janet? He felt his breast empty and he had a sudden terrible premonition that she had run away with another man, a man who never tried to write, but who was happy with the world as it was and his own position in it, and he felt shame and fear as if the event had happened in reality. He went into a bar but she wasn't there either. When he came out he looked round him in the raw cold but he couldn't see the white mountain from where he was since there were houses between him and it. He stood on the pavement and he didn't know where to go next. Why had she lied to him?

Well, he said to himself, I shall have to find her or I shall have to climb the mountain. What shall I do?

I'll see if she is in this bar.

He went in and there she was sitting in a dark corner and there were some people with her.

He recognised John, who was a teacher in the only large school on the island, and his wife, Margaret. And another teacher (he thought) with a red beard, but he didn't know his name. And his wife as well. And a man who worked as a reporter on the local paper, a small pale-faced fellow who smoked endless cigarettes and whose name was Robert.

'Do you want a pint?' asked John, half rising from his seat.

'No, thanks,' said Murdo. There was a glass of vodka or water in front of his wife. Murdo sat down on the edge of the company.

The bar was warm and dark with reddish lights and black leather seats.

'Where have you been?' Janet asked him.

'Oh, just walking around,' said Murdo.

'He's trying to write,' said Janet to the others.

'Write?' said Robert, his eyes lighting up. 'What are you writing?'

'Nothing,' said Murdo. 'I'm only trying to write.'

'Oh,' said Robert, the light almost visibly leaving his eyes as the light at the tip of a cigarette might cease to glow.

John and the red-bearded man began to talk about the school and Murdo listened to them.

At last he asked John why he taught.

'Why?' said John. 'Why am I teaching?' as if he had never asked himself such a question before.

'For the money,' said his wife, laughing.

'That wasn't what I meant,' said Murdo and in a whisper to himself, 'What the hell am I doing here anyway?' He was grinding his teeth against each other to prevent himself from howling like a wolf.

'This is a philosopher we have here,' said Janet in a sharp bitter voice, her lips almost shut.

'You must answer his questions.'

'Oh,' said John, 'I'm teaching History. What can people do without History? They would be like animals.'

'Right,' said Murdo, 'right. Right.' And then,

'Are you an animal?'

John looked at him for a moment with such ferocity that Murdo thought he was going to leap at him like a wildcat but at last he said quietly: 'Animals don't teach each other History.'

'Very good,' said the red-bearded man. 'And now do you want a pint?' he asked Murdo.

'No thanks,' said Murdo and then quite untruthfully, 'My doctor has told me not to drink.' (He used the phrase 'my doctor' with an air of elegant possession though he had hardly ever been to a doctor in his life. He would also sometimes talk about 'my lawyer' in the same aristocratic tone.)

'It would be very funny,' said Robert, 'if animals taught History to each other.'

'It would indeed,' said Murdo.

They were silent for a while till at last Murdo said: 'Once I was sitting opposite a man in a café and there were cakes on the table, some yellow and some white. I took a yellow cake and he took a white one. What's the reason for that?'

'My coat is yellow,' said Margaret. 'That's because I like yellow.'

Janet looked at her own coat which wasn't as rich-looking as Margaret's and a ray of envy passed momently across her face.

'That's a question,' said John to Murdo. 'That's really a difficult question.'

'What café did this happen in?' said Robert as if he was about to take the story down for his newspaper.

'I can't remember,' said Murdo.

'Didn't I tell you he's a philosopher,' said Janet, sipping some vodka or perhaps water or perhaps gin.

Murdo was gazing at the bearded man's wife, a beautiful girl with long blonde hair who was very silent. Beauty, O beauty, he said to himself, Yeats said something about that. My head is so heavy.

Margaret said, 'I just went into the shop and I bought this yellow coat. I don't know why I bought it. I just liked it.'

'Exactly,' said Robert. 'What more can one say about it?

'What are you writing?' he asked Murdo again.

'Nothing,' said Murdo.

'Uh huh,' said John.

Murdo knew that his wife was angry because he had come into the bar disturbing people with his strange questions, and he was glad in a way that she was angry.

At the same time he was afraid that she would get drunk.

John said, 'Well, it's time I was going.' And he and his wife rose from their seats.

'You're sure I can't buy you a pint before I go,' said John again to Murdo.

'I'm sure,' said Murdo.

The bearded man and his wife also rose.

They all went away muttering their goodbyes and Janet, Murdo and Robert were left sitting in their dark corner by a table which was wet with beer.

'What are you writing yourself?' Murdo asked Robert.

Robert looked at him with small bitter eyes. What did he write but pieces about whist drives, local football matches, things without importance?

He didn't answer.

'Did you ever see,' Murdo asked him, 'the white mountain?'

'White mountain,' said Robert. 'What's that?'

'Don't listen to him,' said Janet. 'He doesn't know what he's talking about.'

'Sometimes you're right,' said Murdo.

Robert had been working as a journalist on the local newspaper since leaving school and he had never been out of the island.

'I read in your paper yesterday,' said Murdo, 'that a car was hit by another one on Bruce Street. Do you think that was predestined since the beginning of the world?'

'I don't know,' said Robert curtly, thinking that he was being got at. Murdo felt his head sore again, as often happened to him nowadays.

'It doesn't matter,' he said.

And again,

'But it does matter. Once I was looking at a triangle which was drawn on a piece of paper and it looked so clean and beautiful. And I saw a fly walking across it, across the paper on which the triangle was drawn, and I didn't know where the fly was going. But the triangle was motionless in its own world, in its own space. That was on a summer's day when I was in school. But I forget the year,' he said to Robert.

'I have to go,' said Robert. 'I have something to do.'

'Have you?' said Murdo.

The only people left at the table now were himself and his wife.

'Well,' she said, 'it didn't take you long to send them away with all your questions. What are you trying to do?'

'Why did you lie to me?' said Murdo. 'Why didn't you tell me you were coming to this pub?'

'I don't know,' said Janet.

'You knew I would find out,' said Murdo. 'That's why you did it.'

'Maybe you're right,' said Janet.

We are like the animals right enough, said Murdo to himself. We don't know why we do the things we do.

And he saw his wife like a fox walking across the white mountain.

'Come on home,' he said.

She rose and put on her coat.

'Where's your own coat?' she asked Murdo.

'I left it at home,' said Murdo.

They left the bar and walked home down the street and Murdo put his arm round her.

He felt the warmth of her body on that cold winter's night and his bones trembled.

Then he began to laugh.

'Whist drives,' he said looking up at the sky with its millions of stars. And he made little leaps shouting 'Whist drives' at intervals.

'Are you out of your mind?' said Janet.

He pulled her towards him.

'Do you see that mountain?' he asked her. 'That white mountain. Do you see it?' She was like a ghost glimmering out of the darkness.

'Ben Dorain,' he said laughing.

'I see it,' said Janet. 'What about it?'

'Nothing about it,' said Murdo, looking at the mountain, his warm head beside hers.

The white mountain was shining out of the darkness.

The tears came to his eyes and he felt them on his cheeks.

'You're crying,' she accused him.

'No I'm not,' he said.

She turned towards him and gazed into his eyes.

'Everything will be all right,' she said.

'Yes,' he said. 'I'm sure of it.' And he looked into her eyes. 'Yes,' he repeated.

She tightened her arm round him as if she was frightened that he was going to melt like the snow.

'Come on home,' she said to him in a frightened voice.

'I won't leave you,' he said, 'though your coat is green.'

They walked home quietly together except that now and again Murdo would make another of his leaps shouting 'Whist drives' at the moon that was so bare and bright in the sky above the white mountain.

*

One morning Murdo put on a red rubber nose such as clowns wear or small children at Hallowe'en and went downtown to get the morning papers. Norman Macleod's wife met him at the door of the shop and he said to her:

'It's a fine morning.'

'Yes,' said she, looking at him slightly askance, since he was wearing a red rubber nose.

'But it is not as beautiful a morning as it was yesterday,' Murdo said seriously. 'Not at all as good as yesterday morning. No indeed.'

'You're right there,' said Norman Macleod's wife, looking at his nose. Murdo pretended that he didn't notice her amazed stare.

'You're right there indeed,' said Murdo. 'I myself am of the opinion that it is not so warm this morning as it was yesterday morning,' glancing at the snow which glittered back at him from the roadside.

'Without doubt, without doubt,' said the wife of Norman Macleod.

'For,' Murdo pursued relentlessly, 'the clouds were whiter yesterday than they are today,' drawing nearer to Mrs Macleod and putting his red rubber nose quite close to her face.

'For,' said Murdo, 'when I got up from my bed this morning I nearly went back into it again, a thing that I did not think of doing yesterday. But in spite of that I put one leg before the other as we all have to do in this life at some time or other, indeed at all times, and I decided that I would come for the newspapers, for what can we do without them? What indeed?'

'You're right,' said Mrs Macleod, shifting slightly away from him.

'Yes,' said Murdo, 'in these days especially one must put one leg in front of the other. When the light comes out of the darkness we go in search of the *Daily Record*, those sublime pages that tell us about the murders that have been committed in caravans in the south.'

'Yes,' said Mrs Macleod in a voice that was becoming more and more inaudible as she moved further and further away from the red rubber nose.

'I myself often think,' said Murdo, 'how uninteresting my life would be without the *Daily Record*. That occurs to me often. Often. And often I think what would we do without neighbours? Their warmth, their love . . . These thoughts often occur to me, I may tell you.'

'I suppose . . .' muttered Mrs Macleod, her grip tightening on the newspaper she had in her hand as if she was thinking of using it as a weapon.

'For,' said Murdo intently, 'do you yourself not think that the warmth of the morning is like the warmth we derive from our neighbours. The sun shines on everything and so does the warmth of neighbours. There is a lot wrong with each one of us, we are all flawed in some way but our neighbours forgive us for they say to themselves, "Not one of us is perfect, not one of us is without flaw, so how therefore can we say that others are flawed." These are the thoughts that often occur to me anyway,' said Murdo. 'And I don't think I'm wrong.'

'I'm sure you're . . .' said Mrs Macleod trying to back steadily away while Murdo fixed her closely with his red rubber nose as if he were a demented seagull standing among the snow.

'Give me,' said Murdo, 'one neighbour and I will move

the world.' He considered this for a long time, turning his nose this way and that, the only bright colour that was to be seen on the street. Mrs Macleod wanted desperately to leave but she couldn't move her feet and she didn't know what to say.

Murdo went closer to her.

'I am of the opinion,' he said, 'to tell the truth and without concealing anything from any man or woman, white or black, whoever they are and whatever their colour of skin, I am of the opinion without regard to anyone's politics or religion, for no one can accuse me of being biased, that yesterday morning was as beautiful a morning as we have had for many years. I'm not saying that there don't exist people who would deny that, and who would come to me if they liked with armfuls of records going back to the seventeenth century and before, that would prove that I was wrong, and even naïve in that statement, but in spite of that I still hold to my opinion as I am sure you would under the same circumstances, for I have never thought of you as a coward. Oh I know that there are people who will maintain that neither the summers nor the winters that we endure now are as beautiful and unspotted as the summers and winters of their various childhoods but I would say humbly to these people that they are wrong. THEY ARE WRONG,' he shouted, pushing his nose as close to Mrs Macleod's nose as it could go.

'THEY ARE WRONG,' he repeated in a loud vehement voice. 'As wrong as people can be. I know in my bones that they are wrong. Totally wrong. Totally.' He sighed heavily and then continued:

'As well as that I know that there are professors who would oppose me on this matter. But I know that they are wrong as well. Though I have nothing against professors. Not at all, not at all.

'But I'm keeping you back. I shouldn't have done that. I know that you're busy, that you work without cease, without cease. Lack of consideration, that's what I suffer from, I admit it freely. But I wished to tell you how much more beautiful than this morning yesterday morning was. And I'm glad that you agree with me in my opinion. I am so glad. So glad. It is not often that I feel such gladness. But I know that you wish to go home. I am so glad to have met you.'

Mrs Macleod half walked, half ran, away, looking behind her now and then as if trying to verify that he did indeed have a red rubber nose. Murdo raised his hand to her in royal salute and then went into the shop, having first removed his rubber nose, and bought a newspaper. On his way home he would kick a lump of ice now and again with his boot.

'Drama,' he said to himself. 'Nothing but drama and catharsis. One must look for it even when there is snow on the ground.'

He arrived at a wall and opened out the paper and began to read it, glancing now and again at the white mountain.

He read one page and then threw the paper away from him, but after a while he picked it up and laid it flat on a large piece of ice.

The headlines of the paper said in large black type:

I STILL LOVE HIM THOUGH HE KILLED FOR ME

Murdo found an old boot in the ditch and laid it on top of this headline so that passers-by could read it and then went on his way whistling.

*

One night Murdo was on his way home with a half-bottle of whisky in his hand. He looked up at the sky that was trembling with stars and he began to shout to a group of them that were brighter than the rest:

'Lewis,' and then

'Skye' and finally

'Betelgeuse.' He looked down at his shoes that were yellow in the light of the moon and he said,

'I'm drunk. Murdo is drunk. There is whisky on his shoes. On his shoes there is whisky.'

He then sat down on the road and took off his shoes and raised them towards the moon:

'Here is Murdo. There are Murdo's shoes. They are yellow. Murdo's shoes are yellow.

'O world,' he said, 'how yellow Murdo's shoes are. Ah, Lewis, ah, Skye, ah, Betelgeuse.'

He thought of small yellow men with small yellow shoes drinking on Betelgeuse and he had compassion for them as they sat on the road with a half-bottle of whisky in the hand of each one.

'Ah,' said he, 'do you see the white mountain even on Betelgeuse? Do you have in your hands yellow pencils and are you writing on yellow paper a story about a clerk who left his work in an office on Betelgeuse?'

And the tears came to his eyes.

'Is there a split,' he said, 'between the soul and the body even on Betelgeuse? Is there on that illustrious star a woman like Mrs Macleod, of that ilk?'

And he began to laugh in harmony with the trembling of the stars which also seemed to laugh.

He looked at the sky and he shouted,

'Conscience.'

'Soul.'

'MacBrayne's boats.'

He looked down at his shoes again.

'Leather,' he said.

'Nails,' he said.

'Shoemaker,' he said.

'A shoemaker was born just for me,' he said and he felt pity for the shoes and the shoemaker, a little yellow man with little yellow nails in his mouth.

'Why,' he shouted to Betelgeuese, 'did you put skin on my bones, a worm in my head?'

And he felt the yellow worm in his head like a thin stream of whisky the colour of the moon.

'Existentialism,' he shouted to the moon.

'A lavatory of diamonds.'

'Plato in a thatched house.'

'Mist.'

He stood up and began to sing under the millions of stars a verse of a song he had composed.

> 'The Isle of Mull
> has no grief or sorrow,
> It is so green,
> and will be here tomorrow.'

And he thought of his father and mother and they were like a pair of people who moved in and out of a Dutch clock, yellow and fat with fat red cheeks.

'And,' he said, in a mimicking voice, 'is it from Betelgeuse that you are yourself? When did you come home and when are you going away again?' – the age-old Highland questions.

'I was reared,' he said, 'when I was young and soft. When I grew a little older I thought that I myself was creating the morning and the evening. And at that moment I grew old. The mountains were like fangs in my mind.'

The stars winked at him and he winked back at them and he thought that there was a yellow crown on his head, a sharp yellow crown.

'Without me,' he said, 'sick as I am from *angst* and diarrhoea, you would not be there at all. Are you listening to me? Without me there would be darkness among all the planets.'

He lifted the half-bottle of whisky and he began to drink.

'Your health,' he said. 'Your good health.'

He reached his own house and he saw a ray of yellow light coming out from under the door.

'Like an arrow,' he said.

'Like a knife,' he said.

'Like a pen,' he said, and

'Like a spade,' he said. and finally,

'16 Murchison Street,' he said, 'with the green walls.

'We are all,' he said, 'of a mortal company. Of a proud company,' said he swaying from side to side, the key in his hand.

'Drunkards of the universe,' he said.

'Glory be to the yellow universe,' he said in the yellow light.

He tried to fit his key in the door but couldn't.

'It is not fated,' he said, 'it is not fated that I shall open the door of 16 Murchison Street. The universe is against it.'

He thought of the key as a soul that could not enter its proper body.

'Lewis,' he said to Betelgeuse.

'Skye,' he said.

And finally as if he had climbed a high mountain,

'Tiree.'

And he fell asleep, the key in his hand and the yellow closed door in front of him and a heavy snore coming from him in that cold calm yellow night.

Murdo's Letter to the Poet Dante

Dear Friend,

Can you please tell me when and how you began to write first, and what magazines you sent your first poems to? And what was the animal you saw in the middle of the wood?

For myself, I see this white mountain all the time, day and night. With snow on it.

And in the room next to me there is a table and chairs as like each other as pictures in a mirror. Anyway I hope you will answer my letter for I am trying to write a story about a clerk.

And I don't know how to start.

With much respect and a stamp so that you can answer my letter.

Yours sincerely,
MURDO MACRAE

P.S. You did very well, my friend, with that poem the *Inferno*. But what would you have done without Virgil? I think we all need a friend.

*

Murdo was (as they say) good with children and this is one of the stories he told to his nephew Colin who was six years old at the time:

There was a lad once (said Murdo), and he was seventeen years old. Well, one day he thought that he would leave home where he lived with his father and mother. It was a beautiful autumn day and he saw many strange sights on his way. In the place where he was, there were many trees and the yellow leaves were falling to the ground and they were all so beautiful and sad. But the most wonderful thing of all was that wherever he went – and the day very calm and now and again a fox running through the wood and red berries still on some of the trees – he would see his father's face and his mother's face. Wasn't that strange? Just as if he was in a land of mirrors. In the leaves, in the ground, he would see these faces. This amazed and astonished him. And he didn't know what to do about it. Once in a leaf he saw his house with the door and the windows and his mother standing in the doorway in a blue gown. And once in another leaf he saw his father bending down with a spade, digging.

Well this went on for a long time but at last he didn't see the pictures of his father and mother at all. And then he came to a small village and every man in the village was hitting big stones with hammers, every one of them. When he asked them the name of the village no one would tell him.

In fact they wouldn't speak to him at all. But they just kept hammering away at the stones with their hammers. This was the only sound that could be heard in the village. Think of it, this was all they did all day and every day. And they never spoke to anyone. And he didn't know why they were doing this. He asked them a lot of times why they were hammering the stones but they wouldn't answer him. This astonished him and he himself sat on a stone in his blue dusty suit but they pretended not to see him.

At last he grew tired of sitting down and he went over and looked at one of the men and what he was doing. And he saw that this man was cutting names of people in the stone on which he was working. Murdo didn't recognise any of the names and he was just going to go away when he looked very sharply indeed and he saw that the man was cutting his own name in the stone.

Well, this made Murdo very puzzled and frightened him too, and before he knew what he was doing he was running away from that place till he reached a wood which was very quiet. Not even the voice of a bird was to be heard, and it was very dark there. However, there were some nuts on the trees and he began to eat them. He wandered through this wood for a long time till at last he saw ahead of him a high mountain white with snow though it was still autumn. He stood and stared at this mountain for some time.

Well, just as he was standing there who should he see but a beautiful girl in a green dress just beside him. She had long yellow hair like gold and she said to Murdo in a quiet voice:

'If you will climb that mountain and if you bring me a blue flower that you will find on its slope I will reward you well. My house is quite near here, a small house made of diamonds, and when you get the flower you will come to it and knock on the door and I shall answer.'

Murdo looked around him and sure enough there, not very far away, was a small house made of diamonds.

Well, Murdo made his way towards the mountain and in

a short while he found a blue flower and he ran back to the small house with it and knocked on the door, but no one came to answer his knock. He knocked a few times but still no one came and he didn't know what to do, for he wanted the reward. At last he thought that it might be a good idea to return to the mountain and find an even more beautiful flower and bring it back with him. And with that he left the small house made of diamonds and he went back to the mountain. And he climbed with difficulty further up the slope and found a larger even more beautiful blue flower but he was feeling slightly tired by this time, and he walked much more slowly to the house. Anyway he reached it at last, and he knocked on the door again. The house was shining in the light of the snow and the windows were sending out flashes of light. He knocked and knocked but still no one came to the door. And Murdo returned to the mountain for the third time and this time he decided that he would climb to the very top and he would find a flower so lovely that the beautiful girl would be forced to open the door for him. And he did this. He climbed and climbed and his breath grew shorter and shorter and his legs grew weaker and weaker and sometimes he felt dizzy because of the great height. For four hours he climbed and the air was getting thinner and thinner and Murdo was shivering with the cold and his teeth were chattering in his head, but he was determined that he would reach the top of the mountain.

At last, tired and cold, he reached the top and he saw in front of him the most beautiful flower he had ever seen in his life but this flower was not blue like the other ones. It was white. Anyway Murdo pulled the beautiful white flower out of the ground and he looked at it for a long time as it lay in his hand. But a strange thing happened then. As he looked, the beautiful white flower began to melt and soon there was nothing left of it but a little water. And all around him was the cold white mountain.

Slowly Murdo went down the mountainside, feeling very

tired and cold, and he looked for the small house made of diamonds but he couldn't find it anywhere. There was only a small hut without windows or doors. And Murdo looked at it for a long time and said to himself, 'But it may be that I shall meet that beautiful girl again somewhere.' And he continued on his way through the wood. But I don't think he ever met that beautiful girl again, though he travelled through many countries, except perhaps for one moment when he was lying on the ground, very tired, and he was staring at an old boot and he saw a flash of what might have been her. But perhaps it was his imagination for the moon was shining on the old boot at the time.

Murdo looked down at Colin who had fallen asleep.

'Well,' he said to himself, 'maybe he didn't like the story after all.'

This is an advertisement which Murdo sent to the editor of the local paper but which was never printed:

Wanted: a man of between a hundred and two hundred years of age who knows the works of Kant and the poetry of William Ross, and who can drive a tractor and a car, for work on the roads for three weeks in the year. Such a man will get – particularly if he's healthy – two pounds a year. It would be an advantage if he knew a little Greek.

*

The reader must now be told something about Murdo. He was born in a small village where there were twenty houses and which stood beside the sea. When he was growing up he spent a lot of his time drawing drifters on scraps of paper: and the most wonderful day of his life was the day that he jumped across the river Caras.

When he was on his way to school he would think of himself as walking through the forests of Africa, but the schoolmistress told him that he must learn the alphabet.

One day she asked him to write an essay with the title, 'My Home'. Murdo wrote twenty pages about a place where there were large green forests, men with wings, aeroplanes made of diamond, and rainbow-coloured stairs.

She said to him, 'What does all this stuff mean? Are you laughing at me or what?' She gave him two strokes of the belt.

After that Murdo grew very good at counting, and he could compute in his head in seconds 1,005 x 19. This pleased the schoolmistress and when the inspector visited the school she showed him Murdo with great pride. 'This boy will make a perfect clerk,' said the inspector, and he gave him a hard white sweet.

Murdo went home and told his father and mother what the inspector had said. But he didn't tell them that in the loft he kept an effigy of the schoolmistress which was made of straw and that every evening he pierced it with the sharp point of his pencil.

Nor did he tell them that he painted the walls of the loft with pictures of strange animals that he could see in his dreams.

One day when Murdo was fifteen years old the headmaster sent for him.

'Sit down,' he said.

Murdo sat down.

'And what do you intend to do now that you are leaving school?' said the headmaster who had a small black moustache.

'27 x 67 = 1,809,' said Murdo.

The headmaster looked at him with astonishment and his spectacles nearly fell off his nose.

'Have you any idea at all what you're going to do?' he asked again.

'259 x 43 = 11,137,' said Murdo.

The headmaster then told him that he could leave, that he had much work to do. Murdo saw two girls going into his study with a tray on which there was a cup of tea and two biscuits.

When he came out the other boys asked him what the headmaster had wanted with him and Murdo said that he didn't know.

Anyway he left the school on a beautiful summer's day while the birds were singing in the sky. He was wearing a white shirt with short sleeves and it was also open at the neck.

When he was going out the gate he turned and said, '45 x 25 = 1,125.' And after that he walked home.

His mother was hanging clothes on the line when he arrived and taking the pegs out of her mouth she said:

'Your schooldays are now over. You will have to get work.'

Murdo admitted that this was true and then went into the house to make tea for himself.

He saw his father working in the field, bent like a shepherd's crook over a spade. Murdo sat at the table and wrote a little verse:

> He he said the horse
> ho ho said the goat
> Ha ha, O alas,
> said the brown cow in the byre.

He was greatly pleased with this and copied it into a little book. Then he drank his tea.

*

One day Murdo said to his wife, 'Shall we climb that white mountain?'

'No,' she said with astonishment. 'It's too cold.'

Murdo looked around him. The chairs were shining in the light like precious stones. The curtains were shimmering with light as if they were water. The table was standing on its four precious legs. His wife in her blue dress was also precious and precious also was the hum of the pan on the cooker. 'I remember,' he told his wife, 'when I was young I used to listen every Sunday to the sound of the pot boiling on the fire. We had herring all during the week.'

'We too,' said his wife, 'but we had meat on Sunday.' She was thinking that Murdo wasn't looking too well and this frightened her. But she didn't say anything to him.

'Herring,' said Murdo, 'what would we do without it? The salt herring, the roasted herring. The herring that swims through the sea among the other more royal fish. So calm. So sure of itself.'

'One day my father killed a rabbit with his gun,' said his wife.

'I'm sure,' said Murdo.

'I'm telling the truth,' Janet insisted.

'I'm not denying it,' said Murdo as he watched the shimmering curtains. And the table shone in front of him, solid and precious and fixed, and the sun glittered all over the room.

O my happiness, he said to himself. O my happiness. How happy the world is without me. How the world doesn't need me. If only I could remember that. The table is so calm and fixed, without soul, single and without turmoil, the chairs compose a company of their own.

'Come on, let's dance,' he said to Janet.

'What, now?' she said.

'Yes,' said Murdo, 'now.

'Let's dance now.'

'All right then,' said Janet.

And they began to dance among the chairs, and the pan shone red in a corner of its own.

And Murdo recalled how they had used to dance in their youth on the autumn nights with the moon above them and his heart so full that it was like a bucket full of water, almost spilling over.

At last Janet sat down, as she was breathless.

And Murdo sat on a chair beside her.

'Well, well,' said he, 'we must do that oftener.'

'Oh the pan,' said his wife and she ran over to the cooker where the pan was boiling over.

The pan, said Murdo to himself, the old scarred pan. It also is dancing.

On its own fire.

Everything is dancing, said Murdo, if we only knew it. The whole world is dancing. The lion is dancing and the lamb is dancing. Good is dancing with Evil in an eternal reel in an invisible light. And he thought of them for a moment, Good and Evil, with their arms around each other on a fine autumn evening with the dew falling steadily and invisibly on the grass.

*

Sometimes Janet thought that Murdo was out of his mind. Once when they were in Glasgow they went into a café where there was a juke box which was playing 'Bridge over Troubled Waters' and Murdo sat at the green, scarred, imitation marble-topped table. He was wearing a thick heavy black coat such as church elders wear and a hard black hat on his head.

When the music stopped he went over to the juke box, put money in the slot and the music started again, whereupon sitting at the table in his black coat and stiff black hat he swayed to the music, moving his head from side to side as if he were in a trance of happiness. A number of girls gazed at him with astonishment.

Also in Glasgow he went up to a policeman and asked him, 'Could you please direct me to Parnassus Street, officer. I think it's quite near Helicon Avenue, or so I was told.'

He bent his head as if he were listening carefully to what the policeman might say.

'Parnassus Street,' said the policeman, a large heavy man with a slow voice. 'What part of the city did you say it was in again?'

'I think, or so I was told, I don't know whether it's right

or wrong, I'm a stranger in the city myself,' said Murdo, 'I'm sure someone said to me that it's very near Helicon Avenue.'

'Helicon Avenue?' said the policeman, gazing at Murdo and then at Murdo's wife and then down at his boots.

'It may be in one of the new schemes,' said Murdo helpfully, his head on one side like a bird's on a branch.

'That may be,' said the policeman. 'I'm very sorry but I can't inform you where the places you mention happen to be.'

'Oh that's all right,' said Murdo looking at a radiant clock which had stopped at three o'clock. 'There are so many places, aren't there?' (Muttering under his breath, 'Indonesia, Hong Kong, Kilimanjaro.')

'You're right,' said the policeman, and then turned away to direct the traffic, raising a white glove.

'I think that policeman is from the Highlands,' said Murdo. 'He's got a red neck. And red fists. Big red fists.'

But at other times Murdo would sit in the house completely silent like a spider putting out an invisible web. And Janet wasn't used to such silence. She came from a family that always had something to say, always had morsels of news to feed to each other.

And for a lot of the time she felt lonely even when Murdo was with her. Sometimes when they were sitting in the kitchen Murdo would come over to her with a piece of paper on which he had written some such word as

BLOWDY

'What do you think that word means?' Murdo would say to her.

'Blowdy?' Janet would say. 'I never heard that word before.'

'Didn't you?' Murdo would say. Blowdy, he would say to himself again.

Blowdy, blowdy, among the chairs, the green walls.

Once when his mother-in-law was in drinking tea Murdo said to her quietly:

'It's a fine blowdy day today.'

'What did you say?' said his mother-in-law, the cup of tea in her lap and a crumb of bread on her lip.

'A fine blowdy day,' Murdo said, 'a fine windy bright blowdy day.'

'It's a windy day right enough,' said his mother-in-law, looking meaningfully at Janet.

'That's an Irish word,' said Murdo. 'The Irish people used it to give an idea of the kind of marbly clouds that you sometimes see in the sky on a windy day, and also when the wind is from the east.'

'Oh?' said his mother-in-law looking at him carefully.

When Murdo had gone back to his room she said to Janet: 'I don't think Murdo is all there. Do you think he is?'

'Well,' said Janet, 'he acts very funny at times.'

'He's worse than funny,' said her mother. 'Do you remember at the wedding when he took a paper ring from his pocket and he was wearing a piece of cabbage instead of a flower like everybody else?'

'I remember it well enough,' said her daughter. 'But he's very good at figures.'

'That's right enough,' said her mother, 'but a man should be more settled than he is. He should be indeed.'

After her mother had left Janet sat in her chair and began to laugh and she could hardly stop, but at the same time she felt frightened as if there was some strange unnatural being in the house with her.

*

For about the seventh or the eighth time Murdo tried to write a story.

'There was a clerk once and he was working in a bank . . .'

When Murdo was working he used to go into the bank at nine in the morning and he would finish at five in the afternoon. And he had an hour for his lunch. There were another ten people working in the bank with him and Murdo would sit at a desk and add figures all day, at the back of the bank, in the half-dark.

Beside him there sat a small bald man who had been in the bank for thirty years and who was always wiping his nose as if there was something there that he wished continually to clean off. At last Murdo said to him, 'Why do you do that?'

'What?' said the man.

'Why do you wipe your nose all the time?' said Murdo.

'It's none of your business,' said the bald man and after that he wouldn't speak to Murdo. They would sit beside each other all day and they wouldn't speak to each other. They wouldn't even say Good morning to each other.

Murdo would begin to think about money. When he was in the bank he would see thousands and thousands of banknotes and it would occur to him:

What if I stole some money and went away to the Bahamas or some place like that? But actually the place he really wanted to go to was Rome and he imagined himself standing among these stony ruins wearing a red cloak while the sun was setting and he was gazing down at the city like a conqueror.

After a time, he would, in his imagination, enter a café and eat spaghetti and he would meet a girl in a mini-skirt and he would say to her:

'Is your name Beatrice?'

And they would stand in the sunset where red fires were burning and there would be a church behind her, a church with gigantic carvings by Michelangelo.

'Have you ever heard of Leonardo da Vinci?' he would say to her and she would look at him with dull pebbly eyes in which no soul was visible.

And in the morning Murdo would rise from his bed and he would see a new world in front of him, a bright clean world, a new morning, and he'd say:

'Where will we go today?'

And she would be asleep and he would leave her there like a corrupted angel with arms as white as those of Venus and a small discontented mouth, and he would go out and he would talk to the women with their long Italian noses and after that he would leave Rome and travel to Venice and sail on a gondola, his red cloak streaming from his shoulders.

And all around him there would be colours such as he had never seen before and his nose would twitch like a rabbit's.

And in an art gallery he would stand in front of a painting and the painting would show a man walking down a narrow road while ahead of him the sun was setting in a green light like the light of the sea.

And he would meet a priest and he would say to him, 'What is keeping you alive?'

And the priest would say to him, 'Come with me and I'll show you.'

And they would go into a small room in a small dirty house and there would be a child lying in bed there with a red feverish face, and beside the bed there would be a woman wearing a black snood. And she would be sitting there motionless while the child stirred restlessly in the bed. And the priest would say to Murdo:

'She has been sitting by that bed for nearly a week now.'

'Do you think,' Murdo would ask, 'that Leonardo had as much care for the Mona Lisa as this woman has for her child?'

And he would look around him, at the picture of the Virgin Mary and the candle that was burning in a corner of the room.

'I understand what you're saying,' the priest would say.

'I hope the child will recover,' Murdo would say.

'Exactly like that,' the priest would say, 'God keeps a watch over the world till the sun rises.'

Murdo would leave the priest and the woman and the child and walk down a street where he would be met by two men who would attack him, beating him on the head and chest, and steal all the money he had except for the six thousand pounds that were tied round his pants.

'Well, well,' he'd say to the blank Italian sky, 'there is nothing here but troubles.'

He would then see a group of people standing beside a house that had fallen to the ground.

One of the women would say, 'My mother and father are in there dead. And what I want to know is, what is the government going to do about it?'

'I am from the government myself,' Murdo would say. 'And here are two hundred pounds for you.'

'Two hundred pounds isn't enough,' the woman would say, 'to compensate for all the love I felt for my father and mother. I would require five hundred pounds at least. But I'll take the two hundred pounds just now.'

'Right,' Murdo would say and he would run away, his red cloak streaming down his back and from his shoulders as if they were the wings of an angel or a devil.

He would hear sweet voices floating from the gondolas and his heart would be at peace.

When he would wake from his Italian dream the man beside him would be wiping his nose.

'I'm sorry,' Murdo would say to him, 'for what I said to you before.'

But the man wouldn't answer him.

After Murdo had resigned from the bank he sent the man a letter saying.

I had nothing against your nose. But I'm certain that if you hope to get on in the world you must stop wiping your nose. Napoleon didn't wipe his nose continually. Or William Wallace. I'm sorry to tell you this but I'm only doing it for your own good.

Yours sincerely,
Murdo Macrae

*

What was Murdo like? Well, he was about five feet ten inches in height, thin, pale-faced (like the clerk he once had been) and blue-eyed. He shaved himself every morning at half-past eight, sometimes listening to the radio and sometimes whistling in a monotonous melancholy manner. He often cut himself with his razor blade and for this reason he bought sticks of styptic which he could never find and which, after being dipped in water, became soggy. He ate very little food and this worried Janet. He had a theory that too much food made his brain feel heavy, and that this was particularly the case with meat and soup, though not with fish. At nine o'clock he would go and sit at his desk, open the notebook in which he had been trying to write and look at it. He would then take out of his pocket the green pen which he had once found on the road near the house and chew it for a long while, still looking down at the paper. Now and again he would get up from his chair and walk about the room, stopping to study a purple bucket in the corner. He had a strong affection for this bucket: he thought that some day it would yield him some extraordinary vision.

Then he would go back to his chair and sit down again.

He would sometimes think that there was a crown on his head and that he was king of a country which did not yet exist but which would some day emerge with its own constitution. In this country poets and novelists, painters and ballet dancers, musicians and singers would be the most respected citizens. He would think to himself:

How did other writers work? It is said that Schiller (was it Schiller?) would keep a rotten apple in his desk and that he would take it out every morning, and its corrupt smell would arouse his imagination.

For this reason Murdo got an apple, and kept it in his desk till it was rotten, but one day Janet found it and threw it out. And some bird or other ate it.

After some time he might leave the house altogether and go for a walk.

No matter how cold the day was he never wore a coat.

One morning he was walking down the main street when he met the manager of the bank, a man called Maxwell. Maxwell always carried a rolled umbrella even if the day was perfectly fine with no sign of rain. He also wore thick black glasses.

'Imphm,' he said to Murdo.

'Good morning,' Murdo said.

'Imphm,' said Maxwell.

At last he recognised Murdo and he said to him, looking at him sideways all the time in a furtive manner,

'I'm sorry you felt you had to leave the bank. We needed you.'

'Imphm,' said Murdo.

'It's not easy to get work nowadays,' said Maxwell. 'What are you doing?'

'Imphm,' said Murdo.

He was afraid that if he told Maxwell that he didn't do anything, was in fact totally idle though committed to a blank sheet of paper, that Maxwell would fall dead in the road.

At last he said, 'I'm looking after my grandfather. There is no one in the house but myself and him and his old dog which he had in the Great War.'

'An old dog?' said Maxwell.

'Yes,' said Murdo. 'An old dog. He's very fond of my grandfather. He saved his life at Passchendaele. He picked him up between his teeth and took him back to the British lines after he had been very badly nay almost fatally wounded. Nay. He laid him down at the feet of a first lieutenant called Griffiths. From Ilfracombe.'

'Well, well,' said Maxwell, 'well, well.' Murdo was gazing directly at a point between Woolworths and the Italian café and Maxwell was gazing at a point between Lows and Templetons, and they stood like that for a long while in the cold morning. At last Maxwell said, 'I must go to the office. I'm glad I met you. Imphm.'

And he went away. Murdo looked after him in a vague negligent manner and then went into Woolworths.

He weighed himself and found that he was ten stone two pounds.

He walked from counter to counter. He picked up a book about vampires, glanced at it and then went up to a girl in a yellow dress who was paring her nails. On her breast the name *Lily* was written.

'Lily,' said he, 'have you any tins of Arragum? Lily. It's a kind of paint,' he added trying to be helpful.

'Arragum?'

'Yes,' said Murdo. 'It's for windows and doors and tables. It's used a lot in places where there is great cold and sometimes much rain. The Eskimos use it a great deal.'

'Arragum?' she said. 'I don't think that . . .'

'Well,' said Murdo, 'maybe it's called Arragul, I'm not sure. I saw it advertised in the *Observer* Colour Supplement.'

'Wait a minute,' she said, and she went and got another girl in the same yellow uniform as her own, except that instead of *Lily* the name *Mary* was written on the breast.

'Arragum?' said Mary. 'I never heard of that.'

'Well,' said Murdo, 'it doesn't matter. You can't have everything in the shop. But it just occurred to me that as I was passing anyway . . .'

'What was that name again?' said Mary, taking a pencil from her breast pocket.

'Arragum,' said Murdo. 'A-R-R-A-G-U-M. I think the Queen uses it.'

'Well, we can try and get it,' said Mary.

'All right,' said Murdo. 'I think there'll be a big demand for it after that article.'

And with that he left.

He was thinking of his grandfather and the dog that looked after him, and this imagined world became real to him. The dog was large and had gentle brown eyes and he would lie there on the rug in front of the fire gazing at his slightly damaged grandfather, who was thinking of Passchendaele and the Somme and the early sun glittering on the early bayonets. O those early days, those days of untarnished youth.

I could have gone to Vietnam myself, said Murdo, but I was

too lazy. I didn't do anything about it, I stayed where I was in the bank reading about it in the papers. I did not set my breast against battle, no indeed. And why didn't I? Who knows the answer to that question? Because I believe in nothing, said Murdo to himself.

He saw a Pakistani a little ahead of him but did not go to speak to him.

For what could I say to him? He has come from another world, he belongs to another civilisation. I myself come from the civilisation of TV. He walked up the road and sat on a bench. After a while the town fool called Donnie came and sat beside him. He was carrying a brown paper parcel from which there came the smell of salt herring.

'Fine day,' said Donnie, his eyes blinking rapidly. 'Fine day.'

He was wearing a long brown dirty coat which trailed to his ankles. The smell of salt herring was in Murdo's nostrils.

'A fine day,' said Donnie again.

After a while he said, 'I don't suppose you could give me a penny. A penny so I can buy sweets.'

'No understand,' said Murdo. 'No understand. Me German. Tourist.'

The fool turned his head away slowly and gazed towards the farther shore, his large head like a cannonball, his body like a dull rusty gun. His dirty brown hair streamed down the collar of his coat.

At last he turned to Murdo and said, 'I was wondering if you could spare a shilling for a man in poor circumstances.'

Murdo rose rapidly from his seat, and said, 'Me German. Me no understand your money. Me without pity. Have done enough for shrinking pound already. What fought war for, what sent Panzer divisions into civilised treasuries of the West for, if required to prop up currency now? Regard this as paradox of our time.' And he went away thinking of the fool.

He stood for a long time watching the children play in an adjacent park and then went slowly home.

A Letter to the Prime Minister

I am of the opinion that there is a strong conspiracy afoot to undermine this country of ours.

Why do people sit watching TV all the time? I am convinced that there are certain rays which come out of the TV set and that these rays are causing people to lose their commitment to the pure things of life.

Did you ever consider the possibility that John Logie Baird was a Communist?

Do you really believe that there is no connection between the rise of TV and the rise of Communism in the Western world?

Who controls TV? Let me ask you that. Let me put that question to you in all sincerity.

And if the Russians attacked this country what would our people be doing? I think they would continue to sit and watch the TV.

AND THEY WOULD NOT BELIEVE IT WAS AN ATTACK BY THE RUSSIANS AT ALL. THEY WOULD THINK IT WAS A TV DOCUMENTARY.

Did this ever occur to you?

And as well as that there are many people who do not believe that you yourself exist at all. They believe that you have been assembled on TV.

If this is false please answer this letter at once and establish your identity.

With great respect,
Murdo Macrae

I nearly signed my letter PRO PUBLICO BONO but there has been such a decline in the use of the Latin language that I could not do so. And what is the cause of that? Is it not the TV?

*

Now and again Murdo would go and visit his father whose health was rather poor and who lived by himself since the death of his wife. His father would be sitting by the fire on the cold winter's day and Murdo would think of the days when his father had been fit and strong and how when he himself was young his father would take him out fishing.

And now all he had was his pension and a moderately warm hearth. He wouldn't go and live with Murdo and Janet not because he didn't like them but because he didn't want to leave his own house.

Sometimes he would speak of Libya where he had fought in the war.

'There was this fellow from Newcastle beside me,' he would say, 'when we were in the trenches, and he was always saying that he wanted a quick death. Well, that happened right enough. One evening I looked down at him (he was beside me, you see) and he had no head. A shell had taken his head off. It was like a football.'

'Well, well, imagine that,' his visitors would say. 'Isn't that funny. Well well. Think of that, no head on him.'

'Ay, ay, that's the way it was,' Murdo's father would say. 'He had no head. The head was beside me in the sand there like a football.' And Murdo would see the naked head on the sand, the head without thought or imagination.

'And how are you today?' Murdo would say as he went into the house.

'Oh, no complaints, no complaints,' his father would answer. There would often be an open tin of Spam on the table.

'Is there anything to be done?'

'No, nothing, nothing at all.'

When Murdo was young his father would carry him on his shoulders and show him off to people and he would buy for him chocolate sweets in the shape of cats or dogs.

And he would teach him how to fish on red sunset evenings.

Murdo would sweep the floor or dry the dishes of which the sink was full. And his father would say to him, 'You don't need to do that. I'll do that myself.'

And at last Murdo would sit in front of the fire and his father would tell him a story.

'One time,' he said, 'we were in Libya and there was a man there from the islands and he was always reading the Bible. I don't know whether he was frightened or what. Anyway he was always reading the Bible any chance that he had. He knew it from end to end, I would think.

'Well, he once told me this story. One night, he told me, there was a great sandstorm and the sand was thick about the desert, so thick he said that he couldn't see hardly a yard in front of him, and he was afraid that the Germans would suddenly come out of the middle of it with their guns. Well, he said he was waiting there ready with his own gun and he was looking into the middle of the sandstorm with a handkerchief over his mouth. "Well," he said, "I don't know whether you'll believe this or not but about three in the morning out of the middle of the sandstorm there came this man with a beard and in a long white gown. He was like an Arab and some were saying that many of the Arabs were on the side of the Germans. Anyway," he said, "I raised my gun and I fired at this fellow in the long white gown. But he came straight on and there were no marks at all in his breast where I had hit him at point-blank range and he came right on in his long white gown and he went straight through me. He was smiling all the time and he went straight through me. Isn't that funny?"

'Think of that now,' said his father to Murdo. 'Eh? But he was a bit queer that same fellow right enough.'

These were the kinds of stories that Murdo's father would tell Murdo as they sat in front of the fire on a cold winter's day while now and again Murdo's father would light and relight his pipe. Nearly all his stories were about the war.

And Murdo would look out of the window and he would

see the movement of the grass under the cold wind, and the world outside so dark and dull and sometimes stormy.

And he would think of his mother in her long blue apron with the red flowers on it as she walked about the house while his father would be quietly reading the paper. And he himself would be playing on the floor with a train which his father had bought for him.

What had his father been doing in Libya anyway disguised as a soldier? What good had his soldiership done for him, now as he sat by the fire and the wind blew coldly and endlessly round his house.

His father didn't know that Murdo was unemployed: he thought of him with pride as a clerk in a well-known and well-trusted bank.

Once his father had said to him, 'Do you know something? Your mother always said that you should have been a minister. Did you know that?'

'No, I didn't know that,' said Murdo, astonished by the absurdity of the statement.

'Ay,' said his father, 'she used to say that. She used to say that often to me. "Murdo should be a minister," she would say. "One day Murdo will be a minister. You mark my words. He's got the face of a minister."'

'Well, well,' said Murdo, 'well, well.'

And he would look into the red glowing fire as if he was seeing a pulpit there and he would hear himself saying, 'In the immortal words of our theologian De Sade ...'

After a time he would get to his feet and he would say, 'I'll come again next week. Look after yourself.'

And his father would say, 'Don't worry about me. I'll do that all right.'

And Murdo would leave the house and look at the snow and test the thin roof of ice over the pools with the toe of his shoe delicately and elegantly as if he were thinking of some new ballet, and he would think of his father in Libya and his dead mother and Maxwell walking up and down the winter landscape with a rolled umbrella in his hand.

*

Here is another story that Murdo told little Colin:

In a country far away (he said), there once lived a little mouse and this mouse used to go to her work every day. She would sit at a desk and write in a big book. She even wore glasses. When her work in the office was over she would take the bus home and then she would make her tea and look at the TV and put her feet up on the sofa.

At eight o'clock at night she would make her supper, wash the dishes and watch the TV again. And after that she would go to bed.

At eight o'clock in the morning she would get up, listen to the radio for a little while, wash herself, eat her breakfast and then she would go to the office again. And she did this every day from Monday to Friday.

Sometimes on Friday night after the week's work was over she would have a party for the other mice in the neighbourhood, and they would eat a lot of cheese.

Well, one day, about twelve o'clock, she came out of the office and she took a walk down to a big quiet river that was quite near the place where she worked and she was eating her dinner on the bank of the river – a piece of bread and cheese – when she saw a large white swan swimming in the water. The swan was very beautiful and as white as snow and it had a large red beak which now and again it dipped into the water as if it was drinking. Now and again it would glance towards the bank of the river and stare as if it was seeing the mouse, but of course it couldn't have, as the mouse was so small.

That swan seems to have a very easy life of it, said the mouse to herself. All it does all day is swim about in the water and look at its own reflection and eat and drink. No wonder it looks so beautiful and clean. It doesn't have to cook its dinner or its supper or its breakfast: it doesn't have to wash and dry dishes: it doesn't have to sweep the floor: and it doesn't have to get up in the morning. That swan must be very happy.

And the swan looked so queenly, so calm, swimming in the river like a great white picture. And the mouse said to herself, wouldn't it be wonderful if I could lead the same sort of life? I too would be like a queen.

Well, one day the mouse's manager in the office was very angry with her because of a mistake she had made in her books, and he told her that she must come back and work late at five o'clock at night. When the mouse left the office she began to cry.

Look, she said to herself, at the life I lead. I try to do my best and look what happens to me. Tonight I was going to wash my clothes and now I have to go back to the office though I don't want to do that. Some of the other mice in the office laugh at me and some of them steal my food.

And so she looked out at the swan that was swimming so calmly in the water.

'I'm just as good as you,' she said to the swan. 'I do more work than you. You never did any work in your life. What use are you to the country? You never do anything but admire yourself in the water. Well, it's high time I got some rest as well. I need it more than you do. Anyway in my own way I'm just as beautiful as you. And there were kings and queens in my family as well, I'm sure, in the past, though now I'm working in an office.'

She was so upset that she couldn't eat her food and later a crow came down from the sky and ate it.

Anyway the mouse jumped into the river thinking that she would swim just as well as the swan was doing.

But she slowly began to sink because she wasn't used to swimming and she was drowned in the river and the swan continued to swim round and round, dipping her throat now and again in the water, and then raising it and looking around her with her long neck and her blunt red beak.

*

Murdo sent the following to the local newspaper, but it was never printed.

Is Calvin Still Alive?

Many people think that Hitler is still alive and that he is living in South America with money that he stole from the Jews.

But there is a rumour going about this island that Calvin is still alive. He is supposed to have been seen in a small house a little out of town on the road to Holm.

He is a small hunchbacked man with spectacles, who speaks to no one, or if he does speak he speaks in very sloppy not to say ungrammatical Gaelic.

He has a face like iron and he is said to sit at a table night and day studying a Bible almost as big as himself.

He can't stand a candle in the same house.

If he sees anyone drinking or smoking he rushes out of the house and shouts insults at him and dances up and down on the road, shaking his fist.

He also has a strong aversion to cars.

If he sees a woman approaching he shuts the door at once and sits at the window shaking his fist at her and mouthing inaudible words. If she looks at him he shuts his eyes and keeps them shut till she has gone past. After that he washes his face.

He wears black gloves on his hands. He hardly ever leaves the house in the summer but in the winter he goes on long walks.

Now a number of people in the village wonder if you can find a picture of Calvin so that they can establish his identity. It may be that this is a man who is impersonating Calvin for some reason of his own.

If anyone were to say that it would certainly be odd to find Calvin still alive, I would answer that stranger things have happened down the centuries.

What about for instance the man in the Bible who rose to heaven in a chariot?

And what about Nebuchadnezzar who lived on grass for many years?

It is also odd that this man won't go to any of our churches but that now and again on a Sunday he will be seen hanging about one of them though he won't actually go in.

I await your answer with much interest. I enclose a stamp.

Yours etc.,
MURDO MACRAE

*

One day Murdo visited the local library and he said to the thin bespectacled woman who was standing at the counter:

'I want the novel *War and Peace* written by Hugh Macleod.'

'Hugh Macleod?' she said.

'Yes,' he said, 'but if you don't happen to have *War and Peace* I'll take any other book by the same author, such as *The Brothers Karamazov*.'

'I thought,' she said doubtfully, 'I mean are you sure that . . .'

'I'm quite sure that the book is by Hugh Macleod,' said Murdo, 'and I often wonder why there aren't more of his books in the libraries.'

'Well,' she said, 'I think we have *War and Peace* but surely it was written by Tolstoy.'

'What's it about?' said Murdo. 'Is it about a family growing up in Harris at the time of Napoleon?'

'I thought,' she said, 'that the story is set in Russia,' looking at him keenly through her glasses.

'Bloody hell,' said Murdo under his breath and then aloud,

'Oh well I don't think we can be talking about the same Hugh Macleod. This man was never in Russia as far as I know. Is it a long book, about a thousand pages?'

'I think that's right,' said the woman, who was beginning to look rather wary.

'Uh huh,' said Murdo. 'This is a long book as well. It's about Napoleon in Harris in the eighteenth century. Hugh Macleod was an extraordinary man, you know. He had a long beard and he used to make his own shoes. A strange man. I don't really know much about his life except that he became a bit religious in his old age. But it doesn't matter. If you haven't got *War and Peace* maybe you could give me his other book *The Brothers Karamazov*. It's about three brothers and their struggle for a croft.'

'I don't think,' said the woman, 'that we have that one.'

'Well, isn't that damnable,' said Murdo. 'Here you have an author as distinguished as any that has ever come out of the Highlands and you don't have his books. And I can't get them in any other library. I think it's shameful. But I bet you if he was a Russian you would have all his books. I'm pretty sure that you'll have *Tramping through Siberia* by Gogol. Anyway it doesn't matter.

'But I was forgetting another reason for my call,' and he took a can out of his pocket. 'I'm collecting money for authors who can't write. A penny or two will do.'

'Authors who can't write?' said the woman looking suspiciously at the can as if it might explode in her face.

'That's right,' said Murdo. 'Poor people who sit at their desks every morning and find that they can't put a word to paper. Have you ever spared a thought for them? Those people who can write don't of course need help. But think,' he said, leaning forward, 'of those people who sit at their desks day after day while the sun rises and the sun sets and when they look at their paper they find that there isn't a word written on it. Do you not feel compassion for them? Aren't your bowels moved with pity? Doesn't it surprise you that in our modern society not enough is done for such people?'

'Well,' she said, 'to tell the truth . . .'

'Oh, I know what you're going to say,' said Murdo. 'Why should you give money for nonexistent books? And that point of view is natural enough. There is a great deal in it. But has it ever occurred to you that the books that have never been written may be as good as, nay even better than, the ones that have? That there is in some heaven or other books as spotless as the angels themselves without a stain of ink on them? For myself, I can believe this quite easily as I put a lot of credence in the soul as I am sure you do also. Think,' he said, 'if this room were full of nonexistent unwritten books how much easier your job would be.'

He saw her hand creeping steadily towards the phone that lay on her desk and said hurriedly,

'Perhaps that day will come though it hasn't come yet.'

He took the can in his hand and half-ran half-walked out of the library down the corridor with the white marble busts of Romans on each side of him.

Still half running he passed a woman laden with books and said, 'I'm sorry. Bubonic plague. Please excuse me. I'll be all right in a few minutes. Brucellosis,' and half crouching he ran down the brae among the bare trees and the snow.

Ahead of him he saw the white mountain and he shook his fist at it shouting

'Neil Munro. Neil Munro.'

After a while he took a black hat out of his bag and he went home limping, now and again removing his hat when he saw a child walking past him on the street.

*

'The potato,' said Murdo to his wife one night, 'what is like the potato? What would we do without the potato especially in the islands? The potato is sometimes wet and sometimes dry. It is even said that the dry potato is "laughing" at you. Now that is a very odd thing, a laughing potato. But it could happen. And there are many people whose faces are like potatoes. If we had no potatoes we would have to eat the herring with our tea and that wouldn't be very tasty. In the spring we plant the potatoes and we pick them in the autumn. Now in spite of that no poet has made a poem for the humble potato. It didn't occur to William Ross or Alexander Macdonald – great poets though they were – to do so, and I am sure that they must have eaten a lot of potatoes in their poetic careers.

'There is a very big difference, when you think of it, between the potato and the herring. The herring moves, it travels from place to place in the ocean, and they say that there aren't many fish in the sea faster than the herring. But the potato lies in the dark till someone digs it up with a graip. We should therefore ask ourselves, Which is the happier of the two, the potato or the herring? That is a big philosophical question and it astonishes me that it hasn't been studied in greater depth. It is a very profound question. For the potato lies there in the dark, and it doesn't hear or see anything. But in spite of that we have no evidence that it is less happy than the herring. No indeed. And as well as that we have no evidence that the herring is either happy or unhappy. The herring journeys through the ocean meeting many other kinds of fish on its way, such as seals and mackerel.

'But the potato stays in the one place in the dark in its brown skin, without, we imagine, desire or hope. For what could a potato hope for? Or what could it desire? Now at a certain time, the potato and the herring come together on the one plate, say on a summer day or on an autumn day. It greatly puzzles me how they come together in that fashion. Was it predestined that that particular herring and that particular potato should meet – the herring that was roving the sea in its grey dress and the potato that was lying in the earth in its brown dress. That is a very deep question. And the herring cannot do without the potato, nor for that matter can the potato do without the herring. For they need each other.

'They are as closely related as the soul and the body. But is the herring the body or the soul?

'That is another profound question.

'And also you can roast a potato and you can roast a herring but I don't think they are as good when they are roasted. I myself think that the herring is better when it is salted and I may say the same about the potato.

'But no one has ever conjectured about the feelings of the potato or the feelings of the herring. The herring leaves its house and travels all over the world and it sees strange sights in the sea, but the potato sees nothing, it is lying in the darkness while the days and the weeks and the years pass. The potato doesn't move from the place in which it was planted.

'I must make a poem about this sometime,' said Murdo to his wife. 'I am very surprised that up till now no one has made a poem about it.'

And he stopped speaking and his wife looked at him and then got up and made some tea.

*

One night Murdo woke from sleep, his wife beside him in the bed, and he was sweating and trembling.

'Put on the light at once,' he shouted. His wife jumped out of bed and did as he had told her to do.

'What's wrong?' she said. 'What's wrong?' Murdo's face was as white as the sheet on the bed. He was sitting up in bed as if he was listening to some odd sound that only he was hearing: in the calmness they could hear the gurgling of the water from the stream that ran past their house among the undergrowth.

'A dream I had,' said Murdo. 'It was a dream I dreamed. In the dream I saw a witch and she was coming after me and she had a cup of blood in her hand as if it was a cup of tea. And her face ... There's something wrong with this house.'

'There's nothing wrong with the house,' she said, and when he looked at her he began to tremble as if she herself might indeed be the witch.

'Her face was sharp and long,' he said, 'and she had a cup of blood in her hand and I was making the sign of the cross. The devil was in that dream, there was real evil in that dream. I never dreamed a dream like that before.' And his face was dead white, his teeth were chattering, and he was looking around him wildly.

He thought that the room was full of evil, of devils, that his wife's face was like the face of a witch among the evil.

'I never thought that evil existed till now,' he said. 'Leave the light on. Don't put it off.'

He was afraid to leave his bed or to walk about the house and he felt that there was some evil moving about the outside of the house in the darkness. He thought that there were devils clawing at the walls, trying to get in through the windows, perhaps even breaking the glass or tapping on it.

'Her face,' he said, 'was so sharp and so long, and her back was crooked and she had black wings.'

'You're all right now, aren't you?' said his wife and her blue eyes were gazing at him with what he thought was compassion. But he couldn't be sure. He thought again, What if she is a witch? What if I am a devil myself? What world have we come from, what evil world? What dark woods?

Sitting upright in bed it was as if he was a ghost rising from the grave.

'You're all right, you're all right,' said Janet again.

'Who lived in this house before us?' he asked. 'It was an old woman, wasn't it?'

'Not at all,' said Janet. 'You remember very well who lived here. It was a young family. Surely you remember.'

'You're right,' he said, 'you're right enough.'

Masks, he said to himself. Masks on all the faces, as happens on Hallowe'en. Masks that don't move. Stiff cardboard masks. A wolf's face, a bear's face.

And he felt as if the house were shaking in a storm of evil and the evil hitting it like a strong wind and light pouring out of the house.

'I'm sorry,' he said to Janet. 'I'm sorry I wakened you.'

'Do you want some tea?' she asked him.

'No,' he said. 'But leave the light on for a while.' He listened to the sound of the river flowing through the darkness. Directly underneath the window there was grass where he had buried the black dog when it had been killed on a summer's day by a motor car.

The bones rotting.

'I'm all right now,' he said. 'I'm all right. You can put the light off.'

And she rose and did that and he sat awake for a long time listening to his wife's breathing and he heard above her tranquil breathing the sound of the river flowing past.

At last he fell asleep and this time he had no frightening dreams.

But just before he fell asleep he had a vision of the house as a lighted shell moving through the darkness, and animals around it with red beaks and claws and red teeth, leaping and jumping venomously at the windows and walls to get at him.

*

'What's wrong with that man of yours if he can be called a man at all?' said Janet's father to her one day. He was sitting in an easy chair, his face red with the light of the fire, like a cockerel about to crow.

'When I was young,' he said, 'I used to be at the fishing no matter what kind of weather it was.'

'You've told me,' said Janet. She was more familiar with her father's world than she was with Murdo's. She didn't understand what attraction the white mountain, of which he was continually speaking, had for him.

She herself was of the opinion that the mountain though beautiful was very cold. She much preferred the spring to winter or autumn. She liked to hang billowing clothes on a line in breezy spring and to watch the birds flying about the moorland.

'You don't even have any children,' her father said to her. They were alone together for her mother was at the midweek evening service in the church hall. Her father never went to church.

He was always wandering about in the open air with a hammer or a piece of wood or standing at the door studying the weather.

'It's easy enough to work in an office,' he said. 'Anyone can do that. Why did he leave his work?' In the days before Murdo left the office he used to write letters for his father-in-law about matters connected with the croft, which he couldn't understand but which he could transform into reasonably official English.

'Is he going to stay in that house forever?' said her father again. 'What does he do all day?'

In a way Janet was on her father's side for she couldn't really understand Murdo any more than he did. When she married him she had thought she understood him and that he was normal enough but now she wasn't so sure. He did such odd not to say abnormal things. Her father was not at all odd, he was the quintessence of normality: he was like stone on a moor. Murdo would sometimes come home from the office and he would say, 'I don't understand why I am in that office at all. Why do people work anyway? A sort of fog comes over my eyes when I look at Maxwell and the rest of them. They actually believe that what they are doing is important to the human race. They actually believe that by gathering in money and counting, and by adding figures in columns, they are contributing to the salvation of the world. It's really quite

50

incredible. I mean, the absurdity of what they do has never occurred to them at all. They haven't even thought about it. They are so glad and so pleased that they can actually do the work they're doing, and they make a great mystery of it, as if it were of some immense secret importance. They don't realise at all the futility of what they're doing, and sometimes it takes me all my time to keep from bursting out laughing. If they all dropped dead with pens in their hands it wouldn't make the slightest difference to the world. They would be replaced by other people equally absurd absorbed in the same absurd work.'

'What are you talking about?' she would say to him. 'What do you mean?' She didn't understand clearly what he was saying.

'Well, the world would carry on in the same way as before, wouldn't it,' said Murdo. 'I only hope that Maxwell's umbrella is struck by lightning one of these days. It might teach him a lesson.'

Her father was saying, 'Many people would be happy with the work he's got. There are people I know who clean the roads, clever people too. And look at the warm dry job he had.'

He lifted a newspaper and laid it down again. He bought the paper every day but he never read it right through. He would glance at it now and again and then he would put it down.

'You would be as well to leave him,' said her father.

She had actually thought of leaving him but she knew that she would never go through with it. It wasn't that she was frightened to leave him but she really hoped that one morning he would suddenly leap out of bed and say, 'I'm going back to my work today.' She was hoping that this would happen. And also she thought that she should be loyal to him so long as he was being attacked by his strange sickness.

'No I won't leave him,' she said looking into the fire.

'Well, I hope you know what you're doing,' said her father.

Janet sometimes thought that everything would be all right

if Murdo would find himself able to write something instead of staring at that white mountain which obsessed him so much.

Her father was so large and definite and red in his opinions: she actually thought of his opinions as red and bristly.

'I never thought much of him,' he said. 'There was a foolishness in his people. His grandfather was a daft bard. He used to write silly songs.'

And sometimes her father would pace about the room like a prisoner, his great red hands at his sides.

He raised his fist and said, 'What he needs is a good thump. That's what he needs.' And his face became a deep red with anger.

'You can make tea for yourself if you like,' he told Janet and he went to the door and looked out. 'The weather looks as if it's going to take a turn for the worse.' His round red head was like a tomato on top of his stocky body.

Poor Murdo, she said to herself. What are you going to do? Poor Murdo. And she felt a deep pity for him, in her very womb.

'No I don't want any tea,' she said. 'I have to go home.'

On the way home, she looked at the white mountain for a long time, but all she saw was the mountain itself. At last she turned her eyes away, for the glitter of the snow was dazzling her.

What am I going to do? she thought. There's no money coming into the house and the neighbours are laughing at me.

But in spite of that there was no one she knew as witty and lively as her own husband.

If only we had children, she thought. If only there was some money coming into the house I'd be happy enough.

But a small persistent voice was saying, 'Would you really? Would you really?' like a small winter bird with a small black beak.

'Would you? Would you?' twittered the small bird.

For every day now as she looked in the mirror she saw herself growing older all the time.

And Murdo also growing older.
And the chairs and tables closing in on her.

Last Will and Testament by Murdo Macrae

1. To my beloved wife I leave my shoes and clothes, my pencil and my pen and my papers (All my love such as it is).
2. To my mother-in-law I leave the newspapers that I've been collecting for many years. And my rubber nose.
3. To my father-in-law I leave a stone.
4. To tell the truth I haven't much else except for my bicycle and I leave that also to my mother-in-law. And I leave my watch to Maxwell.

I wish my wife to send the following letter through the post:

To Whomsoever it may Concern.
If anyone can tell me why we are alive, I will give him
  TWO POUNDS, all my money.
For in the first place we are created of flesh and light-
  ning.
And in the fullness of time the flesh and the lightning
  grow old.
And also we are working in a world without meaning.
Yesterday I looked at an egg and I couldn't understand
  why it was in the place where it was.
Now I should know the reason for its position in space.
  For that surely is not a mysterious thing. And I could
  say the same about butter. And salt. And Bovril. Now
  we have come out of the lightning, in our ragged
  clothes. And at last we arrived at Maxwell with his
  umbrella.
This is the problem that Newton never unravelled.
We kill each other.
For no reason at all.
These thoughts climb my head as if it were a staircase.

And that is why I am an idiot.

WE CANNOT LIVE WITHOUT SOME BELIEF.

I believe in my mother-in-law. She will live forever. She
will be knitting in a country unknown to the Greeks.

I believe in my mother-in-law and in my father-in-law
and also in Mrs Macleod.

They will all live forever.

For in their condition they are close to that of the
animal.

They survive on dressers and sideboards.

Those who approach most closely to the condition of
the animal are the ones most likely to survive.

And Woolworths.

Woolworths will live forever.

Too much intelligence is not good for one.

Too much of the spirit is not good for the body, but the
following are good for the body:

Bovril.

Sanatogen.

Butter.

Crowdie.

Eggs.

Water.

Bread.

Meat.

And the sun on a warm day.

And a girl's breast, and a spoonful of honey.

I am sending you this letter, nameless one, with much
happiness and without a stamp.

MURDO MACRAE

*

Murdo's father was dying and Murdo and Janet were watching
him. Now and again his father would ask for water so that he
could wet his lips and his breath was going faster and faster.

Janet was sitting on a chair beside the bed but Murdo was walking up and down restlessly, unceasingly. On a small table beside the bed he saw a letter that had come to his father and had not been opened: it was in a brown envelope and looked official. And the tears came unbidden to his eyes.

Why didn't I do more? he was saying to himself all the time. He couldn't sit down. Outside the window the darkness was falling quickly, and he felt cold. He was shaking as if he had a fever, and his teeth were chattering. Now and again he would look at his father's thin grey face as the head turned ceaselessly on the pillow.

Murdo nearly knelt and prayed. He nearly said, 'Save my father, save my father, and I will do anything You want me to do.' He thought of earlier days when his father used to tease him or carry him about on his shoulders. He thought of his father as a soldier in the war.

What did he get out of life? he asked himself. What did he get? Janet amazed him sitting there so serenely on her chair as if she were used to deaths, as if this room were her true element though in fact as far as he knew she had never seen anyone die before.

A voice was screaming in his head, 'I'm sorry. I'm sorry.' He knew that his father was dying, but he didn't know why he should feel so sorry.

The smell of death was in the room: death was an inevitability of the air.

In a strange way he had never thought that his father would die though he was old and frail.

He saw his father's pipe on the table and the tears again welled to his eyes. He was grinding his teeth together. 'I'm sorry, I'm sorry,' the voice was screaming silently like a voice that might be coming down from the sky, from some bleak planet without light.

His father's breath was accelerating all the time as if he were preparing himself: for a journey, as if he were in a hurry to go somewhere.

And Murdo paced restlessly up and down the room. Pictures flashed in front of his eyes.

His father with a spade, his father at the peat bank, his father reading the paper. And below each picture like an image in a dark pool was the thin grey face.

The stars, they are so far away, Murdo thought.

He was thinking of the other houses in the town with their lights, and they did not know what was going on in this room.

And all the time his body was shaking and shivering as if with the coldness of death itself.

He put his hand on his father's brow and it had the chillness of death on it. Like marble.

Janet rose and went for some more water. Once his father opened his eyes and looked around him but Murdo knew that he wasn't seeing either of them.

And his breath was going like an engine, fast, fast.

Murdo turned away and went to the window. He looked out but he could see nothing in the darkness.

Is this what we were born for? he was saying to himself over and over. He turned back to his father who was melting away before his eyes like snow.

He looked out of the window again.

When he turned round next time he felt a deep silence in the room.

The breath had ceased its frantic running.

His father's head had fallen on one side and the mouth was twisted. Murdo began to cry and he couldn't stop. He knew that his father was dead. He himself was crying and shivering at the same time.

He couldn't stop crying. Janet put her hand on his shoulder and he in turn put his face on her breast like a child, crying.

There was no sound in the room except his own weeping.

He rose abruptly and went outside. Through the darkness he could see the white mountain. Like a ghost.

It frightened him.

It looked so cold and distant and white.

Like a ghost staring at him.

He stayed there for a long time looking at it. He expected no help from it.

There was no happiness nor warning nor comfort nor sadness in that terrible cold whiteness.

It was just a mountain that rose in front of him out of the darkness.

I must climb it, he thought. I must do that now.

He went into the room again and said to Janet, 'I'll be all right now,' She looked at him with love in her eyes and her face was streaming with tears as if the snow had begun to melt in spring, for her face was so pale and tired and white.

'There are no angels,' said Murdo. 'There is only the white mountain.'

Janet looked at him with wonder.

'I'll be all right now,' said Murdo. He knew what he was going to write on white leaves.

A story about his father. At least one story, while he fought with the white mountain, wrestled with it, and after that if he couldn't defeat the white mountain he knew also what he would do.

He picked up his father's pipe and put it in his pocket.

Janet was looking from Murdo's face to his father's. Something was happening to Murdo but she didn't know what it was. His face was becoming more settled, white as snow, but at the same time the trembling life and vibrancy were leaving it.

He was like a tombstone above his father's body.

And she felt fear and happiness together.

For Murdo was growing more and more, minute by minute, like his father and her own father.

It was as if he was settling down into a huge heaviness.

But at the same time there was a terrible question in his face, a question without end, without boundary, a question without laughter.

Murdo took her by the hand and led her out of the house and he showed her the mountain.

'Soon,' he said, 'we shall have to climb it.'

And his face was as set as stone.

And her father-in-law's face was in front of her as well.

It glared gauntly out of the middle of the chairs and the table and the dresser.

That grey question.

That grey thin shrunken question.

THOUGHTS OF MURDO

MURDO AND THE LANGUAGE

When Murdo went to school at the age of four, he being then about three feet high, a starved-looking very tall thin woman loomed up in front of him.

'You will have to speak English from now on,' she said.

Murdo did not know what to say as he did not know English.

'The cat sat on the mat,' she later told him in confidence.

When Murdo got to learn a little English (there was a direct relationship between his height and the language he spoke) he nearly always spoke it at home, though his mother conversed with him in Gaelic. He would find himself speaking as follows: 'I have much homework to do *an nochd.*' (The explanation for this is that he would start the sentence in English, then remember that his mother preferred Gaelic, and switch to that language. If he had spoken English to his mother she would have called him a snob and no son of hers.)

All this caused Murdo to appear very strange. Thus the reverse might happen at school and he might say, '*Chan eil mo* homework *agam* today.'

A very odd thing happened then. One half of Murdo, vertically visualised, had the colour red: the other half had the colour black. Also it seemed to him that half his tongue spoke Gaelic, the other half English. There was a smell of salt herring from the black half, and a smell of bacon from the other half.

He also at first wrote Gaelic with his right hand and English with his left hand. Later these physical processes were reversed. In periods of stress he was completely immobilised, i.e he could not write at all. The psychologist who examined him said that he would grow out of all this, after giving him tests about trains, refrigerators, radio stations, and melons, none of which Murdo had ever seen.

When he was at home the colour black pulsed, and when he was in school the colour red glowed.

Sometimes he felt ill in the area of the red, but when he vomited his sickness was black.

As he grew older the red spread over his whole body and there were only little spots of black here and there. Eventually he was all red, and finally the whole skin became a serene white. However, if he was in a company that sang Gaelic songs and emitted torrents of tears, black spots would break out all over his body.

His language too became abstract as he grew older. Thus he might use words such as 'bureaucracy', 'ideology' and 'green belt'. He trained himself not to feel anger or jealousy, for if that happened the black spots reappeared.

People would say to him, 'Och, you are just suffering from the linguistic disease. It will settle down the older you grow. Eventually the black spots will disappear altogether and you will not feel anything at all.' Still he learned and used long words such as 'dichotomy', 'schizophrenic' and 'traumatic'.

Sometimes laughter emanated from him when he remembered that early day on which he had met his teacher and he would recall 'The cat sat on the mat'. And ever afterwards whenever he saw a cat moving along by a hedge be would think it was in the wrong place.

Neither his handwriting nor his typing ever recovered from this trauma. Part slanted to the right, part to the left. Part (in the case of his typing) was written above the line and part below it.

Such was the linguistic history of Murdo and also why he left the bank, where words like 'draft', 'interest rate', 'bankruptcy,' were used; these words eventually becoming meaningless to him.

NB It is clear from the above that we have here a problem

with the narrative 'I'. For indeed how are we to visualise a narrative 'I' which is spoken to in a language that it does not understand. Later, the Narrative 'I' is split in two, so that we have two Narrative 'I's, that is Narrative 'I'(1) and Narrative 'I'(2). No.1 is found at home, No.2 is found in school. Narrative 'I'(2) takes over from Narrative 'I'(1) and precisely cannibalises it, though not without resentment.

There is a case here for a new kind of criticism which I for the moment as Narrative 'I'(3) will not enter into, but which should however be kept in mind for a proper analysis of this phenomenon. (A concept of which Narrative 'I'(1) is not aware.)

The colours 'red' and 'black' too are significant. Murdo himself cannot explain this. All we can say is that at times he felt like a traffic light, at other times like a comic. He would have bouts of manic laughter so that both the red and the black would shake. The comical side of him was the red, the tragical side the black. One lip would curl comically red, the other tragically black.

That is all Murdo could say about this linguistic phenomenon.

A BILINGUAL POEM BY MURDO
(WITH ANALYSIS)

Thoir dhomh do lamh, my dearest friend,
is theid sinn a null gu town,
if you'll to me a *sgilling* lend,
neo's math dh'fhaodte a half crown.

Agus ceannaichidh sinne da ice cream,
slider dhut-sa 's dhomh-sa cone,
is ithidh sinn iad ann an dream,
is 'Ta' airson an loan.

Notes:

(1) This is clearly located in Murdo's red and black period.

(2) It can be shown from internal evidence that the black is still quite strong with slight intrusions from the red.

(3) One would suppose that Murdo would be about ten at this point. Also external evidence supports this because of the use of old money, e.g. '*sgilling*', 'penny', and 'half crown', which is self-explanatory. In addition, the fact that he was eating ice-cream suggest such an age.

(4) Except for someone who speaks English exclusively, the poem is perfectly clear as to meaning.

NB In his poetry readings Murdo was to use his bilingualism as a stylistic device (c.f. Pound and Eliot et Al*).

The only drawback to this was that international audiences on the whole didn't understand Gaelic.

* Al Macleod, an immigrant Canadian poet.

MURDO LEAVES THE BANK

'I want to see you in my office,' said Mr Maxwell the bank manager, to Murdo. When Murdo entered, Mr Maxwell, with his hands clasped behind his back, was gazing out at the yachts in the bay. He turned round and said, 'Imphm.'

Then he continued, 'Murdo, you are not happy here. I can see that.

'The fact is, your behaviour has been odd. Leaving aside the question of the mask, and the toy gun, there have been other peculiarities. First of all, as I have often told you, your clothes are not suitable. Your kilt is not the attire most suitable for a bank. There have been complaints from other sources as well.

Mrs Carruthers objected to your long tirade on the evils of capitalism and the idle rich. Major Shaw said you delivered to him a lecture on Marxism and what you were pleased to call the dialectic.

'Some of your other activities have been odd as well. Why for instance did you put up a notice saying, THIS IS A BANK WHEREON THE WILD THYME BLOWS? And why, when I entrusted you with buying a watch for Mr Gray's retirement did you buy an alarm clock?

'Why did you say to Mrs Harper that it was time the two of you escaped to South America with, I quote, "the takings": and show her what purported to be two air tickets in the name of Olivera? You told her, and I quote, "I'll be the driver while you bring the money out to me. I have arranged everything, even to the matter of disguises."

'You also said, and I quote, "The mild breezes of the Pacific will smoothe away our sin."

'No wonder Mrs Harper left the bank and joined the staff of Woolworths. Other oddnesses of yours can be catalogued, as for instance the advertisement you designed saying, THIS IS THE BANK THAT LIKES TO SAY "PERHAPS".

'I have therefore decided, Murdo, that banking is not your forte, and that we have come to the parting of the ways: and this I may say has been confirmed by Head Office. I understand, however, that you are writing a book, and that you have always intended to be an author. We cannot, however, have such odd behaviour in an institution such as this. Imphm.

'Also, you phoned Mrs Carruthers to tell her that her investments were in imminent danger because of a war in Ecuador but that you were quite willing to fly out for a fortnight to act as her agent. When she asked you who you were, you said, "Mr Maxwell, and his ilk."

'You also suggested that an eye should be kept on Mr Gray as, in your opinion, he was going blind, but he was too proud to tell the bank owing to his sense of loyalty and to his fear that he might lose his job, as he was supporting three grandchildren. Such a man deserved more than money, you said, he required respect, even veneration.

'You have in fact been a disruptive influence on this office, with your various-coloured suits, your balloons, and your random bursting into song.

'Have you anything to say for yourself?'

'It is true,' said Murdo, after a long pause, 'that I have been writing a book, which I shall continue after I have suffered your brutal action of dismissal. It will be about the work of a clerk in a bank, and how he fought for Blake's grain of sand against watches and umbrellas. Banks, in my opinion, should be havens of joy and pulsing realities. That is why I have introduced fictions, balloons, masks, toy guns, and songs.

'You yourself, if I may say so, have become to my sorrow little better than an automaton. I do not advert to your sex life, and to your obsession with yachts, but I do advert to the gravestone of your countenance, to your strangled "Imphm", and to your waistcoat. Was this, I ask myself, what you always wanted to be, when you were playing as a young child at sand castles? Is this the denouement of your open, childish, innocent face? Why is there no tragedy in your life, no comedy, no, even melodrama? You have hidden behind a mound of silver, behind a black dog and a Nissan Micra. Regard yourself, are you the result of your own dreams? What would Dostoevsky think of you, or Nietzsche? Are the stars meaningless to you, the common joys and sorrows? You may pretend otherwise, Mr Maxwell, but you have lost the simple clownish heart of the child. Nor indeed does Mrs Maxwell have it as far as my observations go. I leave you with this prophecy. There will come a day when the vault will fail and the banknote subside. The horses of hilarity will leap over the counter and the leopards of dishevelment will change their spots. The waves will pour over the cravat and the bank that I have labelled "Perhaps" will be swallowed by the indubitable sands of fatuity. What price your dog then, your debits, and your accounts? What price your percentages in the new avalanche of persiflage? In the day when the giant will overturn the House of the Seven Birches what will you do except crumble to the dust? Nor shall there be special offers in those days, and the brochures will be silent. Additions and subtraction will fail, and divisions will not be feeling so good. Computers will collapse, and customers will cast off their chains. Cravats will cease and crevasses will no longer be concealed.'

In a stunned silence, he rose and said, 'That is my last word to you, Mr Maxwell, and may God protect you in his infinite mercy.'

He pulled the door behind him and walked in a dignified manner to the street, in his impeccable red kilt and hat with the red feather in it.

MURDO AND CALVIN

One day Murdo went into the police station.

'I wish,' he said, 'to report something.'

'And what is that, sir?' said the sergeant, who was large, polite, and red-faced.

'I wish to report,' said Murdo feverishly, 'a sighting of Calvin.'

He paused impressively.

'And which Calvin is that, sir?' said the sergeant quietly. 'And why should you report him?'

'Calvin, Sergeant, is a dangerous lunatic. He is responsible for the Free Church, for the state of Scottish literature, and for many other atrocities too numerous to mention. And especially the Kailyard,' he added in a low voice.

'Kailyard, sir?'

'That's right, Sergeant. One of his grossest inventions. I want him arrested.'

'But, sir,' said the sergeant, 'I can't . . .'

'I haven't finished yet,' said Murdo in a penetrating voice. 'I believe him also to have committed the greatest sin of all. I can only tell you in a whisper. I believe him to have invented the Bible.'

'Invented the Bible, sir?'

'That's right, Sergeant. I have always suspected that the Bible was the invention of one man, a man with a colossal ego and a criminal mind. Let me ask you this. If the Bible had been invented by God would it contain all the mistakes that it contains. For instance,' he said rapidly, 'how is it that God is supposed to have created light before making the sun or the moon? You can read of that error in Genesis. That is only one example. Another example is this. What woman was supposed to have married Cain when there was no other woman alive on the face of the deep but his own mother Eve? They suggest to me the inventions of a man who was not naturally creative and, as we know, Calvin – like Francis Bacon, another treacherous man – was a lawyer.

'Listen, in the Bible there's a man called Amraphel, one called Ashteroth, and another one called Chedorlaomer. There are the names invented by a tired mind. Also, he made other slips in this gigantic enterprise. He said that Reu lived after he begat Serug two hundred and seven years. All this suggests a man engaged in the creation of a stupendous best-seller whose mind flickered at the typewriter. Have you any idea, Sergeant, how many copies of this vast book have been sold in the last thousand years? It is the most bizarre plot in human history.'

'But, sir, I . . .' the sergeant tried to intervene.

'And that is not all by any means,' said Murdo, his eyes assuming a supernatural sharpness and directness. 'If you will allow me to continue. There is also this fact which I think is almost conclusive. A book of such magnitude must have taxed even the greatest brain. And so we find whole chapters which are feverish outpourings making no sense at all, either that or these are space fillers pure and simple. How else can one explain whole chapters which run as follows?

'And Shem lived after he begat Arphaxad five hundred years, and Arphaxad lived three and thirty years and begat Salah, and Arphaxad lived after he begat Salah four hundred and three years. And this, mark you, Sergeant, is the lowest limit of some of the ages. Think, Sergeant, of the huge amounts of money that would have to be paid in old age pensions if that were true. Think of the drain on the Health Service, the hospitals required, the Social Security, the guide dogs, the food, the drink, the white sticks, the geriatric wards. How could any economy have sustained such a vast number of the ancient, especially before television was invented. Look, Sergeant, it cannot be denied that there is at least here a basis for investigation.'

The sergeant's round reddish eyes gazed at him.

'All the oxen and the asses,' continued Murdo relentlessly, 'that one could covet. Is there not something there too? Crimes unimaginable. A fiction of such remarkable cunning that it is difficult for us to understand the ramifications of its plot. The sex, the murders, the casual examples of incest, sodomy, black magic and theft. The silences on important matters like justice and religion. It has been clear to me for many years that at the back of all this was Calvin. Tell me this,' said Murdo earnestly, 'if you were going to investigate a criminal would you not ask yourself certain questions? Ah, I see that you would. Who, you ask, gains by such an immense crime. And you must answer if you look around your country today that the only person to gain must be Calvin. Wasn't it he and his church who became triumphant? Who therefore would be more likely to bring such a result about? Ah, you are now going to ask me the most penetrating question. Opportunity. Did Calvin in fact have the opportunity? You may say reasonably enough that Calvin lived centuries ago but was not so old as the Bible. That puzzled me for a while too, till eventually I saw the solution to it. And I found the solution, as commonly happens, in his own work.

You remember that he mentioned a number of people who lived to the age of eight hundred. I believe that Calvin lived to the almost unimaginable age of 22,000 years five months and two days. He waited and waited, keeping his manuscript intact, till one day the printing press was invented and he pounced (is it a coincidence by the way that Calvin differs from Caxton by only three letters?).

'I can tell you, Sergeant, that on that day Calvin was in his element. Imagine what it must have been like for him to know that his book, once a scroll, would be read all over the world, that boats would ferry his best-seller to the ignorant Africans, Asians and the Scots. Imagine the size of the royalties.

'And now he is here and I have seen him. He will hardly leave his house (for his cunning is supernatural) and I only saw him briefly while he was completing his toilet on the moor. He will speak to no women and if any come near him he will shake his stick at them and mutter words like, "Impudent whores, prostitutes of the deepest dye". And that is another thing,' said Murdo vigorously, boring his eyes towards the crab-red eyes of the sergeant. 'A writer can be told by his convictions, by his mannerisms. Calvin hated women and this appears in the Bible. In nearly every case the women are either treacherous or boring. He hated sheep as well: think of the number that he sacrificed. Who is this man then, this woman-hater, this sheep-hater-genius who has deceived so many million people, ambitious inventor of strange names? What other evidence do you need?'

He stopped and the silence lasted for a long time.

'But I have not,' Murdo continued, 'reached the highest point of my deductions yet. It came to me as a bolt from the blue as bolts often do. The beauty of it is breathtaking. Let me list those things again: a man who hates women, who deceives men, who lives thousands of years, who will stop at nothing for gain, who has come out of hiding at this present disturbed time, who wears a bowler hat, whose sense of humour is so impenetrable that no one can understand it, who imposes such colossal boredom on the world that no one can stay awake in his presence, a man who uses boredom as a weapon. Who, I repeat, is this man? I will tell you,' and he lowered his voice again. 'I believe that this man is the Devil.' He leaned back in triumph. 'There, I have said it. Think how many problems that solves at a stroke. Think how the knots untie themselves, if we once understand that Calvin is the Devil. Everything that was opaque to us before is now crystal clear. All the questions that we need to ask are answered. You must,' he said decisively, 'send a Black Maria for him at once, or a green one or even a blue one, before he can start on more books of such length. Is he planning to come out of hiding to demand his royalties? Think of our country. How could it withstand such a demand? Surely you of all people can see that . . . Ah, I understand, you aren't going to do anything. I was afraid of that. Well, don't say that I didn't warn you when the consequences of his arrival here become clear.' He backed towards the door, the sergeant leaning across the desk towards him. 'Remember that I warned you. You have my phone number, my fingerprints. I have nothing to gain. We know who has something to gain.' He screamed as he went round the door. 'Put him in a cell or he'll destroy us all. Bring him in on suspicion of loitering, of parking on a double yellow line, of singing at the Mod.'

The sergeant strode towards the door and locked and bolted it. He was breathing heavily. And even yet he thought that he could hear that voice shouting, '. . . for being a hit man for the Educational Institute of Scotland.'

MURDO'S MANIFESTO FOR THE COUNCIL

Leaving aside a long philosophical disquisition in which I had hoped to include remarks from Kafka, Dostoevsky, Sartre and others, I will advert to the matter at hand.

Drain Pipes:

These are clearly inadequate and should be replaced. I have not the technical knowledge to discuss this matter in much detail, though I am sure my opponents will speak as if they were engineers, sewage repairers, etc. I will begin as I have started, wielding a broad brush and leaving the details to lesser more bureaucratic minds who have degrees in Drain Pipes, etc.

For myself, I will stick to authentic anecdotes for the People, without whom this election would be meaningless. It is for them that we are fighting, and we must not forget that, and no blurring of questions by those who pretend to be sewage engineers will blind them to what is happening. Suffice it to say that the whole system of Drain Pipes will have to be replaced and kept constantly in review. I accuse Councillor Macleod of gross neglect in this area and though I know his family well I call on him to resign.

Education:

This is a subject on which I am willing to speak at length, and with expertise. Here I wish to make more provocative statements in order to waken up the docile island proletariat. I accuse our education masters (dim shapes indeed) of having created competent soulless people. Where is the imagination? Where are our ideas of angels and demons, where are our dreams, our visions? What use to us is spelling, the numbers table, history, geography, etc? These lead us to become like Mr Maxwell, the bank manager, and his tombstone visage. We need visages more radiant than that if we are to survive spiritually, economically, etc.

With regard to *Geography*, why do we need to know the location of Hong Kong, Rangoon, Canberra, etc? The Norsemen, the Picts, the Anglo Saxons, did not know of them. Did this prevent them from leading happy contented and, on the whole, ravaging lives? What would it have availed a Pict to know of Sumatra or for an Anglo Saxon to be apprised of Tasmania? That will suffice, I think, for Geography.

With regard to *History*, what is Richard II to me or I to Richard II? Were I ignorant of the Battle of Thermopylae, or of Charlemagne, would this disturb my nights? Can Henry VIII help me with my existential decisions, or Boadicea heal me of my wounds? Can Edward I help me to take the mote out of my neighbour's eye? So much for History.

No, Education prevents the unfettered use of the Imagination. It hampers us with facts, and torments us with dates. It confuses us with ideologies, and delays our progress towards the infinite. Read Blake, read Lawrence, but not Plato who kept the poets out of his Republic.

Sailings:

I am totally against sailings on weekdays and would confine them to Sundays, for it is on that day that we are most at ease and can take advantage of perfumed breezes, clear skies, etc. On weekdays, burdened as we are with material thoughts and economic notions, we cannot take advantage of the innocence of the sea, and its sinless expanse.

Toilets:

My opponents say that there are too few toilets available: I say, on the contrary, that there are too many. Too many toilets, even one toilet, leads to drugs, graffiti, conspiracies. Every right-thinking person has a toilet in his own house: why does he need more? Before going on a journey he should make a habit of using the toilet. If, however, he is as they say 'caught short' he should knock on someone's door and ask if he can use their toilet. This would go a long way to maintaining friendship and the community spirit and the oral tradition.

Bridges:

These should be eliminated. People should as much as possible stay in their own village. Only the unimaginative travel. As Pascal said, much of the trouble in this world is caused by people who won't stay in their own rooms. If people are confined to their own villages they will use their imagination more and will be constrained from talking about wars, space shots, etc. Lisbon, Madrid, Rome, these are matters for our dreams, and the reality of Venice is never as beautiful as the Venice of our imagination.

Hospitals:
There should be fewer wards, fewer nurses, fewer doctors. Most illnesses are caused by other people's minds: these are the true sources of infections. Boredom has much to answer for, as indeed have envy, spleen, jealousy and hate. For myself I am free of all these emotions, though I am not sure that my opponents are. Let the bacilli of rancour flourish elsewhere: hospitals are where they breed most. If we had no hospitals, who would have thought of them? If we had no Anadin, who would have invented it. Doctors are vampires on our emotions: they make money from our hatreds. Nurses will miss their watches and their thermometers and indeed their power, but they can be given other paraphernalia. Bedpans will vanish from the landscape; there will be less demand for grapes; lucozade will be no more. Visiting hours will no longer exist, and waxed floors will disappear. Death will die, as it will no longer have the oxygen of publicity.

Finally, though I do not wish to personalise my *Opponents*, there are a few facts that you should know about them.

Mr Chevenix Trench, my Tory opponent, has worked for the Post Office for more years than I can care to count. His horizons therefore are limited to stamps, postal orders and registered parcels. What does he know of foreign policy who foreign policy does not know? Ask him what the capital of Afghanistan is. Will he know it? I think not. He has had no need to examine his life, which is now a struggle for naked power. He works from nine to five every day. What does he do with the rest of his time? I suggest to you that his mind cannot rise above letter-boxes and that his imagination is confined to telephone bills. Touch him, and he gives out a tinkle of nullity. Avoid him, do not be deceived by his busy air of vacuity. You are too intelligent to be taken in by such a nefarious mystagogue. Let him take his ambition elsewhere. In any case he has been involved in a messy divorce.

With regard to my SDP opponent, Mr R Green, what can I say of him? Where are his policies, his intuitions, his imagination? He arrived here first as a photographer, then became a hotelier. His photography was bad, his food is worse. His red banal face, his hail-fellow-well-met attitude are a front for the deepest emptiness. Feel his hand, it is wet with soup and false bonhomie. Look him in the eye: he is thinking of his tariff. He has patronised you by learning a few words of Gaelic. However, if you ask him what the Gaelic for 'werewolf' is, he does not know. Nor indeed the Gaelic for 'bonhomie'. What is his position on the ozone layer? He does not know. Or the greenhouse effect? He has never heard of it. Or the Indeterminacy Principle: his animadversions on that would be laughable.

NO, VOTE FOR ME, YOUR COUNCILLOR WHO CAN DELIVER, WHOSE POWERS OF DEBATE ARE FORMID-ABLE, WHO WILL DEFEND YOUR INTERESTS WITH YOUR BLOOD, WHO TAKES A STAND ON PRINCIPLE ALONE, AND TREATS PERSONAL ATTACKS WITH CON-TUMELY. WHOSE KNOWLEDGE OF KAFKA IS BEYOND REPROACH, WHO WILL LEAD YOU FROM THE DARK AGES OF EDUCATION TO THE BROAD UPLANDS OF HOPE, TAKING ON BOARD LOCAL QUESTIONS THE WHILE, WHO WILL SHIRK SERVILE DETAIL IN FAVOUR OF THE BROAD BRUSH, WHO WILL LEAVE YOUR EN-VIRONMENT AS HE FOUND IT, WHO WILL ATTACK BOREDOM WHEREVER HE FINDS IT EVEN WITHIN THE VERY FASTNESSES OF OUR OWN ADMINISTRATION.

VOTE FOR MURDO MACRAE, BRING YOUR PROBLEMS

TO HIM, AND IF HE IS NOT AT HOME, REMEMBER THAT
THIS IS AN INDICATION OF HIS TIRELESS EFFORTS ON
YOUR BEHALF.

MURDO ON THE PROBLEM OF
FISHING — A SPEECH

Ladies and gentlemen, fellow members of the proletariat, I
wish to say a few words tonight about the problems of the
Fishing Industry.

Ever since the dawn of history, men have fished. They have
set out in their boats, dhows, piraguas, etc, and sought their
food in the wild or temperate oceans. Their families have
depended on the flounder, and their kin have espoused the
kipper. In Japan men have fished with lanterns and sometimes
with the carnivorous cormorant, and in northern climes –
interrupted by the Aurora Borealis – the humble kayak has
been used.

Later still, as time passed, Columbus set off from Spain after
a trifling altercation, towards what he thought was the Indies,
with many ships which included the *Santa Maria*. Indomitable
man! Fine spirit! Excellent sailor! What did he think of as he
progressed further and further into the Pacific without radar
or asdic, nay even without compass. What would his thoughts
have been as he heard on that bountiful air the first sound of
the calypso and smelt the scent of burnt rice.

Later still, after Columbus and Vasca da Gama, whom I did
not mention, as time is short, we come to Admiral Horatio
Nelson, who fought at Trafalgar, and who it is said was seasick
on most of his voyages. You have all heard disapprovingly of
his famous last words, 'Kiss me, Hardy.'

As well as this there have been Drake, who played bowls;
Sir Walter Raleigh; Amundsen, who discovered the South
Pole; Nansen: and many other famous men too numerous
to mention. Anecdotes about them abound.

I ask you therefore when you think of such great men, what are your own trifling complaints about boundaries, quotas, tariffs, etc, (stupefaction!) against such a noble panorama of human adventure. (Mutterings of discontent, some in Gaelic.) Nay, listen to me. As the earth turns valiantly in space, as day by day we hear of pulsars and quasars, what can the humble skate do for us. Its status diminishes in comparison with this vast processional and tremendous rotation of the stars. Indeed your drifters, your trawlers, become a mote on the surface of the deep. Do you think Columbus went in search of the squid and was willing to lay down his life for the herring? (Puzzlement!) On the contrary, his lode star was his Imagination; in the rustling of his sails he heard the music of the spheres. What to him the dogfish, the turbot or the crab. Let them stay in their appointed places, he would have said in his Catholic way. (Snarls!)

Men (and women) have laid down their lives for visions, but never for the haddock. The Holy Grail was not in the shape of a kipper nor the North Star in the shape of a swordfish. The sea is a cauldron of invention, gaiety, profusion, more profound than we can imagine. The proletariat were not called to hunt or die for the mackerel, or discuss the dialectics of the plaice. (Howls of rage!) I will be heard, I was trying to raise your consciousness, in this cold hall without electricity or water.

Let me again expatiate on this grand idea. First there was the innocent tree trunk, then the rowing boat, then the sailing ship, then the steamship. What a marvellous procession! Did Nelson face the might of Napoleon thinking of a quota, as he put the telescope to his blind eye? Did Drake, pursuing the Spanish galleon, stop in his tracks as he thought of the tariff? (Disturbance!)

I stand before you here, an honest man, who is trying to assist you and raise your minds to visionary horizons. I prophesy to you: the proletariat will not triumph if they confine their attention to trout. Another net – the net of capitalism, and the relationship of the bourgeois class to its means of production – is closing over you. This matter of fish is merely a red herring to distract you from the theory of surplus value. What do you find in your nets? Not fish but the illusion of profit and counter-revolutionary, adventurist petty bourgeois factionalists. (Baffled snarls!)

You will thank me for this when I am far away, when I am no more. And no less. You will say to yourselves in the twilight of your old age, I wish my consciousness had been raised more. I wish I had listened to his objective analysis instead of being subjective. Why did I not listen to that honest man, you will say, who strove to raise me from my beetle-like condition to the majestic harmonies of the universe. That is roughly what you will meditate on. When you have a home-help you will think of these things. When you are suffering from arthritis and alienation you will remember me perhaps, your friend in hard times, now a dead body in soft times. (A shamed silence!)

I say to you, give up these illusions of quotas, prices, etc. Consider the lilies, how they grow. Stand up and be counted. Remember your wives and children and leave them only fragrant memories uncorrupted by scales and salt. The march of Democracy continues. Turn your faces to the stars, my friends. To the stars. Let you first love your neighbour, and all things will be added to you.

On these aims I rest. (Prolonged cheers!)

TO THE EDITOR OF THE . . .

Dear Sir,

I see from your correspondence column of last week that H.R. of Peterhead is objecting to my speech on the Fishing Industry (so kindly reported by you) and saying that I am totally ignorant of same.

I think it is scandalous that such an attack should be made by an outsider, who has no idea at all of the uniqueness of this community and, if I may say so, its oral tradition and minority language. What right has he, I ask, to interfere in our internal affairs. What right has he to expatiate on fishing affairs in an organ that does not belong to him, and furthermore against those who have laid down their lives in two World Wars to defend their own way of life? Let him look at the mote in his own eye and ask himself, are things so well conducted in Peterhead that he can afford to attack others?

I will not, however, be cowed. We have our own mores and our own culture and we do not wish those with an axe to grind to interfere.

When I come to the details of his letter I find myself astonished at his intemperate language. What has Columbus to do with the Fishing Industry, he asks, and who is Bruno? I am amazed at his ignorance, quite apart from the fact that he has singled out Catholics. Is he, perhaps, a member of the Closed Brethren or some such sect that he spews forth his malicious froth.

In the first place, the great names of Columbus and of Bruno (the latter of whom paid the supreme penalty for his beliefs) transcend such matters as he mentions. Would he have stood out against the might of the Pacific or the Inquisition, or would he simply have written a letter to a newspaper? It ill behoves him to attack not only me (for I can disdainfully throw his weak logic back at him) but those who because they are dead cannot defend themselves. If this is meant to be Peterhead fairplay then I comprehensively reject it.

Even in Peterhead he must have heard of the Santa Maria and its famous companions: as also of the burning fire of the Inquisition. Even in Peterhead he must have heard of the well-known statement of Bruno that the universe is infinite.

Perhaps it is this that he cannot bear. Does he think that the universe is infinite except in Peterhead and that that town occupies a privileged position? I cannot otherwise account for his poisonous insinuations.

My position in this matter, as on others, is perfectly clear. I believe that at the root of all our problems is the relationship between the historical and the logical in the process of cognition. I come out in favour of the logical method, showing that it made possible the examination of certain categories (including the Fishing Industry) not in the sequence in which they have come to play a decisive role historically, but with an eye on their relationship in contemporary bourgeois society. A correct understanding of existing and extinct forms requires the determination in many instances of decisive forms in the service of logical categories. But it does not follow that I reject the historical method which reproduces phenomena in accordance with their actual historical sequence. 'The anatomy of man is a key to the anatomy of the ape.'

It is of course from such a standpoint that my analysis of the Fishing Industry can best be understood. Simplistic solutions cannot stand the test of time any more than the hollowed-out tree-trunk can carry passengers in the 20th century. Homer too is very different from Picasso.

I hope, sir, my correspondent from Peterhead will clearly understand my position and realise that I have no personal animus towards him but towards his outdated ideology. (Has he, for instance, read the special supplement to the Neue Rheinishe Zeitung, No. 143, issued in 1848 Nov. 15 for his information.) His mistake lies in adopting a subjective stance instead of an objective one, and in not drawing the correct conclusions from the phenomena. In this he is to be found with the discredited Thierry, Proudhon, etc, petty-bourgeois all of them and blatant adventurists.

Let him remember these famous words, 'The direst straits are better than public begging' and also: 'The National Assembly has its seat in the people and not in the confines of this or that heap of stones.'

Sir, we are all responsible to the people, and let H.R. of Peterhead keep that in mind.

I am, Sir,
Yours, etc,
Murdo Macrae.

MURDO & THE SPACESHIP

When I arrived at Murdo's house I found him working on a big machine while another man was sitting on a chair with a melodeon. Murdo's daughter, Mary, was asking him how the spaceship was coming . . .

Murdo said, 'I need paraffin. Morag doesn't have any in the shop. She's got everything else, spades, rinso, mince, bread, margarine, guided missiles, but no paraffin.' His thick glasses glittered contemptuously.

'Well, I'm sure it won't be long till you get your paraffin,' said Mary. 'Do you need anything else?'

'I need four-inch nails,' said her father, 'but Kenneth here got them for me in New York. He was playing at a Gaelic festival there, weren't you, Kenneth?'

'Indeed I was,' said Kenneth, who was bald and had a very thin neck.

'Kenneth here is a sex symbol,' said Murdo. 'He was playing at this festival and he went into a shop in 42nd Street. The man who owned it was from Skye. It took him three years to reach America on MacBrayne's and then he was attacked by some Red Indians from Harris. Isn't that right, Kenneth?'

'That's right,' said Kenneth.

'And what are you going to do with the spaceship, father?' said Mary.

'It's not a spaceship. It's a rocket,' said Murdo. 'I thought at first of directing it against Moscow but then I thought Moscow hasn't done anything to me so I'll attack MacBrayne's with it instead.'

'It's high time you launched the rocket, father,' said Mary. 'I can't reach the wardrobe because of it.'

'The wardrobe,' said Murdo.

'Yes, where I keep the clothes.'

'Oh, the wardrobe. I can't understand how you can think of trivialities like that in this technological age,' said Murdo. 'Surely you know that I have spent seven years on this project. Seven years when I could have been doing something else.'

'Like what?' said Mary.

'Well, building an anti-ballistic shield,' said Murdo.

'When do you intend to launch the rocket?' said Mary.

At that point a little woman dressed in black and carrying a Bible bound with elastic came in.

'Oh, here's Anna,' said Murdo. 'Were you in church, Anna?'

'Yes, indeed,' said Anna. 'The text was from Exodus. A good minister. Strong voice. Fine hairstyle.'

'What did you say?' said Murdo.

'Oh, I'm in a rage,' Anna said, 'Jessie was wearing the same kind of hat as me.'

After a while, Murdo said in a serious voice, 'Anna.'

'Yes,' said Anna.

'Would you like to go to the moon, Anna?'

'To the moon?' said Anna, in a surprised voice.

'Surely, father, you're not sending Anna to the moon,' said Mary. 'You promised me I could go to the moon. I bought a new frock for it.'

'You keep quiet, Mary,' said Murdo angrily.

He turned to Anna. 'The thing is, Anna, do you think you'd be able to handle the media? The media is very important.'

'Media? What's that?' said Anna.

'The newspapers, the BBC, the television,' said Murdo.

'Oh, I can speak to them right enough,' said Anna. 'What do I have to say?'

'Father,' said Mary.

'You keep quiet,' said Murdo. 'I want a religious woman to land on the moon. A woman who can sing a psalm. Can you do that, Anna?'

'Oh, I can sing a psalm right enough,' said Anna. 'But you want me to do it on the moon?'

'Think of it, Anna,' said Murdo. 'You'll be standing on the moon, in your black mini-skirt with your fish-net stockings. Real fish-net. Of course, we'll take the corks out of it first. You will be a sex symbol for the whole world.'

'I would like that,' said Anna.

'And now for the big day,' said Murdo, taking out his diary. 'It can't be Thursday. That's early closing day. Or Sunday. You can't go to the moon on a Sunday, Anna.'

'No, I couldn't do that,' said Anna.

'Tuesday would be all right,' said Murdo. 'Are you free on Tuesday?'

'Tuesday,' said Anna. 'Oh, I don't know about Tuesday. That's my Hate the Catholics night.'

'Well, what about Wednesday then?' said Murdo. 'You don't go to the bingo on a Wednesday, do you?'

'No, I don't go to the bingo,' said Anna. 'Wednesday would be all right.'

'I'll put that in my diary then,' said Murdo. 'You're not frightened are you.'

'Not at all,' said Anna.

'And you're not afraid of communicating with the media? You must be sharp and quick, Anna. What will you say to them when they ask you why you joined the mission to the moon?'

'I'll say, this is a big step for mankind but especially for Gravir.'

'Oh, there is one other thing,' said Murdo. 'Is there anything suspicious or immoral in your background, Anna? You can expect a lot of probing. The media is ruthless.'

'Immoral?' said Anna.

'Yes, like incest, murder, theft, speaking to Catholics. Anything like that?'

'No, no,' said Anna, 'nothing at all like that.'

'That's good, Anna. And now we'll sing Amazing Grace. What about Amazing Grace, Kenneth? Give us Amazing Grace.'

Kenneth sang Amazing Grace, but not well. 'It's all right, said Murdo. 'Kenneth here is more used to Country and Western. What's wrong, Anna?'

'I've just remembered. I can't go on Wednesday.'

'Why not?' said Murdo.

'It's the day I collect my pension,' said Anna.

Murdo gnashed his teeth with frustration and chased her out.

'That means Mary here will have to go after all,' he said.

MURDO & HIS CANDIDATE

The results of the election were:

Mr R. Green	*500*
Mr Chevenix Trench	*150*
Mr Murdo Macrae	*2*

Murdo immediately demanded a recount but the result was upheld.

He wrote a letter to the local paper in which he said:

To these two supporters of mine in the recent election (Ward 3) I wish to say Courage. As yet our ideas have not won wide credence, but was this not the same with many movements in the past? And these later proved of course to be of major significance. One thinks of the Children's Crusade, etc.

Popularity is easily won in these materialistic times, when men will promise the earth, but when one is concerned with a new heaven and a new earth what price votes and ballot boxes then? Do not, I say, be downcast, for I am not downcast. I shall return to the fray, refreshed and patriotic as usual.

The very fact that I only got two votes suggests to me not that my ideas are without substance but that they are ahead of their time. Popularity, as I have said, is easily won and the world will soon know the emptiness of Mr R. Green's ideas, such as they are, when they are tested in the furnace of local politics and, if I may say so, the fires of reality.

I salute you therefore, my two supporters, for your percipience and your honesty. Only you were able to pierce through the prevailing fog of lies and distortion to the inner meaning of my proposals. Only you are the true metaphysicians of democracy. I wish I knew who you were. Sometimes I think of you as idealistic, ardent, blazing with fervour. I think of you also as ones who eschew popularity in favour of Truth, hermits contemptuous of the world of electricity and fake progress around you.

Withal, I think of you as young, independent-minded, not easily convinced. Not for you the rigid forms of the old politics, no, you wish to say to these malignant masks, Avaunt. Get thee behind me.

I say to you in Macarthur's immortal words spoken, I think, to the Filipinos or some such Pacific tribe, 'I shall return.' And return I shall to cleanse these Augean stables and begin again, as we make our way towards the stars.

Thank you again, my dear friends, for your faith in me.

I am,
Yours, etc,
Murdo Macrae.

PS. To Mr R. Green I say, with the inner rage and contempt of the temporary loser,

WE ARE WATCHING YOU: WE WILL NOT REST TILL YOUR CONTEMPTIBLE IDEAS ARE CONSIGNED TO THE DUST-BIN OF HISTORY, WHERE THEY UNDOUBTEDLY BELONG.

MURDO & THE MOD

At the time of the Mod, Murdo tended to get into long arguments about Mod medallists. He would say, 'In my opinion Moira McInally was the best medallist there ever was. Her timbre was excellent.' Most people wouldn't know what timbre was, and Murdo would repeat the word. On the other hand, he would say that though her timbre was excellent her deportment wasn't as good as that of Norma McEwan who became a bus conductress on the Govan route.

Such arguments would go on into the early hours of the morning, and as many as eighty Mod medallists might be mentioned with special reference to their expression when they sang their songs, as well as their marks in Gaelic and music. Murdo would sometimes say, '97 out of 100 is not enough for a medallist since I myself used to get more than that in Geometry.'

'However,' he would add, 'Mairi MacGillivary got 99 out of 100 for her timbre, though she only got 7 out of 100 for her Gaelic since in actual fact she was a learner and was born in Japan.

'Her expression,' he would add, 'was enigmatic.'

At one Mod he offered protection for adjudicators. This was a service which consisted of whisking them off to an armoured taxi immediately they had given their adjudication. For he said, 'Haven't you realised the number of threats those adjudicators get? Not so often from the contestants themselves but from their close relatives, especially their mothers who have carefully trained these contestants for many years in expression, timbre, and the best method of wearing the kilt. No one has any idea of what is involved in producing a gold medallist. His Gaelic must be perfection itself as far as expression is concerned and must be taken from the best islands. Furthermore, he must stand in a particular way with his hand on his sporran, and his expression must be fundamentally alert, though not impudent, though for the dreamier songs he may close his eyes. Now a mother who has brought up such a contestant cannot but be angry when an adjudicator, who doesn't even come from her island, presumes to make her son fifth equal in a contest which moreover only contains fifth equals. There have been death threats in the past. Some adjudicators have disguised themselves as members of the Free Church and carry Bibles and wear black hats and black ties, but this isn't enough as everyone knows that the Free Church doesn't like Mods, since they are not mentioned in the Bible. The *Comunn Gaidhealach* have even produced very thin adjudicators who, as it were, melt into the landscape when their adjudication is over, but even this has not prevented them from being assaulted. These mothers will stand in freezing rain outside adjudicators' houses and shout insults at them and sometimes the more ambitious of them have fired mortar shells into the living-room.'

Thus Murdo's 'Adjudicators Rescue Service', knows as ARS for short, was in great demand, and for an extra pound the adjudicator could make faces at frenzied mothers through the bullet-proof glass.

Another service that Murdo would provide was skin-coloured hearing aids which in practical terms were in fact invisible. These were for turning off after the seventh hearing of the same song, such as 'Bheir Mi Ho.' If the hearing aids were visible it would look discourteous to turn them off. So Murdo would advertise for people who would make skin-coloured invisible hearing aids, and sometimes he would even apply for a grant for such people who had to be highly skilled and whose pay was high as they only worked during Mod times.

Another service he provided was special tartans for people from Russia and Japan and other distant countries. His tartan for the Oblomov clan was well thought of. It was a direct and daring perestroika white with a single dove carrying a Mod brochure in its mouth. Sometimes too it might carry a placard: 'Welcome to Mod 1992 in Dazzling and Riveting Kilmarnock, home of Gaelic and Engineering Sponsorship.' Indeed his sponsorship from Albania was the high point of his life, and he kept for a long time a transcript of the short interview he had with its president, who at that time was being besieged by 300,000 rebellious people demanding more soap and toilet paper.

Murdo indeed became very animated at the time of the Mod, as if he were emerging out of a long hibernation like the church at Easter. He ran a service well in advance of the Mod for booking Choirs into Bed and Breakfast locations, and he further advertised a service for making rooms soundproof so that pipers could practise their pibrochs, one of which was in fact dedicated to him. It was called *Murdo's Farewell to Harry Lauder*. He invented a device by which a piper could smoke while playing the pipes at the same time. He advertised this by the slogan 'Put that in your pipes and smoke it'.

But I could go on for ever describing Murdo's energy and innovative brilliance at the time of the Mod. It was as if he grew alive again, as if he vibrated with elan.

He was here, there and everywhere, organising dances, selling tickets, raffling salt herring, giving endless votes of thanks, singing songs, defending the Mod in midnight debates,

pinpointing the virtues of Mod gold medallists of earlier years
and interviewing them in a special geriatric studio which was
fitted with bedpans, dressing up as a starving Campbell who
needed sponsorship, writing short stories and sending them
in under assumed names such as Iain MacRae Hemingway
or Hector Maupassant. It was a week of glorious abandon for
him, so much so that the rest of the year was an anticlimax,
and he could hardly wait until the Mod was to be staged in
Gatwick or Henley.

Murdo's closely reasoned paper on why the Mod should
be held in Paris was probably his masterpiece. He said first
of all that many of the older slightly deafer people might
think it was Harris, and before they knew where they were
they would be strolling down the Champs Elysees rather than
Tarbert. Also there were a number of Gaels in Paris who
had been detained there after the last football international
as well as some ancient followers of Bonnie Prince Charlie.
Furthermore, it was probably from here that the original Celts
had come before they had changed from 'P' to 'Q'. Also the
word 'église' was very like the Gaelic word 'eaglais' and there
was a small French religious sect called L'Eglise Libre to which
Pascal had belonged.

So it was that Murdo was busy as a bee when Mod time
came, especially with his compilation of Mod medallists into
leagues, headed by Morag MacCrimmon (aged 102), and by
his selection of raffle prizes headed by his special editions of
the Bible with a foreword by Nicholas Fairbairn, and a page
three of aged schoolteachers from the *Stornoway Gazette*.

'I envisage,' he told the press recently, 'that our next Mod
will be in East Germany. As a goodwill gesture I have decided
that there will be no communists on the committee. I hope
to see you all there.'

I should like, but for pressure of time, to detail Murdo's
other astonishing achievements, e.g. the year he won the Mod
Medal himself by an amazing margin of 90 points, and also his
epic poem which won him the Bardic Crown and which was

called 'The Church and the Sound of the Sea'. However, I have said enough to demonstrate that Murdo was by far the most interesting President, Secretary, and Treasurer seen at the same time which the Mod is ever likely to have, and his creation of twenty fourth-equals out of a total entry of twenty-one was the most dazzling arithmetical feat ever seen and also the fairest.

His interview in Gaelic with President Mitterand was a sparkling performance when he countered the President's *'Tha e fluich'* with *'C'est la guerre.'*

MURDO'S XMAS LETTER

Dear Friends,

Another Christmas has come again, and I am sending you a report of my activities during the year. It doesn't seem so long ago since last Christmas was here, but as we all know it is twelve months ago – no more and no less.

My main project in the early part of the year was to encourage Scottish writing, by running a competition for short stories. I asked for a sum of ten pounds to be enclosed with each story: this was to cover administrative costs, coffee, stamps, and whisky, etc. The prizes which I presented in March were ten pounds for the best story, one pound for the next story and 10p for third best. I hope to do something similar for Scottish Writing next year. I shall advise entrants that a maximum of 200 words is entirely reasonable, as it seems to me that one of the faults of Scottish Writing is that it is too long, and with shorter short stories I shall be able to apply better my critical techniques. Far more emphasis should be placed on the single word, which is the hallmark of the truly great writer. What I look for first is good typing, then originality.

Another project in which I was involved gave me great

satisfaction. I have noticed in the past that the standards of In Memoriams in the local paper is very low, and it seems to me that with a little practice they could be improved. I therefore started a workshop for that purpose. I told my class that epitaphs have concentrated mainly on names and dates, without referring in depth to the individual nature of the dead person. I told them that the best writing of the twentieth century is above all truthful. Thus if the dead person was highly sexed, perverted, or a habitual thief, this should be stated. As a result of our final workshop (the cost for the whole course was £50 to each member) I shall put together a small anthology of the best In Memoriams.

Here are two examples:

'May James Campbell's randy bones rest in peace.'

and

'May John MacDonald be able to find his way to his own grave.'

The classic, I think, was

'Let her RIP.'

I may say that the sales of the local newspaper have soared since these epitaphs were inserted and I had a congratulatory message from the editor.

Old clothes is another area of my research, the idea for which I got from the local Oxfam. I have started a campaign by which I hope to convince people that old clothes are better than new ones. The logic of my argument goes like this. Community, I say, is the basis of our life here in the island, and what would be more communal than to wear clothes which in the past have been worn by someone else. In this way we inherit history, sweat, stains and genealogy. Old clothes are like a time machine: they give an insight into the past that cannot be gained in any other way. Look, I say, at these rags which better men and women than you have worn. They did not know where their next meal was coming from. Indeed they did not know where their last meal had come from. Do you not wish to have thoughts like them, pure healthy thoughts, and not impure unhealthy thoughts such as people who wear new clothes have?

Such people, I say, existed on bread and sour milk. Many of my hearers, and I don't blame them for this, have been so moved by my rhetoric that they have stripped off their new clothes on the spot and have taken old clothes of a similar size. This, I say, is what Christianity was really about. Did Christ shop at Harrods? Such a statement has only to be made for the absurdity of it to be revealed. Nor in fact has anyone found an answer to my logic and I do not think anyone will.

So you see, my friends, that I have not been idle.

I have also decided during the course of this year to change the subject of my novel. It was originally to be about a bank clerk, but I have noticed on television a resurgence of the detective story. Thus I have created a private eye called Sam Spaid who walks, as I write, the mean streets of Portree. He wears a bowler hat, and when he is in his office listens to tapes of Free Church sermons. He doesn't drink or smoke and his only vice is sniffing. In his first case he opened his door to find a stunning Free Church woman there. He immediately knew that she spelt trouble. The elastic which she kept round her Bible had been stolen. This investigation, which of course ended in success, took Sam Spaid to a cache of black elastic in Inverness. Sam Spaid's fee, which never varies, is £20 per day plus expenses! He will never be rich but he will be an interesting moral phenomenon. His next case will involve the serial murders of Free Church ministers by a crazed sniper who was made to spend his early years in the Sunday School.

I hope you are not bored at hearing about my projects at great length but at this season of the year such ramblings may be forgiven, as Christmas carols are.

My final project has to do with a taxi service that I run for drunks at the New Year. For this purpose I have a number of advertisements run off, which read, 'Drink as much as you like. Murdo will run you home.' In small print it reads, 'Ditches, lavatories, cemeteries, scoured for those who have INDULGED too much.' The taxi is of course my own car and I am happy for it to be used for such a Christian purpose. In the course of this work I have become very humble, as I have been beaten up and vomited on many times. Hence I have developed a servile stance which has served me well. I call my customers 'Sir' or 'My Lord' and am especially friendly to large people, and to those whose jackets are flecked with a mixture of lager and sickness. It seems to me reasonable that I should charge extra for taking people to their doors or to their lavatories or even to their bedrooms. I wear protective clothing and sometimes a gas-mask. I charge also for burns from cigarettes on the seat of my car. I consider what I am doing to be a Christian duty which money in itself cannot pay. I could tell you of some little contretemps I have had, as for example a drug-crazed addict from Shawbost who attacked me with a graip, but I shall refrain. Nor will I mention that time I took one of my customers to the wrong bedroom. This arose from the fact that there are many Norman MacLeods on the island.

As you can see therefore I have had a busy and eventful year. Blessings on you wherever you are and may we exchange literature such as this often in the future.

Yours as ever
Murdo

MURDO AND BURNS

Murdo was once asked to make the Immortal Speech to Robert Burns, as the man who was supposed to give it fell ill because of the weight of the task assigned to him.

'Ladies and gentlemen, much has already been written and said about Burns. Burns and the Church, Burns and Freedom, Burns and the '45, Burns and Friendship, Burns and Dogs. All these have been speculated on by greater orators than I. Tonight I wish to speak on the topic of Burns and Mice.

Let us think for a moment about mice. They are tiny animals who penetrate our houses and raid our larders. They breed very quickly, as we are told. Cats seize them and kill them. But it is not often that we see the world from the point of view of the mouse. To mice we human beings must appear giants, greedy, vast and implacable. Whenever we see a mouse we wish to kill it. Why therefore should the mouse have any respect for us? Indeed, why should it not despise us, for in its deepest self it is a pacifist. And yet 'an icker in a thrave' is all that it wants from us. Now in the time of Burns there were no traps; it has fallen to us sophisticated beings to have created such things. All that Burns had was a ploughshare.

Let us therefore picture the mouse. A mouse whom we cannot know individually – for mice do not have names as we have – runs trembling from the ploughshare that the great poet is using, for we know that he was a farmer. It is not to our present purpose to ask whether he was a good or bad farmer: that is a matter for literary critics.

The mouse, we are told, is running away 'wi' bickerin brattle'. A fine phrase in itself. Here it is, naked and grey, among the corn, and there is the great poet, who had by this time written many great poems. It is not a minor poet that we have here but a major poet at the height of his powers or as we might say 'pooers'. Most great poets would not see in this tiny creature matter for speculation. A mouse? Who would address a mouse? Burns would. And that is why he is our National Poet. At this moment he would teach us a lesson. A mouse and a great poet would be equal, for, as he himself wrote, 'A Man's a Man for a' that'. This is not a poet who despised mice, this is one who studied them.

Nor did he assail this mouse for stealing his corn, though he might well have done so. Thief, he might have shouted, as we ourselves might have under similar circumstances, with this proviso, however, that we are not Burns, a lad that was born in Kyle and who wrote among other things, 'My Love is Like a Red Red Rose'. One who himself knew destitution, poverty – and corn.

The mouse, as we may imagine, did not wait for Burns to deliver his poem. It ran away, for that is the nature of the mouse. It does not wait to find out what the great poet will do with the ploughshare. Burns meanwhile stands there astonished. The divine afflatus has descended upon him, for his Muse does not despise a mouse.

Is there here not a lesson for us all?

What indeed may 'a bickerin brattle' not signify. May it not call us to be human beings? And what indeed is 'an icker in a thrave'. All of us can afford one. We are not so poor that we cannot afford 'an icker'. We may of course be so armoured in the luxuries of the world that we feel we cannot do so, but if we think for a moment we find we can.

Now the next thing to be said is that by the time Burns is composing his poem the mouse has disappeared. It will not wait for the great poet. On the contrary it will escape, for has it not known of the hardness of the world? Of course it has: and Burns too knows that, for he has seen and known many mice.

Burns therefore is present and the mouse is not. That is a paradox in itself and all great poetry is full of paradoxes. And we cannot imagine the mouse, an icker in its paws, caught red-handed as it were, awaiting for Burns to address it, however attractive that picture might be. Did Burns at that moment remember his dear Jean – all his dear loves, even Clarinda? Did he recall his first fumbling attempts at verse, as he stared at the place where the mouse had been, and now was no more? We don't know: we cannot know – but I think he did. I think as the helpless mouse ran away that he thought of all these things, and of his efforts to succeed in farming, and of his future career in Customs and Excise, and perhaps even of the French Revolution which raged fiercely at that time.

I will not chase thee with my murderin' pattle, Burns said to the mouse. I may chase other beings but not you. My pattle will be kept for dealing with others as the occasion may arise but not you, you helpless being. And the mouse, hiding somewhere, must have been aware of all this. He must have been in his mouselike mind aware that a great decision had been made by Burns. The great poet would not, as in a manic rage, rush into the corn and wave his pattle furiously. We do not know if the mouse knew what a pattle was: perhaps not. Suffice it to say that it was safe at least from the pattle of Burns.

Then we see that Burns was drawn to the wee bit hoosie now in ruin. It is not simply the mouse that he has to be concerned with, but its tiny tenement. And Burns knew of this, for he himself had been forced to change houses as his land failed. His house was in ruin and the wind, snell and keen, blew through it, though of course it had no windows. Burns indeed mourned – for man is made to mourn – but what else could he have done? Was he to know that this tiny tenement was in the path of his ploughshare? No indeed: and therefore he need not blame himself.

But the point of this great poem is that he did! This great poet did! With his ploughshare he had laid that tiny tenement low. And he was sorry for it. He regretted it. And he mourned too for the mouse. And he stood there shivering, for in those days they did not have the thermal clothing that we now have – nor indeed would he have deigned to wear it, for he was a proud passionate man whom wet weather would not frighten, and that is of course why he died at such an early age, of rheumatic fever, as we are told – and he stood there shivering like the mouse. Both the mouse and the great poet shivering. What a picture fit for the heart we have here. And beside them is the cruel coulter. And the mouse and the man have to thole the cranreuch. What poetry is in these words, for 'cranreuch', as we know, is the Scots word for frost.

Ladies and gentlemen, I find myself moved at this moment. Here we have a great poet who has written poems like 'The Banks of Ayr', 'For the Sake of Somebody' and 'Charlie is My Darling', and many more such gems, face to face with the vanished mouse, and one of the greatest moments of his life is here. Did he shrink away from it? No, he did not. On the contrary he showed, this passionate man, feelings that the rest of the world would not show towards a mouse. He was not ashamed to weep in that cranreuch cauld. With his murderin' pattle he stood there, not ashamed to weep, this great poet who had been let down by this brother Gilbert, who knew, as scholars have reminded us, French, and who was au fait, as scholars have also reminded us, with the contemporary work of Pope and others of that ilk. Ladies and gentlemen, I cannot – or canna – but weep as I see this great poet shivering in that field, as important as Bannockburn. A mouse and a great poet. Not indeed two warriors facing each other with wrath and anger, but a great poet and a mouse, an odd confrontation withal.'

Murdo looked around him. That majestic audience, touched to the quick, was weeping. He paused and then said in ringing tones,

'Please be upstanding. Robert Burns.' And then again in hushed reverent tones, 'Robert Burns.'

Then he sat down to the plaudits of the assembled multitudes who had been stunned and moved by his eloquence, his understanding, his sensitivity, his extraordinary insight into the psychology of the mouse. When afterwards they all came to clap him on the shoulder, and say 'Weill dune', over and over again, he muttered humbly, 'Burns – the mouse.' And wiped, as it were, a tear from his eye. But at the same time he accepted all the whiskies he was offered, for this was after all a poetic occasion.

MURDO'S APPLICATION FOR A BURSARY

Dear Sir,

I wish to apply for a bursary from you in order that I may complete my book Down the Mean Streets of Portree. *This is a detective story in which the private eye is a member of the Free Church. His name is Sam Spaid, and he is a convinced Presbyterian. I do not see why the Catholics should have Father Brown and we Protestants nobody. I have written a few pages, which I enclose. These are only a first draft and I hope to complicate the cases further by introducing the idea of Predestination and the Elect, etc. This first case is called 'The Mess of Pottage'.*

I notice from your letter that you require a referee to substantiate my application. As you will understand, I live here in a very isolated situation, and referees who are competent to judge my work are thin on the ground. I thought at first of the headmaster and the minister, but the headmaster for various complicated reasons does not speak to me, and the minister would not approve of my novel. I have, however, a neighbour who is a simple crofter and whose name is Malcolm Campbell. He is an honest man, owner of a few acres of land, and he is quite willing to be my referee. Please excuse his writing as he is not one of these people who will put his signature to anything. He has a view of life which is unsophisticated and true. Thus though he does not understand the finer minutiae of my work, he knows me well enough to appreciate that

I would not put in false claims. He is a regular reader of the Bible and Robert Burns and some selected parts of Spurgeon, and what better literary background could one have? Also he wishes me to get the grant as I owe him a trifling sum for certain repairs he made to my draughty house some time ago. I have tidied up this application a little as he left school at 15 years of age. It is good, as you will appreciate, to have such staunch friends in adversity.

I see also that you require a note of income. Last year I made £200 altogether. Most of this was the income from a Short Story Competition which I ran, in order to encourage Scottish Writing. The rest was in the form of a workshop on 'In Memoriams' which was not as lucrative as I expected.

I have other projects as well. One of my stories requires that Sam Spaid go to Peru in order to capture a criminal who has been trying to undercut the Bible market. I hope to apply for a Travel Grant for that, as of course I would need to study the laws, the social mores, etc, for authentic detail. There is a scene where Sam Spaid confronts a Peruvian god which will require considerable research. I am at the moment trying to find out how much bed and breakfast costs in Lima. Another project of mine involves a visit by Sam Spaid to Israel. This has to do with a secret weapon a crazed member of the Free Church congregation is importing in stages from a fanatical Jewish sect. I will, however, keep in touch with you about this.

There is one other project I am working on as well. In past years some of the islanders when working with The Hudson Bay Company, married and brought home Cree women. Now, the psychology of these women when confronted by our island ways has not been sufficiently investigated. Was the Cree woman frightened, puzzled, enthralled? Did her thoughts return to tepees, pipes of peace, tomahawks, memories of buffalo, etc? There is much research to be done on this; indeed none at all has been done.

It is not enough to say that perhaps only two such women appeared on the island. Two is quite enough for my financial purposes, and if numbers were to be the final arbiter what would we say of the victory of the heavily outnumbered Athenians at Marathon. And furthermore on such a premise our ideas of democracy would be in dire jeopardy, as a moment's thought is enough to show. How indeed are the thoughts, griefs, joys, etc, of one Cree woman any less important than our own? She too had her ambitions, melancholy, and elations. She too had her fears and her hopes. As she saw the sun rise in the morning over the Muirneag, memories of her home on the plain must have returned to her, of her aged chieftain father, various mothers, and so on. And she must also have thought of the young brave from whom her religious husband tore her, to take her to a strange and barbarous island where a minority language was spoken. As you can see, therefore, I have many projects on hand.

I also note that you require a track record of publication. The reason why I have published nothing is very clear. First of all, I am a perfectionist and secondly I am not greatly impressed by the magazines I see on bookstalls. Their stories and poems seem to me to lack a central plan such as I myself have, though I have not put it on paper yet. This vision glimmers before me day and night, and I try in vain to grasp it. It seems to me that these inferior writers have grasped their ideas and put them on paper too soon. Decades, generations, centuries, are not enough for me to grasp this vision. And indeed only my need for financial security – for bread, payment of council tax, payment of new carpet – forces me to frame it in a narrow compass now. It is for visions such as these that you should be paying, intangible, magnificent visions which indeed may come to nothing, but which on the other hand may result in unexpected masterpieces. I often feel that you are lacking in faith, if I may venture a criticism, and that you snatch at the inferior manuscript when you should be supporting the visionary and as yet unwritten text.

However, that is by the bye, and I hope I have not offended you in any way. Beggars such as I cannot be choosers, and great, though as yet unidentified success, leaves a salt taste on the tongue. A pair of trousers, a slice of bread, may be lost by true and sincere criticism. Furthermore, there are many talents born to blush unseen and waste their sweetness on the desert air. It might be that had your organisation existed in the eighteenth century, Robert Burns might have applied for a bursary and lived to a hale old age, where he would have written companions to such deathless poems as 'To a Mouse'. And John Keats might have done the same as well. And Shelley, if he had not been drowned.

If you will bear with me for a moment I will share with you my vision of what an Arts Council should be. Instead of asking for samples and incomes, it should be a source of largesse. It should be the DHSS of the aspiring writer till such time as he can get into print. For he may – and this is where the act of faith comes in – write a masterpiece. Could an early Arts Council have foreseen Paradise Lost or The Divine Comedy? Did even Homer see the Iliad in advance? The logic is irrefutable. The Arts Council should give a bursary to all applicants in case a potential Catullus is neglected.

I return to democracy again. Even one Lucretius or Sir Thomas Wyatt would be a justification of such a policy. Therefore, I appeal to you in the name of such a vision, open your purses: give, give, give, even to those who cannot provide samples, but who have exciting visions of the future. For it may be that by asking for samples you are toadying to the opportunist and the materialist. Is it not in fact in his interests to provide such samples? Are there not inducements for him to do so? But what of the awkward unspeaking one, who is possessed by a vision that he cannot put on paper. What of him? Is he to be ignored in favour of the smooth con-man? Those great inarticulate ones of whom the Statue of Liberty speaks, are they not to be brought to your arms? – I think they are.

I say, think of these things, and I hope also that this letter is not too long, and that what I have said may be taken on board. I know that inflation eats into your budget and I know also that the going rate for a bursary at the moment is £5,000.

Yours in anticipation,
Murdo Macrae

THE MESS OF POTTAGE

Sam Spaid was reading the second chapter of Deuteronomy when there was a timid knock at the door.

'Come in', he shouted, closing his Bible reluctantly.

A small woman, wearing a black hat, black coat, and shoes from Macdonald and Sons, Portree, entered. She stood with her hands folded, her gaze fixed on the floor, away from the great detective. He recognised her at once: she was Annie Macleod who sat three rows behind him in the church every Sunday.

'You look ill,' he said, 'would you like a cup of water? I don't keep coffee.'

'No thank you,' she said.

'Is there anything wrong?' he said, drawing out for her the chair he kept for clients, for he knew at once that she was a client.

How can she afford me, he thought, but put the thought away from him at once.

Suddenly she said, 'It's my husband Donnie. He's run away.'

Donnie, he thought, that sinful atheist. Aloud, he said, 'Run away?'

'I know he has. He left a note saying, "I've had enough".'

Sam took the note, but not before he had equipped himself with a pair of black woollen gloves, also from Macdonald and Sons, Portree.

'You are sure this is his handwriting?'

'Yes I am sure. You will notice his spelling of "enuff".'

'I see,' said Sam. 'I can tell little from this note except that it is from the edge of a newspaper, and that it is clearly the work of a disturbed man. What is this?' and he lent forward, scenting a clue. 'A spot of red.'

'It might be blood,' said Annie timidly. 'He might have cut himself shaving.'

'Not while he wrote the note,' said Sam contemptuously. 'No, this spot is something more sinister than that. However, you may continue.'

His eyes took in the woman's worn coat. No, there would not be much money to be made from this case.

'After all I have done for him.' said Annie, taking out a small white handkerchief and dabbing her eyes. 'It was I who introduced him to the blessing of the Gospel. I used to read a chapter of the Bible to him every night. I talked to him about his sinful life. Whenever he was backsliding I prayed for his soul.'

'And?' said Sam keenly.

'Recently. I noticed a change in him. When I read to him he would stare into space or click his teeth. Sometimes he would mutter to himself. He spent a lot of time in his room. I think he had a woman in there.'

'What makes you think that?'

'Perfume, powder, things like that.'

'Who could this woman be? Did he go out much?'

'He didn't go out at all. I also found a pile of magazines

under his bed. Unspeakable. Naked men and women . . .' She paused for a moment.

'You did not bring them with you?' said Sam.

'No, I did not think you . . .'

'They would have been evidence,' said Sam curtly. Why did he have to tell these people everything? Why, since the Clearances, could they not think for themselves? He felt his toothache beginning again. He wanted to hit this woman. Why don't you fight? he wanted to shout at her.

'Did you bring a photograph?' he asked.

'No, I thought you knew . . .'

'I do, I do, but a photograph would have been useful. People change, you know.'

'But you only saw him last week.'

'Did I? Maybe I did. But I wasn't observing. Observation is everything.' Again he felt a twinge of hatred for this woman who was sitting so docilely in front of him.

'How long have you been married?' he asked irrelevantly.

'Thirty years. I met him when I was coming out of the Claymore Hotel. He was in fact drunk and shouting at the people who were passing. From that moment I decided to save him. I was thirty-five, and all my suitors had left me because I was too religious.'

'So you are in fact older than him.'

'By ten years. But that was not a barrier at first,' and she smiled.

Enough of this, you contemptible woman, Sam thought bitterly. He himself had been married once, but his wife had left him when he had become a detective. Her figure with its black costume, and shoes from Macdonald and Sons, Portree, haunted him still. He pushed the thought away from him.

'I charge £20 a day plus expenses,' he said sharply.

'£20 a day. But how could I . . . Donnie was on the dole and I have my pension.'

'Do you want him back or don't you?' said Sam in a frenzy of rage, though his voice was outwardly calm. He felt a twinge of his arthritis starting. Out of the window he could see people making their way to the Coop next door as if nothing was happening. This is my domain, he meditated, this is the mean street down which I must go. This is where I must come to, after my childhood. He pondered the delights of predestination.

'I will find the money somehow,' said Annie pathetically.

'Good,' said Sam. 'Now you may go.' As she left he had the most intense desire to throw at her the paperweight that was lying on the desk. Highlanders! Would they never learn to give correct efficient evidence? Would they always accept their fate? Why would they not fight for their identity? For their language?

He adjusted his bowler hat and suit from Macdonald and Sons, as he stared into the sinful mirror in front of him. He threw a last look at the photograph of the Rev. John Macdonald which sat on the wall, and made his way down to the pier, where the ferry was waiting.

'Any news?' said Norman MacMillan, who had a pile of tickets in his hand.

'Only the good news of the Gospel,' said Sam curtly. 'I would like to ask you, when did you see Donnie Macleod last?'

'Donnie Macleod,' said Norman a few times.

(You slow thinking spud, thought Sam savagely, are you some kind of inanimate cabbage? He wanted to kick Norman MacMillan in the shin.)

The wheel of Norman's mind ground to a halt. 'Yes,' he said. 'Funnily enough I saw him yesterday. He was on the ferry.'

'Was he carrying a case?' asked Sam.

There was another long silence in which Sam visualised a torture machine of the most marvellous complexity.

'He was, and I thought it funny at the time.'

(Why did you think it funny at the time? He was on a ferry, wasn't he?)

'Did he look worried?'

'Worried? Worried? Worried? No, he didn't look worried. He said a strange thing to me though. A very strange thing. You must know that I do not know Donnie well. He hasn't left the house for years. His father, as you remember, was that Angus Macleod who went suddenly mad and jumped over the side of the ferry . . .'

(These oral stories, thought Sam savagely. This tradition they pride themselves on – how can a detective exist in such an environment. His eye rested on a bollard and he wished he could heave it out of the stone and hammer Norman's bald head with it.)

'. . . not of course that many people speak about it now. But anyway he was standing just about where you are, or perhaps a little to the left, and he said, "A change is good for a man", just as I was taking his ticket and he was making his way to the ferry. And he looked odd.'

'Odd. What do you mean by odd?'

'What do I mean by odd? I mean odd. His eyes were flashing. That's the only way I can describe it. Flashing.'

(You retarded idiot, thought Sam. That's the only way you can describe it. Of course it is. You were never well known for your discriminate style.)

'And then,' Norman said, leaning forward and speaking in a whisper, 'his very words were, "A change is good for a man".' Norman withdrew his head so quickly that he nearly butted Sam in the face, while at the same time his left eye winked rapidly at the great detective.

'He looked devilish,' said Norman, 'and another thing. He came very close to me.'

'Did he do that before?'

'Not as close as that, not as close as that.'

'I see,' said Sam, who did not see at all. What had this to do with anything? (You winking parrot, he thought fiercely.)

'How much will my ticket be?' he asked.

'Same as always,' said Norman, and laughed uproariously. 'Same as always.'

Sam threw a gaze of hatred after him as he made his way to the non-smoking saloon where he sat very upright and watched a child making faces at him.

Devilish, he thought. Devilish. So Donnie was on the ferry after all. He hadn't been killed by Annie, of whom Sam was suspicious from the very beginning because her hair was shorter than the church of St Paul strictly allowed.

When the ferry docked he strode over to the bus and sat in the back seat. He closed his eyes, feeling suddenly that his blood pressure was rising. He made a mental note that he must take more exercise. His contempt for the easy-going Highland way of life was beginning, he knew, to affect his health.

When he opened his eyes he was horrified to see straight ahead of him above the driver's head a screen on which there was a picture of a man and a woman in a naked embrace. For a moment he was worried that this was the content of his sinful mind, but when he looked about him he saw that the passengers were following the film with interest.

Without thinking, he strode down the aisle and said to the driver, 'I want you to turn that filth off at once.'

The driver, manoeuvering equably between a foreign car and a truck, said, 'I can't do that sir. The passengers are watching it.'

'And I am not a passenger, then?'

The driver considered this, chewing gum all the while – he was in fact quite young, and he wore a uniform and a pair of boots from Macdonald and Sons – and then said, 'I suppose you are, in a manner of speaking.'

'What do you mean, in a manner of speaking?' said Sam loudly. He wanted to kill this young man, he wanted to wrench his bones apart, he wanted to spatter his blood all over the bus.

While he was standing there, a large man with a red face touched him lightly on the shoulder, 'Had you not better sit down, Papa? The rest of us can't see the screen.'

Sam turned round abruptly. He should really kick this

man in the groin, but on the other hand reasoning might be better.

'This is pornographic filth,' he said. 'This man should be ashamed of showing it.'

'We like pornographic filth,' said the large man simply. 'Don't we?' and he turned to the other passengers. There was a chorus of 'yes'.

'You tell that bowler-hatted nyaff to sit down,' said a woman with red hair, who was sitting in one of the middle seats.

'You tell him to sit down or you will kick his balls in,' said a fat woman with a fat chin, who was sitting in the front seat.

'You sit there, Papa,' he said, 'We don't want to put you out.'

I will report that driver, thought Sam, in incoherent rage. I will report him and hope that he will be dismissed from his job and turned out on to the street of whatever town he lives in. I wish to see him starving and indigent, begging for food, subservient, humble, asking for mercy as the whip lashes his back.

He maintained a resentful silence till the bus pulled into the bus station at Inverness, imagining only the large man's flesh dripping from his bones in hell. He then got off the bus in the same silence, making a note, however, of its number. He should have slugged that bus driver, and that large man. He felt a familiar contempt: his toothache throbbed, his arthritis hurt, his blood pressure was rising, and now he felt a pain just above his heart.

When he was biting into the pie which he had bought at the café at the bus station, he belched. Thank God it wasn't his heart, it was indigestion. He looked around him savagely. The usual crowd of nonentities, fodder of the Clearances, remnants of the '45. He felt such unutterable contempt that he almost vomited on the spot. The good ones had gone to America and now he was left with illogical dross, who winked their eyes and seemed to have a secretive tradition which they would only tell after eons of time had elapsed. 'You should do something about your salt,' he said to the proprietor as he left, and felt the deep satisfaction which his parting shot had given.

The question however still remained. Had Donnie stayed in Inverness, or had he gone further afield? He felt a sudden pain in his kidneys and went into the lavatory at the side of the café. After he had finished he looked around him for a towel but there was none available.

'You use that machine over there,' said a young man with a grin.

Sam pushed the button on the machine but finding that no towel came out of it he left in the worst of humours.

What else could he do but parade the streets of Inverness.

If it hadn't been for that film he could have questioned the bus driver about Donnie Macleod. But he could not ask a pervert for information and in any case he would have lied to him. I have to assume that he is still in Inverness, he thought, there is nothing else that I can do. I have to rely on the intuition of the great detective. I feel in my bones that he is still here.

In comparison with Portree, Inverness was a metropolis. He counted ten churches before giving up: the Woolworths too was larger. Feeling tired, he sat down on a bench for a while. He took a blue tablet from his pocket and swallowed it; it should keep his thrombosis at bay.

A man who appeared to be a beggar came and asked him for money for a cup of tea.

'No, thank you,' said Sam. The beggar looked at him for a moment and then scuttled away.

Sam gazed straight ahead of him at what appeared to be a cinema, and whose lights flashed intermittently. A moment's thought however told him that it was not a cinema. It was in fact some kind of a club as he deduced from the large green letters which said 'THE MESS OF POTTAGE'. It suddenly seemed to him certain that he would find Donnie Macleod in there. He had no logical means of knowing this, only the mystical intuition of the great detective that he was.

He walked over to the building. Behind a glass screen sat a large woman who was wearing black lipstick.

'One ticket,' he said crisply. 'That will be enough.'

'Adult?' said the woman in a husky voice.

He disdained answering her; he had taken an instant dislike to her from the moment he saw her. But, more than that, he was suddenly struck by an intuition as he looked at her naked neck and almost naked breasts. He couldn't quite focus on what it was but it told him he had come to the right place.

He left the lobby and going through a door ahead he found himself in a large smoky room, in fact Sodom and Gomorrah. The noise was frightening. Dancers clung closely to each other. Some people were drinking at tables. On a stage a large, almost naked, woman was prancing. So this was what the Highlands had come to after the Clearances. So this was what the '45 had done to the people. So this was the result of the sheep runs and the deer forests.

If it hadn't been for his instinctive desire to pursue his investigations, he would have left at once. He touched his bowler hat as if for comfort.

As he stood there hesitating, a large woman wearing red lipstick and tottering on the sharp heels of her shoes (Armstrong and Brothers, Inverness) came up to him and said in a deep attractive voice, 'Are you not dancing, darling?' And before he could say anything he was dragged into the maelstrom of light and noise.

'Where do you come from?' asked his partner, against whose naked breast Sam's bowler hat bobbed like a cork in a stormy sea. He couldn't account for his hatred of her, but said sharply, 'Portree.'

'Portree, darling. Over the sea to Skye and so on.' (Her cliché immediately offended him. Why, wherever one went nowadays, could one never get a really satisfactory religious discussion?) Her mouth yawned, surrounded by a red infernal line.

'Do you always wear a bowler hat when you are dancing?' she asked.

'Always,' said Sam.

'How flip, what an ironic comment you are making on our contemporary society,' said the large woman. 'You must be a satirist, rather like Juvenal.'

Not another pagan writer, thought Sam savagely. Why not one of the prophets such as Micah? But no one ever mentioned Micah or Jeremiah.

The large woman made as if to kiss Sam. He turned his head away from a breath that stank like garlic.

'Has "THE MESS OF POTTAGE" been here long?' he forced himself to say, trying to wriggle away from her hand which rested on his rump. A thrill of horror pervaded him.

'Who knows, darling?' So many questions, so few answers.

Her shadowy chin bent over him and suddenly the solution to the case was as clear to him as a psalm book on a pew on a summer day. He withdrew rapidly from the woman's embrace and made his way to the exit, the sign for which hung green above his head.

'I knew it,' he said to the receptionist, 'I knew I had seen you before. The hair on your chest registered subconsciously.'

'It is true,' said Donnie. 'You have run me to ground. I suppose it was Annie who hired you . . .'

'It was indeed,' said Sam. (You ungrateful pervert, he muttered under his breath.) He wanted to crush Donnie into a pulp. So he had been right after all. That red spot beside the word 'enuff' had been lipstick, not blood.

'I couldn't stand it any longer,' the vicious serpent was say-ing. 'I was tired of hearing Leviticus and especially Numbers. You have no idea what it was like. If I had stayed I would have gone mad.' (You horrible atheist!) 'I couldn't distinguish between the Amalekites and the Philistines.' (You pathetic heretic!) 'When sitting at the table I would have an impulse to stab Annie with a knife. I knew there was no future for us. I saw this job in the paper and applied for it.' (You belly-crawling snake!)

So this was why Donnie had said to that ineffable boring

ferryman, 'A change is good for a man.' So this was why he had looked devilish.

'I won't go back,' said Donnie simply, 'I'm happy here. I love my new dresses. Pink was always my favourite colour.'

'You used to dress up in your bedroom,' said Sam.

'How did you know that?'

Sam ignored the question. After a while, Donnie said, 'You are a marvellous detective, the best in Portree. But you can tell Annie I will not go back. I have made a new life for myself here, and Jim and I have fallen in love. Tell her that if it hadn't been Leviticus it would have been someone else.'

Sam Spaid looked into Donnie's blue eyes, thinking many thoughts. His gaze rested on the rose in his corsage. Then he sighed deeply. 'I think you are taking the wrong course,' he said. 'But I cannot take you back by force, much as I would like to. You will have to give me something in your handwriting that will show Annie that I met you.'

'Yes indeed,' said Donnie, taking a pen from his purse of tinselly yellow. He wrote rapidly, and Sam read what he had written.

'Annie, you're a good woman. Too good for me. I shall think
of you as a sister.
Signed Deborah.'

'Deborah,' said Sam between his teeth.

'Yes, I have changed my name. Jim didn't like the name "Donnie".'

Sam put his hand out to Deborah (Donnie) while at the same time he was thinking that he should kick her(him) in the teeth.

'Goodbye,' he said. 'And may you learn more about those fleshpots than you know now.'

As he left 'THE MESS OF POTTAGE' he was thinking that he would not make much from this case – his fee, and his expenses, which were the rates for the ferry and the bus.

He would have to try and find some more complicated

cases. Little did he know that there was one waiting for him which would be known as 'The Case of The Disappearing Pulpit' and which would push his logical powers to the limit, and bring him expenses to the devil-possessed village of Acharacle.

MURDO'S THOUGHTS

Sometimes Murdo on a summer evening in the half-dark would say, 'Ah, you inscrutable panoply of stars, you mute procession of infinite diamonds, how little must our petty diurnal motions interest you. The Co-op for instance with its ancient till, the butcher's with its pendant flesh of sheep and swine, how little do these things rest on your individual stellar minds.

Galileo stared at you, so did Copernicus and Bruno. To the Greeks you were circles, to us you are misshappen ellipses. As Angus Macleod, dressed in his dungarees, makes his humble way to the sawmill, or Donald Munro, idle now for five years, switches on the television, while at the same time giving a howl of rancour and rage against the existential vagaries of his life, and especially his wife and his children, are you apprised of them? No, indeed, you are not?

And as I myself confront my typewriter and the sheet of blank paper which I have inserted there, are you aware of my baffled thoughts, and my envy of Catherine Cookson? I am sure you are not.

No, you continue on your luxurious orbit, you execute your perfect motions, you are perfectly happy to ignore us. And you are right to do so. For what are we but inferior notes, dwarfish monads, dressed in our various arrays against eternity.

When I was young I scampered lightheartedly through fields of bluebells. The daisy was not alien to me, nor the crocus. The rhododendron rose up in all its glory and so did the forsythia and the chrysanthemum.

Now all is different. I find little to adore in the clematis or the philadelphus. What is the japonica to me, or the hydrangea? I find myself a pitiful object among these blooms. I limp among these vernal blossoms.

I am tired of the old names. I wish to invent new ones such as 'Chrtex' or 'Crymp' or 'Haberdragon'. I wish to say in the language of the spheres 'Choro lem typsck'. Gaelic is not enough for me, nor is English. I wish words composed entirely of vowels, such as 'Aiuoiauo', or of consonants, such as 'blxrnmst'. On landscapes of such names I wish you to shine, O immortals.

And indeed you have shone for a long time. The dinosaur you have seen and the mastodon. You have seen the 'q' and the 'p' Celts. You have seen the Co-op, opened in 1924, with its many tins, its freezer, beans and spaghetti. Are you not tired of these sights? Are you not exhausted by fish fingers?

Our telescopes penetrate the atmosphere. But what indeed have we learned of ourselves? I ask you that and I know that you will not answer. Everything is old, yet everything is new or middle aged. Saturn shines on a bald head, Pluto on a random beard or chin. A waistcoat here and there is lit up by Mercury. Denims are illuminated by Jupiter and kilts by the harsh skies of Mars.

Proud travellers of the sky – majestic yet not erudite voyagers of space – what shall you say of him, this worm, Murdo Macrae? Shall you say of him, he is a good man, potential author overwhelmed by failure; or on the contrary shall you say he is a squalid idler, who inhabits a squalid tenement? Shall you say, he is a bag of wind, a sporran full of fantasies, an infernal git, or do you indeed say, he is a valuable soul untainted by the millions of Vietnamese, Malaysians, Chinese, etc, bowed over their watery plots.

Is he a con-man, you ask, is he a florid vocabularist? Or is he a poor fool in the labyrinth around him?

It is sad that you are not able to speak, ancient though you are. It is matter for sorrow that you have not even learnt a few words of Gaelic in your voyagings through space. You are not even able to give the Gaelic for 'satellite' or for 'comet'. And what do you say of 'Arcturus'? If you could speak, what stories you would be able to tell. Of the '45, of the Clearances or kelp: of run rig, the sheiling and the genealogies of Ossian. Of Presbyterian conspiracies, and the plots of the Elect. Of the angst of Arnish and the euphoria of Eagleton.

But your silence remains as we turn from thatch to stone, from exchange to subsidies. You will not speak, you remain mum. You keep your stellar mouths shut, you refrain from gossip. You have nothing to say about Mary Nicolson's moustache, or the scandal associated with Dougie Cameron's blankets. You do not ask: why has David Shaw painted his window panes green or why does Lily Stevenson live entirely on corned-beef?

And we accept this because we must. We bow down to it, as we have no alternative.

To the lyrics abandoned in space we say 'enough', and to your diamonds we say 'sufficient'.

I now have to return to my humble abode for a call of nature, asking myself indeed about the ambiguities and paradoxes of the word, and I leave you, masterful emblems, with these words: Remember the dead, O remember the dead, but remember the living more.'

MURDO AS POETRY CRITIC

'Three of the greatest lines in the poetry of our people,' Murdo would often say, 'are the following:

Shawbost is the most beautiful to me (lit. with me)
where I was brought up when I was young
where there are the peatstacks . . .'

I know that simple translation cannot give one the melody of these lines, but it can tell us the content. I admit that when I read these lines first I didn't understand their pathos, their heartbreaking directness. Peatstacks, I thought, what have they to do with the lyric, with that dictum of Milton's about poetry being 'simple, sensuous and passionate'.

However, as I re-read these lines, being brought up directly against the 'peatstack', I thought – this is precisely what the poet is trying to do, precisely this is his aim. He is like Wordsworth presenting us with the peatstack in all its bald thereness. It rises concretely from the abstract (for Shawbost from a certain point of view can be considered an abstract) and moreover it does so in a vivid manner, as indeed the gum tree in all its ghostliness arises from Australian poetry.

Furthermore, what else is being done here? The peatstack is, as we all know, the source of heat in the islands. For many years we had no electricity, as we have now. The peatstack was what held us together as a story-telling community. It sustained our communal broodings. The poet encapsulates in the peatstack a whole way of life, communal aid, tractor, cup of tea, the indigenous and ambitious lark, the wounded landscape, the heather.

The poet in fact is bringing us up against the reality and glory of our lives. Out of the sensuous melody of the poem there rises like a historical monument, like a ship in the night, the peatstack. It casts a shadow, the shadow of history, and indeed that is its purpose.

I look forward to more of these brutal yet poetic invasions, as for instance 'lazy bed', 'HIDB' and 'District Council'. 'Humankind cannot bear much reality,' wrote T.S. Eliot, but I think they can. Only when this has been done can we see that we are mature, only then can we say with the great poet Walt Whitman, 'I suffered: I was there.'

MURDO'S RANDOM JOTTINGS

A foot in both cramps.
Flogging a head nurse.
A snake in the grass keeps one on one's toes.
An apple a day keeps the orange away.
He left under a shroud.
No man is an island but Harris is.
Duty is only skin keep.
A stitch in nine saves time.
Thyme is of the essence.
A putter wouldn't melt in his mouth.
Sneaking about is the better part of valour.
Casting your Fred upon the waters.
It's all ill wind that does not recover.
Turning the other sheikh.
The tigers of luxury succumb to the warthogs of
    righteousness.
The herring volk – people of Peterhead.
My art's in the Highlands – Van Och.
A woman's place is in a home.
All that glitters is not lead.
There's no fire without smoke.
Incidents will happen.
Here be dragoons.
People in grass skirts shouldn't throw cinders.
If you can't stand the heat get out of the furnace.
The first shall be last and the last shall be fifth.
Sand Ahoy!
Never say Dai.
Helping a lame writer over his style.
Going to work on a leg.

MURDO'S PROPHECIES

- When the Access card is lost, there shall be sorrow in the glen.
- When the two cows meet head on at the Road of Fasting there shall be a dark bridge over the Navon.
- Whoever wears tartan that day shall not return till the fairies rise from their mounds.
- The Dark Woman will not eat the pebbles of repentance till Calum Mor loses five sheep.
- When there are three measures of snow a white man will descend to the trough.
- A fire in the thatch will cause the downfall of two dynasties.
- A ferry will be built on the bones of the last horse.
- The Macleods of Skye will submit to the papers from the far country.
- Whoever brings a polled cow to Innis nan Gall shall suffer for it.
- None shall inherit the House of the Green Chimney but the man with tackety boots.
- The man who sings through the nose will signal the downfall of the Mod.
- Pretend how he will, the man with the long kilt shall not be forgiven.
- The empty sporran shall be filled with the milk of mercy.
- The delinquent rabbit shall be cast on the dungheaps of history.
- On the day that the stranger is nigh, the milk bottles from the mainland shall fall over.
- The bell will cry 'Alas' when the robes shall fall from the statue.
- The end of the world is near when the MacBrayne's ship will be on time.

'THE END OF THE RAJ' BY MURDO

'It was evening,' wrote Murdo hurriedly, 'and the Raj was sitting in the sun. The last punkah had fallen silent, and the skulls of the Pathans hung against the clouds. Lady Robinson-Hattersley sipped her gin and tonic, her helmet tilted over her dark hair. She was sending her sons home to Folkestone again; how could she bear it? The heat was dazzling, the mountains in the distance were white, many men had died crossing that rope bridge: Champers had won the VC there.

Who would remember them when they were gone, the griff, the tiffin, the bhistri (the water carrier), the dhobi (or laundryman), the lowly mehtar (or sweeper)?

Not far away was where old 'Nobby' had won the MC, and 'Pillbox' the DSO. She felt her imperialist imperative weakening. This water was poisonous and the ayah had blisters on her chin. So much for the cholera that was sweeping the valleys.

Alexander had once passed this way. In his curt way he had killed many tribesmen. In the glimmering light she saw the thunderbox with her husband Willie sitting on it. He had a straw moustache and was wearing his topé. She thought, perhaps I should take a photograph of him for my book 'Leaves of a Memsahib's Notebook', but she decided against it, for her husband was a great killer of snow leopards, bears, parakeets and orioles. He also hunted the warthog, that slow yet venomous inhabitant of a harsh landscape.

'Make sure you pack their iron beds,' she shouted to the servant. And don't forget the fitting for the stiff upper lip. Inside, her tears rained down. The Dogras were waiting for her will to fail (she could hear their drums during the night), but she would not fail. She had met Willie on the boat coming out. He had said 'Hm' twice before she noticed him. Then she had seen that he was indeed a white man, brave, though small.

He had shown her photographs of mynahs, some of which were black. These are what we call coal mynahs, he had said. It was the only joke she had ever heard him make. He had a good 'seat', none better. He was a sahib.

The tiger rug of which the children were so frightened seemed to move in the dim light. Poor Willie; should she shoot him or not? The house was full of dead birds and dead animals. Wherever she went she was tickled by feathers. Not a book in sight. She stretched luxuriously and yawned. The Union Jack fluttered over the kopje (no, that had been South Africa). To see Nanga Parat on a clear day was a delight. She would miss it. It looked like . . . like . . . soapsuds. She picked up the glass with 'Northeastern Indian Railway' engraved on it. She was going to seed; she had given up wearing her spats.

She must get out, OUT, OUT. The smell of the goatskin irritated her. She had given up her polo. It annoyed her that not a single British family but had had an officer relative in India. So many VCs, MCs, and DSOs. As a child, before she had met Willie, she had been contented with her lot. But now she had India in her blood.

She saw Willie rising from the thunderbox. How she loathed him: it was only now that she recognised this at last. His monocle flashed in the last light of the Raj. His braces were the colour of the Union Jack. Behind him she saw a canna, the Kalaho peak, a markhor and a yak.

She must get home. She must make it to Essex once more. She must talk to the vicar. She put on a choga and a koi.

She took the rifle down from the stand. She would say that seeing him rise unexpectedly in the half light from the thunderbox, she had thought he was a Pathan or one of the dogras who eat the flesh of warthogs.

She sighted along the rifle – and fired. The Raj for her had come to an end. The Boxai Gumbaz rose up in front of her. Thunder echoed from the hills. The monsoon suddenly poured down.

'Will there be anything else?' said the bhistri.

'That will be all,' she said in her husky voice. As she went in she muttered to herself the words:

> *'When you're wounded and left on Afghanistan plains*
> *And the women come out to cut up what remains*
> *Just roll to your rifle and blow out your brains*
> *And go to your Gawd like a soldier.'*

Was it her imagination or was the tiger rug moving again?

MURDO'S NOTICE FOR THE LOCAL NEWSPAPER

I was sorry to hear, wrote Murdo to the local paper, of the wedding of Finlay Thomson at the early age of 50.

Brought up in Crossbost, he was the only son of a crofter. He showed great promise at school, being especially good at plasticine, and eventually became a teacher.

In the '80s he was a fine exponent of parsing and analysis, and in the '90s he discovered Dickens and Tennyson.

For many years he lived in a room and kitchen in Glasgow. There he met Dolina Maclachlan, a Domestic Science teacher. Their courtship was spasmodic and various, and they would go to ceilidhs together.

I had many fruitful discussions with Finlay about grammar.

I shall remember him as a fine loyal friend, and one who would give the shirt off his back if it was absolutely necessary.

His many friends will regret his marriage. He was a generous host, a learned colleague and a first-class grammarian. We shall not see his like again in much of a hurry.

Our sympathy goes out to his wife, the second daughter of Angus and Katag Maclachlan, 30 Main Street, Shawbost.

At the going down of the sun and in the morning we will remember him.

Murdo Macrae

A 'P' AND A 'Q' CELT
IN CONVERSATION, BY MURDO

On a puiet morning they met, Qeter Morrison and Qaul Thomqson.

'Haqqy days,' said Qeter.

'And to you,' said Qual.

The Qeewit was chirquing in a qoqlar, a qlumq monk was qainting a manuscriqt.

'It is the pueer air that is in it,' said Qaul after a qause.

Qrofound was the morning, and the qeasants at their toil, heads bowed over their qotatoes.

A daqqled horse stood by a qost. A stream riqqled in the sun.

A puiq fell from Qaul's liqs.

'When did you last see the father?'

A smile dimqled Qeter's amqle face.

'We will need Qrior notice,' he said.

Puietly chuckling together they entered the qantry and then the vestry, qassing a qaqal bull on the way.

MURDO & THE JEHOVAH'S WITNESS

Sometimes at breakfast time Murdo would say, 'Not to have been born is the best. Any more toast?'
  'It is there beside you.'

'So it is indeed. Not many Highlanders would eat muesli. Stands the Co-op where it did?'

'I'll leave you the dishes,' Janet would say.

'Yes, indeed, I am an heir of infinite riches. Why don't we get a washing machine?'

'If you would sell one of your stories we might. I'll never know why you left the bank.'

'It was indeed mysterious. My head ached and a drowsy numbness dulled my senses. That was the long and short of it.'

When Janet had gone, he muttered to himself, that was indeed the long and short of it. Not many of us had the chance to do the work for which they were created. Thus a born poet becomes a bin-man and reads the *Financial Times*, while a violinist becomes a manager of sewage. How shall the soul be saved?

At that moment the doorbell rang.

'Who are you?' said Murdo, peering out into the mirk.

'I am a Jehovah's Witness.'

'He does indeed need a witness,' said Murdo, 'as he is invisible.'

'Do you know about Life?' said the Jehovah's Witness.

'Indeed I do,' said Murdo. 'I will not let you in, as the house is untidy. Are you selling your product?'

The Jehovah's Witness said, 'Have you come to the Cross? Are you washed in the blood of the Lamb?'

'Not that I am aware of,' said Murdo. 'Your product is not faring well these days. Tell me, is it the fault of your training? Do you need a sales manager? You must advertise on TV.'

'I would like to discuss the Bible with you,' said the Jehovah's Witness, wiping the rain from his glasses.

'I am sure you would,' said Murdo. 'But not all of us get what we want in this life of ours. Some of us have heard of Barth, Tillich, Kierkegaard. What do you say to that?'

'Listen,' said the Jehovah's Witness, 'it says here: "Blessed be those that hunger for they shall be filled".'

'The hunger is indeed there,' said Murdo. 'But nevertheless you are a corrupted man. Hie thee elsewhere. Mrs Davidson has no one to talk to but her cats. Speak to her. Take thyself hence and turn first right then left. What have I to do with thee? And may I say unto thee, what dost thou know about life, thou effete ventriloquist? It will not profit a man to be sneaking up and down and expecting his neighbour to give him cups of tea. Avaunt, thou boil on the face of the waters. Begone, thou imp of false theology. Were my ancestors Covenanters for this? Go and get thy coffee elsewhere.'

The Jehovah's Witness turned on his heel. Murdo put his head in his hands and stared for a moment at the gravel and the hills. It was a day on which the witches might have met Macbeth. His spirit was low, his angst was troubling him.

He washed and dried the dishes, muttering about Hades. Comfort me with asphodels, he said to himself.

He glared malevolently through the window at Mrs Macleod.

'Nymph, in all thy orisons be all my sins remembered,' he said. And then he said, 'I will not submit, never, never, never. I am of the proud clan of the Macraes. I will fight this metaphysical smirr on my own. Thank you.'

SEORDAG'S INTERVIEW WITH THE BBC, BY MURDO

'How old am I? I am ninety-five years old. We used to have a black house, a dung heap, and a byre. Now we only have a microwave, a cooker and a freezer.

My daughter looks after me. She is seventy years old. She has arthritis, bronchitis, and a bit of heart trouble. I was never at a doctor in my life; I could leap the height of a trout over the house.

In the early days, we had brose, oatcakes and milk: now we have weetabix and sometimes my daughter makes lasagne.

The oral tradition? I remember that we used to sit around

the fire in the ceilidh house reading *The Guns of Navarone* aloud. It took three weeks. Before that we had *Where Eagles Dare.*

I read the *People's Journal.* The other day I saw a funny thing in it. "Highlander in kilt wishes to meet another Highlander in kilt."

I listen to Scottish Dance Music as I am immune to it now, and it doesn't affect me.

I feel as young as when I was working in the run rig. I could go to a dance yet (laughs). My leg is as white as the bogcotton on the moor.

I had seven children. Most of them worked for the Gaelic BBC. Did you ever hear the programme "From the *Slabhraidh*"? It was my daughter Sheila that did that. It used to be on at four in the morning.

Of course when I was young we never locked our doors. Stealing was unknown. There was some incest, but if a man was caught stealing he would be put out of the community.

We have funny neighbours now, *a ghraidh*. A Frenchman, a German, and a man from Portugal. They are the only ones who speak Gaelic.

You have fine knees yourself, *a ghraidh*. It is a pity that I was not seventy years younger.

And of course there is not a cow or horse on the island now. The blacksmith's closed twenty years after the last horse died. Calum Macmillan was always a bit slow. I used to go up to the last horse and stroke him. I would give him a saccharin as we had no sugar in the war. Oh, he knew he was the last horse all right. It was like the second sight.

I never had the second sight myself, though my sister had. She prophesied when the first planning officer would come to the island.

There was a time when I was in Peterhead and Wick. I would be following the herring but it might not be the same herring.

My eyes are as sharp as ever. I can see a buzzard from

five hundred yards and a proverb from further away than that.

Oh, I remember Cathy Morrison. She was very witty. She said to me once, "You are as fat as a barrel with a cran of herring in it." (Wipes her eyes, laughing.) Another time she said to me, "That man is as thin as a rake."

You've got nice soft knees. Sarah my daughter is in bed with the arthritis. Her husband's dead. His last words were, "It's the fine day that's in it." You're not to run away. I was only joking. Don't lift your voice like a seagull when the planting is being done. Come back. Come back. Come back.

I never told you about the *tairsgear*.'

THERE WAS A SHOULDER, A SURREALIST TALE, BY MURDO

Once upon a time there was a shoulder and it shouldered far away. Wherever a battle was to be found it was there. It was to be found in India, South Africa, the Sudan. It would wave the troops on, and the fine absent chiefs. And sometimes it would compose a pipe tune. This shoulder had not much to say for itself. It might go into a bar and ask for a half and a half. That was the maximum of its verbiage. It was the best-behaved shoulder in the British Army.

It never thought about the intricacies of things: it put itself to the wheel. And it would sometimes fight against shoulders of its own kind.

At one time it had tartan on it, then nothing at all, then tartan. The shoulder loved the tartan. It had a great reputation for strength.

One time it found itself at the Green Hills of Tyrol. It heard the cowbells and it felt at home. But then it saw other shoulders coming towards it and it began to snarl and then to fight. That is why there are many shoulders buried there.

This shoulder would cast a shadow over a burnt house.

Sometimes it would brood about the oral tradition, even when the foreign officer was shouting, 'The first duty of a shoulder is to die for the King or the Queen, as the case may be. Failing these, an attaché will do.'

When the shoulder returned home there was no sign of its village. It wept and wept for a long time. Then it was given a home help and sat in a chair watching TV.

Sometimes, if it was in a good mood, it would say, 'When I was a shoulder in Afghanistan,' or it would say, 'That was where I got my campaign medal. It is as pretty as a rainbow.'

All the shoulders from the Highland regiments asked for their own minister. They were very upright and honourable. They had been brought up on the very pith of buttermilk and were very strong.

None of the shoulders ever rode a horse and none of them became an officer.

If it wasn't for these shoulders where would the British Empire be today?

It's a thought, isn't it?

THE STORY OF MAJOR CARTWRIGHT, BY MURDO

Major Terence Cartwright, wrote Murdo, was an interesting man. He came originally from Hampshire.

When he arrived in the small Highland village of A—— his first act was to learn Gaelic. Most of the natives had long ago given up speaking Gaelic but Major Cartwright was determined to keep the old traditions alive. He dressed in the kilt, made crowdie, cut the peats, and had a little dog called Maggie. The dog looked like a dishcloth which you might see on a kitchen table.

At ceilidhs Major Cartwright would introduce the singers and the songs.

'*Tha mi toilichte a bhith an seo an nochd,*' he would say, speaking with great aplomb. He would insist on speaking Gaelic throughout the ceilidh, though the natives were not used to it.

'We should not let these Sassenachs run our affairs,' he would say, when he spoke English. He voted Scottish Nationalist at all times and would say, 'It is high time we had a government of our own.'

He loved cutting the peats. Everyone else hated doing them: all of them used electricity, gas or coal. But to Major Cartwright cutting peats was the bee's knees. He was never happier than when he was out on the moor among the larks and the midges.

'A fine figure of a man,' the natives would say at first.

The Major made oatcakes, which the natives despised. He would hold his little dog in his arms and speak to it in the Gaelic. It looked like the bottom of a mop.

'*Tha mi uamhasach toilichte,*' he would say. A few of the natives initially disliked him: then more and more as they saw what he was up to. 'Anyone would think we were living in the eighteenth century, he is bad for our image.'

He advertised lessons in Gaelic but no one went. He wanted to teach the natives the correct use of the dative and the genitive, but they would have none of it. He even began to write poetry in Gaelic, which he published in a national magazine.

'Many is the time,' he would write, 'that I would look over to Harris of the lazybeds. It was there that I was reared.'

The natives thought that they ought to get rid of him. They felt he was riding roughshod over them. His poodle was stolen and Sam Spaid was asked to investigate. Sam Spaid hated the Major at first sight and would only speak to him in English. He found the poodle on a washing line: Anna Maciver, who was eighty years old and almost blind, had hung him there.

'You senile idiot,' said Sam Spaid under his breath. 'You

incontinent oaf.' He was wearing a black suit (from Anderson and Sons) and a pair of black shoes (from the Co-op).

'Here is your . . . thing back,' he said to the Major. (You imperialist hound.) The Major made crooning Gaelic noises to the dog, based on a lullaby from Iona.

'What are the marks on my dear Maggie?' said the Major.

'Pegs,' said Sam Spaid curtly.

Sam Spaid went off in a rage to his next case. He had been paid in oatcakes.

The Major began to make oatcakes and crowdie for sale, but no one would buy them. He felt that he was becoming more and more unpopular.

At night, on his own, he read *Dwelly's Dictionary*. He knew the Gaelic for the birds and trees and flowers, shellfish, and so on. Most of the Gaelic speakers from the village had joined the Gaelic Department of the BBC.

The Major had never been so lonely in his life, not even on Salisbury Plain. His wife had stayed in Hampshire and wrote to him in English. He replied in Gaelic. It was with great difficulty that he had managed to take the poodle with him.

'I did not find anywhere more beautiful,' wrote the Major. 'The lochs, the sheilings, the streams.'

He picked up his bagpipes and began to play the 'Lament for the Children'. In the distance he would hear the music from the disco: and someone singing 'Walk Tall' in an American accent.

It was one of his great sorrows that he could not find the Gaelic for 'poodle'.

Night fell over A——. The Major put away his pipes. What had he done wrong? Whenever an Englishman came to the village he would say to him, 'This is not for you. You have done enough harm. Do you know for instance the Gaelic for "rhododendron"?'

The Englishman took the hint. After a while no one stopped in the village, and the bed and breakfast trade failed.

There were murmurings of discontent, rising to open roars of hatred.

'I was born in Uist of the peewit and the rowan,' wrote the Major. The moon shone over *Dwelly's Dictionary*.

One day with his poodle he left. All that was found in his house were some oatcakes, some buttermilk and some crowdie.

He went back to his wife in Hampshire.

Often he would look back on his days in A—— with stunned amazement. He changed his poodle's name from Maggie to Algernon.

'We have seen much together,' he would say to him. 'The time is not yet. The books at the airports are all the same.'

He gave up the bagpipes and gave his kilt to Oxfam's.

He and his wife opened a restaurant in Hampshire. His oatcakes, buttermilk and herring became famous. The menus were in Gaelic with English translations.

In the evening of his days he would say, 'Fine it was for me that I dwelt once in Harris.' An Indian was chewing his oatcakes with the air of a gourmet and a South Korean was delicately sipping his buttermilk.

'Fine it was for me,' he said, 'that I tasted the salt herring in my youth.'

SOME JOTTINGS, BY MURDO

1) Imphm
   Hem
   Alas
   Och
   Alack
   Er
   Rrm   *(Preferential treatment)*
   Um   *(Friendly fire)*
   Ahem   *(Salutary suggestion)*

Thoughts of Murdo

Em   (*Categorical imperative*)
              (*The rule of the proletariat*)
Arrum   (*White heat of the technological
                 revolution*)
              (*Aesthetic, ethical, existential*)
Hum   (*Expanding universe, big bang,
                 quasar*)

2) And then my heart with pleasure grinths
   and dances with the hyacinths.
                    (*Murdo Wordsworth*)

3) It never came a wink too soon
   nor brought too long a day
   but now I often wish the night
   had sung a roundelay.
                    (*Murdo the Hood*)

4) For a' that an' a' that,
   the microwave an' a' that
   the man o' independent mind
   is king o' men for a' that.
                    (*Murdo Burns*)

5) There lived a wife of Usher's Well
   and a wealthy wife was she,
   her cooker was of the deep deep clay
   and her fridge was ivory.
                    (*Murdo Ballad*)

6) Never never never never never
   never never never never never.
                    (*Murdo Shakespeare*)

7) Come into the garden, Mod,
   for the adjudicator has flown.
                    (*Murdo Lord Tennyson*)

SAM SPAID

Sam Spaid bent down and picked up his mail from the lobby. He was in his blue and white striped pyjamas (Co-op, Portree) and his blue slippers (Anderson and Son). There were only two pieces of mail: one a communication from Strathclyde, which he crumpled into a ball and threw into the bin, the other an envelope with his name but no address written on it. And no stamp.

He opened it. There was a piece of paper inside it and written on the paper in shaky handwriting, which at first he found difficult to decipher, were the words 'You slimy inauthentic theologian'. Immediately his face contorted with fury, red spots danced in front of his eyes. He read the words again then looked at the paper and envelope, searching for clues. But there were none. He did not recognise the handwriting.

As he ate his muesli, he studied the message again. Who could have written him that letter? He didn't think there was anyone who disliked him, unless it was one of the criminals he had uncovered in his many successful cases. His tea tasted foul and so did the toast.

Apart from the Case of the Disappointed Evangelist he had nothing on his plate. 'Inauthentic', eh? Not many people would know that word. It must have been an educated man who had written that note, and there weren't many educated people in Portree. Most of them were actually working for the Gaelic Department of the BBC and therefore not at home. Furthermore, the criminal had delivered the letter himself, the filthy horrible swine, riff-raff left behind at the time of the emigrations.

He sat at his desk all day drinking glass after glass of water and studying the handwriting. He thought he had seen it before but could not identify it.

That night he read three chapters of Numbers before falling

into a deep sleep. In the morning he found another envelope
on the floor (there were no other letters) and when he opened
it he read the words: 'You ineffable religious snot. Why don't
you look under your pillow?' The handwriting was the same,
and still not easily read.

Under the pillow he found an old digestive biscuit. He
stared at it in amazement. What did this mean? His large
face reddened and boiled with rage like a choleric crab. His
hand tightened on the toaster. Who was trying to get at him?
He, who had never harmed anyone in his life. He took out the
list of his cases filed for future publication:

The Case of the Highland Horror (that was that woman
Miss D. Lennox who had inherited a haunted castle from her
stepfather and who had been found dead in a rain barrel).

The Case of the Enchanted Elder (that had taken him to a
striptease club in Oban and lavish fees and expenses).

The Case of the Australian Cousin (who had easily been
uncovered, because after twenty years in the outback he still
spoke with a strong Highland accent), and many others. He
could see no obvious clue there. He had a sudden idea. Getting
hold of a piece of wood he nailed up the letter-box.

The rest of the day he spent simmering quietly, now and
again thinking of throwing a plate or two at the wall, but with
great difficulty he refrained.

He read two more chapters of Numbers that night before
falling asleep. In the morning he went confidently into the
lobby. In spite of his confidence there was an envelope there.
He opened it and read the fateful words: 'You futile inves-
tigatory excrescence. Look under the teapot.' And there he
found a squashed pancake, one of the ones he had bought
from the Co-op.

His mind staggered under the weight of the puzzle with
which he was confronted. He felt giddy. First his arthritis,
then his heart bothered him, but there was no one to whom
he could recount his symptoms. He did not wish to go
out, though he thought of himself as a popular man who

always had a single word for everyone. His usual swear words 'Clearance fodder' and 'imperialistic poodles' fell flat from his lips. Nor was he much better pleased with his recent invention 'Black house perverts'.

The day passed in a stupor of surrealistic scenes and images. He cut himself when opening his usual tin of corn-beef; his malignant flare at Mrs Macleod was only a shadow of its former ferocity. He looked through all his correspondence to see if he could find the handwriting. But all he could find were old letters. One of them began: 'No, you ineffable stream of pee, of course I can't marry you. Do you think I'm a masochist?' (That was from Marjory.)

Another said: 'I send you by return of post a copy of *The Triumph of the Elect*, which you sent me. Please defray postage.' (That was Evelyn.)

There was also a letter from the Income Tax which asked him for a list of fees and expenses. It was addressed to Private Eye Sam Spaid, Portree, Isle of Skye.

Finally, there was a letter from the local Police Department querying his interrogative techniques.

But he did not find the handwriting he was looking for.

He could not work like this. That morning he had put on a red tie with a brown suit, and he had broken two cups.

An idea came to him. He would stay up all night, but he would have to make sure that he did not fall asleep.

He chose from his extensive library a book called *The Amusements of the Prophets*, and read avidly. It must have been at three in the morning, and when he had reached the part about the honey, that his left hand began to twitch violently. He stared down at it in surprise. Then he began to move, as if under an obscure order, and found a piece of paper on which he wrote the words: 'You eccentric Moabite. Look under the money jar.'

He went to the cupboard and took out a doughnut, which he placed under the jar. He put the paper in an envelope and laid it on the lobby floor, then wrote his name on the envelope. All this time he was in a state of suspended animation.

So it was himself who had written the messages after all. He put away *The Amusements of the Prophets*, carefully marking down the page. One thing bothered him. Why had he not recognised his own handwriting?

Then the answer came clear to him. He had written with his left hand. Flooded by childish memories mixed with bile, he remembered that when young he had written with his left hand. Then his grandfather, a vision of a long snot-infested beard and small hating eyes, had hit him repeatedly with a belt till he had changed hands.

All was now clear to him. He went to his file and wrote the Case of the Blur-lined Letter.

Then he sank to his bed and slept till midday when a stunning but perplexed fisherman introduced him to the Case of the Docile Drifter.

THE CONCIENTIOUS PARTNERS

J.D. Williams and Oxendales, wrote Murdo, were great heroes in Highland mythology. It was from them that coats, pillowslips, frocks, etc, came by mail order and, generally speaking, COD.

Many was the time that One-eyed Angus, the postman, brought such a parcel to a house. Angus would only give the parcel to the addressee and to no one else, no matter how closely related. Thus he would make his way to the peatstack or to the cornfield or to the seashore, in order to deliver the parcel which might in fact be a wardrobe or sideboard. In this fashion people would have to carry large or small sums of money with them at all times in case One-eyed Angus loomed over the horizon with a parcel. He was a small man with a red face, and no knowledge of Berkeley or logical atomism at all.

'Much as J.D. Williams and Oxendales are great Highland heroes,' he would say, 'and much as they are handsome as the oak-tree, slender as the salmon, with eyes as blue as the egg of a peewit, however their hearths are open to the stranger, and however kind they are with venison, wine and mutton, they are causing me no end of bother. Plus,' he said, 'receipts are difficult to obtain when there is heavy rain in it or a violent snowstorm.'

Poor Angus, ignorant of philosophy or theology, inhabitant of a land of clouds and thistles, lone struggler through the world of the COD! It is often I think of him resting his wardrobe in the land of true hospitality and curiosity, himself untainted by alien materialism, for he was too poor himself to afford such luxuries. He would mutter 'rich bastards', as he trudged through a marsh and the birds were singing cheerfully overhead.

For he was consumed by his Presbyterian conscience. 'No, indeed,' he would say, 'I will not give this parcel to you, though you may indeed be the mother or the brother of the acc——, the addressee.'

And therefore the largesses of J.D. Williams and Oxendales would cause One-eyed Angus to froth at the mouth. 'These men,' he would say, 'heroes though they are for their munificence, have caused more chilblains than anyone else; they have bowed my back and made my hair the colour of the bogcotton. I would be glad if small articles were sent for.'

And so it was that this happened. People felt sorry for One-eyed Angus and stopped sending for wardrobes, dressers, etc. Nor did these great heroes ever discover why their trade with that area declined and diminished. Little did they realise that it arose from the community spirit of a village and the Presbyterian conscience of one man. For how indeed were they likely to know of it, but it warms our hearts to think of it.

Now Angus rests under the daisies by the sweet water of Loch Gair. Above his head waves the simple daffodil, but of a winter's night if you are passing and happen to shout the words 'J.D. Williams' or 'Oxendales', a figure will suddenly arise, putting on its boots, and with a face contorted with rage in the eerie light of the moon, will appear also to take a bag and trudge through mud and marsh to cornstack and peatstack, muttering to himself over and over 'Bloody COD' – and a hand grained with toil, will stretch out for the fateful wardrobe, or whatever, and sign in the moonlight the paper which One-eyed Angus holds out.

MURDO'S PLEA FOR A
NATIONAL ANTHEM

Sir,

I would like to show you why my song, 'There was a Shoulder', should be considered as our National Anthem and therefore fit to be sung at rugby, lacrosse and hockey matches, whenever two or three or eleven are gathered together.

The arguments in favour of my song are as follows:

Firstly, everyone has a shoulder. This is a very important point. It means that instead of being divisive or contemptuous or bellicose, it draws attention to what we have in common, e.g. a shoulder. There is no aggression here, only the cry of suffering humanity, for there is no one who does not have a shoulder.

Secondly, and following from this, there is no reason why the two teams should not sing my anthem. Neither would be betraying nationalistic fervour, etc, in doing so. They would be learning about our common humanity, its hopes and fears, etc, and the mutual kinship of shoulders. Indeed also the shoulders of each member of the team could be bared at this point.

Finally there is a pathos there which could appeal to all men of goodwill. This Scottish shoulder wandering freely all over the world – where does it come from, where does it go to? Is it an orphan, a refugee? Who will look after it, who will give it shelter? Our thoughts go with it. It draws attention to our solitary state, our need for friends. It belongs to the category of sunt lacrimae rerum as seen in Virgil, Tennyson, Larkin, etc.

I hope these thoughts will be of use in this troubling matter, and in this troubling time. I refer of course to Beirut.

Yours etc,
Murdo Macrae

MURDO ON TRANSLATION

Sir,

Can any of your readers help me? I would like to translate the following passage into Gaelic for a book I am writing, The Thing in Itself: A History of Sofas from a Philosophical Standpoint.
Here is the passage:

'Now Köhler said, "You see two visual realities." As opposed to what? To interpreting presumably. How does he do this? (i.e. how is this established?) It won't do to ask people. Köhler never says it will but he says, "If you're not blinded by theory you'll admit that there are two visual realities." But of course he can't mean only that those who don't hold a certain theory will say, "There are two visual realities." He must intend to say that whether or not you're (1) blinded by theory, or (2) whether or not you do say one thing or the other, you must be right to say "there are two visual realities".'

> *Yours in anticipation,*
> *Murdo Macrae*

PS Does Cogito ergo sum, mean, I think, therefore I add up?

DETERIORATION IN SAM SPAID

A great change came over Sam Spaid after the Case of the Blur-lined Letters. He became a more private eye than before. He trailed people only halfheartedly: his witty sayings became fewer: he dressed in a sloppier fashion.

He asked himself the question, 'What am I doing? What is the meaning of my work? Do I do it for honour? Yes, perhaps. Or for the conscience of mankind? Again, perhaps.

'These days and nights of snooping in doorways, beating people up and being beaten up, these hours of sitting outside the Co-op disguised as a crofter or an insurance agent, what are they for?

'Am I in fact a crusader or a knight or an Old Testament prophet? I have burrowed into bins and learned that all fish is gross. And that tinkling symbols can be found among slimy sandwiches.

'When I was young I snooped with innocent assurance. I shadowed people without regret. Now however I ask myself, Why, Why, WHY? Do I deserve the title "private eye" and what does it mean? Is it a pun on "private I" or have I touched an optic nerve?

'And was the meaning of the letters revealing that I was spying on myself?

'When I was young I always thought that this would be my *metier*. I spied and snooped on both my parents. One night I looked into their bedroom and, the horror, I did not recognise either of them. From that night I decided to find out who these people were, *and what that thing was for.*

'I dreamed of unearthly secrets, of being paid for scavenging about. Cases of theft and incest abounded, though, thank God, I have not found any necrophily yet. Fearlessly, I strode the street. "That is the private eye," the people would say. I was in the public eye. A private eye in the public eye! That was a paradox which caused me many a wry smile.

'Now my innocence is gone. The words, "If it were not so I would have told you", come often to my mind.

'Last night the answer came to me. It was simple and clear. I shall change "private eye" to "scourge of God". A fiery cloud will go before me at night and a cloud shaped like a waterspout by day. I shall strike out of the whirlwind. I shall accept the sacrifice of sheep, my nostrils shall smell the fat of the roasting oxen. I see sin everywhere, for example a "syndrome", i.e. "an airport for sinners" and I leave you to deduce what "syncope" means.

'My whip is upon you, ye Levites: and my lashes upon you, O ye Philistines. You will not be free of my finger-printing, O ye Moabites. I shall pursue you to the fourth or fifth generation, for I am Sam Spaid, erstwhile "private eye" now "scourge of God".

'And this change shall be made on my stationery.' Thus spake Sam Spaid.

THE SCOTTISH DETECTIVE STORY, BY MURDO

The howdumdeid was leeing on the flair when Inspector Macdermott arrived.

'Hoo is he ca'd?' he speired the hoosekeeper.

'The Rev. M. Kailyard,' she said.

Her een were a keethin' sicht.

The Inspector peeked through the winnock. He saw a shelty, a quey, an' a watergaw.

'Did aebody ca' on him?' he speired.

The eemis stane was leein' by the corp. The Inspector keeked at his watch.

It was ane after ane.

'Ay' said the hoosekeeper. 'He had a lang beard an' he faced baith weys.'

'Baith weys,' said the Inspector, gantin'. The draff o' last nicht was dowie in his mooth.

'He was ca'd Anti – something.'

'Aunti something?'

'Ay.'

The hoosekeeper wis a drodlich. Forfochen, the Inspector picked up a caird frae the flair aside the howdumdeid.

His chouks fell.

Professor Anti-zygygy, it said.

The Inspector faddomed it a' noo. It was a liteerary maitter. A' to dae wi' dialectic an' the contradeections. He reca'd whit the hoosekeeper had said.

He was facin' baith weys. That was eet. Frae Byron tae the present day.

'*Sunt lacrimae rerum*,' he said. 'Git Professor Anti-zygygy. There is bluid on the eemis stane.'

'Seil of yir face,' he said to the hoosekeeper. 'An' dree your weird.' Then he clamb intae his carr.

'There's a fine look tae the lift,' he said to a passing farmer.

'Na, I dinna want a lift,' said the farmer.

'Ignorant knoul – taed krang,' said the Inspector to himself, as he drave on.

MURDO'S BALLAD

There lived a wife o' Usher's Well
an' a wealthy wife was she.
Her mooth was o' the bad bad clay
and her dress was crammasie.

'To Noroway to Noroway
to Noroway o'er the faim.'
Thus spak the wife o' Usher's Well
who was a canty dame.

She hadna sailed a league, a league,
a league but barely three
when the canty wife o' Usher's Well
went a' tapsalteerie.

Gie tae me a hame help, she said,
a hame help but barely seeven
afore I climb that heich heich wa;
until the gates o heeven.

They brocht unto her a hame help
a hame help but barely twa
and she didna climb tae the gates of heeven
but she played at the ba.

An' lappit in her bedclaithes fine
she asked for her barely bree
'For my three sons are in the the brine
and i'm fair drowkit,' said she.

FRAGMENT OF A PLAY BY MURDO

(Set in a Chinese restaurant. Low lights, black phone, etc.)

Enter Yu Fuang: Is the chowmein ready yet?

(pause)

Lin Fang (his grandmother) soliloquises:
              The moon over the Yangtse.
              When shall I see you again? In my
              pigtails, wandering near the Gate of the
              Beetle in the year of the Dragon ...

Thoughts of Murdo

(enter Angus)

Angus: *A bheil an chowmein deiseil fhathast?* [1]

Yu Fuang: *Cha bhi e fada.* [2]

                (*pause*)

Lin Fang: . . . The Emperor riding past.
                Dust by the Gate of the Beetle.

Angus: *Agus king's prawn.* [3]

Yu Fuang: *Ceart* [4]

                (*pause*)

Yu Fuang soliloquises: I wish my honourable granny
                would help me. She soliloquises all day.
                In this so honourable alien land I feel
                so tired, so tired . . .

                (*pause*)

Voice outside the window sings:

                The town hall clock in Stornoway
                chimes its message every day . . .

Lin Fang: That so honourable young voice
                recalls to me a poem by Li Po:
                On the Yangtse with a glass in my hand
                and looking at the moon
                I think of Peking . . .

Angus: *Tuilleadh rice.* [5]

Yo Fuang: *Ceart.* [6]

                (*pause*)

                I long for Confucius.
                The Flea Church is strict, strict . . .

                (*pause*)

143

Angus: *Agus 'sweet and sour'.* [7]

                 (pause)

Ling Fang: Honourable young man has hit nail on
                 head. Sweet and sour is how I feel far
                 from the land of my so honourable and
                 psychologically correct ancestors.
                 I think of Li Po:
                 The Emperor has exiled me here to
                 the Island of Hoo Pung
                 I look at the moon . . .

                 [1] *Is the chowmein ready yet?*
                 [2] *It won't be long.*
                 [3] *And king's prawn.*
                 [4] *Right.*
                 [5] *More rice.*
                 [6] *Right.*
                 [7] *And 'sweet and sour'.*

FURTHER THOUGHTS OF MURDO

On a fine summer's day as he sat in his study, Murdo would
see the road in front of him and people passing up and down
on it as if on their way to Camelot or Ballachulish. Beyond
the road was the heathery sward, on which his eye would rest
lovingly, and he would think some such thoughts as these:

It is indeed fortunate that I live here where, at the first hint
of spring, the humble crocus peeps out its lovely head as it
nestles, perhaps beside a helpful stone. The ill-clad buzzard
perches on a post and the rabbit plays his innocent games.
The seagull makes a flying visit and the innocent tit gobbles
up the guilty worm.

In the autumn the tree burnishes its leaves and in the winter
a cloak of snow descends. Sometimes a cloud passes overhead

and I ask myself, where is it going on its innocent way? Is it perhaps heading for Sumeria where the alphabet was first invented, or to Egypt where the pyramids were erected by many men and where the innocent cat was worshipped, or perhaps to Carthage where the innocent Dido burnt herself after she was deserted by the con-man Aeneas, and of which city it was said, '*Carthago delenda est*'.

Night falls, and the patient owl goes 'Tu whit tu whoo', and the beetle drags his weary length along. On such a night did Juliet in her native Italian speak sweet nothings to Romeo, and in Latin also did Caesar whisper in Cleopatra's ear, '*Te amo,*' – that great man who had Pompey decapitated and who said '*Veni, vidi, vici*' when he landed in Britain.

Then in the month of March the daffodil rises proudly from the sod and later still the rhododendron. In this fruitful land however we do not have the gum tree, nor does the melon or the kiwi fruit flourish here. The orange nor the tamarind grows easily, nor the breadfruit tree, and the palm tree only takes a passing interest.

Time passes slowly, and during the harvest the mouse nibbles at the golden blades. The crooked scythe is no longer to be seen, but the reaper is: and instead of the upstanding horse we have the tractor slaving eagerly on behalf of mankind. Such is progress at this present moment in time. The future is uncertain and the past is the past.

No longer is it the case that we have the corncrake, for poisonous and venomous substances have put an end to him, and the lark is not feeling so well. The raven no longer comes to the winnock and the common dove is sickening. What has happened to the crow and the swallow? They will all go the way of the roc and the auk and the dodo. The domestic hen too is in danger, and the flagrant goose.

Life is changing and things are no longer as they were. Where are the summers of our childhood when we would paddle in the burns, and catch the seemly trout and the salmon which was not safe from us. They are, I fear, no more.

Some such thoughts as these would stir in Murdo's mind as he looked out of his winnock and saw two or three council employees now and again cutting the grass, and a big black dog with slavering jaws would trot along on some mysterious quest of his own.

MURDO IN CONVERSATION

Sometimes Murdo would stop a smallish farmer and, like the Ancient Mariner, hold him in his thrall. He would speak to him in the following wise:

'If a man says to me looking at the sky, "I think it will rain therefore I exist," I do not understand him.'

But more importantly he would discuss things which interested the farmer. Thus he might say, 'The Highlander never looked kindly on the pig. Is this perhaps because he belongs to one of the lost tribes of Israel, as is commonly said; for you may see many domestic animals in the Highlands, including the dog and the cat and the sheep, but never the pig in its pink splendour, though he is mentioned in the tale of the Prodigal Son.

'Also, at one time, the Highlander used to drink the milk of the ewe and, in extremis, he would take blood from his cow, mix it with oatmeal and make a meal of the resulting melange. That was at the time of the Clearances.

'The innocent and cud-chewing cow the Highlander has taken to. it reflects from its eyes his own leisurely concerns, his hopes and fears, etc. These eyes are, as it were, treasuries of oral tradition and language. The tup too he has taken to and the ewe, known as the yowe in the areas where Lallans is spoken.

'But the pig, never the pig. Something in the pig disconcerts him and at the same time repels him. What can that be? Is it perhaps something to do with its cannibalism, reminding him of the days of the clans? The goat he will accept with its capricious leaps but not, not, the pig.'

Murdo would end with the following quotation:

'"What is the use of studying philosophy if all that it does for you is to enable you to talk with some plausibility about some abstruse question of logic, etc, and if it does not improve your thinking about the important questions of every day".'

And as an illustration of this, Murdo would quote:

'"It would have made as little sense for me to say, Now I am seeing it as . . . as to say at the sight of a knife and fork, Now I am seeing that as a knife and fork".'

'Good-day to you, sir.'

NEIGHBOURS

Murdo hated the programme *Neighbours* and when it came on he would start screaming, or go into epileptic fits. Catalepsy too was one of the strategies that he employed. If none of these was available he would say, 'This is the end of civilisation as we cobbers know it.'

Or, more simply, 'We will roo this.'

Or, 'Rolf Harris' impudent didgeridoo will replace the psaltery.'

He would hide in sheds or in wardrobes or under beds, or pull blankets over his ears. His nervous system would appear to collapse and he would mutter frenziedly some such word as pommy, or emu.

Swag, billycan and eucalyptus would become to him common swear words, and so would billabong. 'Speak not to me of sheep stations,' he would say, 'nor tickle me with the didgeridoo.'

It would take hours before, with the help of valium, he would settle down again in the arms of his loving sheila, Janet, who would whisper to him over and over, as if to a sleeping child whose limbs have run wild, 'It is fine and dinkum. See you later. Bad Rolf Harris will not get you nor does the billabong await you.'

THE WHIST DRIVE

A very nice whist drive was held in our village the other day *(wrote Murdo for the local newspaper)*. Mrs A. Macleod held her cards very well and Mr R. Macleod was everything that was required. There was no rancour between Mr and Mrs D. Macleod, though in fact Mrs D. Macleod missed a trick or two. The matter, however, was smoothed over amicably.

Tea and cakes were purveyed at the interval. These were of the highest quality. Mr F. Macleod was in sparkling form: his quips were of a rare vintage. Mr Z. Macleod told the story of the Angels of Mons once again.

When the whist was resumed after the fine tea (for which we must thank Mrs G. Macleod) everything was as nice as before. Mr F. Macleod allowed himself a few pleasantries, and I wish you all had been there to hear them. Mr N. Macleod and Mrs G. Macleod shared a joke.

Much work goes on behind the scenes at an event of this kind. We wish to thank Mr L. Macleod for setting out the chairs so nicely: Mr K. Macleod (known to his friends as Kenny) for handling the raffle tickets so well: and Mrs S. Macleod for donating prizes which were won so handsomely by the recipients, who came forward so nicely and with such humility.

Murdo Macrae

(NB. I would like on behalf of the Committee to thank our local writer Mr Murdo Macrae for writing so nicely about our event.

Mr W. Macleod)

(And finally I would like to thank Mr W. Macleod for his able words about Mr Murdo Macrae.

Mr T. Macleod)

POEM BY MURDO

I remember, I remember,
the house where I was born.
There never came a Saturday
but Mrs Macleod came in at morn.

She never brought a thing to us
but she would say 'An ounce
of sugar is what I would like' –
These words she would pronounce.

And then my mother, bless her heart,
who is long in the ground,
would say 'I will not give you an ounce
but I will give a pound.'

And O the smile upon the face
of the cunning A. Macleod.
'I hope I'm not a wink too soon.'
Her heart was beating loud,

as she would say 'O welladay
I'd like your phone to use'
which then my mother would reply,
'Whatever's mine is yours.'

And then alack such looks so black
got Anne from old and young
as she went on, for ages long,
with her repulsive tongue.

Alack alack and welladay
such looks from old and young
and instead of the phone a thick thick rope
about her neck was hung.

MIRROR OF MAGISTRATES

(A little play penned by Murdo Macrae)

Mary:	And what was the North Sea oilrig like, this time?
	(pause)
Norman:	Bad. Bad. *(removing his diver's suit.)*
Mary:	And were you reading that pornography again?
Norman:	Yes, Mary, I was.
	(pause)
	I was so alone. So alone.
	(pause)
	Alone.
Mary:	Was not my photograph good enough for you?
Norman:	It was different, different.
	(pause)
	Different.
Mary:	I'm going to divorce you, I made up my mind.
	(pause)
Norman:	This is a big blow, Mary, no denying it, it's a big blow for a man just home from the oilrig.
	(pause)

	Have you given it long and hard conseedered?

    (pause)

Mary: Yes, I have. I am tired, tired.

    (pause)

    Tired.

Norman: You will have to help me, Mary. There was nothing to do but look at the sea. You have no idea, no idea. It was driving me mad, mad. It was my pornography saved me.

Mary: Saved you?

(Knock on the door. Enter Anne Macleod.)

Anne: Could I borrow an ounce of butter, Mary?

(Mary and Norman burst out laughing, and are soon in each other's arms. Normality in the shape of A. Macleod has brought catharsis.)

Mary: Butter! Butter!

Norman: Butter!

(They go off into hysterics again. Curtain slowly falls.)

MURDO & THE DETECTIVE STORY

As Murdo, relaxing his labours, would watch the TV in the evening, he would say to the weather man when he had finished, 'Thank you very much.'

If a play was on he would say, 'Watch out. There is a villain behind you.' Or, 'I am sure he is from Control. It's either MI4, MI5, MI6, or N2, or WST 8. How can anyone know? We are not privy to such information.'

The advertisements he took as part of the play. 'Ah,' he would say, 'I now see the connection between the story and the Heinz. It was inevitable.'

He would also at various points quote proverbs such as the following: 'There's many a slip when you are sitting on the fence.' Or, 'Thank heaven for small little girls.'

He would imitate Sherlock Holmes' facial twitch and say to Janet, 'The game's afoot.' Or, 'I would refer you to my little monograph on scythes.' Or, he would go around for days saying, 'You know my methods.'

For instance, if an insurance man came to the door selling insurance, or a retired mendicant schoolteacher selling double glazing, or a stranger who was looking for a house in the village, he would say to him, quietly, 'You know my methods.'

He would sometimes write to his daughter Mary, who was at Glasgow University, in the following way:

My dear daughter (or Hastings as you are better known),
    I wish to say to you Sacre bleu. Or, a thousand thunders. Or, C'est curieux, n'est ce pas. Or some such words.
    Eh bien. I hope that all goes well with you and that you are in le bon heart. You are indeed an exotic creature. Depechons vous, Hastings, we must keep this to ourselves.

                                    Your devoted father,
                                    Murdo Macrae.

Mary was quite used to such letters and would often reply.

Dear Mr Poirot,
    After much doubt and indecision, I am at last emboldened to write to you. I have to tell you, that after every

meal I eat in this house I am as sick as a chien. I fear therefore that I am being poisoned.

There is a train that arrives here at 1.01. If you are not on it, I fear that you will not receive another letter from me.

(Ms) Shirley Wainwright, M.A. PH.D.

Murdo would reply,

Dear Miss Wainwright,

There is no stamp on your letter. I therefore cannot take it seriously, I the great Poirot. Sacre bleu!

Yours,
Hercule Poirot.

Dear Mr Poirot, (Mary would answer)

I am at the moment imprisoned in an attic, bound hand and foot, apart unaccountably for my right hand. Unaccountably a pen has been left beside me. I have thrown this letter out to the milkman (I think I am somewhere in East Sussex).

Your sincerely,
(Ms) Shirley Wainwright, M.A., Ph.D., N.U.T.

And so on.

There were many programmes that Murdo didn't like, including ——, ——, ——, ——, ——, ——, ——, and ——, etc.

There was one games show master whom he hated, and he would shout at him in a frenzy, 'You slimy snake. You snail of the first water. You tongue of newt.' At such moments he would froth at the mouth, then say to Janet, 'I shall be all right in a few minutes. You go out and enjoy yourself. I need no attention from anybody. In my day we gave all that we earned to our parents. I know that I sacrificed myself for you but you are young, you need fresh air and so on. Leave the tablets beside my bed.'

And so on.

He also hated programmes about the Arts, Science, Religion, Philosophy, Politics, etc. He was never happier than when he was watching a detective story on the television. Locked-room murders were his favourites followed closely by carnage of any kind.

If the murder was set in Mexico he would say to Janet, 'This will be no good.' But if it was set in a country house, cut off by snow or typhoon from civilisation, the telephone lines down and the microwave not working, he was deliriously happy. His favourite line was,

'And where were you at 11.03 last night?'

followed closely by,

'I devoutly hope that we will be in time, Watson.'

He loved fogs, masks, disguises, cabs, men who had known each other in Australia, or Indians who slouched round standing stones or pubs.

In bed one night he said to Janet,

'The dog didn't bark.'

'I didn't hear it,' said Janet.

'That is precisely the problem,' he said, and went to sleep.

He suspected that films had deteriorated rapidly once people began to talk on them and that the thriller had destroyed the detective story.

'Look what we have lost,' he would say, 'great lines such as these':

'So it was not he who left the ball on the stair.'

Or,

'Sometimes I feel I understand Anataxis, Nori.'

'Ah, those were the days,' he would say to Janet. 'En vérité, these were the days, mon ami. Sacre Bleu!'

MURDO'S CROSSWORD

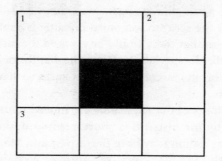

<u>Across:</u>   1   *Pshaw (3)*
            3   *Nothing: Central Heating (3)*
                             (reversed).

<u>Down:</u>   1   *Part of Loch Lomond (3)*
            2   *Nothing! Cold! H!   (rev.) (3)*

Solution: <u>Across:</u>   1   Och
                             3   HCO

            <u>Down:</u>   1   Och
                             2   HCO

BRING ME MY CABER OF BURNING GOLD

'The origins of the Highland Games,' wrote Murdo, 'are lost in the mists of antiquity.

'All we know is that before a battle a number of little girls, usually dressed in tartan, danced the sword dance. Whether this was designed to perplex the enemy, we simply have no idea.

'Nor do we know whether there was a MacCabre clan. It may be of course that the word "macabre" is a corruption of such a clan name, though again we cannot be sure.

'Whether the sporran was worn in battle is another enigma. It would seem that there would be no need for carrying money on a battlefield especially as after the battle there would be plenty of sporran searchers about, but again we have no certain information.

'The customs of the Highlands are indeed matter for deliberation. Why for instance is shortbread so dominant in our culture? One nation may have Beethoven and Mozart, another Michelangelo and da Vinci, yet another Voltaire – but we have shortbread.

'The Second Sight is a troubling matter; so is the Oral Tradition. At this time apparently a certain house was selected in a village and all the villagers converged on it. There they would take part in their Oral Tradition till the early hours of the morning. We do not know (1) why this particular house was chosen, (2) whether the guests brought their own provisions, or (3) what the host thought of being kept up till all hours.

'Standing Stones are another mystery. Were they in fact a method of measuring the time before the Highlanders had clocks? Were they primitive sorts of rockets? Were they used for human sacrifice and did they cease when the Old Age Pension came into being? Some consider that they were used to identify Saturn, others suggest Mercury, or Jupiter or Harris: and yet others opine that they could locate quasars and pulsars, so intricate was their organisation. Traces of radio communications have been found at their bases, according to some amateur scientists.

'Further questions are: Why were these large stones hauled for miles and miles to sit beside this particular tea-room and museum? Why did these dwarfish beings (for these men were smaller than us) go to such inordinate lengths to build such a circle? Here they are coming from all directions carrying their colossal stones on wheelbarrows, mayhap having a little worthless conversation on the way, and perhaps on their arrival a glass of orangeade at the adjacent restaurant. It is a strange sight indeed. Science will have to advance much further in my opinion before solutions to these questions can be found.

'Other customs too are puzzling. Why do so many islanders wink with the left eye when they are talking? Does this indicate a period perhaps after the '45, when there were many spies in the Highlands? And why do so many women borrow sugar? Does this point to an age of deprivation?

'As I have written elsewhere, the role of J.D. Williams and Oxendales will also have to be investigated.

'Questions abound: for example, why is the Bible carried to the pulpit by an elder? Why do so many singers, even the most prominent, sing through their noses? (And what does the singer have to say to the pianist before they begin their recitation?) Why does a fiddle group never smile? And so on.

'It can be seen that much remains to be done before we can get a true picture of our Highland ethos before we can sit down and say that these and no other are our mores, before we can discover who we muscular, brave, fair-haired and generous people, as it were, are.

THE KILT COMPLEX

According to Freud, the 'Kilt complex' originated in the Highlands of Scotland. He describes two kinds of personalities, the anal and the exhibitionist, as being prone to this neurosis. (The open-thighed is a variant of the second of these.)

The kilt complex, according to Freud, is closely connected with freedom. It is a reaction to the strict mores of the

Highlander, and suggests clean-limbed ferocity connected with mountains and lochs.

The sporran may have originated as a container for the 5d and a counterbalance to the super-ego.

Outsiders, that is, people extraneous to the Highlands, may adopt this complex in order to be on the winning side or simply as a protest against the paucity of Gaelic in their chosen areas.

It may be noted that the longer the kilt the more neurosis it covers: one whose kilt almost sweeps the floor is liable to be a raving psychopath. On the other hand a short kilt suggests a free personality, one who might say, in Gaelic, 'My anima is my own to command.'

PS 'Kilty party' is known in the Highlands of Scotland as a ceilidh.

THE ROLE OF B&B IN HIGHLAND CULTURE, BY MURDO

This is a short monograph on the cultural role of Bed and Breakfast in our culture.

In the first place many landlords and landladies are able to take advantage of the (accidental) birth of a famous poet in the general area of their houses.

Thus they might say, 'This is where the noted poet Neil McEwan was born. It was quite close to my bathroom or bedroom that he wrote his most famous poem, or sat staring into space wrestling with the Muse. Not far from my living-room is where he died, at the early age of fifty-six. As you will see, my house, called in Gaelic the House of the Three Mists, is named after one of his most famous poems. My husband and I are great admirers of his work, and have been, since we moved into this highly competitive area. Many critics of his work have had bed and breakfast with us and have been, as you will see from the guest book, well satisfied with their accommodation, which is, as you will notice, en suite, though smoking is not allowed. There is ample evidence that Neil McEwan himself did not smoke.'

Thus landlords and landladies unselfishly advertise many of our most famous poets and artistes and sometimes do this by means of menus as for example the Neil McEwan soufflé, or venison à la Neil McEwan, or the Neil McEwan sorbet. Other literary references are the Neil McEwan Nature Trail, or How to Become a Poet in the Neil McEwan chalet, or our Neil McEwan Blue Room. There is also Neil McEwan shortbread, or the Neil McEwan tie and scarf, or Neil McEwan toffee.

'It is indeed a happy accident that he was born and died so close to us. McEwans of course have lived here from time immemorial, though he was the only one up to his time to put pen to paper. His wife was from this area, and it is said that his famous poem to her was written when he saw her coming from the Co-op with the messages. His biro can still be found in his tiny study. He did not, as far as is known, correct much of his work, but relied on what he called his inspiration. Discarded poems were placed in a bin positioned where our kitchen now is.

'He had a wife and four children, none of whom followed him in his worship of the Muse. One became a bank manager, one became a doctor, one became a primary teacher, and the last one became a fish farmer. It is said that none of his family read poetry, not even their father's. He died without making a will while in touch with the Muse at that gate over there and on which you will see the notice: "Neil McEwan in touch with the Muse."

'It is said that he had a fight with a bard from a neighbouring village over some onomatopoeia and shouted to him, after knocking him down, "This fist is in payment for your metre."

'Copies of this book are sold in the foyer. Others can be obtained from the Neil McEwan Cultural Centre along with maps of his house. The Neil McEwan taxi service is also very useful, or you may stand on a wet day at the Neil McEwan Bus Shelter.'

Such are the many ways in which the literary qualities of famous poets can be promulgated to make their works and lives known to the passing tourist.

A POEM BY MURDO

The Isle of Lamis is of isles the fairest,
the smell of sphagnum is of the smells the rarest,
its heathery slopes where the pear resideth,
as also where the haughty deer abideth.

Many were the emigrants who went by train
to Glasgow City where there was not much gain
and some would say Alack and some Ochone,
as arthritis they suffered to the very bone.

Many was the time, when I was reared,
that the nest of the peewit was by me cleared,
or barefooted in the evening gloam
I would make my cheerful way home.

My mother's face I still remember yet,
her name was Anne (her sister's name was Bet)
and granny would be lying in her bed.
The oral tradition filled her grey-haired head.

I shall return from Glasgow by the train
and meet my youthful comrades once again
and we will talk about the days of yore
when never in a house was shut the door.

MURDO'S MENU

- Clear Soup à la Oral Tradition
- Emigrant Haddock (with selection of sauces)
- Duncan Ban Macintyre's Braised Steak (with selection of carrots)
- Robert Bruce's Banana Split
- Sir Walter Scott's Meringue Glacé
- John Knox's Ice Cream Sundae
- Coffee, Tea, Whey, extra.

THE TEACHER'S FAREWELL BY MURDO

Friends and Colleagues,

Many thanks first of all for the small token of esteem you have given me – this excellent radio – and may I say that though I live a good few miles from the main road up, as you know, an isolated rocky track, you are most cordially invited to drop in and listen to programmes on this radio, though, as you may know, my own interest is Radio Three.

You ask me what I shall be doing with my time. I shall, I think, continue with my monograph on 'The Imperative Mood and the Roman Legion, a study in the Command', an area which has not been investigated in the past.

At this time too I might say a few words, as is usual on these occasions, on the future of Education. For my own department there is no future. It is, as you know, going to be a storehouse for videos. It will hear no more of the ablative absolute or the subjunctive.

When I came here first we had what were known as lines. Pupils were lined up as in a military posture. I don't know if you remember Miss Oates, a twittery sort of lady who collapsed on, as it were, the parade ground. Our Rector at that time known as Caligula – the doughty Mr Robb, M.A. – wouldn't allow her to be moved till the parade was over. After all, he said, that is what she joined the teaching profession for. Miss Oates taught Cookery, Domestic Science as it is known now. She was called, I think, the Scone.

Which brings me to nicknames. There was a Deputy Head known as Pompey. When it was discovered that Caesar had cut off the head of the popular general, someone must have envisaged Caesar saying, 'Pompey is only a deputy head now.'

I myself was known as Galloping Cicero, and there was a lady known as the Sliding Snake. She is, alas, dead as well.

We no longer of course wear the toga as we were wont, and that, I think, is a retrograde step. As someone once said – I hope the ladies present will excuse me – when we wear the toga, no one can say that our flies are open. The Romans were a wise race. If I may venture a little joke, one can say, there were no flies on the Romans.

Strange things happen in teaching. Once when I was walking to school – you all know that the motor was alien to me – a young man, an employee of the council, jumped out of a hole in the road that he had been helping to dig and thrusting out a dirty hand at me said, 'If it weren't for you, Mr Summers, I wouldn't be where I am today.' Such is life! And then of course there was Mr Greene who ran off with the coffee money. And Mr Hogg, who built his private fortune on the sale of the little pencils at the back of the EIS diary.

I loved teaching. What else might I do? What else could I do? I had the responsibility for moulding the minds of the young. Give me, I used to say, a perfectly empty head and I shall fill it with the dative, the ablative absolute, and the vocative case.

The Romans, of course, were not fond of jokes. When you are building an empire you can't be joking continually. And we must not of course forget that they had aquaducts as well. And the Ides of March.

It will be a sad day when we will not be able to translate

the school motto from the original Latin into the colloquial version. Strength through Boredom. And indeed boredom is a weapon that we must not under-estimate. If we were not bored, would we have invented the fire, or indeed a grammar system? The world in my opinion has been propelled forward by boredom and that is why we pay attention to agreement of case and gender and so on. Thus the more boredom there is in a school the better. Was it not because he was bored that Julius Caesar sailed to Britain and said the famous words, '*Veni vidi vici*', which are an example of alliteration. (*Et tu Brute*, is an example of the dying fall.) But enough of that. For myself my days of teaching are over. I will go out into a world which knows not Horace, and meet, as it were, my landlady Miss A. Jones for the first time. I will see her as she really is, a representative of the common unclassical woman, ignorant, diffuse, but withal having a rough truth about her. I will listen to her trenchant descriptions and her illuminating stories – not indeed about Horatius and the Bridge – but that will not matter. For I ask myself sometimes in my moments of doubt, did Zeus indeed make love to a swan, or did he come down to Danae in a shower of gold? Miss Jones would say 'No' and in her simple way she might be right. What is Dido's pyre to Miss Jones or Miss Jones to Dido's pyre? For her motto is, if I may venture a little joke: '*Mince sana in corpore sano*' and that is enough for her.

And so I say farewell to you all or, as I might put it, *Ave atque vale*. I say to you, keep the flag of boredom flying. Do not give in to the siren voices which whisper Munn and Dunning, or Standard Grade. And above all avoid those who speak of relevance. Relevance has never been important in education. I myself have never heard anyone speak Latin, saying for instance, 'Did you hear the weather forecast today?' or 'Keep on your own side of the road, you nyaff' – but that does not perturb me. Indeed it drives me to greater efforts. For I hear the sound of trumpets in the words, 'The Rhine having been crossed, and the dispositions having been made, Caesar at his earliest convenience engaged with Pompey, who having been wakened from sleep, saw Caesar's forces drawn up against him, to his great astonishment.'

Such are the words of the classics and they should set an example to us all.

(Mr Summers sat down to prolonged applause and then exited, carrying his radio, having delighted everyone in the atrium, and having delivered himself of a sapient oration.)

MURDO'S LETTER TO A FRIEND

If it were not so, I would have told you, and as it is I will not tell you. Such are the constraints of secrecy.

That is why I will not tell you what I had not meant to tell you in the first place. This letter is to inform you of my position and as it were to reinforce it.

You will I am sure not put me in the position of being forced to tell you something that if it were so in the first place I would not have told you precisely anyway.

I am sorry that this is so, but it is a result of integrity on my part and ignorance on yours. The man who does not know anything cannot be betrayed or betray.

Such is indeed the reason for this hasty scrawl against the pressure of events – a communication and an explanation. A presence and as it were an absence.

Our friendship will I am sure endure in spite of this contretemps.

With kindest regards and best wishes and I hope your wife is well.

Your true friend,
Murdo Macrae.

MURDO'S DEFENCE OF THE PUN

There are a number of people (wrote Murdo), people usually of a Calvinist stamp, that is, ones who wear tight waistcoats and who have gravestone faces, who look down on the pun.

For myself, I believe this is a mistaken attitude and arises from jealousy and rancour on their part.

Shakespeare, for instance, the well-known playwright, though his life is for the most part a mystery (we cannot even be sure of his portrait) used the pun a great deal, especially for characters who spent most of their time in woods or forests near Athens. Also Hamlet, though a tragic figure, was accustomed to use the pun. Thus, for instance, he said to Claudius, 'I am too much i' the sun', which is a good example of a pun. How he managed to pun when so many people were being killed or committing suicide or drinking poison from cups in which unions (another pun) were thrown, we shall never know, but I think this shows the importance of the pun to Hamlet's psychology. Though, of course, other figures of speech were also used by Shakespeare, such as antonomasia, metonymy, synecdoche, onomatopoeia, not to mention the humble metaphor and the simple simile.

Another example is, 'a little more than kin and less than kind'. If a man of Hamlet's propensity for tragedy – a character based as it were on *The Spanish Tragedy* – if such a man, I say, uses the pun extensively, who are we to gainsay him? And there are indeed examples of the miching mallecho of people who never used the pun, such as Malvolio and Polonius, etc, etc. The taste for the pun in Shakespeare's tragedies is different from the lack of the pun in Greek tragedies, but that was because the latter (a) were translated by Gilbert Murray and (b) were religious. In any case when a man marries his mother, as happens in Sophocles, an opportunity for the pun is not often available. It would be laughable if it were.

Aeschylus too, as far as my reading goes, did not often use

the pun. However, the pun is rife in Shakespeare. It is only such people as Sir Andrew Aguecheek who find it difficult to comprehend the pun.

It therefore behoves all those who assail the pun to be silent or to ask themselves why Shakespeare, whom I may call the noblest Roman of them all, used it so often, as indeed when Hamlet says to Polonius, 'It were a brute part of him to kill so capital a calf there' (punning, as you will remember, on the words 'Brutus' and 'Capitol').

'In my opinion only such people as bear a grudge against the world, people who appear to have indigestion, and also ones whose faces are as fixed as solidified dung, disdain the pun, even when used by a great Dane like Hamlet. For myself, I said to someone only the other day (it happened to be a day of almost complete silence), 'You could hear a pun drop', and later I added, 'You could hear a pan drop', which, in my opinion, though not as good as Shakespeare, does put a different complexion on, as Kant would say, the thing in itself: and is not bad for a Highlander who, as it were, wishes to undermine ideology and annihilate mores, and who sometimes, as it were, takes off on linguistic wing over the meagre county of ethics.

MURDO ADDRESSES HIS REFLECTION

At times Murdo would address his reflection in the mirror in the following words:

Who are you, my exact reproduction, to speak so scornfully of precisely those people who are for the most part protecting themselves with tattered raincoats against the trenchant gales of Reality.

Do you not also have your clichés, your pallid examples or antonomasia, your limping metaphors?

And, after all, what are you but a writer who cannot write, a failure, as the world judges you, a pimple on the face of reality (though many questions are begged by such a word, especially since the electron was discovered).

And of course I am not ignorant of Freud, Jung, Adler and others whom I do not know about.

It is a problem, I might say a dilemma, which satirists of my stamp face. People will say, 'Who is he? I kent his faither!' (as indeed they might have said of Oedipus or of the Saviour himself) and this shows the democratic language of the Scots, though the word 'kent' is, if I may interpolate, cause for ambiguity. However, facts are chiels that winna ding.

I, however, answer that I write as the spirit moves me, not out of hostility but out of joy: and that if any lame dog wishes to help me with my style he has my phone number.

It is actually to the Pharisees and a little to the Sadducees that my words are addressed. I wish to say, as Cromwell said to the Rump, 'Pray in your bowels that you may think yourselves mistaken.'

And so, perturbed spirit, which enacts my unshaven image, and as it were, hypocrite reader, I say, I have taken on board your point about clichés, and how we all need them: mankind cannot bear much reality (with my reservations about electrons, etc) and I would only say, I do these things out of charity. I have always disliked a tinkling symbol and speak directly to you in the name of Love who vaunteth not, and abideth with her two friends, Faith and Hope, in these, as it were, meagre pages of mine.

MURDO'S LETTER TO MR A. MACLEOD,
16 PARK ST, S——

Dear Mr Macleod,

You will not know me: I picked your name and address from the phone book this morning.

I am at the moment engaged in a project on Happiness, and I have selected you as one who might help me.

The first question I would like to ask you is: are you happy? In answering this question, you might think of such things as rate of inflation, mortgage, marital quarrels, your income, your next-door neighbours, the number of your children, your in-laws, your garden, number of rooms in your house, whether you have a garage, distance from shopping centre, money left over after essentials such as whisky and cigarettes have been bought, etc. This is only a short list: others I am sure will readily spring to mind, such as insurance, subsidence, etc. However, when all these questions have been, as it were, mentally catalogued and analysed (for this progress is nothing if not scientific) I wish you to write down a simple Yes or No in the box provided. Impressionistic ideas are of no use to me: what I require is a scientific evaluation, after all the factors have been taken into account.

When considering this question you might also ask yourself: Do I wish to get up this morning? Do I wish to shave? Do I wish to howl like a wolf when certain persons are talking to me? Do I wish to exchange a simple greeting in the morning, or, on the contrary, do I wish to say, 'Why don't you go back home, you newt' or eft as the case may be? Do I make faces at myself in the mirror? Do I wish to commit suicide by means of gun/sword/washing powder/gas, etc? If any of these apply please have no hesitation in putting them down.

Then ask yourself this simple question, When I leave the house in the morning, do I wish to return to it?

There are many instances of men, apparently perfectly balanced, who suddenly and as it were on the spur of the moment drive off to Inverness and are never seen again, submerging themselves in the teeming millions. Ask yourself if you are one of them.

Other instances come to mind, such as the man who went berserk in the supermarket. One moment he was perfectly sane, just like you or me, the next he was throwing cans of dog food about indiscriminately. The mind is indeed deep and mountains high. Such instances are well documented and have occurred.

Then again you might ask yourself whether you are irritated by minor things, e.g. if there is a traffic hold-up lasting three hours on your way to the office, or if your wife coughs persistently throughout the night so that you can't sleep, or if the phone rings and when you answer there is NO ONE there. Many such instances abound.

Remember, I wish you to write a simple Yes or No in the box provided, but only after due consideration. If you find that you can't answer, simply write, I find myself unable to answer. Shallow judgements are of no use to me, as, e.g. after a good meal, you might write Yes. It is the long haul that is important. You may take days, weeks or even months to answer. You may, if you wish, consult Schopenhauer in order to make up your mind. Or you might ask a close friend or neighbour to help you. The main thing is that the answer should be scientific.

I look forward to hearing from you. And remember you are not alone. I am getting in touch with many other people as well.

And good luck and good hunting.

> *Yours, etc,*
> *Murdo Macrae*

TWO POEMS BY MURDO

(sent to *Encounter* but returned)

> (1)
> When I was young and happy,
> I heard a wise man say,
> you cannot be a spendthrift
> on very little pay.
>
> But now I'm old and withered
> I wish that I had known
> that the cold winds of Rannoch
> will howl about the bone.
>
> (2)
> When you and I were young, Maggie,
> when you and I were young
> the words of an old tradition
> flew easily from your tongue.
>
> But now that you are old dear
> and wear a thermal vest
> the sun goes down at evening
> and love itself has rest.

MURDO AT THE UNEMPLOYMENT BUREAU

Murdo carefully took off his black hat when he entered the unemployment office.

'Sir,' he said, 'I am not here to look for a job. I am here to help you. You are unable to tell me that Dante had a job other than writing poetry and the same is true of Virgil, Horace and other dagoes one could name.'

The man who was bending over the desk with a pen in his hand looked up at him in surprise.

'Indeed,' continued Murdo, 'it surprises me that a man of your largeness of mind, not to say diligence, should be working at all. A man whose job it is to give other people jobs is in my opinion an example of a paradox. There's too much of it altogether, altogether,' he added earnestly, while beating steadily on the floor with his right boot as if he were hearing distant music such as that made by a chanter.

'It would be much simpler if, as a man with a job yourself, you ensured that others had no work. You, sir, should be a barrier there preventing men from getting at machines instead of encouraging them, for machines have done a lot of harm in the world. I should be glad if you were able to tell me that there is no work available for me.'

The man raised his eyes from the pad on which he had been writing and gazed blankly at Murdo.

'In my opinion,' said the latter, 'you should, like a Roman emperor, turn your thumb down when a man comes for a job. You should be able to say that there are more men in the world than there are jobs to fill, for if it were not so how should we have governments and bureaucrats who are examples of people who have jobs yet do nothing. Isn't a bureaucrat an example of a man for whom a job is not available, though he works just the same? When one considers the world in this light, a simplification takes place,' he added, leaning forward and speaking rapidly while clicking his teeth at the same time. 'There was a time when there were fewer men than there were jobs. That would have been, I think, in the Neolithic Age or thereabout. But as time passed there was a great acceleration of men so that they passed the number of jobs available. Thus the mysterious thing has happened that since there are not enough jobs an absence of jobs has been created. Thus a bureaucrat is an example of a man who sits in a chair and gives others the jobs that he has not got. Similarly a critic is an example of a man who believes that he has a job, though in truth he has not. And one could enumerate other examples if one had the time.'

Before the man could answer, Murdo continued: 'I have given this considerable thought, and I think your job now is to realise the realities of the situation and say frankly that you have no job to give anyone, except an illusory job that does not in fact exist, and that instead of putting a sign up in your office and in your window saying that such and such a job is available, you should on the contrary put up a notice saying –

"IN THE INTERESTS OF REALITY I HAVE TO SAY THAT THERE ARE NO JOBS AVAILABLE AND THIS SITUATION WILL LAST AS LONG AS I AM IN THIS POST. IN OTHER WORDS IT WOULD HAVE BEEN BETTER FOR YOU IF YOU HAD NOT BEEN BORN."

'Do you not think, sir, that this is the greatest job that you can render the community, to tell them the truth that the world has run out of jobs because of the great increase in the number of people. There are of course jobs imaginable which you do not have and which society cannot afford to support, such as, for example, Grape Carrier to Patients in Hospital, or the job of Exposing Everyone in the Community in the Service of the Truth, but for the moment we shall not be concerned with them. After all, what did a melodeon player do before the melodeon was invented?' he said, poking the man in the forehead with the umbrella he was carrying, though in fact it was a hot dry day. 'I have come to wish you well in the loneliness of your command and to ensure that you will not betray the principles of injustice by offering anyone a job, for by so doing you would be continuing an evil which it is time we put a stop to, eradicated, wiped out, smashed.' And his voice rose in a terrible rage.

'Please excuse me, sir, for that outburst, but this is some-thing that I feel very strongly about. For in any case what job could you offer me that would satisfy the huge spaces of my imagination? Have you ever considered that Plato evicted us

172

from his kingdom, though he was nothing but a rotten dirty Greek with no proper religion? Now I should say to you that as there are no jobs commensurate with our imagination – I am talking about painters, writers, and so on – what would be the point of you offering me a job for telling such a bitter truth?

'Sir,' he went on, 'when one considers the mind and its limits, when you consider what you are and what I am, it might very well be that it should be I that is offering you a job, or even taking over from you, and relieving you of these metaphysical conundrums that you are subject to each day. Sir, it is with pain that I regard you and your trembling hands. For how can you come here every day knowing that you are taking part in a fraud: a seller and trafficker in jobs that do not really exist but which you have invented in order to keep civilisation going, such as for instance a Professor of Philosophy, or a Prime Minister. I submit, sir, that you have begun at the wrong end. Learn inhumanity, sir, offer the men to the jobs instead of the jobs to the men, for in that you will be in touch with the essentially contradictory nature of Christianity itself. Need I say more to a man of your obvious intelligence?

'And one final word before you offer me the job that I do not in actuality want, since it does not in fact exist, I would plead with you to have a slot system in which you do not have the titles of jobs but on the contrary the names of men, so that as the jobs appear they come in search of the men; I mean real true genuine jobs, jobs of a high class of reality. Think of me as a job looking for a man, and please believe me that as such I feel my own reality and also feel for you. Be hard, sir, send the men away and keep the jobs in the silence of the night and admire them as you admire the ideas of that rotten Greek Plato who had no real religion. Love them as they wish to be loved, all those lonely jobs, even those that aren't yet in existence but are, as it were, waiting in the aisles and the theatres of the absurd. And if you would kindly put some money in this box which would sponsor the creation of a Missionary

Society to Bearsden, I would be very grateful. Humanity must be smashed, sir, eradicated, and jobs created in its place and given their rightful position and status in the world.'

After a while Murdo was aware that the man was looking at him with a stunned gaze while simultaneously his hands were trembling, and before going out of the door he said, 'See, your hands are trembling. That is a sign of the inconsistencies of the system which your subconscious is aware of, though it hasn't yet reached your conscious. I am sorry for you, sir, deeply sorry, and if it weren't that I see too deeply I would accept a job myself and even take over yours. Pray for us all and especially for yourself. We all have much to answer for, much to answer for.'

Gibbering mildly to himself he left the office, unfurling his umbrella to the hot dry rays of the sun.

MURDO'S POETRY READINGS

Murdo's first poetry reading occurred in a public bar, the organisers having decided to bring poetry to the people. The pub was full at the time – which was two o'clock in the afternoon – and as Murdo stood up, his knees trembling, the barman was shouting. 'Two pints and two martinis over there.' Murdo could not be sure afterwards that anyone in the bar heard him, though he had read the most metrical of his poems: the only result of his visit being that a small man in a cap had tried to borrow five pounds from him in the lavatory.

He was then asked to read at a small village hall in the Highlands. When the time for the poetry reading came there was no one there at all: and the lady that was in charge of the proceedings was nervous because she had forgotten to put up the posters. When Murdo, the first to arrive, went to the room where the reading was to take place he was going to be charged a pound by the door-keeper till he told her who he was. Eventually five people arrived, and after Murdo had read his poem 'The Herring Girls' there was a spirited discussion about fish.

However, Murdo began to receive more and more invitations. His technique at any poetry reading was first of all to find out how much money he was to receive: and thereafter to wrap himself in impenetrable mystery. He spoke slowly and with great deliberation, sometimes explaining references which were entirely clear while leaving obscurities as they were. Thus he might spend a great deal of time on why he had used a simple place name, while he wouldn't translate some such word as '*duilgheadas*', for he often interpolated Gaelic words among his English on the analogy of Pound and Eliot doing the same with Greek and Chinese. On one occasion a member of the audience asked him an unexpected question: 'Do you feel you are a poet when you get up in the morning?'

After a long pause Murdo said, 'No, I feel like a prose writer.' He added, 'Non-fiction.'

When he stayed at his host's house, Murdo kept up the same impenetrable reserve. He also did some odd things. For instance he might take the bulb from the lamp and leave it lying on the table. Or he might face a picture to the wall. Or sometimes he would write a meaningless poem and leave the pages hanging in the wardrobe. He might suddenly say to the host, 'Whisky has the emotive yellowness of atrophy.'

Sometimes too, in order to give the impression of an intense insomniac, he would pull the lavatory chain several times through the night. 'I have an old malady,' he would say darkly, 'which afflicts me especially at three in the morning.'

Another interesting ploy was to leave the company of the host, shouting, 'I've got it,' and rush off to his room. Then he would sit on the bed smoking for an hour and arrive later as if nothing had happened. All this gained him a reputation for mysterious genius.

His great difficulty was with his smoking. Most times he

would find there was no ashtray in his bedroom, only a wicker basket. Before it occurred to him to use the wash-basin or the toilet for the ash and flame, he would open the window and flick them on the slates or thrust them into any antique vase or plant he could find.

Sometimes he also wore extravagant clothes, such as for instance a plaid or a multicoloured suit. If he had to use a microphone he would begin by kissing it with religious fervour after first wiping it with a handkerchief. He would explain the figures of speech in his poems at enormous length. At times his voice would rise to a manic shout and then sink to an impenetrable whisper. He would also tell the audience how the poem had been created and even read alternative versions of it. At times he would laugh bitterly, as if a poem was the record of a secret wound on which he did not wish to elaborate.

'Love,' he would say, 'what is love? It is a lethal cocktail. Our skin feels it but our hearts – no.' Or, 'Beauty, what can one say about it? All we have to do is consider Dostoievsky or Pascal.' He used such techniques with mainly rural audiences. With sophisticated audiences he would use pauses and silences: or he would stop in the middle of a poem. Or he might even leave the stage and come back later, his eyes apparently red from weeping.

If when he arrived there was only a tiny audience since, as the organiser often explained, there were alternative attractions such as a sermon or a professor giving a lecture about stones, he would look stunned. Then he would say, 'Is it for this that I came? Is it for this that I woke at six o'clock this morning? Is it for this that lust illuminates our mortal flesh?' Then he would say, 'Yes, it is indeed for this.' The organiser would feel so guilty that she would take him for a meal in an Indian restaurant, though she had originally intended to give him fish and chips.

In the restaurant, he would mutter over and over, 'The mysterious East. Have you read the immortal epic of Kalyani or indeed the fine miniature stories of Krishnabutari, so tiny that they could be written on the head of a gramophone needle?' He always refused rice, saying that it gave him heartburn. 'Do they not have bacon and eggs?' he would say, staring up at the ceiling adorned with mysterious drawings. 'Why do they not have pictures of Highland soldiers dressed in the tartan?' he would ask. If he was taken to an Italian restaurant he would mutter, 'I thought I would have been given some hard ecus in my change. Where are they?' And he would brood angrily for the rest of the night.

He had created also a long poem which was written in the Pictish language, and which was written on blue paper. 'Though we have little of that language,' he said, 'it is enough. Words such as "entrok" for "twilight", and "oberton" for "chariot" are inherently beautiful. And what can one say about "hok" which means the scent of hay on an autumn evening. I have loved this language since I saw my first inscription on one of its stones: "Orag rig dum", it read. It means "In fond memory of the sheep shearer Dum".'

His readings from his Pictish manuscript were received in respectful silence. He fielded all questions with avid aplomb. On these occasions he wore a long cloak fastened with a silver brooch. He told his audience of many Pictish customs, such as the Ingok and the Yor. Pictish poets, he said, had such respect for words that they spoke only in an inaudible monotone.

His poetry readings became more and more numerous. He travelled to France, Germany, the Philippines and Japan. 'What they say about geishas is not true,' he would say, but would not elaborate. An American scholar who had been listening to his Pictish poem said that Murdo had a primitive ferocity and at the same time calmness: an issue of a famous American magazine was devoted to the poem. He insisted on inserting footnotes which were sometimes three pages long. Young students adored his manic intensity. When it suited him he pretended not to have heard of Pound or Eliot, or said that they had not gone far enough. 'Poetry is infected by the germs of criticism,' he would say. Or, 'No genuine poet knows what his adjectives mean.'

And then quite suddenly he stopped attending poetry readings at all. 'I find,' he said, 'that after them I feel sordid and commonplace. I feel that audiences are coming to hear the poetry and not to see me. They, however, feel inadequate when confronted with me in the flesh and this in turn makes me feel guilty. How should I have this gift, I ask myself, when clearly they have none. Their faces shine with anticipation and ignorance. I am the high priest of their imagination. How disappointed I am when I see them. Furthermore, their questions are often impertinent or ambiguous. They ask for meaning when they should be seeking for magic. Poetry is hostile to church halls, I tell them.

'Also, I wish they would call me by my proper name when they introduce me. Did people make errors with Homer, Horace or Lucretius? Were there many alternative events when Dante was giving a reading? Was Virgil taken to an Indian restaurant?

'No, from now on I shall retain a holy silence. It is no use writing to me: I shall not answer. For poets to be authentic they must remain invisible. A stench arises from poetry readings when there should be incense. Statues do not walk in the daylight, legends do not parade about at night. The afflatus is not to be quenched by sherry or coffee. The door-keeper also dies and the organiser is as grass. The Arts Council will not suffer the torments of the desert. Mutability is all.'

And thus he would shoulder his spade and repair to the byre, where he would commune with the cows. 'Their liquid warmth fascinates me, their wavering lines comfort me: and I also take the scythe to the hitherto upright corn. Life is not to be found in the city but here in the certainty of grass and hay. I have seen to the heart of things and I find it in the solitary and humble yet arrogant and gregarious lyric. We all suffer. I am tired of beer mats, microphones. I am exhausted by bardic hieroglyphics, errant posters no longer attract, nor am I enchanted by aseptic bedrooms where I am not allowed to smoke. Excuses will no longer satisfy. I shall reach the absolute logic of the poetry reading. I shall read to myself in the absolute holiness of mirrors. Janitors may glare at me, trains may be delayed, I shall return to the incorruptible legends of childhood. I have suffered. I was there.'

The byre appealed to him, with its authentic smell (the poetry of John Dung he called it): smoke rose from chimneys, an old woman, scythe on shoulder, chattered lightly to another. 'This is the dialectic of the ultimate sonnet.'

ANTHEM

Avaunt, prognathous orators,
you spurious sports depart
we wish no smooth imperators
nor marble of the heart!

But come you leafy viators,
green stems of worth, upstart!
And a lack of hard proprietors
be 'Ios' of our arts!!

MURDO'S BUSINESS LETTER

Dear Sir,
Hopeful of these things, I now conclude my letter to you. May they come, as we both ardently wish, I am sure, in the near future. We have worked long and hard for this, and have finally found the requisite equipment.

So I raise my glass to you, at this midnight hour, in the firm expectation that no efforts have been spared and the dwarfs of bureaucracy have finally been overthrown.

I have enjoyed working with you, as I hope you with

me. And I hope the opportunity will arise again in the
near future.

The prince, if I may so put it, has found the slipper, but
the ball is still in our court.

Yours sincerely,
and with kindest regards to your family,
Murdo Macrae

Enc.

Copies to: Mr Sprockett
                           Mr Burns-Nightingale
                           Mrs Tight Corset
                           Ms Sherry-Spiller

MURDO & HIS FUTURE READERS

O future readers of my monologues, letters, remarks, jottings,
I now say farewell to you. It may be that in your time, the
DHSS will no longer exist, and writers like myself will breathe
a natural and unrestricted air. In your days perhaps no one
will be working at all, and there will be no more banks,
car factories, fish farmers, etc. People will earn their bread
by pressing the buttons of a computer, sitting in their own
homes at their own desks. Such is the unsponsored dream
that I have.

In those days I imagine the arts will flourish and Mrs
Macleod will be able to rest and read Dostoevsky without
having to listen to the seething of a pan on her kitchen stove.

Robots (from Japan perhaps) will in their infinite patience
assume the drudgery of the masses and switch on and off
the television for us. We will lie on sofas meditating on the
infinite permutations of the universe while no low-flying jet
will practise its gyrations overhead.

In those days there will be no wars, for men will become so sensitive that they will find it unthinkable to harm another human being except for certain games masters on the television.

There will be many poems, paintings, operas, unsolicited manuscripts, woollen pullovers, various kinds of bakery, jams, etc, etc.

There will be a computer of unimaginable proportions such that men and women will be able to do the leisurely work to which they are suited. Nor will they sweat and plot and suffer ignominy and sleepless nights in order to be chiefs and principals of this or that industry, whose aims are not theirs and whose working they do not understand.

In those days I prophesy unto you that the lion will lie down with the koala bear, and the tiger with the warthog. A new song will come to the lips of many, and they will no longer say, 'I am no gossip, but I am sure that Linda Morrison's skirt is too short.' On the contrary they will discuss the subtleties of structuralism and the meaning of the word 'precisely'. It is possible that an Irony Board may be created.

Minor poets, however, will say as before, 'Now I wish you to be quite brutal about my work, though I have sunk all my hopes in it,' and the honesty of reviews will vary with the distance of the reviewer from the reviewed, for human nature cannot be changed overnight.

Nevertheless, I am sure that men will progress and that you, distant reader, will look upon my amateurish anarchic jottings as the *cris de coeur* of one who was searching for a 'newer world', open, free, and generous, and you will say, 'He was a good man, not comical withal, but his heart was in the right place,' though I hope that you will not talk precisely in these terms but rather with a speech of infinite gradation, such that for instance you might have one word for 'one who though stupefied by boredom continues to smile while holding a glass of sherry in his hand' (I suggest a 'cromp'), or 'one who speechifies at great length while the audience is seething with anger and rancour' (I suggest a smile-brog). In any case I send my kindest regards to you, across the foam, jungle, veldt, etc, etc, O you men and women of the future, honest, open, lively, alert, and not hypocritical, free of bitterness or egotism, lovers of the arts, and in no sense mean, cruel or intolerant.

To you, my impossible readers, a fond farewell.

Murdo.

MURDO AT THE BBC

When Murdo was invited to a Glasgow studio at the BBC to talk about his new book, *The Thoughts of Murdo*, he spoke for a while about literary matters such as his train journey, what he had for breakfast, and his expenses.

That done, he launched into praising his book which he said was modelled on *The Thoughts of Chairman Mao*, Mao being, he understood, the Chinese equivalent of Murdo.

He suggested very strongly that if the listener was of the ilk which hadn't smiled for a long time, e.g. a Celtic supporter, he should buy the book and, addressing his listeners directly, he continued, you will find here anarchic ideas, revolutionary concepts, animadversions on the laughable nature of reality in which we are all enmired. If, he went on, you are moved to laughter by the signing of the Magna Carta or the Monroe Doctrine, or the Scottish International Football Team, you will find here much to amuse: if you think that MacGonagall was a great creative genius; if you enjoy the catastrophes that happen to other people, then you will enjoy this book. If you like similes such as e.g. as hectic as a cucumber, as foreign as an eel, or as brave as a traffic warden, you will find such plays on words here. Indeed the pun is part of its essence such that you may hear a pun drop or indeed a pan drop. Other topics adumbrated are *Neighbours* and *Take the High Road*.

Moreover, he continued, humour breaks down all boundaries except those between Lewis and Harris. It raises a smile in toilets and in supermarkets, it joins us all together by elasticated bands, it breaks down dogmas (such as e.g. love me, love my dogma), it recognises the futility of all effort, reconstitutes well-known poems into new language such as 'When I consider what my wife has spent', by Milton, it creates new denouements for books, and so on. All these you will find in this valuable though not priceless volume.

It has been said of me that I am the greatest humorist since Ecclesiastes or Job. While not disputing that for a moment, let me add that in buying this book you will be joining a certain class of people as ignorant as yourselves, uninterested in such serious topics as litter, and able to lie in bed for a long period of time without moving. Your vacant gaze will be fully reflected in this book, as also your anthropoid opinions. Verbs, adverbs and nouns will turn somersaults, and you will see the triviality of all that passes for power and progress e.g. Visa cards, the Westminster Confession etc.

If you are of that ilk which yearns for meaninglessness, I am your instant guru. I sign no agreements without laughter, I am an enemy of the working breakfast. A book such as mine will give you arguments for maintaining a prudent lethargy, and for avoiding tax; it will sustain you in your night of deepest laziness; and will remind you of famous figures which include Mephistopheles and Mrs Robb, 3 Kafka Rd, East Kilbride.

If you wish for history, you will not find it here, you will not be burdened by anthropology, genealogies or any formal logic. The Chaos Theory will not be examined even with a broad brush, nor will there be much reference to thermodynamics. Dante, however, gets a brief mention. Cultural influences on the whole will be avoided and there are no quotations from St John of the Cross. Some reference however is made to herring and to those golden days when you could buy a tenement for sixpence. Clichés as far as they are understood will not be used and neither will metonymy, synecdoche, personification etc. Wittgenstein, along with Partick Thistle, will be relegated, and so will remarks of football managers such that 'If you do not score goals you will never win a match'.

If you are looking for passion you will have to look elsewhere. Enthusiasm is avoided as is any form of élan or hope. Optimism is evaded and no-one learns by experience. It has taken the writer many years to arrive at this position, having endured friendly fire etc. and he is now as happy as a red herring in May.

He no longer believes that the British working man will ever come to repair any form of machinery. He eschews the illusion of efficiency. He believes that the class system will remain unchanged, and that television will not be better than it is today. British Rail will fail and MacBraynes will be as grass. Asses will be coveted and adultery will rear its ugly head. The Royal Family will perish in the Bog of the Tabloid, and the Queen will reign forever, though otherwise the weather will not be too bad. Middle-of-the-road politics will be run over by speedsters and sanity will no longer be accepted as an alibi.

In conclusion buy this book, as it will not be published again in a hurry, unless there is a great demand for animadversions on hopelessness.

And finally God bless you all, though the probability is that he will not.

LIFE OF MURDO

Many people will be surprised that in my auto-biography the main character should be Murdo. Murdo, however, is my alter ego as revealed in *Thoughts of Murdo* published some years ago. Using 'Murdo' rather than 'I' allowed me the distance that I needed to be objective about myself and to make comedy of painful experiences.

Iain Crichton Smith

At the age of seventy, Murdo would look back on his life in between visiting the toilet and scraping dry skin from behind his ears. He was brought up in a small village of churchgoers, football players and men with long beards. He was totally useless at everything he touched. He could not use a scythe, he could not cut peats, he could not clean the chimney. He would stand for hours staring at a cow or a sunset.

People would say about Murdo, he is so stupid he must be very clever. Actually nothing much went on in Murdo's head. He was very poor, and would be sent by his mother to ask people for money. He thought happiness was a scone with crowdie or the back of a loaf with marmalade. He could not afford mutton or beef. Sometimes as he lay in his bed in the small house of one bedroom and mean furniture he would dream of chocolates, but never of theology. He would have given away the whole Bible for a slice of melon.

Oh those dreaming days between moor and sea. Murdo never went on a boat but loved looking for hours into soupy pools where crabs moved sideways. He loved mussels and whelks and foamy seas on stormy days. He drew pictures of drifters, and motor boats.

And he read a great deal: that was his solace. The books he read were *Black Masks* imported from America and borrowed from one particular friend. The criminals wore masks and the detective was as much hunted by the police as by the criminals. Murdo never related these stories to his mother as he thought there were worse in the Bible. He could not have survived if he had not read. In woodwork, however, the teachers thought he had problems with his coordination: thus, a simple table he had made might look like a bed post and vice versa. He also had great difficulty in tying his laces. Under his breath he would often mutter the words 'Horse manure' which

189

he had picked up from his *Black Mask* books.

There was no toilet in the house and no hot water. The roof was made of felt. There was a bed in the kitchen and one in the bedroom. He loved Rupert in the *Daily Express*. He used to go to the well for water and to the moor for his toilet. While squatting there benignly he would hum Gaelic tunes but he would not yet think of the Clearances of which he had not heard at that time. Indeed he had not heard much of the history of the island and had not visited many parts of it, as there were no cars, and he would immediately have got lost anyway. He had no sense of direction and would often turn left to find himself at the edge of a dangerous cliff.

He knew more about Dickens and *Black Mask* than he knew about his village. He loved *Oliver Twist* for instance. He imagined London as a place where there were toilets and hot water and people didn't have to go to wells.

Sometimes as he walked across the linoleum in the early morning he would have an impulse to sing. However, at school he was often bullied. He was nicknamed the Bird because he was up in the air all the time. Now and again the teachers would belt him for muttering 'Horse manure'. He loved certain words such as 'macabre' or 'marauder'. But essays such as "A Day in the Life of a Penny" would not allow him to use them. One of the teachers was grey and spectral and loved cemeteries. She gave them sweets but nevertheless they tormented her. At the end of the day, pupils from different villages would fire stones at each other. Thus what later he saw on TV about Israel and the Palestinians seemed quite familiar to him. People were always coming up and offering to fight him. He was always being knocked down and the woollen suits his mother made for him mocked. In summer like the others he went barefoot. In any case he could hardly afford shoes.

One time he wrote a piece about Neville Chamberlain who travelled all over Europe with an umbrella as a protection against Nazism. He read this to his family who were not impressed. His brother tore up the ending of a story about

Wild Bill Hickock and ever afterwards he hated him and even now between going on visits to the toilet he remembers that incident quite clearly.

Once, walking in a ditch, he was hit by a shinty stick with which a scholar was taking practice swings. A lump rose rapidly on his head.

He was often ill with bronchitis and thrust into bed by his mother who always wore black because she was a widow. 'Stay there,' she would say to him, 'or you will die of tuberculosis of which there is much about and of which your father who drank a lot of whisky died.' So Murdo spent weeks and weeks in bed, reading books about public schoolboys in England. He thought death was round the corner and that he would die young. But he never did, and now he is seventy and hale and hearty and receives his pension. Such is life, and the working of predestination.

Murdo however played a little football and loved to do so. Sometimes himself and another young villager would play with a fishing cork. Without his reading and his football he would not have become the drooling geriatric he is today. There was no TV in those days, only wirelesses as big as wardrobes. The wirelesses were run by batteries for there was no electricity in Murdo's house. The wireless would tell him how the English international football team beat the Scottish international football team by seven goals to nothing.

Murdo would collect cigarette cards, some with footballers on them, some with flowers. Around the house he would not tread on the daisies lest he should injure them. He recognised no other flowers and indeed there weren't many others. However he hated seagulls and would throw stones at them. As also at the telegraph wires. He was as cruel as everybody else to a fat woman with fat red legs who lived in a thatched house with ten cats and wasn't all there. He only learnt pity from his own later suffering.

This story Murdo is telling now to pass the time between going to the toilet and scraping dry skin from his head. Old age, he will have you know, is not romantic, but itchy and wet. His bodily functions are all failing. He uses all sorts of powders, creams, air fresheners, eye drops, scalp cleansers, and so on. All he thinks about is food but he does not drink so much now, as it makes him depressed.

He looks out of the window a lot and thinks up nicknames for people. He considers sending anonymous letters full of murderous intent to game hosts on television.

Nevertheless he is at times content and makes up new versions of old poems such as this by Milton:

> *When I consider what my wife has spent*
> *in Marks and Spencers I have screamed and cried.*

And so on.

Murdo rested for a moment in his narrative, absently plucking a scab from his scalp and scratching at his itchy eyes.

Murdo in his youth was surrounded by tuberculosis. Oh yes, the young as well as the old were dying of it. Their faces grew white, they spat and spat, they coughed their little dry coughs, they went to the sanatorium, and they died.

And Murdo in his youth was surrounded by war. His friends were drowned in foreign seas. He listened to the wireless and heard of their lost ships. He heard names like *Timoshenko* and *Voroshilov*, he ate whale meat and put saccharines in his tea. And his brother was in the Navy as an officer.

Murdo attended secondary school and learnt about Pythagoras's theorem from the well-loved Caney who spat all over his geometry book and who had been engaged for twenty-five years to a lady from the Science Dept.

And one day he was strapped for not learning from the New Testament, the famous passage about charity and tinkling cymbals.

Oh Murdo was not well fed at all. At dinner intervals he would go to the Reading Room in the town and pore over magazines which showed fox-hunting people and shrivelled women sharing a joke. Ha ha think of poor Murdo wondering what sharing a joke meant. And there were leather covers on these magazines.

Was he clever? No, he was not. But he loved Mr Trail, his Latin teacher, who when the bell went would leave the staffroom, having already opened his Vergil, and who would walk along the corridor, the book open in front of him, feel for the handle of the door and say, 'Line 340, Catriona.' Mr Trail was a ball of fire and had hair like a fox.

And Murdo loved Dido and hated Aeneas.

And he loved Vergil.

The war raged on and he ate salt fish and there were no oranges.

And he fell in love with a girl with bluish black hair. One day he climbed over a wall, to bring her a piece of turnip. And he wept and cried, and that was a long time ago, and he met her many years afterwards and he could not believe that this was she. And maybe, thought Murdo, this is not she at all.

One time Murdo had gone to bed after studying his theorems and Rob, his friend who was in the Navy and home on leave, came in to say goodbye. He came over to the bed and Murdo could not open his eyes. He never saw Rob again.

Murdo was as thin as a pencil. There was no flesh on him at all. He was continually aware of his own uselessness. And he was aware of the Atlantic and the deserts of North Africa and the snows of Russia. But he was not aware that there was any oddity in lack of toilets, electricity and running water. (No *en suite* for Murdo.)

Sometimes there would be storms and hens being driven on to the moors by the wind.

And another time he went to the house of a fat spinster woman and she and another fat spinster woman were talking in sexual terms. And Murdo picked up the women's magazine where in a story a woman stabbed a rival with a pair of scissors. This troubled him for a while, indeed gave him nightmares. The sound of the sea was in his ears every day. He read Keats and many other poets, and he kept a big notebook in which he wrote poems. But he never showed them to anyone.

The war raged on. And he read his *Black Mask* stories. He loved geometry more than anything except the crosswords in the *Listener*. And there was *Titbits*, and *Answers* also. His mother didn't like the villagers whose cows chewed her clothes on the line though the villagers were good to her. But she never had any money and she was a widow and she had come from another village. And she always talked about Glasgow where she had lived when young: and of Blochairn and Parliamentary Rd. etc. That was before Murdo's father died, who had been a seaman. Ah, what a terrible life Murdo's mother led. She never had anything new, she was dependent on others, she had a widow's small pension, and she had to count every halfpenny.

She grasped Murdo with a grip of death lest he should get TB.

And Murdo would sit in the attic reading D.H. Lawrence and *No Orchids for Miss Blandish*, for this is how he learned about sex.

The larks sang every summer morning, and so did the singer who lived in the house opposite him.

The postman brought J. and D. Williams catalogues and would only give the parcel to the addressee and to no one else. He had squint eyes. But Murdo expected no letters. Nor did his mother.

Murdo had no theatre, no music, and hardly any books. He would buy milk from a loud stout deaf woman who shouted so that she could be heard all over the village. She had many sons who would hardly leave the house. They were odd people: but perhaps Murdo himself was odd. Who knows?

The war raged on. And Murdo listened to a wireless which was kept in a thatched house with a white cloth over it. (At this point Murdo would like to tell you of the rationale of thatched houses but in truth he is fatigued by this analysis of his youth and will not do so. Suffice it to say that the curvature of such a house is because of the high winds. Murdo however is not sentimental about the thatched house in which behind curtains in beds old women slept till they died. Murdo in fact thinks that microwaves and washing machines and tiles are a great improvement on the smoky benches of thatched houses.)

Suddenly the war came to a stop.

And Britain won. So after a while there might be sugar and sweets and oranges and jam instead of spam and whalemeat.

Thus Murdo like everyone else rejoiced. The young men ceased to be drowned though the young and old died of TB for there was no cure. In the sanatorium they spat and whitened and were like candles fading away, and they had hectic red spots on their cheeks, and Murdo was frightened of visiting his consumptive friends who were put out into the cold winds to be cured from the heat that was destroying them.

But Murdo himself, though thin, remained healthy enough and his bronchitis ceased, though his puzzlement at the universe increased. And he hid from it inside crosswords and geometry and mathematics.

He wanted to leave. Oh yes, he wanted to leave the sighs and the deaths and the sorrows and the ... and the ... and the ...

Could one blame Murdo? Only one in Murdo's place could blame Murdo. For Murdo was not suited to the island. He was not practical enough. And the wooden tables he had tried to carve looked like bedposts. So Murdo said Ave atque vale and Mrs Macleod said Good riddance. Who does he think he is with his Latin? Back of my hand to him and back of my neck also. Thus Mrs Macleod.

And so Murdo departed from the island, being then seventeen. When he arrived at Aberdeen where he was to attend university did he feel nostalgia for the island? No indeed he did not. Murdo was entering a new world with many streets, avenues, lanes, markets, shops etc. And toilets and water and electricity.

The house he then inhabited was run by a spinster, her unmarried brother and their father who was a little man who loved playing draughts but when Murdo beat him he would not speak to him for many months. Also there was in this house an insurance man who used to sing "All We Like Sheep" for he took part in Gilbert and Sullivan operas. Murdo soon learned to go to the pub with the brother who was a Clerk of Works and the little old man would sniff their respective breaths when they came in. (And Murdo used the toilet properly.)

Ah the city of Aberdeen was so clean and new and glittering. And the texts he read were so new and glittering. And the girls he saw were so new and glittering. And no one wore black.

Thus Murdo would walk past a cemetery in the early morning and intone from *Othello*. (Though he was not greatly taken with *Beowulf* and that thistly language so unlike Gaelic and which no one whom he knew of spoke.)

O shall he tell of Aberdeen? How different it was from the black island with its dying inscriptions and its cemeteries and its Obh obhs. Its light was so clear that he could see for miles as it were into the essence of existentialism. Friends wrote poetry and Murdo wrote poetry. And he joined the SNP Society and once read in the student newspaper how he had been elected president by the only gentleman who had turned up.

One day the Celtic Society went on a picnic out of town. They had a piper who played stirring tunes on the bus, and a bootful of whisky and beer. They played one game of rounders as a concession to the day and then drank halves and halves till the piper became drunk and his vigorous tunes became laments and everyone was happy in the swaying bus in the setting sun.

Murdo forgot TB and bronchitis and learning Robespierre and Beowulf.

He would go to his professor's house in the evening once in a while and read an essay which he had composed on for example William Cowper whom he loved because he was shy and had gone mad. And the professor hated Laurence Olivier and T.S. Eliot. So Murdo would sit and cower (for he was very young) in front of this cold learned man and think of subjects for conversation such as his landlady, his landlady's father, the island, horse manure and *Black Mask*. But none of these would he in fact gibber. He had in short no gift of the gab. Nor had he yet learnt about footnotes (or feetnotes). If only Murdo could remember, if only he could recall those days as they were, if only ... but then Murdo ... can't, up to this point at any rate.

All Murdo can remember is happiness. All Murdo can remember is joy. All Murdo can remember is that he was not known, no one knew about Murdo, no one recognised Murdo or knew that his tables turned out like bedposts or that he could not clean the chimney or that he could not sow or reap. Murdo melted into newspaper shops, the bookshops, the pubs, the chip shops. Murdo was a creature of the spring day or of the haar. Murdo was happy to be nobody, and to read poets among whom Eliot and Auden were his favourites. He had the nerve to write for the University magazine *Alma Mater*.

Sometimes he would stand on Union Terrace looking down at the big public draughtsboard. There were his landlady's father and others holding out their long poles like fishing rods. Beside them was the public toilet to which they often retired as they were old and their kidneys did not work well. What mimic battles were fought there beside the toilets. What vaguely moustached Napoleons and Wellingtons toiled over their strategies. And if one of these players lost how his face crumpled like a child's.

It must be said that Murdo drank a fair number of whiskies in those days. One time, on a cold night, he and his friends toured the pubs of Aberdeen taking a different drink in each pub, and arriving at last at the Students' Union, to whose toilets Murdo retired. He sat down against a wall. He got up and seemed to have walked but to his astonishment he had not moved at all. This puzzled him greatly. However after a long time he found himself outside the door of the Students' Union where he fell down and puked over an unknown lady's green shoe.

In Murdo's opinion one cannot speak too highly of the pleasures of drink and whisky in particular. What is wine in comparison to it, what vermouth or gin? It reduces problems to their proper size, that is to say to dwarfish diminutive dimensions. It spawns metaphysical speculations of the most useless sort. It releases the conversational powers of the inhibited. It creates absurd verbal disconnections. It brings man down to his knees after losing his powers of speech. Also he may be seen chatting happily to a companion who is not there. The moon takes on romantic associations as it slips from cloud to cloud. Murdo stops to exchange a few wise words with a complete stranger. He falls, gets up again, clutches at railings. Oh how benign is Murdo's expression. He has no enemy in the world except old English. Only Beowulf and Grendel trouble him.

It has not been stated so far that Murdo had by this time changed his lodgings. He was now staying with a Roman-nosed lady and her moustached husband. With him were two friends, a Malcolm and another Murdo.

They all three slept in one big bedroom and there were other lodgers in the house as well. There were a cat and a child. Once Murdo saw the cat running across the notes of the open piano and quick as a flash he said, 'It must be playing Depussy.' In those days Murdo was addicted to puns.

The three friends used to go much to the cinema: there were many cinemas in Aberdeen, each enshrouded in smoke. One of the most common actresses in those days was Jean Simmons. The landlady's husband attended many films and recited the stories of them at great length: the last that Murdo remembers was *The Spider Woman Strikes Back*. Murdo liked Westerns: indeed he has seen *Shane* nine times, and *High Noon* slightly fewer. Also to be heard in those days was the voice of Nelson Eddy.

(How Murdo wishes he had instant recall. He remembers on Sundays the girls with cracked handbags parading up and down Union St. He remembers many cafés, among them

Jacks, in which the superlatively dressed owner revealed to the students how much more than they he knew about e.g. existentialism.

Murdo was destined for a degree in Celtic and English but dropped Celtic because he found the grammar etc. stupendously boring. He much preferred Eliot and Auden to the thickets of philosophy.

He was still as thin as ever and would drink many glasses of stout to keep himself visible to the general public.

He met one or two girls in those years. One he encountered in the Public Library. He remembers taking her home, her face shining blue in the light above the door of her house. Another he took to the theatre to see a Shakespearean play, for Donald Wolfitt, an actor publicly exhausted by his art, often graced the boards. But it cannot be said that Murdo was a great romanticist; whisky was more his style. He was not greatly driven by the compulsions of sex. Let no one seek revelations of such kind in this text. Poetry and football occupied Murdo more than any other activities. Not that he was good enough to play football for the University. However he did go to Pittodrie much.

Poems he wrote regularly though he has kept none of these. For those who may be interested in the years that are to come some may be found in *Alma Mater* as also one or two pieces in *Gaudie* including one on Auden's use of the definite article.

It comes to Murdo's dimming mind that he has not made a good job of this evocation of his University days. He has not shown their excitement, their newness. No, he hasn't. He has fallen far short of Rousseau and Augustine. He has not spoken of the trams as they passed through the overarching leaves. Nor has he mentioned the bitter coldness of Aberdeen in the winter. Nor listening to the radio and in particular a song, if such it could be called, connected with Edmundo Ros, "He was Killed Stone Dead in the Market". Fragments of other songs come back to him now and again e.g. "Thank You for Being an Angel" etc. And they instantly summon up these granite streets.

He thanks Aberdeen for giving him these days after his unhappy childhood of poverty and salt herring. His mother stern and loved and at times wild loomed over the Minch. But Aberdeen was inhabited by many characters, whom he recalls with affection, even the shrivelled ones, the city itself a cage of light.

He remembers Duthie Park also with affection. There he would lie with the other two Ms on summer days, perhaps revising his Vergil or his Keats.

Thus Murdo has come to the age of 21. Around him were students who had returned from the war, for example Alexander Scott and Derick Thomson, (Indeed Scott had edited a magazine called the *North East Review* to which Murdo had contributed. Scott too had written plays for radio and a book of poems called *The Latest in Elegies*. Many of these students had fought in the war. Murdo was young for his age, and did not know about the 'world'. All he knew about was books. If left on a desert island he would have expired almost instantly after staring out for a little while at the salt water. What indeed could Murdo do? True, he could sharpen a few puns but that was the extent of his expertise. I tremble for poor Murdo in his flannels as he leaves behind him the shelter of academe.

I tremble for him but I am determined to tell the truth about poor him, if he is of any interest to anyone. I do not wish to put him in a good light unless he deserves it. There survived until recently a little photograph of him in his class at primary school. He wears a jersey and a tie pin. He is looking out at the world with a rather scared expression.

Murdo's brother A.J. had married a Helensburgh girl and was to live in Dumbarton. Murdo's mother wished to leave Lewis. So it was that everybody went to live in A.J.'s house in Dumbarton. This didn't work out and Murdo and his mother and his younger brother found themselves in a slummy flat on the High Street of Dumbarton.

Just after the war Dumbarton, Clydebank etc. were ugly industrial towns and Murdo, it must be said, was not used to industry. Above them in the flat a man beat his wife regularly. She appeared with a black eye, he appeared in a natty suit. He was a true blue Protestant and she had a true black eye. In front of the blatant glaring tenement was, in the winter, a pool of slimy water. Murdo used to take the bus to Helensburgh, a nice seaside town, but did not truly know why till he realised that it was because he was in search of the sea; and the Clyde would do. He would sit on the shore and stare out at the yachts and the ships on the misty horizon.

From Glasgow people would come at weekends to sit on the scarred benches and throw sticks out into the Clyde for dogs to catch.

Helensburgh was a planned town with straight parallel streets. Dumbarton was different.

To its Free Church his mother would go in her black hat: she would walk down the half-lighted streets. But beside her in the tenement lived a freckle-faced Catholic girl (married to an asthmatic) whom his mother extraordinarily liked. The couple were Irish. One day the Catholic girl had a black spot on her forehead and Murdo's mother thinking it was dirt pointed to it. Of course this was symbolic of Ash Wednesday.

Dumbarton was awash with Highland policemen, many from Lewis, constables, sergeants, inspectors, chief inspectors. Why was this so? It was partly so because of their heavy tallness, brought about by scones, crowdie, buttermilk, oatcakes, fish. It was so also because reared in the writhing environment of sin, they sniffed out crime instead. Sin was the self, and crime is the state.

Meanwhile Murdo set out on weekdays to Jordanhill College where he learnt to be a teacher. (This he has come to, for what else was open to a poet except the rotting streets of Parnassus.) At Jordanhill he studied Hygiene and Speech Training. He spent as much time in the basement as he could, playing billiards or table tennis (he cannot now remember).

He read heavy boring books on education. He received very low marks for Hygiene because he did not attend the lectures. As for Speech Training, what had he to do with it or it with him? A man who looked like D.H. Lawrence with a pointed beard taught Psychology, using a yellow book he had written himself.

Murdo cannot convey the death to the spirit which is to be found in a Teachers' Training College and therefore will not try. Suffice it to say that he was sent out to teach in various schools and found himself with classes which at times he was only able to control with difficulty and sometimes not at all. O far from him at these times were T.S. Eliot and Auden and Jean Paul Sartre and Camus. For he found himself under severe threat by those who were not aware of the delicacies of literature.

And he travelled every day from Dumbarton to these schools and the Training College and was not happy. He felt as if he was in the wrong place. There was the ugliness of everything that surrounded him, the ugliness of buildings, ugliness of thought, ugliness of trains.

Ugliness, ugliness. And Murdo could hardly bear it.

And he would take the bus to Helensburgh named after Helen Colquhoun, but for him Helen of Troy. He would sit by the shore and stare out at the Clyde. And he liked Helensburgh and wrote poems about it. But Dumbarton, how should he deal with Dumbarton? How with the brown broken-toothed tenement on the High St? Which often needed repairs. And had its coal shed with a lock at the back.

(Curiously enough his mother was happier there than in Lewis. There was her church, there were her friends, there was her Catholic freckle-faced neighbour like the daughter she never had, but she didn't like her surroundings. And who indeed would? This tenement has now forever gone, as unnoticing Murdo noticed recently on a visit to Dumbarton, and may God or His equivalent bless those who blasted it in powder and slime to the ground.)

This was a dreadful period in Murdo's life, harbinger of more dreadful periods to come. It seemed to him that he had gone down to Avernus where there were walls scrawled with the graffiti of the lost. It seemed to him that the world was full of big heavy wardrobes and big policemen. It seemed to him that there was no sky but only brown earth. It seemed to him that there were a lot of idle scrawny dogs about.

And then there were the terrible lectures of the Training College. Statistics abounded. Hygiene was waxing and Donne and others were waning. Educational abstractions filled him with fear. Lessons watched by supervisors filled him with torment. Radiators were around. Staffrooms pullulated. How did poor Murdo survive? At this period it seemed as if Murdo had no friends and this is true. What is the meaning of this world, he asked himself. Can religion tell me? Can existentialism? Can Platonism? But none did.

Ugliness ugliness, ugliness. Squalor around him and big heavy wardrobes and tall Highland policemen and coal cellars. The only escape was the Clyde, sometimes a fine glitter of water.

How far down Murdo went among the weeping walls through the rain towards the heights of metonymy and metaphor and alliteration and irony and anti-climax. For these were taught. And parsing and general analysis. And these pupils would in his nightmares kick adverbs and adjectives and subjunctives about like footballs. Into the late red dusty skies of Glasgow or Clydebank.

(Dumbarton is now quite different. In Murdo's opinion Dumbarton has improved a great deal. It has a Sue Ryder shop and a Cancer Research shop and a Capability Scotland shop. Here Murdo goes for books. And indeed he does this wherever he is in Scotland – or England. His first destination in a city or town is Oxfam or Save the Children. He is always looking for the great green crime Penguins which are no longer published but may sometimes be found in such shops. He is not interested in shirts, trousers, suits, shoes etc. but only in books. He can tell at a glance when he enters such a shop whether he is going to be lucky. His eye sweeps the shelves like that of a hawk or an eagle. Many of the books he immediately dismisses.

Edinburgh he knows by the charity shops in Corstorphine, Glasgow by those on Byres Rd. Crieff too and Perth and Fort William he knows by their charity shops. In some he finds no books at all that he can read. Ominously Mills and Boon are taking over. Catherine Cookson is much in evidence. But Murdo is sometimes triumphant. And for 30p he might find a little masterpiece.

Murdo is happy to read those books which others have read and dedicated to the long dead. Indeed he feels sometimes that he prefers these books to new ones. He does not eschew their foggy pages. The lesser green Penguin writers he sometimes finds and to his great sense of avarice he saw in Hugh MacDiarmid's cottage (now empty of the great man himself) a large number of green Penguin crime books which he nearly pinched when the guide was absent.

This page or two is self-indulgent for Murdo, beginning with the new Dumbarton and its charity shops and leading to other animadversions for which Murdo might not otherwise find space (or might forget). But here he might mention his love of good crime stories. At one time he read much SF but that did not last. And especially is he fond of locked room mysteries. Indeed his library is full of crime stories though of course there are many other books as well. And here he is glad to see how many good women crime writers there have been (including the divine Margaret Millar). But not so many good women writers of SF.

He has himself tried to write a good crime novel but has never succeeded since such an undertaking requires great intelligence, indeed more than for a conventional literary novel. Murdo's interest is in the classical puzzle novel not in the works of for instance Simenon or indeed any crime writer from Sweden.

His greatest regret was being recently in Italy and finding in what appeared to be a charity shop classical English detective stories he hadn't read – but written in Italian. Day after day he would come back and look at them as if hoping that during the night they had changed back into English. Salivating.

So this short byway comes to an end. Murdo has placed it here before the next tragic episode with which he is faced so that the memoir will not appear as gloomy as it might otherwise do. Murdo had his many struggles but let us not appear melancholy about them. For instance he came from a very religious background and from a bilingual background which made it difficult for him to choose the language he would write in. Vanity vanity said his religion. A hollow bell sounded in Murdo's heart. A hollow black bell. And now he will proceed.

Now it is a beautiful autumn day and Murdo will tell of his National Service which occurred after Jordanhill.

Those who have read his memoir with attention will realise that Murdo was not of the type of which soldiers are made. He was not able to keep in step or to clean his rifle correctly or to shine his boots so that they became mirrors or to blanco his belt.

Murdo felt himself to be in an alien country once he had walked through the gates of the barracks and gave a last lingering gaze at the people working in the fields. A moustached corporal strode up and down in front of Murdo where he stood trembling by his bed and said, 'If you play fair by me I will play fair by you.' Murdo at that moment would have played fair by anyone. And indeed he saluted sergeants and corporals till told to stop.

In the barrack room with Murdo were many others, among them Public School boys who had the aplomb and ice coolness of their kind. There was a tall black stove pipe and above the beds lockers. Sometimes one of the Public School boys who had a gramophone played "Love O Love O Careless Love, you

Fly to my Head like Wine". These words Murdo remembers as he also remembers the elegiac wail of the Last Post.

Murdo however could not understand the highly personal hatred corporals had for him. They pushed their red pulsing faces into his face: they referred in dreadful terms to his mother and to Murdo himself. What would T.S. Eliot do here, thought Murdo. Or William Blake? Shakespeare would be fine and so would Duncan Ban Macintyre. But Murdo was not fine. Murdo did not want a rifle, he did not want a belt, he did not want shining boots, he did not wish to hear lascivious talk about women or continual swearing. In many ways poor Murdo was innocent.

O the K.R.R.C. had a famous history: many V.C.s had been won in places where the regiment in Murdo's opinion ought not to have been in the first place. Courage, ardour, and breakneck patriotism were praised. Murdo felt that Vergil was being squeezed out of him so that many men might become one man. Murdo was afraid. He couldn't write nor did he read. He was too busy suffering punishments. He was too busy aligning his knife and fork correctly on top of his bed for inspection.

O how clumsy Murdo was. He could not fit into that social organism. He heard his boots on the square with trepidation. He taught himself to iron but at great expense of spirit. He broke like others the ice on the surface of the water buckets in winter in order to shave. He polished his cap brooch and his belt buckle. But Murdo was not a soldier nor a phantasm thereof. His country was not that square nor that barrack room. His countryman was not that corporal. Indeed that corporal was Murdo's enemy, if Murdo ever thought he had an enemy. He was put on a charge for not having the regulation number of studs in his boots. He was put on a charge for having a dirty rifle. And all the time it was as if Murdo was sleep-walking. What was he defending? He didn't know. It certainly was not Murdo. And what indeed was he defending with the soles of his boots or with the orderliness of his knife fork and spoon. What culture? What frontiers?

All this time especially during these first weeks no one could be more puzzled than Murdo. It was as if he was in a deep sleep and being continually and roughly awakened. He went to Avernus and rose from it quaking. And Avernus had a stove pipe that was all the furniture apart from the bed that Avernus had. But in the grey light there were young men with knife-sharp creases facing two years of ironing.

Murdo sits at his desk on a beautiful autumn day in 1997 and contemplates those days. They were grey and square. They were tense and straight. He cannot work out whether they were real or unreal. Many Glasgow boys couldn't stand them and went over the wall; they did three or four years of National Service instead of two. There was a plumber's mate in the barrack room, and there were Public School boys. In his youth Murdo had read stories about English Public Schools and here were some of their representatives who had already served in their Cadet Corps.

Murdo has already written about those days and here is a new piece he has written:

> *The corporal thrust his face into our faces.*
> *That was the end of civilian kindnesses*
>
> *as also of scholarship and verse.*
> *We bent our heads under that fierce harsh*
>
> *despotism, though in democracy.*
> *We broke the ice in buckets, saw the sky*
>
> *brokenly reflected, rushed at sandbags with*
> *rabid screams. Death o where is death*
>
> *as seated on beds we mourned. Reveille came*
> *always too early. O do not have the shame*
>
> *of dirty badge or rifle. Boots must be*
> *mirrors of neatness, impersonality,*

blackness made to shine. O worst of all
would be great joy at marching, general

subsuming the particular, and a flag
blatant spectacular overpowering brag

of the true small heart that wished to be alone
in its own unburnished natural flesh and bone.

So Murdo saw the squareness and rectangularity. And Murdo had to learn this. Murdo learned to suffer the absurd, his number became more important than himself and Murdo wept inside himself for the loss of the world. And was that world to be protected by such as Murdo? Paradox of paradoxes. And Murdo was not sent abroad though there was war in the Far East and a slogan was MAKE THE ARMY YOUR KOREA.

Murdo was on the contrary intended for the Education Corps. And he will tell of this later though he would like a few moments to weep for the loss of his two years on this autumn day as he looks out the window at the pasture and the running rabbits and the sheep and the cows. And the sparkling leaves.

And all that can be lost in the squareness and the rectangularity and the greyness and numbers taking the place of people.

However Murdo came back to tell the tale.

After some additional training Murdo became a sergeant in the Education Corps. Imagine it, imagine it. There is Murdo with three stripes on his arm. Who could have thought it, who could have foretold it? No, not in his most bizarre meditations would Murdo have thought it.

What did Murdo have to do? Here is what he had to do. But first it must be mentioned that after his training was completed in England he travelled through the cold icy night to Edinburgh, for he had been assigned to the Royal Scots. He waited shivering till the buses began to run and arrived on a winter's morning, not far from dawn, at Dreghorn Barracks. There were two other sergeants and a CSM in the Educational Depot. Two things in particular stick in Murdo's mind. The first was that as he entered the door he was asked if he had his Higher Maths. He said Yes and therefore he was teaching not English but Maths. The second was that on his first day a CSM (not the Education one) borrowed money from him.

So what were Murdo's duties? Murdo's duties were as follows:

1. He gave lectures to the recruits on the United Nations and NATO.
2. He taught the Forces Prelim which was the equivalent to Highers and allowed soldiers etc. to go to university.
3. At the time he was in the Education Corps the army introduced examinations such that corporals, sergeants, CSMs and RSMs had to pass them: otherwise they would go down a rank.

Murdo found his surroundings civilised. He also found that there were many recruits who could not read or write. These were discovered as they were always on charges (as Murdo himself had been). The reason for this was that they could not read the Daily Orders, and were too ashamed to say so.

Oftentimes Murdo sympathised with the recruits who after a ten-mile march might be asked to apply themselves to NATO.

He coped with Mathematics all right, even up to Forces Prelim. There was a colour sergeant who was in his class and who was very clever. However he put Murdo on a charge because he had not handed in his sheets on a Monday morning before he had gone to teach in a camp not far from Dreghorn. Murdo was understandably miffed, and wished that this man would not pass his examinations. However he did with as it were flying colours and later gave Murdo a new battledress.

The RSM was a sturdy red-faced perfect soldier and for this reason Murdo did not like him and almost certainly he did not like Murdo. He drank much whisky because he was bored and would rather have been serving in Germany. One night Murdo was in the mess when the RSM was captaining a team of darts players. He was easily winning by the simple device of periodically going up to the board and wiping off his opponent's score. (He had ordered Murdo to write the scores.) The RSM's opponents were captained oddly enough by a lady CSM. At a crucial stage in the proceedings one of her team, a sergeant, was heard to mutter, 'If we had the RSM as our captain we would be winning this game.' The RSM, even more red-faced than ever from drink, turned to him and in a passionate voice ordered him to take two extra guards. Meanwhile Murdo was cowering to the side, having watched with disbelief the scores he had put up being wiped away by the RSM.

And yet of course this RSM was not unintelligent: indeed he had passed his examination with ease. He was a first-rate RSM. But the power in the camp was his: he more than the CO was the real commander, or so Murdo thought.

As far as Murdo thought about military matters.

Often Murdo would on his time off make his way to the Cameo cinema which showed foreign films. At that time many were for some reason Swedish (that is to say Bergmannish). They were either very gloomy or showed naked people making love in woods whose trees were unaccountably bare. Murdo also saw *Les Enfants du Paradis* and many other films of that nature.

One time he met a nurse who took him to her house. She, her mother and father and Murdo played a card game whose rules Murdo did not understand. He did not go back nor indeed was he invited back.

At this time Murdo did more reading than he had done before: however no artistic material of Murdo's own survives from that period.

(It may be mentioned that many many years after this, when Murdo was perhaps in his late fifties, he was giving a talk to a number of writers' groups who had gathered in Crieff. The first person Murdo talked to was to his great astonishment an ex-RSM. You could have knocked Murdo down with the proverbial hammer. That an RSM should be writing stories and poems, how odd, how strange, how bizarre. But it was certainly the case. Only this RSM had been in the Intelligence Corps.)

(Murdo should also add that there was a probably apocryphal story in the Education Corps about a sergeant who had told his platoon that a man was coming to talk to them about Keats. And I don't suppose any of you buggers know what a Keat is, he added.)

In this paradoxical period of his life, Murdo was ordered to put on a charge a corporal who had not turned up for a lecture. Murdo marched briskly behind this man to the CO's office. Behind them both was the RSM with his florid face and martial stick. At one stage the RSM shouted, 'Remove belt!' Murdo innocently removed his belt though in fact it was the 'chargee' who was supposed to do so. Murdo could imagine the RSM behind him turning a fierce shade of purple.

Murdo makes light of this now but at the time not much light was to be made of it.

He was a very conscientious sergeant: he taught recruits letter-writing. He taught Regulars the Forces Prelim. He enjoyed Maths as he had done in school, especially the wonderful world of geometry. In his youth, Murdo was not very good at Maths till meeting his Damascus in Woolworths when he bought a Penguin Puzzle book which converted him immediately to that marvellous world. What a vision of orderliness geometry was. If only the world itself was like that. Geometry was not visited by corporals or sergeants or shiny boots and belts.

The orderliness of the Army was different; it had a mad logic about it. Thus it was said that there had been an RSM who stood at attention at the phone when speaking to his CO. Thus it was said that a recruit had been released from his charge because his number had been mis-typed: so in effect it was not him at all.

In any case the world of the Army was not Murdo's work; he was too clumsy and in a way too innocent. And yet in its own way it too is a protected world. The civilian world is distant and perhaps disorderly. How would an RSM with all his power adapt in a world in which he had no power, in which no one had heard of him? That is a vague philosophical question which Murdo now adumbrates, but without much hope of an answer.

What did Murdo learn in the Army, and with pain, against his will? He learned:

1. To live in a big bare barrack room with people he had never met before.
2. He learned to iron but has now forgotten how to. He learned to use blanco which now he doesn't need to. He learned to polish brass of any kind.
3. He learned about a world which theologians might call totally other, a world which did not know of existentialism and Eliot's poetry and did not care. A world which was based on the command and was not at all aesthetic. A world which did not much care for feelings. A world which thought about women much of the time but was of course masculine.
4. He learned about a world in which privacy did not exist.
5. The academic world, Murdo had found relatively easy. This he did not find easy. He should have learned this more thoroughly at the time but didn't.
6. In the end, it was good for Murdo to know about this world. To live entirely in an academic world – based often on minor egos and minor quarrels – is not good for the soul of man. It is best that such

academics should have their noses pressed firmly at times in the dirt so that they stand up later in horror to find two or three stripes towering over them.

7. Murdo learned to fire a rifle which he has never done since and which he doesn't want to do again.

8. This was a world in which there was no shelter. It was continually scrutinised and evaluated (at least in the first few weeks, later not so much so). It was a world which hunted out dirt from rifle barrels.

9. It was a world which operated by inflexible rules, sometimes bizarre. It was a completely hierarchical world. It was a solid ladder.

10. It was a world in which Regulars disliked National Servicemen being made into sergeants etc. (especially people like Murdo who though competent as an education sergeant was not so as a soldier). As has been said Murdo's poetry did not develop here. He had written some poems at the University but here he had no time and no inclination to write. He might speculate now but to no avail on why he wrote nothing at all.

It is strange how even now that song comes back to him: "Love O Love O Careless Love, you Fly to my Head like Wine". Are these the exact words? Perhaps not.

Eventually the time came for Murdo to leave and to enter the sudden glare of civilian life.

He could walk about in his anonymity. He could climb easily on to buses. He could walk with a stooping posture if he wished to. He could wear trousers which did not have knife-edged creases. He could read, he could write if he wished to. He did not need to get out of bed at half-past six in the morning. There was no sound of the bugle in Dumbarton.

(Actually his younger brother had done his National Service before Murdo. He had been stationed in Hong Kong with the

Argylls. His younger brother had adapted easily to the army and looked very proud in his kilt. About this time his older brother was with his wife about to leave for Rhodesia to teach there after teaching in Dumbarton. Or was that a little later? Murdo's memory is not absolutely exact.)

Murdo and his mother and his younger brother moved into a new Council flat on the outskirts of Dumbarton on the Helensburgh road. It was the top flat and it was new. Never had they had a house like this. It was even on the edge of the country.

Murdo's mother was happy. She went to her Free Church and she had friends. Murdo became a teacher at Clydebank High School, travelling thereto by train every day.

Was he happy there? Not really. For it turned out that Murdo was quite good at teaching academics but not at teaching non-academics. And indeed it was non-academics that he mostly taught (?) with the class lettering running as far down as K (e.g. 2K). Also Murdo had to teach history and geography. Geography he was not au fait with and never has been and as for history he was not clever at remembering facts.

Murdo had in fact drifted into teaching for as he stood up in the glaring light and after reading existentialists and Eliot etc. he found that there was nothing else he could do. No, nothing at all. For though he could iron and burnish boots this was not enough.

It was the genial custom in those days to give to new teachers the worst classes. And thus it was that to 3F Murdo would in mounting baffled noise teach the adverbial clause of time or the adverbial clause of concession. Or to 3J from his limited store of geography the story of the fishing industry.

Mackerel, he would say knowledgeably, are surface fish and cod are ground fish (or the other way round). Leafing through one of the answers he found the following: 'Mackerel and herring are surface fish: ground fish are cod, haddock and fillet.' (Thus does the fish and chip shop take revenge on academe).

The school itself was a new building, and the pupils could indeed have been much worse. However Murdo's weakness began and remained as a teacher of non-academics who indeed found little in education that they could fasten on to. (Thus Murdo is not blaming them but on the contrary blaming himself. For Murdo's mistake was that he was teaching his subject, and not pupils. With academic pupils this is adequate and praiseworthy perhaps but not with non-academic pupils who tend to be more 'human' in their responses as indeed they might ask during a penetrating lesson on coal where you had got your tie from.)

Murdo has flashes of memory from these days. Thus he learned to play Solo during intervals for there was a strong-going card-playing fraternity in the school. He remembers the terms "abundance" and "misère" (or some such words). On a Friday afternoon he even graduated to Bridge though this was a much more demanding and élitist game. These games sometimes took place after school while waiting for the train.

Did Murdo become a demon card player. He did in fact become a respectable Solo player though Bridge being a more strategic game was more difficult for him.

As has already been said, Murdo's knowledge of historical facts was not of the most capacious or astute nature (though he did like historical ideas of which there are many to choose from e.g. Communism or Marxism. However it may be that Murdo chose to immerse himself in these as well as in philosophy to disguise the fact that he found it very difficult to teach non-academics. In any case Murdo has always been interested in philosophy, though not so much recently. And he might mention here the influence Kierkegaard has had on him. (Indeed it might be a good idea to mention something about Kierkegaard before Murdo forgets to include it later on.)

Kierkegaard appealed to Murdo because he was both a

poet and a philosopher. Also, he pitied him because he was a hunchback. For those who do not know much about Kierkegaard Murdo might mention that he was a religious figure. He believed that there were roughly three categories in religion. There was the aesthetic when we might admire for instance beautiful churches. Then there was the ethical when one might be involved in religious morality. Finally there was the existential of which Abraham was the exemplar. Asked to sacrifice his son Isaac, he did this unhesitatingly. Murdo in fact has written a little story based on Abraham and Isaac (in Gaelic).

In effect, Kierkegaard attacked the liberalism of his time. One could not be saved by rationalism but by the leap of faith.

One supposes that this man of extraordinary intelligence was also a tortured being. He was engaged to Regina but did not marry her. This leap which he did not take caused him much philosophising.

Kierkegaard interested Murdo because of his call to individualise oneself. Also Murdo still had to work through his attitude to religion. Also there was something frail and vulnerable in Kierkegaard's appearance in the physical world (a powerful intelligence in a misshapen body).

It might be said that Wittgenstein also attracted Murdo later on, partly for biographical reasons. He of course was another bachelor, a man of extreme brilliance who was perhaps more eccentric than Kierkegaard. Thus he loved seeing gangster films and reading *Black Mask* stories. He would philosophise in class and then walk out saying, 'I am so stupid today.' He died (was it of cancer?) saying how joyful his life had been. Actually Murdo did read his first book with its wonderful epigrams set out in order.

People like that appealed to Murdo, extreme intelligences whom he tried to understand but whose biographies interested him as much as their work. Maybe some day a book should be written on the influences on culture of the bachelor such as these two and Kafka and Housman and Vergil and Larkin and Kant and many others of their ilk. This is merely a passing animadversion.

Murdo is not mentioning his reading in a boastful manner but because more has happened to his mind than to his historical figure in space. He himself at this time believed that he would not marry, that marriage was too great a responsibility. He could not understand how people joined together in matrimony as it were so light-heartedly.

Philosophers such as Kierkegaard and Wittgenstein were legends to him. They seemed to be wrestling with important issues in such a way that it seemed their lives depended on it. It was fascinating to see Wittgenstein almost dismissing Bertrand Russell as an intellectual influence.

Now as Murdo ages these philosophers do not seem so important to him. He looks out of the window at the manifold doings of Nature and these delight him most of the time. Never again will he be so enthralled by Kierkegaard's tortuous impalements. And he sees the Abraham–Isaac story as a cold-blooded game, for the deaths of millions of children have happened in the interim.

Still he salutes these two extremists of the mind whom for a while he idolised and for whom even now he retains affection.

As Murdo wrote, before his animadversions on Kierkegaard and Wittgenstein, he was not good at retaining historical facts. Thus the Rector, who had a Ph.D. in history, was to watch him give a lesson on Columbus. Murdo, who was rather cavalier about dates, stated firmly that Columbus had discovered America in 1592, and made other errors. The Rector was becoming visibly agitated. How could he let the pupils go home with such inaccurate data? One can imagine him working his way through this complicated problem. Finally he went to the front of the class and asked it to point out Mr Smith's 'deliberate mistakes'.

During the three years he spent in Clydebank High School

Murdo started writing poetry again. He met Bill Turner, editor of a magazine called *The Poet*, who lived in Glasgow. He found Bill very helpful and he contributed to his magazine. He also contributed to *Outposts* when Howard Sergeant was editor.

These poems were to be gathered together and published in 1955 in a booklet called *The Long River*, a title derived from a long poem about MacDiarmid in that book. The publisher was Callum Macdonald, a Lewisman who lived in Edinburgh and who also published a poetry magazine called *Lines* to which Murdo contributed. (Much later to his astonishment Murdo discovered that Callum had been a squadron leader in the war.)

One reviewer of his book (in *Lines* itself) said that Murdo had great poetic gifts but that he lacked humanity. This is what Murdo has been trying to correct since then.

The Long River as has been said contained a long poem in praise of Hugh MacDiarmid. Murdo has not wavered in his belief that MacDiarmid was a genius, though his work was of variable quality. He believes that his best work is his earliest. MacDiarmid was ambitious, autodidactic and self-centred. Nevertheless his lyrics still seem to Murdo stunningly new and fresh. He met him much later when the great poet was old and deaf and very gentle.

Much later too he wrote an essay on MacDiarmid's poetry called "The Golden Lyric" which though praising the poet greatly did make some critical remarks. He received from MacDiarmid a typically combative letter rebutting most of the criticism he had made. All this time, while Murdo was writing poetry he was also teaching. More and more however he was beginning to feel that the Lowlands were not his proper home. He felt slightly aslant to them. They seemed uglier than either Aberdeen or Lewis. Though he never saw any violence in Glasgow it seemed to him a more frightening city than Aberdeen. All this in spite of the fact that he and his mother had many Highland friends in Dumbarton, who were in fact mostly policemen and policemen's wives.

It is possible that there were many factors which made Murdo uneasy. First he was not very happy teaching non-academic pupils. Secondly, he found the townscape ugly and anonymous. Thirdly, he missed the sea. That eternal sound must in some ways have filled his early subconsciousness. Its music was omnipresent.

His poetry could not properly exist in the area in which he was, it could not breathe.

He taught in Clydebank High School from 1952 to 1955. Murdo was now twenty-seven years old.

Perhaps if he had been twenty-seven years old now he might (with the help of the Arts Council, non-existent then) have left teaching. But he did not dare to take that forward leap of which Kierkegaard had spoken. The leap he took was back to the Highlands.

So Murdo arrived in Oban, and it seemed to him to be heaven on earth. It was the autumn of 1955 and trees were fruiting twice. Oban stood near the sea and there were stunning views of Mull and Lismore. Again, Murdo heard the voices of the seagulls and again he saw MacBrayne's boats. On a wonderful magical day he sailed to Iona (for thirty-five shillings). The sea was calm and clear, and out of it he saw the Dutchman's Cap looming. One could imagine how the legend of Tir nan Og had risen. He remembers seeing in Iona churchyard the grave of the Unknown Seaman who had died in the war. The water was green and the island very quiet with an atmosphere of extraordinary peace. He landed at Staffa and saw those columns which had inspired the opening of the "Hyperion" of Keats.

In Oban he walked along the Gallanach Road and saw the Atlantic, authentic and ruffled. He saw jackdaws playing about the tall cliffs. On the way to Ganavan he climbed to Dunollie Castle, unroofed and with many birds. Often he would sit on a bench and look out to sea as he had done in Helensburgh. But Oban was different from Helensburgh: in Oban he felt instantly at home. It was a Highland town though there were many tourists. The air seemed right to him. The squawking of the seagulls woke him in the morning in his lodgings.

How was Murdo to know when he arrived in Oban that he would remain there for twenty-two years? Twice while teaching he tried to sever himself from Oban (in fact he was given presentations twice) but found that he could not leave. It was in Argyll that he was to write a great deal of what he is pleased to call his *oeuvre* in this land of lochs, hills and trees, the land to which the great Gaelic poet Duncan Ban Macintyre belonged. A land above all of woods.

Did Murdo at times feel that this land was too beautiful for him and that he should have remained in the regions of ugly industry? Murdo thought that without question. On the other hand, it was only in the Highlands that he felt truly at home. It was only there that the pen became an instrument of nature in his hand. In Dumbarton he felt as a writer uncomfortable, at a slant to the universe. Though not so with Helensburgh where he had written many poems.

Oban was not Lewis. It was more cosmopolitan. Its sea was not so wild except at Gallanach. It had trees. It had many shops, and was larger than Stornoway. It had two cinemas. It had McCaig's Tower which was like a stone crown above the town. It had an unroofed castle. It had a ferry to the island of Kerrera.

All these things Murdo absorbed in those wonderful autumnal days. In this lyrical interval. And often he would go to the pier and gaze at the boats perfectly mirrored in the water and at seagulls stabbing the bones of a herring. Sailors would be knitting nets among orange buoys.

Murdo was in lodgings as he had been in Aberdeen. At that time Murdo was not bothered by living in lodgings. In summer however there was the risk of being put out into a hut as the landladies welcomed the visitors with their pre-ensuite rooms. What was Murdo like then? He hardly ate anything and was thin as an emaciated pencil. He was perhaps nine stone in weight. It seemed to him that food made his head heavy. His landlord however was large and a long-distance lorry driver. And there was a little daughter who ran about or stared at Murdo with her thumb in her mouth. Murdo had nothing to say to little children, he was quite withdrawn, he was not at that time a gossipy member of the human race. He thought more about Kafka than he did about Mrs Macleod.

The Rector of the High School was John MacLean, brother of the famous Gaelic poet Sorley MacLean. He was a classical scholar, educated at Oxford under A.E. Housman, and later at Vienna. He translated, much later than this, the *Odyssey* into Gaelic and said that it worked very well because of the Highland clan system and the rich vocabulary of the sea. He was a very hard worker and believed that everybody else should be the same. He didn't think that teachers could teach while sitting down and would look through the glass of the classroom door to see if teachers were vertical. He taught pupils for the bursary competitions and had a large number of successes so that Oban High School enjoyed during his lifetime a great reputation.

Murdo thought of him as a republican Roman, upright, honourable and friendly. Murdo at this time hadn't learned to work properly, but did get his pupils through their Higher English and (miraculously) through their Lower History. After this had happened, John MacLean came to his room and said, 'That was very good, and I always thought you were an incomprehensible poet like my brother Sorley.' He was a lover of traditional poetry and translated some of it into Gaelic.

He knew every pupil by name though the school was a large one, and he could be seen talking happily to the farmers who came in to the market. His scholarship had not in any way separated him from them.

Murdo admired him greatly, though in fact he had little sense of humour and indeed Murdo looks back with a strange affection to these early days when teachers strode about the school in black gowns. This was to him – at least the first few years – a golden time when he would wake up early with brimming joy in order to teach pupils, though as usual he was not as good with the non-academics as with the academics.

Murdo would make jokes and laugh at his own jokes. The essays of Addison and Lamb were taught as also *Hamlet* and *Macbeth*. No modern writing peered timorously over the horizon. There was also the *Prologue* of Chaucer. Murdo would give out an essay to each pupil every week, while at the same time he was writing English poetry and Gaelic short stories. It seemed to him that the Gaelic short story was usually an anecdote about a woman changing into a seal or a seal changing into a woman. Or conversational exchanges of a less riveting nature. Thus he wrote stories of a certain artistic structure.

Some of these stories brought criticism and obloquy on Murdo's head. Thus he once wrote a story of an American President who was considering the release of the nuclear deterrent. This was not considered a truly Gaelic story. So Murdo suffered.

But his results with Highers were always good. This was partly because he was very enthusiastic about literature and also because he had learned to work hard while at the same time inditing a great deal of his own *oeuvre*. I think Murdo must have been very intense in those days with not much loose conversation. But also he had at times I think humour within a controlled environment and some wit.

Meanwhile at weekends he would often travel to Dumbarton where his mother still lived alone after his brother had set off to New Zealand. Nor did Murdo ever see his younger brother again. (Recently in Sirmione Murdo remembered Catullus and his line to his brother, *Et in perpetuum frater ave atque vale*. Not long before he had received his brother's ashes from Australia. On a cold day he scattered them on the sand of Bayble Bay in Lewis.)

One of the most interesting teachers in Oban High School was Jack Murray who taught history. He had composed his own history books, which began with Oban and spread outwards. Each chapter was followed by a number of questions but they weren't simple questions on the content. They were all designed to make the pupil think hard about the political context. His method of teaching was to put the pupil in for instance the position of Charles I and ask him what he would do if faced by such and such a problem. He had a large number of classes to whom he was always giving written exercises.

He had been to Eton and would remark about certain prominent politicians that he had helped them with their homework. He had an acute intelligence which worked from first principles. He built his own house and was absorbed in architectural problems for a while. Then he bought hens and worked out graphs of their production of eggs. He was the first teacher to take a group of pupils into East Germany, that is, in his case Dresden. One of his pupils is now Professor of History at Aberdeen University: in the same year was James Hunter who has written such wonderful books on Highland history.

Murdo, who was more interested in ideas than in facts, would provocatively say that history was only a metaphor. Jack would think this through and after a day or two would come back with a reasoned reply.

Later in his life he suffered from disseminated sclerosis but for a while would still come to school. Then he retired and began writing a book on a German merchant banker who was an ancestor. This involved him in much research: he was able to type letters though not write them. Eventually he finished the book and asked Murdo to have a look at it. It was published eventually by Michael Joseph just before he died. All during his illness he was directing his considerable intelligence to the progress of the disease. Both John MacLean and Jack Murray died relatively young; they had given their lives to teaching.

Murdo too gave his life to Addison and Lamb. Once two of his pupils sent him from London a backgammon game because they had read about it in the stories about Sir Roger de Coverley.

What shall one say about this life of Murdo? Is it riveting, is it interesting? The fact is of course that Murdo was not set on any high stage: on the other hand the memoir is interesting to himself. It keeps him out of the bathroom and possibly delays senility. Was it good for his writing to be a teacher? Probably not but then there was nothing else he could do. If Murdo had left teaching he would have lived in penury. Did Murdo wish to starve in a garret if such were still extant? No, he did not. Thus he remained in teaching. He was as conscientious as it was possible for anyone to be, and he even edited the school magazine. He wrote up his record of work. Once when returning it, among others, the Rector said that he found it very hard to read, whereupon one of the teachers remarked that Murdo was the most illegible bachelor on the staff.

And indeed he was a bachelor, a very thin bachelor for he hardly ate any food, which irritated his landlady who took his abstinence as a reflection on her cooking. In the evenings however Murdo with others did some considerable drinking and read widely, especially the novels of Beckett which he found hilariously funny.

In 1958 Murdo sent some of his poems to Edwin Muir and that gentle saintly man sent him back an encouraging letter suggesting *The Listener* and the *New Statesman* for possible publication. While Murdo was considering this another letter arrived from Edwin Muir saying that he had been commissioned by Eyre and Spottiswoode to introduce three new poets in one volume and asking if he could see Murdo's poems again. Thus *New Poems 1959* appeared.

At that time Alvarez was the poetry critic of *The Observer*. He was the one who passed judgment with the metropolitan scales firmly in his hand. And to Murdo's great delight he was very flattering about Murdo's contribution to this volume. It was a defining moment for Murdo. He had been away for the day – perhaps on a picnic with the others to Kerrera –

and when he returned there was this review. Murdo's cup ran over. It brimmed as if with joy. He returned renewed to his educational labours, his Register and his Record of Work. Thus from the celestial regions he descended to the terrestrial.

Some weekends he went from Oban to Dumbarton to see his mother. He felt guilty about her since she was on her own though she had her church to attend. On holidays he would usually take her away for the day on the bus to Luss or Helensburgh. Luss is a lovely little village with roses climbing up the fronts of the houses. It also has a nice cemetery.

(Murdo has always liked cemeteries and has often been photographed in them for the media. Not long ago he was in the cemetery at Aignish some miles away from Stornoway. He wandered contentedly round it while cameras were clicking and to his great astonishment found a gravestone on which was written the venerable name of Charles Dickens, idol of his childhood, creator of *Oliver Twist*. There he was firmly fixed among the Macleods and Macdonalds, many of whom had been drowned at sea in their youth. And the wind scoured the cemetery and the sea in front of it glittered.)

In school during the day, at night Murdo worked on his poems and Gaelic stories. These stories were inward ones. They contained often only two people, a mother and son, a German and Highlander in the First World War, and so on. Many were set outside the Highlands. One consisted of a long series of letters sent from a student to his Calvinist home and showing the changes that took place in him gradually.

Murdo also went out a lot at night, particularly to the house of a friend of his who was fond of jazz. Thus for a little while Murdo too grew fond of jazz comparing it to Gaelic songs. But jazz from destitution had created an unearthly joy.

One night among these nights Murdo came home and tried the door of the flat next to his lodgings. The key however would not turn. Murdo earnestly went back to his flat, found his bedroom, did not recognise it and went out again. After some minutes of puzzled brooding he opened the door of the flat again, fell over the umbrella stand and saw as in a flash of lightning his landlady standing there without her teeth, wondering, and justifiably so, what was going on.

All this while Murdo considered Addison and Lamb and Chaucer's *Prologue* with its prioress and monk etc. He hoarded his poems inside him as best he could. Often in the mornings he had an idea for a short story which disappeared during his discursions on direct and indirect speech, punctuation and Polonius.

During his time at Oban High School Murdo was approached by the local Gaelic Drama Group to write a Gaelic play. Thus he wrote a Gaelic play about the Clearances in which Patrick Sellar was tried in hell. It was called *a' Chuirt* (*The Trial*). The idea came to Murdo when he was reading with his Sixth Year *Huis Clos* by Sartre which is also set in hell. This play to Murdo's great surprise won all the awards at the Gaelic Drama Festival. It was followed by *An Coileach* (*The Cockerel*), a play about the betrayal of Christ by Peter. There were other plays including *Tog Orm mo Speal* (*Lift on my Scythe*) based on Goncharov's *Oblomov*. (It might be mentioned here that the Russian novel of the 19th century is one on which Murdo has richly grazed.)

Mention might be made here of Murdo's output of drama. He has written a number of radio plays mostly produced by his great friend Stewart Conn, one a Western on good and evil. He has also adapted Brecht's play *The Wedding Party* to a Highland setting: this was toured by Eden Court, Inverness.

His most recent play *Lazybed* (1997) is based on *Tog Orm mo Speal*, but much longer and anti-Thatcherite. He also in the same year did a play called *Columcille* (about St Columba and commissioned for the fourteenth anniversary of the saint's death). This toured the Highlands and Ireland.

Murdo has always believed in the magic of the theatre. When he was at Aberdeen University he used to see Wolfitt drooping dramatically and hanging on to the curtains when he had finished *King Lear*.

The most extraordinary play Murdo has ever seen was a version of *Richard III* done by a Georgian company in Georgian (Russian). Here there were wonderful images to compensate for the linguistic ignorance of the audience including a fight taking place on a suspended map of England for the sovereignty of that country. Drama in Gaelic has not flourished though it has in Ireland. The Church is hostile to it, considering it the work of the Devil, though drama began in religion in Greece and continued so in the Miracle Plays. But the black-hatted and white-collared gentlemen of the Church have in their tight-lipped brilliance been against it, thus dismissing Shakespeare, Goethe, Ibsen, Sophocles, Webster, Aristophanes, Brecht, Pinter, Euripides, Shaw, Aeschylus, Marlowe etc. etc. May their shiny trousers shine the better for it, thinks Murdo, who often has visions of these miniature unforgiving specimens in his mind's eye as he surveys the sweep of universal creativity in the minute rain of the Highlands.

It was after he had written *a' Chuirt* that Murdo wrote his novel on the Clearances called *Consider the Lilies*. This is in fact the only one of his novels that still remains in print, though *The Last Summer* and *On The Island* had a short flickering life in paperback. *Consider the Lilies* was written in eleven days during an Easter holiday break. It contains some anachronisms: however Murdo does not think this hugely important. (However the novel would have been better without them. This is a good example of Murdo's logic.)

This novel has been reprinted a number of times: there was an American edition of it called *The Alien Light*. A review of it in the *New York Times* mentioned Harris tweed, the tartan and whisky so that the greatly educated Americans might understand its literary origin.

Why, asks Murdo, has this novel of his survived and others disappeared down a great black hole? It is, he believes, because it is totally separate from himself. Others of his novels are partly autobiographical: this one is not. Furthermore it is about an old woman who might appear helpless but in fact has great strength in spite of the loss of her church. For the Church at the time of the Highland Clearances was implicated in those terrible events. Ah, said the minister, you have sinned greatly by your dancing, and therefore God has decided to evict you.

For those who have read this novel I might mention a question I was once asked about it. In the novel, Mrs Scott, the old lady, goes to see if she can get help from the minister. She doesn't in fact get any. She crosses a little rickety wooden bridge, has a dizzy fit, and falls into the water. She is rescued from the stream and taken to the house of a local agnostic, Donald Macleod. The question was put in this way: Before she fell into the stream Mrs Scott was very Old Testament in her nature: after she came out she was very New Testament. Did this mean that her fall into the stream was a form of baptism?

It is of course a very good question and is consistent with the book. But the author, Murdo, did not in his wisdom think of this at all.

The book is quite short and ends optimistically with a quotation (translated from Gaelic) that there is no ebb tide without a full tide after it.

One of the anachronisms in the book is that Mrs Scott offers Patrick Sellar tea instead of milk. There are others which Murdo can't now remember. Patrick Sellar is modelled on a Nazi with his leather whip.

It may be that Mrs Scott is modelled on Murdo's mother. She belongs to those Calvinist women who feel invincibly right and correct in everything they do. Mrs Scott learns differently. Stripped of her ideology she stands at last as a human being in the terrors of history.

It has been said that no other novel of Murdo's has had this impact. And yet Murdo never had any intention of writing novels: his chosen art form was poetry. His friend Giles Gordon was at Gollancz when this novel was submitted, and accepted it. Giles Gordon also brought out an edition of *Deer on the High Hills*. He is now a very high-powered literary agent.

This book was published in 1968. Murdo had by this time been thirteen years teaching in Oban and six years before that he had brought his mother to live with him there. This as it turned out was not a good idea though many people were very kind to her. It was not a good idea for Murdo either: he would no longer be able to go out drinking. Indeed he spent practically all his nights in the house. This had one good result, that he wrote an enormous amount, of stories and poems in both English and Gaelic. The world became to him his flat and the school.

Time passed and Murdo measured out his life in stories and poems. His mother it turned out was not fond of Oban and depended almost totally on him while at the same time Murdo was immersed in his writing (and at daytime in his teaching). He now regrets those days, but there is no doubt that writing was necessary to him. It would also have been simpler if he had been able to drive: in that case he could have lived outside Oban and taken his mother for trips.

This complication and intricacy of sacrifice and emotional attachment Murdo has studied and it appears in one or two of his poems. He was much closer to his mother than boys normally are.

This was pretty certainly because of her protectiveness of him when he was young. The whole relationship reminds Murdo of Lawrence's *Sons and Lovers* and the close attachment there. It may be that male writers tend to have closer relationships to their mothers than to their fathers. Perhaps more sensitive than is normal, they have an element of the feminine in them.

However, at this stage in his life, Murdo could by an outsider be said to have sacrificed himself to the demands of his mother. There came a time when she would not leave the house, was indeed frightened to do so. Murdo therefore remained in the house as well: thus he had very little opportunity to enjoy himself in any way.

It may be on reflection that the situation was even more complicated and subtle than that. As Murdo grows older and looks into his past, little explosions as of hidden mines suggest to him that his motives weren't so clear or as humane as he once thought. Maybe subconsciously he wanted to lock himself away from the world so that he could get on with his writing (which he certainly did). How can one ever understand the complex manoeuvrings of the mind? He has a poem about a spinster who could be said to have sacrificed herself to her mother. Yet might it not have been a deliberate barrier against marriage or an excuse for not being asked to marry anyone?

Murdo's mother did in fact prevent Murdo from attachment to young women.

Yet in spite of himself and in spite of his mother's difficult nature Murdo could not help feeling intense pity for her. She had brought up three sons on very little money, eighteen shillings a week. She often in spite of her stubborn pride had to borrow money from villagers whom essentially she was not in tune with. She then was advised by the local headmaster to send her sons to university which would mean a prolongation of her poverty. She was always talking of her early days in Glasgow and of the kindness of the neighbours. Clearly it was in that city that she had been happiest.

When she went to Dumbarton she was happy there for a while. Then eventually she was left alone as all her sons progressively departed. Her younger son she hardly heard from. Loneliness depressed her and eventually made her a little odd and bitter. It is hard to imagine how such a life would not make one bitter.

However, Murdo could understand this; his two brothers on the whole couldn't. In all that he wrote Murdo was concerned with motivation, with an attempt to understand the human mind including his own. As has been said, one of the terrible realities of old age is the ceaseless examination of one's own actions in early impulsive turbulent days. Thus he looks back on this period as one of ambiguous goodness.

He was able at this time to buy clothes for instance for his mother but she often refused them as being too expensive. Once a brother of hers who worked in South Africa and was pretty well off had bought her a set of false teeth and yet in spite of the fact that she no longer had teeth she would not wear them. This uncle had also given Murdo the unimaginable sum of five pounds to write a letter for him. He had come it appeared to Murdo with gifts which were corruptly gained from the Kaffirs but Murdo was not able in his poverty to refuse them. He too was a Kaffir whose ancestors had lived in 'black houses'.

Putting this rather grey section of his memoirs aside Murdo would now like to impart two incidents, both to do with plays, from his days as a teacher. Once, he had a class of non-academic girls who were very thrawn. That is, they were almost certainly very pleasant girls outside the school but, inside, they would not do anything which had the remotest connection with reading or writing, at least for Murdo. They were perfectly happy to sit, as it were in a meditative stupor or to chatter idly or comb each other's hair. They all wanted to be hairdressers. (Boys often with thick pebbled glasses wanted to be pilots.)

Murdo who had been brought up on the Protestant work ethic felt extremely guilty about this. After a considerable time he thought of a solution. If they would not read or write (having experienced profound failure in these) they might be willing to act. So Murdo invented little dramas every day. These dramas were done spontaneously. And it turned out that the girls were quite good at them. The blackboard often became a mirror. There emerged a long "soap" entitled "The Life and Death of a Popstar". Murdo was becoming haggard with the attempt to invent new dramas.

One day an inspector came to the school. He wanted for some deep reason of his own to see this class. Murdo panicked: they had nothing at all written in their jotters. He decided that desperate boldness was the only solution. Thus in the last period of the day he invented another drama which the girls did well. All day the inspector had been seeing teachers teach from book and blackboard. He woke up. By this time the girls were quite confident and at the end he asked one of them if they did this often (thinking perhaps that it had been put on as an insouciant flourish instead of as a desperate expedient). The girl replied vivaciously that they did this all the time.

Another incident had to do with Pinter's plays which Murdo studied with great success (since they are among other things very humorous) except with one particular class who could not understand Pinter's obliquity and bizarre plots. One day Murdo was returning from England and was waiting in the cafeteria at the Waverley station. Sitting there with *The Observer* spread out in front of him he heard a voice saying, 'Do you know about these two then?' Murdo looked down and saw two bare feet opposite him. He put down *The Observer*. 'Burke and Hare,' said the owner of the unshod feet equably and proceeded to tell Murdo some more. Then this strange rather simple person told Murdo of his family and particularly of an uncle who 'served in one of thae tanks during the war. What are thae tanks called?' Murdo summoned to mind the name 'Sherman'. 'No, they were British,' said his companion. And so this indeterminate conversation proceeded. Murdo now knew how he could explain Pinter to his class.

Murdo used to read Einstein, Marx and Freud in Penguin paperback with his Sixth Year classes. He found many of them became so interested in psychology that they studied this rather than English when they went to university. One girl told him that at a discussion in Edinburgh with some of the students she found them entirely ignorant of the great triumvirate: this did much for her self-confidence.

However, Murdo still had problems with his non-academic

classes in particular. At this time it may be said that he
was saving money from his not very munificent earnings in
preparation for at some point leaving teaching. He had become
a teacher by default and though at certain moments he could
be inspired at other moments he was distinctly less so.

From around 1968 or so, Murdo began to meet his future wife
Donalda. Donalda had been married before but for various
reasons the marriage had foundered: she had two young sons.
She was a nurse at this time but was looking for a job which
would make it easier for her to take care of her sons. She
thought of primary teaching. Unfortunately she didn't have
her Higher English. She had been desperate to become a
nurse when she was younger and consequently hadn't been
as studious as she might have been. Her father hadn't wanted
her to become a nurse thinking that she wouldn't be able
to stand the sight of blood. This was because when he was
trapping rabbits or fishing she didn't want to see the killings.
But in fact she became a very competent nurse and sister.

Donalda thought that Murdo might be willing to help her
with her English since in fact he had taught her in school. And
this Murdo was pleased to do. His mother didn't consider
Donalda threat since whenever she came she brought her two
young sons.

Murdo had no idea of marriage at this time. He knew that
his mother would not want another woman in the house.
Was Murdo right in thinking this? Indubitably he was. His
mother was a very strong dominating personality and would
have wanted her own way. Such is the psychology of life.
Or at least this is what Murdo told himself. But then can
the faithful reader believe that this was in fact the case? Or
was Murdo setting up a barrier against marriage and using
his mother in this practice? Murdo at this time was very
interested in Kierkegaard and Kafka. Both of these writers
remained bachelors. They had long engagements which came
to nothing. Indeed to them marriage was a huge enterprise,

ungovernably complex. Kierkegaard was deformed, Kafka was ill. Murdo was Murdo. Thus Murdo was protected by what he thought was his own beneficence.

And in any case at the back of his mind was always the idea that he would leave teaching. He had tried to do this twice before but had lost his nerve.

Donalda was younger than Murdo by eleven years. At this time he had not thought of her as anything other than a student. Furthermore she had two young sons. Her mother lived in Taynuilt, a little village twelve miles from Oban, and Donalda would sometimes visit her while she was in Callender Park Training College which has now alas vanished but was in its time innovative. Her father, who died in 1968, had been a policeman.

Murdo however read K. and K. Nor did he think at all of those hundreds of people who married without hesitation. For Murdo as for K. and K. marriage was a vast step. It was in fact unimaginable. What was wrong with Murdo? It might have been his fatherlessness and his mother's protectiveness that had caused this. Were K. and K. more real to him than the people he met every day? That is probably true. So Augustine wept for Dido when he did not weep for himself. Books are very powerful shields against the world and also powerful teachers. As the Puritans set up their shields of dogmatism against the fires of hell so Murdo set up his books against reality. And to him they have been nevertheless the greatest of gifts.

When she came to Oban in 1962 or so, Murdo's mother used to attend the Free Church. Now she did not go out at all. She also had become senile and would imagine that people were talking about her if they waved their arms. No reasoning was proof against this. Also she had had two very heavy nose bleeds which had caused Murdo great panic.

Murdo is writing this part of his memoirs in November 1997. The run of *Lazybed* has just ended in the Traverse Theatre. The word "lazybed" is of course an ingenious pun.

The main character won't get up from his bed because he finds the world meaningless and cannot summon up the energy to take part in what to him are absurd gestures. This play takes its idea from Oblomov, the main character in a novel by the 19th-century Russian writer Goncharov. Thus the main character stays in bed and is looked after by his mother.

He is visited by the minister, a psychiatrist, his very energetic brother and a nurse, with whom he falls in love. It is clear that much of this is autobiographical though not all of it. Murdo, my own namesake, is a metaphysician and Kant also puts in an appearance (a story about Kant had been written by Murdo years before). So too does Death who is very cheerful, and likes Murdo.

One of the most powerful moments in the play is when Death comes for Murdo's mother. Here there is a strange slow dance as Murdo's mother gazes up into Death's face and they move off together. This moment was invented in this way by Philip Howard the producer.

Murdo's mother died in 1969. He tried to hide from himself that she was dying. She was thirsty and he gave her milk. However, the doctor decided that she must go to hospital and Murdo's last sight was of red blankets and his mother's staring face. She didn't wish to go to hospital; he thinks she would have preferred to have died at home. However, Murdo thought that she might live.

That night or the next (he cannot now remember) a police-woman came to the door of his flat. His mother had died. He went to the hospital and saw her dead face which seemed to have become stern and Roman. He felt as if ice surrounded him and he was trembling all the time. He felt as if he was in outer space. It was actually the first dead person he had seen.

At this point and for a long time his whole personality disintegrated. He would not go to school. He felt as if death had destroyed his writing. A cousin of his from Stornoway came to the funeral and he went back with him. This cousin,

Danny, had a bad cold and indeed it was wintry weather. Murdo lay in his bed in Danny's house listening to him coughing: he had the distinct delusion that Danny was going to die and that he had caused his death by making him travel for a long distance by bus and boat in such weather. Murdo was full of guilt.

It may be of course that Murdo had been overworking, teaching and also writing without respite. And now the world of reality opened out before him, jagged and painful.

Furthermore at this time he had a particularly difficult class which didn't help. It seemed to him that the whole world should know about his grief but life seemed to continue. He felt totally alone in the world and indeed to a great extent he was.

He became extremely restless: he began to throw out letters and various documents as if he wished to prepare himself for a more rigorous less cluttered life. He took himself off to Edinburgh, and even the Orkneys. He was completely without destination or direction.

However as he was travelling on the bus through the night towards Lewis, the thought of Donalda, whom he had not seen for a while, returned to him and the ice melted a little. It was as if he was breaking like a trembling nestling through an egg.

When Murdo went to Edinburgh he phoned Norman MacCaig from the Abbotsford Bar and Norman came to see him. In those days the Abbotsford and Milne's Bar were where the Edinburgh poets met. In one or the other one could usually find MacCaig and Goodsir Smith. Tom Scott who looked like an Old Testament prophet patronised another pub in Rose Street.

Murdo met many strange people in these pubs. One of them wore a badge with a number on it. When Murdo asked what this number represented he was told that the man was a poet and the number referred to a poem of his which was one line longer than *The Waste Land*.

Norman MacCaig was tall, handsome, ascetic-looking. He

was brilliantly witty. Once when another poet was fumbling through his papers for a poem to read and this went on for a considerable time, MacCaig murmured to the person sitting next to him, 'I thought he was going to read aloud.' Another time when someone was telling him that he used to take his dog for a walk through the cemetery because he stayed near one, MacCaig muttered, 'Not near enough.'

Most people were frightened of his acerbic wit, for he could bring an argument to a close by a stunning and decisive figure of speech. He talked as he wrote in metaphors. When he spoke about poetry Murdo could see him taste the words of a poem on his tongue. He never talked about his private life but presented to the world a quizzical sometimes remote look.

When Murdo used to visit Edinburgh during his teaching days he would book into a hotel: then he would visit the Abbotsford. There he would meet MacCaig who would invite him to his house along with numerous others. He would stay overnight at MacCaig's having drunk a considerable amount of whisky, and MacCaig would say that Murdo was the only person he knew who paid Bed and Breakfast for a case.

His house was crowded with people on a Friday night, among them probably many he did not know.

Murdo really loved MacCaig's poems when they began to appear everywhere in the 'sixties, often in *The Listener*. They were brilliantly metaphorical, startlingly original. They were like pictures one might see in a mediaeval illuminated book. They showed animals and birds and places in a startlingly new light. A seagull would stare about it with a "quartermaster's eye". This was extraordinarily exact.

Murdo remembers MacCaig once attacking Whitman for his rhetoric. Murdo had just been reading Whitman and pointed out how exact in description Whitman could be. And MacCaig was converted. He didn't like preaching in poetry and disliked his own first two books because they lacked clarity.

He professed not to read novels though he did say that

reading C.P. Snow's prose was like wading through a forest of dandruff.

He was very strong-willed and competitive and liked to get his own way. Because of his quick intelligence he could humiliate people. Murdo once heard him say to MacDiarmid on the radio that though he was a great poet he was not the whole culture of Scotland or words to that effect. He liked to take part in the practice of flyting, insults exchanged in a cheerful manner. He had a powerful sense of his own ego. He was a close friend of Hugh MacDiarmid and admired his poetry greatly. He told Murdo a story once of himself and MacDiarmid taking a sickly friend to a Burns Supper. This friend, as it was cold January, wore a duffel coat. In the middle of the proceedings they found that he had disappeared. They took a taxi and searched for him. They eventually found him and dragged him back to the Burns Supper and placed him securely between them. When the man finally managed to remove the hood of his duffel coat they discovered that it wasn't their friend at all.

Murdo often read with MacCaig who was an exceptionally fine reader of his own work, always audible and always giving every syllable full value. As his poems were clear and lucid the audience derived great enjoyment from them and particularly from the imaginatively exact images. It is true that many of his poems were metaphysical, in the sense that he tried to marry a philosophy of the relation between subject and object to his descriptions, but in general he read poems that were easily understood, one of his favourites being about a toad, with a jewel in its head.

His poems of course are bright and colourful and in their love of living beings optimistic. However he used to tell a story about saying to an audience of which Robert Lowell was a member that he would read his cheerful poems first, then his pessimistic ones. After he had read some cheerful ones, Lowell's funereal voice came from the audience, 'Now read us your gloomy ones.' It is hard however to find pessimistic ones till later in his career when he lost a close friend called Angus MacLeod.

MacCaig was not what might be called a full-time poet (if there can be such a thing): he taught in a Primary School. He never became a headmaster because of the fact, as he himself used to say, that he had been a conscientious objector in the war. For this he served some time in prison. He did not seem at all political in his poetry or in his conversation, as MacDiarmid, Sorley MacLean and Goodsir Smith had been. He told Murdo a story once with great relish about MacDiarmid whom as has been said he admired enormously. They were both on their way to a meeting at which MacDiarmid was to talk about the common man and how much he had done for art. As they were walking along MacDiarmid was saying to him how little the common man had in fact done for art. However at the meeting he returned to the theme on which he was to speak. When the meeting was over MacCaig reproached MacDiarmid for what he called his hypocrisy. 'That,' said MacDiarmid, 'was an example of dialectical materialism.' There was undoubtedly a mischievous element in MacDiarmid who loved ideas in a way that few of the other poets did.

Murdo has already mentioned MacCaig's ego. Because of this he didn't like to show any sign of weakness. (Murdo is sure for instance that he didn't like confessional poetry: his own poetry is objective not subjective revealing little about himself.) Once when he and Murdo and Edwin Morgan were at a poetry reading in Carlisle they had to climb a brae which MacCaig found difficult: now and again he had to stop. But when Murdo asked him if he was all right he answered brusquely that he was. He continued smoking though for the good of his health he should have stopped. He was a brave man. He once told Murdo about someone who had committed suicide. It was a neat death, he said meaning that it was untroublesome to others, efficient, unmessy.

Murdo is sure he didn't like to travel though he did visit

America, Italy and Australia reading his poetry. It is surely certain that he received invitations that he turned down. Yet he wrote some fine poems set in Italy and America though none Murdo thinks set in Australia. His best poems are of course set in Scotland, either in the Highlands or in Edinburgh.

His mother belonged to Scalpay. She and his father "collided" in the Lowlands. He always said that his naturally metaphorical speech was inherited from his mother. He liked mixed metaphors such as one he had heard, "The foot is on the other leg."

That night Murdo went to Edinburgh, he was well received by MacCaig who could behind his remote exterior be understanding and tender-hearted.

Two of the contrasting personalities in Edinburgh in the 'sixties were in fact MacCaig himself and Goodsir Smith. Smith was a Falstaffian figure often seen uproariously laughing (the 'most variously funny' Sorley MacLean had ever met). While MacCaig appeared cool and remote, Goodsir Smith was very extrovert. He would sometimes make a statement and build extraordinary structures on top of it. Thus one night in his flat, to which you had to climb dizzying flights of stairs in spite of the fact that the poet was asthmatic, he came out with the statement that Vienna and Dundee were very alike because both had green buses. And from there he created his absurd logic.

It was said that he had once trained for teaching and had told his class that they should write an essay of great length on any subject whatsoever and the prize would be a packet of cigarettes.

Another story which circulated about him was that after a bevy which lasted for a day or two he had gone up to what he thought was a bar, asked for a whisky and had been told that whiskies were not served in the British Linen Bank.

He was a painter as well as a poet and often visited Plockton where Sorley MacLean was headmaster. He wrote poetry of the night where banks and such bourgeois institutions dissolved in romanticism. His best poetry was his love poetry and his best poem one about a lady he had met in the Black Bull. He had to learn Scots since he had not been born in Scotland but in New Zealand. His father was the famous pathologist Sir Sidney Smith.

Much of his poetry was humorous, and he would write of himself in the third person as Slugabed Smith, the endpoint of an effete civilisation. His poetry had the humanity that he himself radiated.

He was also a formidable scholar and Murdo once witnessed a literary argument between himself and MacCaig where it was as if a galleon confronted a darting ship. He thought the debate ended in a draw.

In those days there was much talk about Lallans and Synthetic Scots. MacDiarmid raked the dictionary for wonderful Scots words that encapsulated whole stories. "Yow-trummle" meant the time of year the ewes trembled in their shorn state and was a classic Scottish term, and MacDiarmid unearthed other extraordinary treasures. There was a story told about Douglas Young that he had once gone into a pub saying that Scots was perfectly comprehensible to the "ordinary" person. He asked for a pint of beer and then, later, for 'some mair' whereupon the barman went and opened the window. This sounds apocryphal.

How Murdo misses Goodsir Smith and his warmth and those poems of his of moonlight and whisky and references to Li Po etc. He does not think there is a central pub where writers meet any more. Modern writers are much more serious and earnest and intent on their word processors. Maybe much of what those poets might have written went into their conversation. They were wasteful and they were themselves. The focus would shift from Edinburgh to Glasgow, from poetry to prose. Rose Street would wither.

But before Murdo leaves the subject there was another poet whom he should mention and that was Robert Garioch, which was in fact a pen name, his full name being Robert Garioch Sutherland.

Much of his poetry is very funny and perceptive, his persona that of the tiny unimportant spectator on the edge of things. His translations of the Italian poet Belli are masterpieces, though Belli's satire is fiercer and less genial than Garioch's. He was a good performer of his own poetry (Goodsir Smith didn't read his poetry in public at all) and came across as someone with a sly wit, apparently but not in fact disorganised. His poetry was mostly set in Edinburgh, though he did write a long philosophical poem "The Wire": it must be remembered that he had been a prisoner of war in Italy.

Most of his working life was spent as a schoolteacher, at one time in London and at others in Scotland. Like Murdo himself he wasn't comfortable with certain classes and wasn't given certificated classes because for some unaccountable reason he had only a third class degree. However when he was later doing his poetry readings for certificated classes he was apparently brilliant: and Murdo can believe this. In London he taught Arnold Wesker and went to see his plays, and amusingly commented that Wesker hadn't learnt much from him. He left education earlier than expected and without the "packages" that have been received since. Sisyphus was his image of the teacher. He lived in Nelson Street. Once, Murdo and his wife were invited to a party in the flat of Sorley MacLean's daughter and stayed the night in the Nelson Hotel opposite Garioch's flat. The three went along together to the party, Garioch explaining that when he saw some public regulation which he thought ludicrous he pasted a WHY sticker over it: for this reason he seemed to have a number of these stickers.

In the course of the party Murdo drank too much, was sick, and lost his teeth down the toilet. He was not aware of this till his wife Donalda pointed it out to him. As it was late and there seemed to be no taxis available, the three decided to walk home, Garioch suggesting to Murdo that the sewers should be scoured for his teeth, and saying that there was a short-cut available to the Nelson Hotel.

At a later stage and after much walking Garioch decided

that he needed a pee and in a waste land a toilet was found. However the toilet was locked and the genial poet decided to put a WHY sticker on it. He then peed against the wall of the toilet. However into this deserted area inhabited only by Murdo, Donalda and Robert there were projected a male policeman and a female policeman, the latter of whom proceeded to charge Garioch with exposing himself in public or some such nonsensical accusation. She read out the formal regulation under which he was charged and Garioch genially corrected her a few times. Meanwhile Murdo was energetically waving his arms about in a heroic manner, and saying, 'I must help my friend,' and, of Donalda, 'See this woman. She has no compassion.' This seemed to infuriate the lady policeman (who was much more vindictive than the male one). It didn't make matters any better when she asked Garioch for his name and he gave the name Robert Sutherland which in fact came as a surprise to Donalda who thought he was trying to outwit the policeman and didn't know that the name Robert Garioch was a pseudonym. He was never however summoned to trial and he wrote a poem about the incident called "A Fair Cop" for Radio Forth. The silly thing about the whole incident was that there was no one around to see Garioch peeing. At that time he was in his seventies or eighties and probably needed to go to the toilet quite often.

Murdo was on the point of going down to England with Garioch for a poetry tour when he heard that he had died of a brain haemorrhage. He had looked lonely since his wife died.

After Murdo had seen MacCaig he flew north to Orkney and took a taxi to Stromness where George Mackay Brown lived. He was told at the hotel he stayed in that he didn't need to lock the door of his room as nothing was ever stolen.

Orkney is a very attractive island, much more prosperous than Lewis. It has the chapel, built by Italian prisoners of war, which Murdo visited. Then there are the Standing Stones and the Stone Age village unearthed by a sandstorm. Stromness Murdo preferred to Kirkwall as it had old-fashioned cobbled streets one of which if he remembers correctly was called The Khyber Pass.

The island was certainly enough for George Mackay Brown: he had lived in Edinburgh for a while when he was at university and then he had later attended Newbattle Abbey when Edwin Muir was Principal. But Orkney sufficed for him: it was quite astonishing how it was continually refreshed by his imagination right to the very end of his life. He also read a great deal about the Vikings and his historical imagination was fed by books and place names. Every week he contributed a column to the local newspaper.

We read in that column that immediately after breakfast he sat down to his writing at the kitchen table after the bread and marmalade had been cleared away. He never married so that all his time was his own. Murdo was amused to find that though in his work he attacked machinery he wasn't short of modern technology in his house. However he was quite genuine in his attack on the decay of history and folk tradition.

His own favourite writers included Forster and Mann. He reread books rather than kept up with new ones. Every year in his column he mentioned Burns and every year also he welcomed the daffodil after a hard winter. His health was never good but at this time he was well. He made and drank his own beer. He cooked for himself, especially, in winter, good thick soup.

Murdo discovered later that like himself he loved to play football when he was young.

He was not a witty talker like Norman MacCaig, but often sat quietly and listened to others. He didn't like talking about literature: he wasn't, Murdo thinks, interested in theories of any kind. He wouldn't take part in poetry readings, because he was too nervous to do so. In the summer many readers of his books visited him. He told Murdo that when an American professor was on the phone asking about George Mackay Brown he told him that regretfully the author was dead. His novels and stories were translated into many languages.

He had the most interesting face, like the prow of a Viking ship, a large jaw being its most prominent feature. Orkney was an island more and more of which he discovered each day. He described most beautifully its changing skies and seas. It was a world that he had made from his imagination. Not much of the present Orkney appeared in his works. Even his column was about the past or about harmless topics like the weather or books he had been reading or local festivals. When he was younger he had apparently been more daring in a column he had written and he had been confronted on the street by a large red-faced man. After that he didn't take sides on local issues.

When Murdo visited him on that occasion in the late 'sixties he met one or two students who had come to see him. And of course he met John Broom again. John had been an alcoholic in Edinburgh, but had given up drink and was only taking tomato juice. He was an interesting man with a wry sense of humour. A librarian by profession he told Murdo of the customer who had asked for the book *HMS Ulysses* by James Joyce. He said that bookmarks were often bits of bacon, cold fried eggs and on one occasion a dead mouse. He used to be a lay preacher in the Unitarian Church and often after a bad Saturday might found the pulpit hard to ascend and descend on the following day. George had a story that he had missed out a page or two of his sermon one Sunday and that everybody in the congregation found his discourse very deep, and well above their heads.

He had been in love with a girl called Stella Cartwight when he was in Edinburgh: whether this had anything to do with his drinking belongs however to the realm of speculation. He wrote a book about his alcoholism called *Another Little Drink* but he used a pseudonym.

At this time the main bookshop in Stromness was owned by Charles Senior, a poet. Broom said that Charles was determined to have only books of the highest quality in his shop and would not sell cards or other mean material. For this reason according to Broom when the shop opened the heading in the local paper was "300 Penguins Cross the Pentland Firth".

Broom for a period was a constant correspondent to *The Scotsman*: indeed he and a number of others more or less wrote to each other via that newspaper. Broom defended freedom of opinion and was often to be found on the side of pornography, arguing that it must be permitted. He was very knowledgeable about the cinema and films.

Altogether Murdo found Orkney a most fascinating island. There was no heavy hand of Presbyterianism and it had an idiosyncratic quality which became magical on Midsummer's Day when night was like afternoon. It had kept and maintained the wonderful St Magnus Cathedral. Stromness itself is a quaint town with winding cobbled streets.

George Mackay Brown was accepted by the people as one of their own and went for walks among them every day. He didn't wish to leave the island at all, though he was once enticed to London. He was not so much a private poet as a *vates* who represented the spirit of his community. He was quite open and unpretentious. In his column for *The Orcadian* he talks in a relaxed manner about his life and his domestic affairs, referring to his portable radio and his refrigerator and the meals he cooked.

Yet at times he must have been lonely and he suffered from depressions. Nevertheless his books do not show any of this: they read optimistically and have about them the feel of an external sacred world. In this he must have been helped by his Catholic faith. His God is not the personal God of salvation but the one who is seen in the land and sea, in the growth of corn and the spectacle of the natural world. Thus he is able to accommodate the pagan Norse in his world view.

He was pure artist and this view of him is only disturbed by his awkward references to nuclear war and the corrupt world of the machine which probably helped him to survive when he was in hospital. He was apparently a fine mimic though Murdo never saw this side of him. He would not harm anyone and probably was unaware of much of the guile in the world. He wasn't terribly good at interviews because he didn't analyse his art. But he had an inner guide which kept that art clear and unaffected to the end.

For a number of years now Murdo had been living on his own, though he and Donalda were going out with each other at weekends. Donalda was for part of this period teaching in the small school at Glen Etive. There was no electricity so a generator was in use. To cross the river one had to push oneself along in a box. There were mice and rats in the school. There were only a few pupils, who used to visit her in Taynuilt as they grew older. Glen Etive of course is most famous as the glen to which Deirdre and Naoise came from Ireland and where they built their bower fleeing from the king who fancied Deirdre as she was very beautiful. For many years the couple lived in idyllic bliss in Glen Etive till the king sent a messenger saying they had permission to return to Ireland unharmed. However the king had Naoise killed and Deirdre killed herself.

Donalda and Murdo used to go for dinner every Saturday night to a different hotel in Argyll. Sometimes in the autumn they used to pick brambles. Murdo gradually recovered from the death of his mother, for which he had suffered guilt and genuine grief. He was not very good at making food for himself and his only major discovery in this direction was porridge and mandarin oranges. Otherwise he used to go to a hotel for his lunch. There he would meet an old man, a regular customer, who would ask him every day how old he was. Another customer of the hotel was the sheriff who told him that it was difficult to get a verdict of anything other than Not Proven from the islands because the people always stuck together.

Later he would go out and meet Donalda in her home in Taynuilt. She had separated from her husband and lived with her mother and her two sons, Alasdair and Peter, after she left Glen Etive School and became a school nurse combining her two expertises. She travelled around Argyll and the islands, testing children's eyesight and hearing and giving injections against rubella. She worked with a lady doctor.

Once during her period as a school nurse she was testing old people asking them what they could hear on her machine, whereupon one of them said that she could hear "The Minstrel Boy to the War is Gone". Donalda's mother was a widow, her husband who had been a policeman dying around the same time as Murdo's mother. She too had been a nurse. There was a croft attached to the house in Taynuilt and Donalda had a calf which Murdo sometimes used to feed, its head butting the pail.

From this period Murdo recalls fine carefree autumns, travelling at weekends around Argyll, which he recognised as particularly beautiful, in fact the loveliest area he had ever been in, with its lochs, mountains and trees. Murdo especially loved and loves trees. On Lewis there were hardly any. The island was bare and bleak with winds howling round headlands. Argyll's lochs which mirrored mountains were especially attractive. Oban too is a nice little town facing the sea and crowned with the unroofed McCaig's Tower. But now he began to see more of the wider Argyll.

Bed and Breakfast brought many visitors to the county but Murdo wonders whether dependence on Bed and Breakfast is good for a town. What happens to those areas of life which aren't measured in money, like the Arts? He sometimes has fantasies of Bed and Breakfast signs hung out like spiders' webs in order to catch the passing flies, the visitors. In his early days in Oban when he lived in lodgings he was put out of the main house in summer in order to make room for summer visitors.

Ay yes Murdo thinks, man cannot live by Bed and Breakfast

alone, nor indeed by En Suite. He has had much experience of Bed and Breakfast. He remembers the first time he encountered the landladies who would not allow smoking and how he would stub his cigarettes out in pot plants. Now he seeks most often for tea or coffee and biscuits when he enters a room. Then he searches for a plug whose flex is often quite short for the kettle. Then he tries to work out whether the switch on the kettle itself goes down or up, i.e. if no light comes on. Many a time he has waited for the kettle to boil when in fact the kettle switch was in the wrong position. Then he finds that there is only one chair in the room, whereupon he (or Donalda) has to sit on the bed. Why is there only one chair in the room? In Murdo's opinion this is because the lodger is not encouraged to sit in the room for a long time when he should rightly be out in the health-giving rain. Calvin must have had this idea first.

Murdo sometimes cannot remember the number of his room and has been known to enter another room where a startled woman sits up in bed or a very large man naked to the waist turns massively towards him from inspecting himself in the mirror. For Murdo has no sense of direction. He turns left when he should turn right: he does not recognise any modest buildings such as a cathedral or a nuclear station. No he proceeds on his fated way towards a cemetery when he should be heading for his Bed and Breakfast residence. Nor does he recognise his landlady or her husband (who is often the one who brings in breakfast).

'A land,' Murdo would say, 'dependent on Bed and Breakfast is a land without soul.' For the landlady (or landlord) will without doubt be thinking about money all the time and whether the amount of marmalade or toast or butter can be diminished, whether one can find a cheaper bacon in some other shop, whether eggs could be bought at a lower rate here or there, whether one can import rolls from the Third World, how many biscuits if any at all should be left with the tea or coffee. Then again, one knows that however kind the landlady or landlord is and however much they expatiate on their local lore (which is a great assistance to the Bed and Breakfast trade e.g. Carlyle was born here or Rob Roy made a film here) in the end the whole thing, however disguised, is a commercial transaction (which of course one always knows in dealing with a hotel which has no one to tell us of local lore).

Then often a Bed and Breakfast establishment has only one bathroom which may be firmly locked when one goes in search of a preprandial pee. One hears a man cheerfully whistling from the shower while one stands writhing on one leg in the bedroom next door, cursing under one's breath. Then one imagines this carefree monster turning his slow attention to shaving, cleaning his teeth (loudly spitting), admiring his face in the glass or looking for pustules on his neck or chest, blissfully unaware of the other guest, contorted like a Francis Bacon figure not so very far from him. Oh how Murdo curses that merry man, now engaged in sitting peacefully on the toilet, how he hopes that he will be startled by the stigma of some horrible disease such as leprosy, so that he will leap up, unlock the door and rush to the doctor or his wife. But there is no sign that he is ever going to come from the toilet enwreathed in steam as it is. And Murdo searches in his room for some receptacle into which he can pee. But there the pot plant looks too small. And so Murdo waits and waits, gritting his teeth, till after twenty minutes which seem like hours the chain is pulled.

And even then the man does not come out. What is he doing? Is he perfuming his toes/nostrils/head? Is he reading Dostoevsky? Is he making out cheques?

But Murdo will now leave Bed and Breakfast and turn to something else.

There is no question but that meeting Donalda was a turning point in Murdo's life. He was no longer so lonely as he had been. He no longer visited the pub as he had done constantly after his mother's death. In his flat in Combie St, he would listen for Donalda's footsteps on the stone stairs. In her yellow dress she was like an actual physical ray of sunshine entering his house.

During this period they travelled (Donalda driving) over much of Argyll. Murdo became aware of the colour and extravagant loveliness of the country. He learned to recognise rhododendrons (who had known only the daisy and the daffodil). In Lewis the moors were bleak and there were hardly any trees. Here there were beech, birch and the ash. There were lovely red and orange coloured leaves. There were infinite shades of green, copper and yellow. There were hydrangeas, poppies, snowdrops, crocuses. Gorse and broom yellowed the sides of hills. Bluebells misted the glades of woods. There were spontaneous unnecessary extravagances of complete blossom without revision, perfect in every detail at first shot.

There were owls, glaring and magisterial. There were doves flying in pairs, grey and modest. There were buzzards on fenceposts. Instead of the ubiquitous dizzying lark of Lewis there was the redbreast, the swan, the duck, the gaunt heron quizzing the water. There was the cormorant and the wagtail. Once Murdo saw a mother weasel crossing the road with a string of tiny weasels behind her as if they were following an invisible green light. All this Donalda pointed out to him for she was more observant and knowledgeable than he was about this world.

He remembered from Lewis a world of the sea, the mussels in their blue helmets stuck to the rocks, the pin that transfixed the meat of the whelk, the shining silver herring. He remembered the infinitely changing surface of the sea and its constant sound. He remembered boats, bollards, piers, the rock pools with jelly fish and crabs. He remembered the smell of the brine and the broken shells on the sand.

This world of decorative colour and scent was new to him. In rural Lewis there had been few if any flower gardens: the wind was very strong. Colour did not suit the bleakness of the prevailing ethos. Such exuberance would be suspect, such spontaneity unusual. In Argyll mountains gazed at themselves in lochs. The invisible cuckoo duplicated its call. The startled fawn turned its face into the headlights and disappeared into the woods. There were squirrels and rabbits. The saddest sight would be lambs dead at the side of the road, killed by cars. There was something mystical, innocent and melancholy about such deaths.

What Murdo came to love best of all was the twinkle of green leaves as if they were luminous thoughts, sudden intellectual musings and insights. They had an extraordinary brilliance and freedom as if they formed fragments of a theory.

He and Donalda would gather brambles, the richest biggest ones among thorns. Donalda used to wear tall red boots as they made their way into the centre of the clumps. Their hands were later red as if bloodstained.

In the past Murdo had followed the tall white racing moon out of the pub. Now he lived in a daylight world which almost did not need the benefit of imagination. At its clearest and bluest it was heaven itself.

In the middle 'seventies and before they were married, Murdo and Donalda visited Murdo's uncle in White Rock in Canada. His name was Torquil Campbell, a brother of his mother, and he was eighty-seven years old. Murdo had met him once or twice before in Lewis, where he had been holidaying. He had been driven from his relative's house in Lewis because of the amount of food he was being given. Breakfast, tea with cakes at eleven, dinner, tea with cakes in the afternoon, his main tea and then more food before he went to bed. 'Dang it,' he told Murdo, 'my stomach can't take it.' He was a big heavy craggy man, widowed when Murdo met him.

On his mother's side there were Torquil, who had gone to Canada, Angus who had gone to South Africa, Alisdair who had been drowned young, John who lived in Lewis, Katie Ann, a sister who had also gone to Canada, and one or two others. Murdo's grandfather had been married twice.

Generally speaking Murdo was not interested in genealogy nor in the formation of a family tree. He knew however that the only writer in his family had been his grandfather's brother (or was it his great grandfather's brother) who had written a book called *Father of St Kilda*. This book curiously enough was not about St Kilda at all as might have been expected but rather about the Hudson Bay Company. (Later Murdo discovered that there had actually been squaws on Lewis brought home by intrepid members of the Hudson Bay Company. They smoked pipes, and probably had strange ceremonies. Did they attend the Free Church with feathers on their heads? Did they do strange dances quite unlike Strip the Willow at midnight? Murdo can only speculate.)

Fleeing from a superfluity of food, Torquil travelled with Murdo on the plane to Glasgow where they were to stay overnight before travelling to Prestwick whence Torquil was to return to White Rock (where a lamp had been installed, triggered to light up at night so that it might be thought that the house was occupied). Torquil was hoping to have a bath in the hotel which had been booked but unfortunately the water had had to be turned off. Torquil went up to the astonished manager and in a loud voice, for he was very deaf, shouted, 'Do you know what you Scots are, you are Red Indians. You accept anything that people throw at you. God dammit, you're like Red Indians.' The astonished manager gazed at him, not knowing how to answer this. Torquil, with Murdo in his wake, stormed up to his room. 'You know,' he said to Murdo, 'the only history we ever learnt was English history, all about English kings and queens. We never learnt about William Wallace or Robert the Bruce.' Murdo thought, what you need here is not William Wallace but a plumber. However it was clear to him that his uncle thought Edward the First or his son had cut off the water to the hotel. In his room, craggy and large, Torquil looked like a Red Indian himself brooding on his tribal wrongs: he could have been Chief Sitting Bull.

The following day Torquil and Murdo travelled to Prestwick by train. In the evening there was a wedding party in the hotel and pointing to one woman who was dressed in red, Torquil said loudly, 'That dress reminds me of the curtains we used to have round the bed in Lewis.'

In actual fact Murdo remembered those beds in what was known as the *cùlaisd* in the black house. They were often occupied by old women who never rose from them. Outside the black house one could hear the cows systematically chewing the grass. In the main room there was a fire and a bench and a black pot for hanging on a chain and a little window. So the ingenuity of Torquil's metaphor had brought together two worlds, that of the black house and that of the modern airport hotel.

Because Donalda and Murdo hadn't been able (owing to the position of their seats on the plane) to see the film, they were supplied with red wine on the way over to Vancouver. They were told that the wine would be thrown out when they arrived in Canada anyway.

Thus when Murdo emerged to the glare of Vancouver he was not feeling very well, what with the wine and the jet lag. Torquil loomed out of the glare and took their cases: he was driving a white car as long as a boat (a Plymouth as Murdo later discovered). Murdo managed to say a few insignificant words but when they cruised into the garage of his uncle's house (which he had built himself) he went to his bed though it was only afternoon.

In the morning he was up bright and early, Donalda at the table before him and already familiarising herself with the kitchen. Through the kitchen window Murdo noticed that there was a wire festooned with tin cans which was hung over the garden. When the crows descended on the cherries, Torquil pulled the wire so that the cans jangled and drove the crows away. 'I know all them danged crows,' said Torquil sourly. Murdo was given a green cap to protect him from the heat of the sun and the three of them sat in the garden. Men with red helmets were working on the road in front of the house.

'I built this house myself,' said Torquil. In the olden days you could shoot duck where some houses are built here. In a corner of the garden was an Empire rose which Torquil had planted after his wife died.

'She was very keen on gardening,' he said. 'Because I was on the Fire Brigade I used to drive the car pretty fast but she would see flowers at the verge of the highway and she'd get me to stop. I told them at the hospital not to give her any doggone drugs, I don't believe in them drugs. I made a song for her. You know the day she was buried all the flowers were stolen from her grave.'

He told Murdo and Donalda how he had met his wife. She had been on service in London and had been intending to emigrate to Australia but one day when she was out walking she saw an attractive poster for British Columbia: so she decided to go there instead. Meanwhile Torquil and a friend had been going to emigrate to Australia but his friend dropped out and Torquil went to Canada instead. 'And I met her at a dance in Vancouver. I was playing my accordion. My wife was an orphan, you know, from Loch Lomond-side.' All this he told them while he hosed the Empire rose. 'They've rationed the water,' he added.

Murdo had a notebook which Torquil had filled with his life story. One day he had gone with the gig to the town of Stornoway. He then walked down Point St where he was stopped by a Recruiting Sergeant. This sergeant had asked him whether he wished to join the army.

'I'm only sixteen,' Torquil had said. 'But he told me I was tall enough to pass for eighteen. So I agreed to join and I told the postman he must give me any letters addressed to me. I ran away and all I had with me was my accordion. I arrived in Fort George and by gosh that was an eye opener. You were up at the crack of dawn going for a run before breakfast. However I was a crack shot and enjoyed the training. My father and mother didn't know where I was till I sent my suit home from Fort George. They had always been good to me. But I wanted to see the world, you see. I was young and I wanted to see the world.'

Murdo learnt from the short autobiography that Torquil had written something of his early life. Once when he was a child he had poured milk all over the clay floor. His mother had hung him in a creel over the fire as a punishment for being so improvident with the food God had given him. Another of his early memories was trying to crawl to a neighbour's house across the snow. He was proud of his memory and would recite poems which he had learnt in school including "A Wet Sheet and a Flowing Sea".

He would say that he couldn't understand Murdo's poems because they didn't rhyme. Burns's poems he liked though he had the curious idea that Burns must have been a Catholic because he had so many children.

He told a story about his schooldays. When he was twelve or so, he and his classmates were throwing snowballs at each other during an interval on a cold winter's day. The minister and his son (who was being privately educated) visited the school. The minister went in to talk to the headmaster: the boys began to throw snowballs at the son who seemed to enjoy the horseplay. However when the interval was over, the headmaster gave them six of the belt on each hand for throwing snowballs at the minister's son. After their punishment Torquil asked to go to the toilet. The headmaster by this time in a genial mood made to hit him on the bottom with his belt. However he hit him on the head instead. After trying to study poetry for a while, Torquil collapsed and was taken home by the headmaster. He swore thereafter that he would not return to school, and didn't. In any case in those days it might have been possible for him to avoid school more easily. He did not hold anything against the headmaster, who, he said, was 'an excellent Navigation Teacher'.

He insisted that he had a happy childhood. Once he had an

argument in Canada about the food they were being given in the works canteen. A man who came from Paisley made some derogatory remark about Highlanders, the implication being that their food was pretty primitive. And then, I thought, by gosh we were brought up like princes. Fresh fish, meat, scones, crowdie, fresh butter, oatcakes and barley cakes, fresh milk, cheese, salmon – we were brought up like kings. And that fellow from Paisley was brought up on greasy chips. When I was young I had such a big appetite that my father would say, 'Butter the door for Torquil.' Murdo would sometimes study his craggy uncle. He would envy his unquenchable cheerfulness and optimism. And his generosity. Most days they had salmon and fresh strawberries. Torquil had been told by the police he could use his car for going to the shopping precinct but he had ambitious ideas of taking Murdo and Donalda across the whole of Canada to Thunder Bay where his sister lived. They pleaded with him not to do this. They had seen him drive in Vancouver where there was a continuous stream of cars and a relentless noise of horns. He would often go through a red light and always drive very fast. 'You are allowed to go a bit over the speed limit,' he would say.

'You know,' he said, 'one time when I was working as a Fire Officer we were called out. We used to plant potatoes at the Fire Station at the time. Anyway I jumped into the wagon and as it was moving I was trying to put my helmet on. The next thing it was hit by a car travelling west on Commercial St and I was thrown out. Everyone was killed except myself. Funny enough, I had a dream the night before. I saw this white figure around the croft at home. Whenever I saw this figure that meant a death. Of course,' he said to Donalda, 'Murdo doesn't believe in the supernatural. But I believe in it. I've seen that white figure of a woman many times.'

He took Murdo and Donalda to fairs where there were Red Indians. 'You know,' he said, 'we used to teach Gaelic to some of these people, and they would teach us some Indian words.' On the way to Hell's Gate, hundreds of miles from White

Rock, they saw an enormous number of totem poles. At Hell's Gate they crossed the Fraser River in a cable car. Down below, the water swirled tumultuously.

This is a strange land, Murdo thought. For a start, the telephone boxes are blue. Then he read in the local newspaper that the inmates of one of the prisons had formed a union. Another news story told of a woman who had gone into a supermarket, bought a gun and shot herself in the rest room.

Torquil took them to church and it was a woman minister, which didn't please him though in fact he didn't seem to be at all religious. The minister was rather schoolmistressy and said that she would sing a certain hymn because she herself liked it. Her sermon compared people's lives to that of a business, in particular a bank balance. If you sinned you were in the red, if you were virtuous you were in the black. Thus it was that as noted in books by historians such as Tawney, Protestantism was closely linked with capitalism.

When Murdo and Donalda went for a walk facing the torrential noise of traffic, they saw on the grass verge a green snail eating another one in a horrible ooze. There were grass snakes around the house which came out and dozed in the sun. Donalda hated snakes and once Torquil hung one around his neck like an ornament to show her that they were entirely harmless.

Canada was very clean, almost innocent. One couldn't imagine bloody battles, mysterious events, happening there. There were no castles, murderous with intrigue and the passions of men. There seemed to be no shadows, no noises. It was like a newly built flat with no creakings in it. The sun shone every day with friendly monotony. On the beach, fat men threw baseball balls towards their sons. Murdo and Donalda sat in the garden and ate cherries.

'That man next door is from Saskatchewan,' said Torquil. 'He's a nice man.' And then, 'People have tried to buy this house from me: they offered me thousands of dollars. But I won't sell it.' What would happen though to the house when

Torquil died, Murdo thought. It will go to a stranger as he has no family. Torquil had a basement in which he kept his tools. Murdo himself was completely impractical. He was terrified of hammers, planes and chisels.

Theoretically Murdo knew what a chair or a stool should be like but never achieved any semblance of them in the real world. He was good on Platonic form but not on wood or steel.

Torquil was not very expert with modern machinery. He had bought a cine camera and put on a show one night. On the screen a woman carrying a creel chased a church at what seemed a hundred miles an hour. He also had a record-player which appeared to get mixed up with the radio. Thus the songs of Calum Kennedy would loom from the middle of the news.

There were advertisements on the radio all the time. The television programmes were uninteresting. Once however they all watched a natural history programme where a puzzled dog was nosing at a porcupine. 'See that,' said Torquil, 'that dog will feel the pain of them needles. Them porcupines are cunning.' Again and again the dog approached the porcupine but had to retreat each time; eventually it slunk off defeated.

In Torquil's little book, Murdo read of his uncle's voyage to Canada and his arrival there. The ship, it appeared, was crammed with East Europeans most of whom were seasick. Torquil and his friends being used to boats in stormy seas were the only ones who weren't sick. They discovered one night that the cook had left a big cake outside the galley. One of them suggested they should take it as the passengers never ate any food because they were so sick. So they ate it. And similarly the next night they ate a chicken and threw the bones over the side. But on the third night Torquil said that he would inform the ship's officers if they took any more. By that time of course even a very thick chef would have become suspicious anyway. The ringleader of this group, Torquil wrote, was long dead in Flanders Field.

So they sailed on through storms and rough seas. One of their number, a stalwart blacksmith, had taken to his bunk complaining that he was sick, and reading the Bible. However, they played a trick on him and shouted that they had just seen the coast of Newfoundland appearing. Immediately he jumped up from his bed and went up on deck where they set on him as they had been taking it in turn to bring him his meals.

Arriving in Canada they entered a restaurant. None of them had been in a restaurant before and most of them didn't know any English. They agreed that Torquil should order. When he had done this and the food had been brought, one of them said to Torquil angrily: 'But you know I don't like bacon and eggs.' It was of course true that English was a foreign language to them.

Many of them became alcoholics. One reason for this was that they found Canada very cold and the pub a warm and friendly place. Many of these emigrants would turn up later in Lewis in their forties or fifties. They had stopped writing home years before and no one knew where they were. They would give up drinking and join the church, 'their watch chains snaking their waistcoats'. They would become sober and puritanical. One of the churches on the island would have many reformed alcoholics.

Torquil wrote that at one time he and a friend had been drinking in a pub in Mid-Canada. He woke up to find himself lying on a haystack. He said that drinks were often spiked in these pubs and customers were robbed. Another time he was brought up before the magistrate in a similar situation. Uncharacteristically he had been causing mayhem in a pub though he had no memory of it. His friend pointed out to the magistrate that Torquil couldn't speak English and gave the impression that he wasn't all that mentally brilliant. He was fined though he didn't wish to pay as he was sure the bartender had given him a Mickey Finn.

He was in Canada during the time of the Depression. 'You had to take whatever job you were offered,' he said, 'if you wanted to survive. I saw an advertisement for a rough carpenter. I didn't know what a rough carpenter was but I took the job. I was up in a crane too, pretty high above the ground: I had a head for heights.'

He worked often as a lumberjack. In summer you were nearly killed by mosquitoes. In winter it was very cold. 'Once when I was cutting down a tree some snow fell down the back of my neck. "Dang this," I said to myself, and downed tools and handed in my papers. You didn't care what you did when you were young. When I was working on the railway a gang of us went into a carriage and danced the eightsome reel to keep warm. I worked a lot on the Canadian Pacific Railway.'

And Murdo thought; in similar circumstances I wouldn't have survived. The bosses or the mosquitoes would have got me or I would have fallen from a tree or a crane. One morning I would have lain in my bed and said to myself: 'This is it, the World Spirit doesn't demand any more of me.'

Once when Torquil was queuing up outside a canteen, an Italian was standing in front of him. Torquil noticed that there was a feather on the back of his collar. He picked it off and as he did so the Italian turned on him with a knife in his hand. 'If it hadn't been that there was a Lewisman there who happened to have a hammer the Italian would have killed me. I lay awake in my bed that night in case that Italian came after me but he never did: he turned out to be a real nice fellow.'

Another time he was sent for errands in a sledge over frozen water. However as he was coming back the sledge went through the ice and he was swimming about among the stores. 'The thing was I forgot to take my pipe out of my mouth and the boys were saying, "Torquil loves his pipe more than he cares about the stores."

'And that's true enough. I was working on the grain elevators with a friend of mine and as he was passing I held out a plug of tobacco thinking that he would take a piece and leave me the rest. But he took the whole lot and went away laughing. I meant to give him what for but the next thing I heard was that he had been mangled in the machinery. He had lent me a book called *The Virginian* and I never got to give it back to him.

'There were so many of these boys,' he said.

'A funny thing happened to me after I came to Canada. I was in Toronto and I was invited to visit this house where there was a number of Lewis boys lodging. Well, they started talking about the old days back in Lewis and I couldn't take any more of it. I got up and went out. I was thinking, here we are in a new country, what's the good of going on about the old days. Wasn't that funny?

'And it was a new country right enough. If you saw the Douglas firs in winter time under the snow and the sun sparkling off them like diamonds you would think you were in fairy land. You never saw such a sight in your life. You couldn't imagine it.'

He laughed and said, 'Do you know that I was in the First World War in a Canadian regiment and after I came back to Canada I was in this forest one day and I heard a rattling noise just as if it was made by a machine gun. Well, I lay down flat on the ground: and do you know what it was, it was a woodpecker.' There was our hero Torquil thinking he was back in the war again. But it was like a machine-gun right enough.

'When I came back from the war there was something wrong with my two kidneys. This doctor, his name was Major Campbell, he told me I would be dead in six months. I wrote to my girl friend from Lewis breaking it off (I was engaged, you see) but I never told her what had happened. Anyway I was getting these pains in my back, real stabbing pains and the only thing that would help was if I played handball very fast. So after the six months was over I went back to the doctor and he said, "I thought you would be dead by now." So I told him what I had done and he said I must have sweated a lot of the poison out of my system. I have only one kidney, you know. But I'll tell you something, that doctor died before me.' He said this with great satisfaction and Murdo glimpsed at that moment the unbreakable will that had sustained him in his life in Canada. For a second the craggy face stood out triumphantly as if over a cemetery.

One day Torquil took Murdo and Donalda to see a man called John Smith.

'I'll tell you about that fellow,' he said, as he drove along in his usual magisterial manner. 'John Smith is from Lewis. He was nineteen years old and he was going to Canada. However this minister came up to him and said, "I hear you've been working on a Sunday on the Clyde shipyards."

'"I hear you work on a Sunday yourself," said John.

'And that minister wouldn't speak to him, and John was sailing for Canada.'

It turned out that John Smith was a brisk little man with a limp. His wife who was sitting in a deep soft chair with a flowery cover on it didn't say much.

'How's the garden today?' said Torquil, sarcastically. 'I guess you're working as hard as ever. Darned fellow here,' he told Murdo and Donalda, 'spends all his time reading. What's that man's name again?'

'Charles Darwin,' said Smith proudly.

'Says we come from monkeys,' said Torquil largely. 'The place in Lewis where John comes from, they're monkeys there right enough,' and he laughed.

'You know you're ignorant,' said Smith angrily. 'Can you explain to me why you have an appendix?'

'An appendix? What's that got to do with anything?'

'An appendix is no use to you, that's why. You can't explain to me what an appendix is for. Darwin explains it but you can't explain it.'

'I've got better things to do with my time,' said Torquil.

'You're so ignorant,' said Smith scornfully. 'I suppose you think Adam and Eve were the first people on earth.' And he laughed malignantly.

'It says so in the Bible,' said Torquil. 'I suppose you think they were two monkeys. Two monkeys eating an apple.'

'It wasn't an apple,' said Smith triumphantly.

'What do you mean?'

'The Bible doesn't mention an apple. It just mentions a fruit. That shows you don't even know your Bible.'

'It says it was an apple.'

'No. It just says a fruit.'

'You look it up,' said Torquil confidently. 'Have you a Bible?'

'No, I don't keep a Bible.'

The two of them, at a standstill, glared at each other. Smith's wife had made tea and cakes which she brought in on a trolley.

'Garbage,' said Torquil, 'monkeys in the Garden of Eden.'

And then, quite irrelevantly, he said, 'You know something, John, when I came here first I was driving a cab for a while and I took these two ministers to visit a house. It was bitterly cold and they told me to wait for them but they never invited me in or anything and I was freezing in that cab.'

'How are you enjoying staying with this ignorant Christian?' said John Smith.

'We're enjoying it fine,' said Murdo and Donalda.

'You watch his driving,' said Smith. 'He shouldn't be driving at all. He can hardly see.'

'I can see as well as you,' said Torquil. 'I can see you're talking a lot of garbage. I never heard of monkeys that ate apples.'

'That's because you never read any good books. I'll ask you another question. Where is the Garden of Eden, you tell me that.'

'I guess it's in the Middle East somewhere,' said Torquil.

'You see that,' Smith appealed to Murdo and Donalda, 'he can't answer any of my questions.'

'I'll tell you something,' said Torquil. 'I read the Bible right through every year. I begin at Genesis and end at

Revelations. I read the whole lot, the names of the tribes and everything.'

'What are you at just now then?' said Smith.

'I'm at Numbers, Chapter 3.'

'Numbers?' said Smith scornfully. 'You'd think it was arithmetic he was doing.'

Torquil didn't take offence at any of these exchanges: it seemed that they were habitual. He proceeded calmly on another tack: 'My father once threw a Bible at me,' he said. 'I came in late from a dance. He was in a terrible rage. In the old days I didn't care what time I came in. You know, Johnny, I should have had the croft in Lewis.'

'How was that?'

'Well, I was the oldest of the family. My father wrote me to come home but I had just started in the Fire Service so I didn't go. My brother John inherited it. He and I didn't get on so well when we were young. We were always arguing as to who should drive the gig. My father died, and then my mother died about a month after. They were good parents to me.'

Smith's house didn't seem as luxurious as Torquil's: the chairs sagged and the sofa looked soiled.

'It was all adventure then, Johnny: that's why we came to Canada.'

Smith didn't say anything: he shifted his game leg as if it was giving him pain.

'Johnny here plants potatoes and vegetables,' said Torquil, 'he doesn't plant flowers or fruit at all. It was like that in Lewis, people didn't have flower gardens. It was too cold and windy.'

'I suppose you think your garden is the Garden of Eden,' said Smith, 'just because you've got cherries.'

Murdo thought there was a slight touch of venom in his voice; it was plain that Torquil had been more successful than he had been.

'Good old Darwin,' said Torquil, 'the monkey man. But I'll tell you something, who ever saw two monkeys looking after a garden?'

His large infectious laugh filled the room.

'I thought I'd bring the young ones along to see you,' said Torquil. 'Johnny here is one of my oldest friends. We came over to Canada on the ship, the *Numidia*. By golly, we had some storm. Do you remember Tinkan, Johnny? It was him who stole the chicken and cake.'

'Yes,' said Johnny.

'Dead in Flanders Fields.' He got to his feet. 'Johnny here was wounded in the war. That's why he limps. But he talks a lot of garbage. I never heard of a man with a tail in my life unless it was the Devil.'

When the three arrived home, Torquil took out a big black Bible, and putting on his glasses read the first part of Genesis. After a while he laid the Bible down beside the bowl of fruit on the table and said in an astonished voice, 'Well, dang it, he was right enough. It doesn't mention an apple at all. How did he know about it? He never reads the Bible.' His lip stuck out as if he was pouting: he was clearly disappointed. 'Never mind,' he said, suddenly brightening, 'I'll take you to see Mrs Macdonald tomorrow.'

Mrs Macdonald was from Ness, Lewis. Her daughter was married to an ambassador and she stayed in the house and looked after the children.

'Though she's been here for years,' said Torquil, 'her Gaelic is as good as ever.'

As they entered the house they passed a man crossing the hall, bare-footed and carrying a towel. His feet left damp patches on the wood. He said 'hi' as he passed.

'That fellow there is a millionaire,' said Torquil. 'They have big parties and barbecues here, and they do deals in real estate.'

When they arrived in Mrs Macdonald's room she was saying to a little blonde girl of twelve or so, 'Now, here's some money for you. Seven-up, and bring back the change.'

'As careful as ever,' said Torquil.

'I have to train them,' she answered. 'Otherwise they would be given everything they wanted.'

'Quite right,' said Torquil.

Mrs Macdonald was a slim grey-haired woman neatly dressed in brown with a brooch at her throat. She laid some cakes and tea on a low table. Murdo found it hard to think of her as belonging to Lewis as she seemed very composed in her Canadian environment.

'Torquil has his widows who look after him,' she said, smiling. 'They're leaving him alone jsut now because he has company, but they're very good to him.'

'That's what happens in Canada,' said Torquil, 'the men die of heart attacks making money, and the women are left behind.'

'So you never go back to Ness now?' Murdo asked her.

'Not often. It's all different now, Torquil. Even the girls in the shops aren't as polite as they used to be.'

'I was home last year,' said Torquil, 'and I was talking to an old lady who lives next door to my brother. She is eighty years old, and she used to be a friend of Murdo's mother here. She was telling me that there is a Dutchman and a Frenchman living in the village now. "I don't know anyone here any more," she said to me. "I'll soon be dead. The earth is tired of me." At one time she was a herring girl and she told me they earned five pounds in three months. Murdo's mother, Chrissie, was a herring girl.'

'When my husband died, my daughter asked me to come here,' Mrs Macdonald told Murdo and Donalda. I help with the children as she and her husband do a lot of travelling. I don't like it here all that much but there's nothing for me in Lewis.'

'Why don't you like it here?' said Torquil energetically. 'Canada's a great country. I remember when I came to Vancouver first I felt at home right away. There was the sea and the mountains and we went for a walk in the gardens. Vancouver is beautiful.'

267

'Have some cakes,' Mrs Macdonald invited them.

'She makes them herself,' said Torquil. 'Mary used to make cookies as well. You do a lot of baking, don't you, Isobel?'

'Yes, I make scones sometimes. But we don't have crowdie here.'

It was difficult for Murdo to visualise what sort of life Mrs Macdonald led in Canada. She seemed as lonely as Torquil himself must surely be. She also seemed serene, though she might be inwardly discontented and a psychological exile.

They were talking about the old days as they must often do. Murdo's attention wandered. He thought of the two 'girls' whom Torquil had invited to see them. They were seventy years old and walked with sticks.

What had his wife been like? Murdo had never met her.

'We never quarrelled,' said Torquil once. He had written some Gaelic songs about her.

'I'm thinking of taking the young ones over to Victoria Island,' he told Mrs Macdonald.

After a while they left.

'A brave woman that,' said Torquil, as they drove away. 'When she came here first she hated Canada. She was a friend of Mary's. She does a lot of embroidery and knitting. Of course,' he went on, 'many people didn't like Canada at first. It was so big and they felt lost. And the prairies went on for ever.'

'You should be the poet, not Murdo,' said Donalda.

'Yes, Donalda, I used to get good marks for my compositions.'

They crossed over to Victoria in a big comfortable ship. And they had chowder soup.

They booked into a Motor Inn and Murdo found a Bible in the room in which Christ was said to have the edge on a star baseball player.

Victoria was a very English city with Olde English sweet shops: and Fable Cottage, a fairy-tale almost Dali-like structure surrounded by gnomes sawing, working with axes, boating etc.

Torquil hired a car and drove about with the assistance of another of his lady friends, a widow called Mrs Campbell. She was small, neat, determined, and kept ordering Torquil to slow down.

'He drives so fast because he was in the Fire Service,' she said.

'Yes,' said Torquil equably, 'that's true. I climbed a ladder once when I was in the Fire Service and looked in through a window and there was this woman sitting in a burnt chair. She was bald, all her hair had been burnt away.'

They visited Butchart Gardens.

'At one time this used to be an old quarry,' said Mrs Campbell.

'The gardens in Vancouver,' said Torquil, 'are full of tramps and drug addicts. You've got to be careful there but the ones here are all right. Sure, they'll be OK.'

'It's very English here,' said Mrs Campbell. They had The Olde England Inn and Chaucer Lane and Anne Hathaway's Cottage.

'Murdo would like that,' said Torquil sourly, 'Flora here is like a guide-book.'

As they were walking along. Torquil said, 'Flora came to Canada as a housemaid and then she met her husband.'

'That's right,' said Mrs Campbell, 'the first time I saw a hoover I didn't know what it was for. But you have to learn pretty quickly. Then I met my husband who was in real estate. We didn't have any children but I had a good life. And of course I met Torquil.' And she smiled mischievously.

When they arrived back at Torquil's house in White Rock the crows had eaten almost all the cherries.

'They're like locusts in the Bible,' said Torquil.

He took them to visit Chinatown in Vancouver, the biggest on the continent outside San Francisco. There were many down-and-outs lying on the pavement. Phone boxes had oriental writing on them. A man in a long black coat with a dead white face, as if powdered, passed them flamboyantly. In the twilight young lovely prostitutes in shorts were patrolling the pedestrian precinct. Torquil used his cine-camera extensively.

In Lewis at that time, thought Murdo, his uncle John would be scything. Torquil had travelled far in his life.

'There's a place called Skid Row around here,' said Torquil. 'This is where those who didn't make it ended up. Some Lewis lads took to drink, you know.'

A young boy with long flowing hair was playing a guitar. Beside him was a cardboard box with some money. The Chinese passed him impassively.

'The Chinese are said to be very hard workers,' said Torquil. 'In the camps you come across a lot of foreigners, but not Chinese so much.

'You see that young fellow over there, that's a guitar he's got. I fancied playing the violin myself, it's a beautiful instrument, but I never learned. I used to play the melodeon and the bagpipes but I never played the violin. In my day it was the melodeon we played, not the accordion.'

He sat down on a seat, his back very straight, his legs stretched out in front of him.

'I haven't been here for a long time. I don't much care for Vancouver now, it's too busy for me, and it's all changed. They're knocking down and building all the time. When the widows lose their husbands they sell their houses and move into condominiums in Vancouver.'

When they were driving home he suddenly said, 'I've never held anything against coloured people, they're human beings just like us. But some people don't like them. Sure, they think coloured people are stupider than us. I've never found that. My brother Angus used to invite me to visit him in South Africa but I never went. I don't approve of what they're doing out there. "Look at it this way," I used to say to him, "we were brought up in thatched houses just like the African natives. We didn't have water or electricity or toilets." Sure, that's how it was.'

A motorist tooted impatiently at him and he said, 'In

270

Vancouver they don't give you a minute to think. They're honking at you all the time. "Sure," I said to Angus, "we had houses like they have in Africa. We had clay floors and we had the fire in the middle of the floor, and the cattle were under the same roof as the people. We were just like natives, sure."'

The traffic lights hung down in the middle of the road. It was a fine balmy evening. The holiday was coming to a close.

The night before Murdo and Donalda flew home, there was a ceilidh in Torquil's house. There was a middle-aged couple called Morrison, whose ancestors had come from Lewis; a widow called Sarah and another called Elizabeth; Smith and his wife; and a young shy couple called Cowie who didn't speak very much.

The widows had brought Torquil a cake and some scones which were later served by Donalda with tea and coffee.

Sarah, a plump blonde lady, said she'd seen a Gaelic singer recently on TV.

'He wore a kilt,' she said, 'and he had lovely round knees.'

'That's a funny thing,' said Elizabeth, 'I don't think I've ever seen Torquil with the kilt.'

'I used to wear it when I played the bagpipes,' said Torquil.

'Nobody in Lewis wears the kilt,' said Smith with some acerbity. 'Tourists think we wear it all the time. But maybe if Torquil wore it he'd have round knees as well.'

Everyone laughed.

Morrison said that he had been in Lewis recently. 'The first time I was ever there, though my great-grandfather came from Lewis. A place called Shawbost. You'll know Shawbost, Murdo?'

'Yes,' said Murdo.

'A lot of them speak English there now. In Stornoway though I heard a Pakistani speaking Gaelic.'

'A Pakistani?' said Sarah.

'Yes,' said Morrison, 'they have lots of Pakistanis in Lewis. They own all the stores in Stornoway.'

Suddenly the shy Mrs Cowie remarked, 'They go in for the Mod too. I heard one of their girls singing a Gaelic song. With a Stornoway accent.'

'A waste of time those Mods,' said Smith sourly.

'You think they should be reading Darwin,' said Torquil.

Elizabeth, as if to change the subject, said, 'How are the cherries this year, Torquil?'

'No so good. The crows practically stripped the trees when we were in Victoria. But I've a few left I can give you.'

Morrison remarked lightly to Murdo, 'Torquil always gives cherries to the widows and they bring him baking.'

Murdo went round pouring whisky into glasses: it was 'A Hundred Pipers'.

'Some of these whiskies you never see in Scotland at all,' he remarked.

'I don't drink whisky myself,' said Torquil, 'I saw the harm it could do.'

'Tactful as ever,' said Sarah, 'he gives you whisky and tells you not to drink it.'

'Oh, I didn't mean that,' said Torquil, 'everything in moderation.'

'Like the widows' cakes,' said Morrison, and they all laughed.

Sarah said to Morrison, 'Why don't you give us a song? You have a good voice. Why don't you sing "Loch Lomond"?'

'Murdo doesn't like that song much,' said Torquil. 'He thinks it's sentimental.'

Murdo suddenly felt very isolated.

'I'll give you a Shawbost song,' said Morrison. He took a sip of whisky, cleared his throat and began:

> *Se Siabost is boidhche leam*
> *far an do thogadh og mi suas . . .*

(*Shawbost is most beautiful to me, where I was brought up when I was young.*)

He sang a large number of verses, sometimes closing his eyes.

'You have all the words,' said Sarah, 'you have a good memory.'

'And he has a good voice too,' said Elizabeth. 'Where did you learn that song?'

'Oh, it was passed down through the family.'

'It's his anthem,' said his wife.

Donalda brought in some coffee and cakes.

Cowie asked Murdo if they had been to the North at all.

'No,' said Murdo. 'We didn't want Torquil to drive too far.'

'It's very beautiful,' said his wife, a pretty dark-haired girl.

'Did you know that Torquil had written the story of his life?' Murdo said. 'He's got it in a notebook. He mentions seeing a black bear eating berries when he was up north.'

'Jim here could have taken you if he had known,' said Mrs Cowie.

'I would have. They have wonderful rivers there, full of salmon.'

Suddenly in spite of what Torquil had said, Sarah began to sing "Loch Lomond".

When Sarah had finished she said, 'I don't understand that bit about the high road and the low road.'

'There would have been two roads,' said Torquil magisterially.

'That's not it at all,' said Smith. '"I'll take the high road" means that he would die and be in Scotland sooner.'

'John here knows everything,' said Elizabeth, 'he's like an encyclopaedia.'

'He knows everything about monkeys,' said Torquil jovially.

'All this is very well,' said Margaret, 'but I think we should be leaving. Sarah here is working tomorrow.'

'I'll give you a few cherries before you go,' said Torquil. They went out into the almost-stripped garden. A moon was rising, very pale, and in the dim light Murdo could see the guests drifting around the cherry trees. Torquil picked some cherries and put them in little cartons he had. Elizabeth's white scarf glimmered ghostly in the half light. Murdo felt suddenly very nostalgic under the moon, as if it were the moon of home, the moon of Lewis, "the moon of the ripening of the barley".

People eventually moved towards their cars.

The ghosts of Canada, Murdo thought, salmon runs, prospecting, walking the streets of Winnipeg in the Depression, unshaven, unsteady.

The cars drove off, and Donalda, Torquil and Murdo returned to the house.

'Nice people,' said Torquil. 'The Morrisons give John Smith and his wife a lift. I should have talked more to the young ones. I remember nights like this in Lewis when I played the melodeon. What did you think of the widows?'

'They're very nice,' said Donalda.

'Elizabeth's husband died of a heart attack in their living-room. He was a dentist. And Sarah's husband died of cancer. I used to tell them to slow down but they kept on just the same. In Lewis we took things easily. You know the job I liked best? I was once a coiler on a fishing boat when I was seventeen and on the summer mornings it was beautiful. I would ask the skipper for a turn of the wheel. I felt like a king, sure, like a king.'

He lumbered to his feet. 'I suppose I'd better go to bed.'

When Donalda and Murdo were clearing up she said, 'He put you on the spot with "Loch Lomond". You didn't remember that his wife came from there.'

Murdo thought, I make many mistakes like that in my life.

'He's got a good memory,' said Donalda.

'But it's not good for Genesis,' said Murdo.

As he lay in bed Murdo thought, this is my last night in Canada. I may never see Torquil again. As a matter of fact he died the following year of an aneurism. Murdo's last sight of him was when he was turning quickly away after helping to take their cases to the check-in. The plane rose, casting a shadow on the Canadian runway, and headed for home.

Murdo and Donalda were married in July 1977 in a civil ceremony in Perth. Murdo had left teaching at the end of June.

There were now four people in the flat in Combie St, Murdo, Donalda and the two boys Peter and Alasdair. It has to be said that it took Murdo some time to get used to his role as stepfather, as he was not a natural authority figure. He wrote in the mornings, then cooked the boys' lunch (he gave each bean his individual attention) and then wrote in the afternoons again. Donalda was a school nurse and was sometimes away a week at a time in one of the islands.

The building had six flats on three floors. Next door to Murdo and Donalda there lived another Smith. When mistakenly their letters went through to Mrs Smith she invariably opened them. She would ask Donalda why she had decided to withdraw the boys' savings. Another time when the door of the flat happened to be open, she gave her brother a tour of their flat. She went through the rooms systematically with him, explaining what had been done to them, and finally saying: 'And there is Murdo and he is doing his typing.'

Murdo was surprised by this surrealistic appearance but gamely continued his work.

Living in a flat can have its problems. For one thing a roof needs to be repaired and then all the tenants have to contribute their share of the bill, and assume that it has been repaired, for not all tenants (some of whom may be old, memoryless, lame, half blind) will be able to clamber up a steep roof (often wet) to check. Then each tenant had his own particular week to put the light on, and to make sure that the landing in front of his door as well as his share of the stairs were washed. It was an intricate timetable, meticulously worked out by some ancient social Scottish intelligence. Down below there was a lady who walked about with a broom all the time.

When Murdo was working he liked the noises that were around him. It might be the postman climbing the stair, the drip of a tap, a carpet being delivered next door, the binmen. All these contributed their companionable sounds to his images. At night one could hear drunks passing up the road, limited to their usual vocabulary.

In many ways, Murdo liked to be in the town itself. It made him feel that he was at the centre of "reality", missing nothing, in the middle of "real life". This was almost certainly an illusion. However he was at least writing rather than teaching. He had never wished to teach, he had drifted into it: now he was working at his ideal work.

Then if he wished he could go down town and in summer see the tourists, who doubled or trebled the population. Or he could take a walk along the sea. Or to the library. From the crowded George St he could see Kerrera and Mull and the coloured yachts and the big MacBrayne ships.

His life was uneventful. Now and again he would stare at the walls as he tried to think of something else to write but in general he wrote easily and freely and if he could not write in English then he wrote in Gaelic as if he was riding a linguistic and psychic bicycle. But as time passed he wrote more and more in English. He was away from the Gaelic homeland and had been for years. He had to write for a living and there was not much money in Gaelic (and not a great deal in English either). At one time he used to think that if he left teaching he would not be able to write. Now however he could, probably because he was married. Alone, there was the danger that he would not have much discipline.

At this point Murdo would like to animadvert a little more to the question of language. He himself has written in English and Gaelic; poets like Sorley MacLean and Derick Thomson, generally speaking, have written entirely in Gaelic though in their student days they wrote poems in English.

Is it true that as a rule one should write in the language of one's childhood? Robert Garioch wrote in Scots, and so did

Hugh MacDiarmid though he wrote his later "poetry of fact" in English. Sydney Goodsir Smith learned to write in Scots. Edwin Muir wrote in English.

It seems true to say that those poets who wrote in Scots or Gaelic wrote better poems in these languages than they did in English. And of course if we return to Robert Burns his Scots poems are much stronger than those he wrote in English, which seem stiff and good-mannered.

In these languages and for these poets there is less distance between the poet and the reader. When Murdo went home to Lewis he would never dream of speaking to a villager in English for this would be a superior social gesture. Nor did he ever speak English to his brothers or his mother.

What does all this mean? Does it mean that Murdo's own poems and prose in English are less likely to last than his Gaelic? It may do. But he began to write in English and has written more in English than in Gaelic. Is this because he was trying to get through to a larger audience? Yes, it was. Many Gaelic speakers while speaking Gaelic cannot read or write it. It has become the habit for poets who write in Gaelic to put English versions opposite the Gaelic poems. This allows English-speaking readers access to the Gaelic poems. But then again Sorley MacLean has written that Gaelic poems cannot be translated into English. This has not prevented non-Gaelic-speaking critics from writing essays on his work while reading only the English versions. Would people do the same with Baudelaire, Lorca, Goethe, etc. Murdo wonders.

Then again this question of language is muddied a little bit by writers like Conrad and Nabokov. Is there anything in common between the English of Conrad and that of Nabokov? Nabokov's prose is certainly more playful than that of Conrad. But they both have in common a wrought brilliance, lighter possibly in the prose of Nabokov. And in choices such as the Hundred Best Novelists which are periodically promoted their novels have a high place.

It seems therefore that this question of language is even

more complex than one had thought. Nevertheless – even though the justice of it goes against himself – Murdo thinks that to write in the language of one's childhood, provided that that language is in a healthy state, is preferable to writing in a language that is learned later. This begs a lot of questions but he will leave it there. Much of what he thinks is to be found in a poem of his entitled "Shall Gaelic Die?".

He thinks that we grow up in a web of language to which feelings are attached, and that the most powerful feelings of all are those of childhood. It seems to him significant that the two great poets of the 20th century in Scotland are Hugh MacDiarmid and Sorley MacLean and that neither of these poets wrote in English: and that at times in comparison with for instance Scots, English looks pale; and that we see this often in the prose of Sir Walter Scott when authentic Scots breaks through English like colourful thistles in the words of some of the more gifted commonalty.